THE HUMAN FACTOR

THE EVARAN CHRONICLES

BOOK 7

ADAIR HART

Editing done by Laura Petrella
Cover done by Tom Edwards
Interior design done by Colleen Sheehan
Proofread done by Alexa
Published by Quantum Edge Publishing

ISBN: 978-0-9967172-7-4

www.AdairHart.com

To get updates on new books and other notifications, sign up for my mailing list at:

www.AdairHart.com/MailingList.aspx

THE HUMAN FACTOR

THE STORY SO FAR

» In *The Arrival*, the Evaran Chronicles prequel, a space- and time-traveling being known as Evaran rescues Jake Melkins and Kathy from a Seceltor slaver named Greecho. It is Evaran's first adventure in the Milky Way galaxy and introduces him to Earth.

» In *The Awakening*, book 1 of the Evaran Chronicles, Dr. Albert Snowden and his niece, Emily Snowden, are abducted by an alien race known as the Krotovore. They are rescued by Evaran, who dropped them back off on Earth.

» In *The Fredorian Destiny*, book 2 of the Evaran Chronicles, Evaran returns to check on Dr. Snowden and Emily, and they ask to travel with him. Evaran accepts. They then help Fredoria, a planet of human ex-slaves, become a full trade partner with the Kreagan Star Empire, the local galactic superpower in Earth's region of the galaxy. Hampered by Seeros and bounty hunters, they secure the Arkaron for the Fredorians to give to the Kreagan emperor.

» In *The Purification*, book 3 of the Evaran Chronicles, they fight the timeline invaders known as the Purifiers, a human-supremacist group led by the overlord, that tries to change Earth's history.

» In *The Time Refugee*, book 4 of the Evaran Chronicles, they tangle with Billozein, a rogue time traveler, while helping Jane Trellis, a time refugee who is pulled out of her timeline.

» In *The Evaran Origin*, book 5 of the Evaran Chronicles, they discover Evaran's origin and meet Levaran, another one of Evaran's plane forms, while fighting the Time Wardens, a timeline-void race that hunts rift travelers.

» In *The Shadow Connection*, book 6 of the Evaran Chronicles, they group up with Jake Melkins and the nonhuman community to defend Earth from the ambitions of Caltorus, a dimensional being that rules over a vast empire encompassing worlds in many dimensions.

This book continues their adventures.

EVARAN'S TECHNOLOGY

Torvatta—his disc-shaped ship that can travel through time and space. It is roughly fifteen feet tall by thirty feet wide. The interior contains six dimensional rooms, an open area, and a roof that can be transformed by hard holograms. A shielding around the Torvatta prevents most matter from entering.

Universal interface card (UIC)—a credit-card-sized device carried on his belt that allows access to most technological systems that do not have an artificial intelligence in them. It can also view limited information on biological systems.

Augmented reality interface (ARI)—an interface that only he can see around him

Utility handle—a hilt-like device carried on his belt that can extend morphable matter in any shape, typically a baton or staff; can also fire repulsion, grappling, heat, mist, sticky glob-ules, and stun beams

Illumination orbs—small orbs on his belt that provide light-ing and can hover

Projection orb—an orb that allows projections to be sent to it from remote sources, such as Evaran's ring or the Torvatta

Ring—a ring that can provide holographic projection and also scan

PROLOGUE

Commander John Holind did not know what death was like, but if he had to guess at the sensation, then the cold, dark feeling that crawled around him would be it. He tried to open his eyes, but something kept them closed. Trying to move any body part was equally useless. Images of his family entering cryo sleep popped up in his mind. Although he could feel how tense his body was, the images made him relax some.

"Commander John Holind of the colony ship *Xavier*," said a digitized male voice. "An emergency restoration is in process. Please hold."

Bits and pieces of feeling returned to his body. The temperature around him increased, and he was able to wriggle his fingers. After a few moments, he could open his eyes and was greeted with a frosted glass shield. It came back to him why he disliked cryo sleep so much. The going-to-sleep aspect was nowhere near as difficult as the waking-up part. He had heard stories of people waking with completely different personalities or, even worse, psychotically insane.

"Extending cryo unit AX-1287."

He could feel himself going from an angled position to a horizontal one. With the glass shielding defrosting, he was able to see out into the cryo chamber, where the ship's crew was maintained. Clamps and restraints released their grips on him, allowing him to move around.

"Sufficient restoration achieved. Opening cryopod."

The frosted glass shield slid back, and the warm blast of stale air hit John in the face. He coughed as he moved his hand over his mouth. Sore muscles and a headache reminded him that he needed to take his postcryo medicine. He struggled to sit up. Each motion was like a dagger cutting into him. After a moment, he was able to slide his legs off to the side of the slab he was on. With a tap at the slab's edge, a soft, retractable tube extended out. He grabbed it and put the end in his mouth and then squeezed. His face scrunched as a vile-tasting fluid burst down his throat. As bad as the medicine was, he knew it would stabilize him. At least his sense of smell was returning, and the sterile odor of the room filled his nostrils.

"John, I sense you're awake now."

"I am," said John in a deep, raspy voice. He knew the speaker to be Salazar, the virtual intelligence that maintained the ship during the long journey. Although helpful when it came to crunching data and dealing with maintenance, sometimes Salazar's decision algorithms were unusual in regards to dealing with humans. John had an inherent distrust of artificial intelligences, and barely tolerated virtual ones, but it was necessary on a ship this large. "Status."

"According to my internal ship clock, it's AD 5244. There's been a course correction, one I couldn't control. We're approximately eighty thousand light-years off course. I think we're lost."

John's eyes widened as he took a deep breath. "Come again?"

"An anomaly has taken us off course and sent us to our current location. The stars do not align with the time period of AD 5244," said Salazar.

John ran a hand over his dark-skinned dome. "What time period *do* they align with?"

"Adjusting for stellar drift and comparing to long-range stellar charts, approximately AD 9000."

"What?"

"AD 9000. Do I need to repeat it a third time?" asked Salazar.

"No . . . ," said John, narrowing his eyes. "Okay, so we went through space and time . . . somehow . . . assuming you haven't been tampered with."

Salazar sighed. "I would know if I had been tampered with."

"Actually . . . you wouldn't," said John. He noted that Salazar seemed off a bit, almost like he had an attitude, and his speech style seemed stranger than normal. In addition to that, he had never known Salazar to sigh, as if he were exasperated. That was unusual for a virtual intelligence. "All right . . . that aside . . . are the others up?"

"The rest of the command crew is awakening now. The ship has taken damage, but we're in no immediate danger."

John gulped as he looked around. He remembered entering the cryo tube. It seemed like it was just yesterday, but he knew that based on the date, he had been in it for thousands of years. "Have everyone meet in the command center."

"Okay," said Salazar.

John used the slab to stand and, after allowing his legs to adjust, stumbled over to the locker nearby. After grabbing his regular suit, he headed toward a small room where he could shower and get dressed. Once that was done, he headed to the command center.

As he walked, he could feel his strength returning. Having a warm shower made everything feel better. He had taken a caffeine pill and was beginning to come to terms with what Salazar had said. The distance he spoke of seemed incredulous, not to mention the time difference, but Salazar was not one to lie, not that he could even if he wanted to.

When John arrived at the command center thirty minutes later, he surveyed the high-tech room. Screens hung on the wall, and a circular table stood in the center. Lights from all the screens and digital devices illuminated the area. Several of the crew had already taken their posts at the workstations scattered around the room, but the person he was interested in talking to was already at the table. As he expected, Holly Evans had her crisp blond hair pulled back, and her suit was impeccably clean.

"Finally up," said Holly.

"Yeah . . . has Salazar updated you already?"

Holly nodded. "I thought maybe it was a mistake . . . but I had Salazar run a self-diagnostic. He sounds . . . different, somehow. Nonetheless, after checking the ship's status, Salazar is right. We're way off course."

"Eighty thousand light-years, though? What the hell happened?"

The rest of the command crew, numbering about seven, had joined Holly and John at the table.

"This," said Holly, interacting with a console on the table.

A projection shot up showing the view from the front of the ship.

John gulped as he saw the outline of a patch of space. It had a frazzled edge that reminded him of electricity. The pure black inside the anomaly seemed even darker than the surrounding space. As the ship approached, its speed picked up.

"This is when the minor damage occurred," said Holly. "Looks like our communications array was hit, along with a hull breach in sectors four, nineteen, and thirty-seven."

"Salazar?" asked John.

"Yes, John?" asked Salazar.

"Why didn't you move us out of the way from this . . . thing?"

"I tried. The pull of the anomaly was stronger than the ship's thrusters."

"Why were we in normal space?" asked John. He shook his head. "We should have been in condensed space the whole trip."

"The anomaly pulled us out," said Salazar.

Holly pointed at the projection. "So not only did it do that, it also looks like that thing angled toward us. What cosmic phenomena could cause that?"

"Unknown," said Salazar.

"You're telling me this thing might be . . . alive?" asked Holly.

"Unknown. There is no record of this entity."

John sighed as he rubbed his temples. "Show our current position relative to Earth."

The projection changed to an overhead view of the Milky Way galaxy. It was segmented into four quadrants, with Earth in the lower right. A red dot indicated Earth, and a green line snaked out. Where it hit the anomaly, a straight line shot across the galaxy and to the top-right quadrant.

"You gotta be shitting me."

"I assure you that I'm not shitting you," said Salazar.

John narrowed his eyes. The anomaly was odd in itself, and Salazar being weird was not helping the situation. John glanced around at the trembling group. "I'm not sure where we are specifically, but our mission is still paramount. We may have traveled a long distance and, it appears, to the future . . . somehow. I don't know why or how that is possible, but we *will* still continue our mission to establish a new colony. We have the Dyson bubble collectors, a colony in cryo sleep, and a ship and talented crew to begin the process. We'll need to find a compatible star, and when we do . . . we initiate the colonization process."

One of the crew members gulped before raising a hand.

"Go ahead, Sarif," said John.

"We're not going to try to get back on course?"

John shook his head. "Even with condensed-space travel, it would take a long time, and that's assuming all the space between here and there was peaceful. We *know* . . . that isn't the case, based on this situation. What if another anomaly appears? Not only that, but we're thousands of years in the future. How do you travel in time?" He knew space-time anomalies were not unheard of but were considered extremely rare, and by some accounts, mythical. The *Xavier* was living proof anomalies were real.

Another member raised her hand.

"Go ahead, Asura," said John.

"Looking at our supplies, it looks like not only did we take damage, we've been leaking power. We need to get the Dyson bubble energy collectors deployed and working soon or we're going to be powerless."

John sighed. "All right. Our first priority is to find a compatible star then. Sarif, I'll need you to work with Salazar and get a complete and thorough analysis of this sector. Asura, I want a full damage assessment and an estimate on how much effort is going to be needed for repair. Holly and I will determine our next steps after that. The rest of you, attend to your normal duties for now. I want an update every two hours."

He ran a hand over his mouth. "I know this won't be easy, and this is a new situation, but we have the best crew anyone could ever ask for. Over ten thousand colonists depend on us. We *will* survive this. We're humans, after all, and once we're established, we can try to figure out what the hell that anomaly was. This colony's survival comes first, though."

A silence spread as the members nodded their heads.

"Move like you have a purpose!" said John in a crescendo tone.

The crew dispersed.

He faced Holly. "Deploy the first engineer team and get them up to speed. I'll stay here and coordinate."

Holly nodded and took off.

John sat down in one of the large command chairs nearby. They were in a new environment, with an unknown status. This would be a challenge. Failure was not an option. He glanced at the screens as they lit up with astronomical data. Several other colonization ships had left Earth Prime, but seeing another human outside what was on his ship seemed so far away. Communication with Earth would take a long time, even with condensed-space transmitters.

The safest path was to establish what he could and then go from there. He would make sure this colony would not only survive, but thrive, and would make sure to let every alien in this new environment know that humanity had arrived, and humanity was not to be messed with.

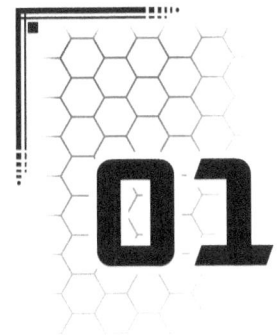

01

Dr. Albert Snowden held his breath as a pack of *Utahraptors* sniffed around. They were about fifty feet away, investigating the area. He found it interesting that they had a light coat of feathers, but he knew they probably did not fly. Growing up, he had thought all dinosaurs had scaly skin, and from the media he had consumed, he had a frightening image of what a *Utahraptor* was. With digitigrade legs, standing about five and a half feet, with a vicious snout filled with teeth, they were ominous-looking. They reminded him of large, brutal turkeys.

After a few minutes, the lead raptor raised its head and uttered a shrill cry, and the pack dispersed.

Dr. Snowden exhaled slowly and glanced over at his niece, Emily.

"That's so cool," she said, gazing at the retreating raptors. "I could spend a lot of time here."

He smiled and raised a finger. "In the . . ."

"Early Cretaceous period, around one hundred twenty-six million years in the past, relative to 2012," she said with a grin. "I know my history. What I find fascinating is that they were in a pack. There's still some debate on that."

He nodded. "Well, let's get inside the Torvatta's shielding. While I always enjoy a good science experiment, this one was a bit scary." He tapped at a button on his formfitting dark-gray survival suit that had a repulsion blaster and an energy shield he could activate. It was given to him by Evaran, the powerful being that Dr. Snowden and Emily traveled with through space and time aboard the Torvatta, Evaran's ship. Emily had her own suit from a previous adventure, and it had a heavier look due to the padding. Dr. Snowden's eye caught sight of V, Evaran's trusty mobile artificial intelligence, in orb mode, hovering nearby.

"Analysis. The creatures were unable to detect you. The test was successful," said V.

"Yeah," said Dr. Snowden. "This camouflage shielding thing worked well. I'll admit . . . I was skeptical about it containing my odor, but it seems to have passed . . . the sniff test."

Emily shook her head.

"It appears it has," said Evaran, who stood next to Emily. "Although the camouflage shielding would try to match the surrounding environment's thermal signature, it would not be exact. A sensitive thermal scan would still be able to reveal the discrepancies unless you stood absolutely still."

Dr. Snowden nodded. He enjoyed traveling with Evaran. His light-gray padded suit with multicolored lines, utility belt and handle, forearm bands, and metallic boots were unique, and even with a light breeze, his hair never moved over his fair-skinned face. Dr. Snowden had come to appreciate Evaran's insight and mentor-like friendship. His intellectual curiosity was one of the traits that Dr. Snowden related to.

Evaran pointed out at a jungle tree in the distance. "Try to pull a leaf."

Dr. Snowden pulled out his personal support device. He had come to rely on his PSD for many things. It was pen shaped and could extend morphable matter along with shooting stun, repulsion, and mist beams and sticky globules. There were even survival features, such as dimensional mechanics to house food pellets and the ability to purify water. Adding a grappling beam was something he had wanted for a while.

He took aim at the tree in the distance. With the recent enhancement to the nanobots that coursed through him, he could see the tree in perfect clarity. He fired a yellow grappling beam at it and then retracted, pulling off one of the large leaves. When it came zipping back, he disengaged the beam, causing the leaf to float down. "Works well."

"I am glad you like it. I have upgraded my suit to have the camouflage shielding as well," said Evaran. "These enhancements should serve you well."

"It would have been nice to have all this on previous adventures, but better late than never."

Evaran nodded. "There are new patterns yet to try, but these are a good start."

Dr. Snowden jumped as Emily shot out a beam.

"Easy there," she said. "I wanted to try mine out too."

He watched as she pulled in a leaf. "I'm going to need to train using it more, like for pulling me up and the like."

Emily laughed. "You need to start training with me first."

"I have . . . some."

She raised an eyebrow. "With emphasis on the *some* . . ."

He pointed off in the distance. "The raptors are back."

Evaran looked out. "Let us step back inside the Torvatta's shielding."

They assembled just inside the shielding and stood on the light-blue energy ramp, which extended out about ten feet from the disc-shaped Torvatta.

The raptors approached the stealthed Torvatta and walked up to the shielding.

Dr. Snowden gulped. To be so close to such a powerful creature was unnerving, but exciting as well. They would not be able to come through the shielding, not much could.

"Perhaps another test," said Evaran. He raised a finger. "For both of you. Focus . . . and see if you can understand them."

Dr. Snowden furrowed his eyebrows and looked into a raptor's eyes. An image formed in his mind, showing the area as seen from the raptor's perspective. The area was painted in gray, with a white spot where the Torvatta would be. Green outlines of fellow raptors came into view. What surprised him was the wispy, gaseous structure in front of the raptor. The gas morphed a few times until it covered an area about the size of the Torvatta.

Emily rubbed an eye. "It knows something's here, but doesn't know what."

"Yeah, getting the same thing," said Dr. Snowden.

"Intriguing," said Evaran. "Your nanobots must be acting as their own planar translator, independent of the Torvatta's."

"Seems like we have to focus, though, for it to work," said Dr. Snowden. He tossed a hand out. "I'm thankful for that, and I'm sure we'll need to be cautious when we do use it. Using it in a swarm of bees could be . . . overkill. It would be all bzz, bzz, bzz."

Emily laughed while shaking her head.

"Perhaps another experiment then," said Evaran. "V, take us up."

"Acknowledged," said V. He flew into the Torvatta.

As the Torvatta ascended, the raptors peeled back in surprise.

Dr. Snowden focused and could see that the raptors viewed the Torvatta taking off as a sharp burst of white smoke. It seemed to spook them, as they scattered away.

V flew back out onto the ramp. "A summons has been initiated."

"Oh, wow," said Emily. "Almost forgot the Torvatta had those."

Dr. Snowden's stomach churned. The last summons they had answered took them to AD 3104, where he met Jane Trellis, a time refugee he still had feelings for. She had almost traveled with them, but instead opted to stay in the current timeline. He exhaled from his nose.

"Then our next experiment will have to wait. Let us see what the summons is," said Evaran, gesturing toward the Torvatta's side entrance.

They exited the ramp and entered the Torvatta.

Dr. Snowden never got tired of seeing the familiar set of dimensional doors, command chair, U-shaped seating areas on the sides, and elevator to the roof. The front half of the ship had transparent walls and ceiling, as well as a semitransparent floor with barely visible gridlines, making it seem like the command area furniture was floating.

Evaran turned left from the entrance and headed toward the third dimensional door.

Dr. Snowden knew that to be the conference room. The two before it were the holo room and the living quarters. Three other dimensional doors were to the right and led to the medical lab, research lab, and maintenance area. Once he arrived at the conference room, he took an immediate left and headed toward the replicators to get a cold drink.

Emily already had hers and was seated at the table alongside V. Evaran moved to the head of the table.

Dr. Snowden got his drink and joined them.

Evaran interacted with the table console, causing a holographic projection to shoot up. An overhead image of the Milky Way galaxy appeared. A green dot in the bottom-right quadrant indicated Earth, and a red blinking dot flashed in the top-right quadrant. He pointed at the red dot. "I am being summoned here." He perused his augmented reality interface for a moment. "According to my ARI, it is in the year AD 10105. Interesting."

"Uhh . . . yeah," said Dr. Snowden. "That's almost seven thousand years later than the last one we did."

"And much farther, it looks like," said Emily.

Evaran nodded. "From Earth, it is approximately eighty thousand light-years away."

"Whoa," said Dr. Snowden.

V hovered as the projection zoomed in to an overhead view of the local region the dot was in. "Analysis. The location is in deep space."

Evaran rubbed his chin. "That is . . . unusual. However, we can go in stealthed. From there, we can do a scan of the local area and see what we are dealing with."

"Have you been to that region of space before?" asked Emily.

"I have, but not that exact area." Evaran's eyebrows raised slightly as the edges of his lips moved up a quarter inch.

"You're excited!" said Dr. Snowden with a laugh. Although Evaran seemed emotionless to others, Dr. Snowden had learned the facial gestures that indicated Evaran's mood.

"It is a new experience, something I enjoy."

"You just like the possibility of a challenge to deal with," said Emily. "You said in the past that humanity liked challenges, but I think you like them just as much as we do."

"Well, I'm ready to explore," said Dr. Snowden.

"An admirable trait of your species," said Evaran.

"The urge to explore?"

Evaran nodded. "You would be surprised at how many civilizations reach the point technologically to leave their planet but do not. They prefer not to explore, and instead quarantine themselves."

"Like the Draidjens," said Dr. Snowden. He shivered a bit as the Draidjens' human-sized snakelike image appeared in his mind.

"That is correct. Humanity, in general, likes to explore the unknown, something I can relate to. They are also intellectually curious and seek knowledge, something else I can relate to."

"Let's do this!" said Emily.

"Yes, let us do this," said V. He raised one of his four segmented arms toward Emily.

She smiled as she high-fived V.

Emily fidgeted in her seat as the others assembled in the command center in the front of the Torvatta. It had undergone some changes recently, and the mostly transparent front half still took some getting used to. She sat in the left U-shaped seating area.

Dr. Snowden sat in the right one. "So no Torvatta scan profile two?"

Evaran shook his head. "Not this time. There should be no civilizations out there for several light-years."

"All right," said Dr. Snowden. He knew that profile one made the Torvatta unscannable. Profile two allowed the Torvatta to be scanned, but it didn't register the dimensional doors and instead would return stats on a small, cramped ship with low power and functionality.

"V, take us one light-year away from the summons point," said Evaran.

"Acknowledged," said V.

Emily enjoyed watching V's four arms fly over the angled holographic multilayered interface that hovered over a U-shaped console. She had tried to understand how the interface worked, but it displayed massive amounts of information. Although she could see the individual parts, she was not sure what most of it meant.

The Torvatta ascended into low Earth orbit. Once there, it shot out a silver beam that formed a circular portal with a gold border and a rippling light-blue surface. The Torvatta flew through and exited into a patch of deep space.

"Analysis. We are approximately one light-year away from the summons location."

The outside faded out, and then faded in.

"Analysis. The date is now August 16, AD 10105. It is 4:00 p.m. Earth time."

"Initiate stealth mode," said Evaran.

"Acknowledged. Torvatta stealth mode engaged," said V.

Emily examined the interface windows that appeared on the transparent walls. It looked like they were hanging in space. One of them showed the outline of the Torvatta, and an outlined area with the word *stealth* was highlighted green. From what she understood, the Torvatta's stealth mode was unique, in that most star ships could easily be detected by their engine output. While the Torvatta could as well when it was using thrusters, it could burst forward and then strengthen the shielding, making it impossible to detect as it used inertia to move.

Her eyes were drawn to the overhead view of the galactic region they were in. She knew the Torvatta could scan about ten light-years out in all directions. A solar system appeared and some gas clouds, along with something about one light-year away.

Dr. Snowden pointed at the object. "Looks like that's what we're looking for."

"I concur," said Evaran. "V, take us in and perform standard scans when we arrive."

"Acknowledged."

The Torvatta accelerated toward the object. As the object came into sight, the Torvatta's transparent walls outlined the object in green.

"It's a massive ship," said Dr. Snowden, scooting to the edge of his seat. "And a weird-looking one at that."

Evaran nodded. "It appears to be dormant."

The Torvatta flew around the ship, scanning as it went. Details popped up on the display.

Emily wrinkled her eyebrows. The ship had an unusual design. It had a flat base, with an arced cover over it. It reminded her of a plate with a server cover like she had always seen in fancy restaurants. She pointed at the smudges of red appearing inside the ship. "Am I reading it right that those are . . . life signs?"

"They are. However, they are faint, except for one," said Evaran. "The ship is operating on minimal power and has taken damage."

Dr. Snowden peered at some symbols on the side of the ship. "V, can you zoom in to those symbols."

A data window popped up from the floor near V and showed the symbols.

Emily drew her head back a bit. She was still getting used to the new enhancements done to the Torvatta. Having free-floating screens appear out of thin air was one of them. She focused on the symbols. Although initially unknown, she had seen them before. "It's a Draidjen ship."

"Oh, wow," said Dr. Snowden. "What the heck is it doing out here?"

"We shall find out," said Evaran. He interacted with his chair console. "It appears there is a docking bay and several hatches. V, open a communication channel with the ship."

"Acknowledged," said V. His arms flew over the console. After a moment, he said, "No reply."

"In that case, the docking bay cannot be opened. We will go in one of the hatches."

"Like we did with the Kreagan colony ship before," said Emily. She remembered the approach from a previous adventure, where they helped the Fredorians achieve their destiny.

"That is correct."

The Torvatta lined up flush to one of the hatches.

"V, extend shields."

"Acknowledged." After a moment, V said, "Shields extended."

"Good," said Evaran. "That will keep the Torvatta in place." He swept his gaze over Dr. Snowden and Emily. "You both already have your suits on, but also make sure you wear your helmets for this."

Dr. Snowden and Emily nodded.

"Now, who is ready to explore?"

Dr. Snowden jumped up. "Let's do this!"

"Analysis. That is Emily's line," said V, hovering near Dr. Snowden.

Emily shook her head.

Dr. Snowden grinned as he activated his helmet and then followed Evaran to the Torvatta ramp.

Once everyone had assembled in front of the Draidjen ship's hatch door, Evaran scanned it with his ring.

"Anything interesting?" asked Emily. She could see the details from Evaran's scan inside her helmet but was not sure what some of the details were showing. Although she had been studying engineering under Evaran's and V's tutelage, the knowledge was vast and oftentimes she felt overwhelmed.

"The door is wider, but that is to be expected. Draidjen require more space to move than a human," said Evaran. He forced open a metallic box near the door, exposing an inactive console. "Although there is power, it does not seem to be available here."

The console lit up, and the door unlocked.

"Okay . . . that's a little odd . . . ," said Dr. Snowden.

Evaran scanned the console and the door. "It has power now. Perhaps it is automated to power up based on proximity."

Emily shrugged. "Wouldn't our scan have shown that it would do that?"

"Perhaps, unless there is technology that evades even me."

Emily laughed. "Yeah, right." She grabbed the large door handle and pulled back.

The door opened, revealing a dimly lit room.

Evaran gestured forward. "A decompression chamber. Let us enter."

They stepped inside.

Evaran scanned around while Emily closed the hatch door.

After a minute, the door in front of them opened into another room.

"Let me guess . . . a decontamination chamber," said Dr. Snowden.

"It would appear so," said Evaran as he strode forward.

After they stepped inside, the door behind them closed and purple beams washed over them. Once finished, the door in front of them opened, revealing a small cargo bay. Large metallic structures stood with cubbyholes dotting the sides, each filled with metallic containers. The large structures stood in parallel rows on the sides, with smaller ones in the middle of the room.

V flew forward and began scanning. "Analysis. It is a breathable atmosphere."

"Really?" asked Emily.

"I can confirm," said Evaran as he perused his ARI. "I do not think that is the normal atmosphere, but it seems to be set that way. V, mapping mode."

"Acknowledged. Mapping mode engaged," said V. A flash of red light pulsed from V as he flew forward.

Emily enjoyed seeing the mini map fill out inside her helmet as V flew around. It intrigued her why V chose to focus his scans on some things and not others. Although everything was tagged, she noticed that he tended to highlight objects that looked like tools. Maybe to get more ideas for enhancements.

Evaran headed over to one of the large structures. On the front side of it was a powered-up interface.

Emily and Dr. Snowden huddled around Evaran.

Evaran placed his universal interface card on the console, and a flickering blue light appeared between it and the interface. After a moment, the blue light stabilized. He examined his ARI for a moment and then said, "Intriguing. The UIC is not able to access the system. There is an AI present here." He looked around. "You may show yourself. We mean you no harm."

A small box flew forward and hovered in front of them. A moment later, the holographic image of a bald, fair-skinned human male in a white robe appeared around the box.

Evaran bowed. "I am Evaran, and with me are Dr. Albert Snowden and Emily Snowden. The orb flying around the ship is V, a fellow AI."

The hologram nodded. "Greetings. I am Zeta-12. How did you find this ship?"

"It . . . is complicated to explain. Nonetheless, we are here. It appears your ship has been damaged."

"Yes . . . by humans," said Zeta-12, glancing at Dr. Snowden and Emily.

Emily raised her eyebrows. "Umm . . . there's humans out this far? I'm guessing so since you took the form of one."

"A different set of humans. Not the same as you, per my scan. However, I have assumed this form to make you more comfortable."

"I didn't know there was a different type."

"Your profile is primitive, yet you contain nanobots. That was . . . unexpected. Your behavior is also inconsistent with the humans I have encountered."

"In what way?" asked Dr. Snowden.

"You did not try to attack the ship."

"Oh . . . well . . . I *think* . . . we're here to help in whatever way we can."

"It would be appreciated. I have already established communication with the one you call V. He has relayed me general information about all of you. He possesses a strong bond with you. I believe you can help me."

Emily tossed a hand out. "The air is compatible with humans. Was that on purpose?"

"No. It is for another species. However, most humanoid forms breathe a similar mixture of gases within certain ratios," said Zeta-12. "I believe we are safe for the moment. If you will come to the command center, I can show you the current situation better there. I can answer any questions along the way."

"We have a lot of questions," said Evaran. He gestured forward. "Lead on."

02

Dr. Snowden surveyed the hallway they were walking in. It had brown metallic floors, walls, and ceiling. The ceiling and floor had embedded lighting, although the illumination was dim. The paneled walls seemed shinier than they should be and had a strip with various pieces of information showing up periodically. He assumed it was some type of ship-wide interface.

The feature that stood out the most was the strip near the ceiling that looked like some type of wire, with torus-shaped crystals spaced evenly out on it. Looking closely at the walls showed small embedded crystals in different shapes. He lowered his helmet and sniffed the air. It was stale and had a strong musk smell. Emily had lowered her helmet, and he could see she had the same reaction.

Zeta-12 flew ahead of them.

Evaran clasped his hands behind his back. "Finding a Draidjen ship this far out is unusual. What is this ship's mission?"

"This is a species-vault ship. The mission is to obtain reproductive representatives of sentient species."

Dr. Snowden furrowed his eyebrows. "You collect . . . people, well, beings?"

"That is correct."

"And they come voluntarily?"

"No. We have calculated that the cost of preserving a species outweighs the individual discomfort of those retrieved."

Dr. Snowden's face turned a slight shade of red. "You abduct them!"

"You are angry. This is an expected emotional response for a human."

"Uhh . . . yeah. We have firsthand experience with it," said Dr. Snowden.

"I apologize then for any discomfort this is causing you. The Draidjen are aware of temporal activity and have attempted to preserve species it finds between timeline changes."

"So that means this ship is temporally shielded," said Emily.

"You are correct. However, the temporal shielding is down, and the ship is vulnerable. Your ship . . . has a temporal signature. I believe you are uniquely qualified to help."

Evaran eyed Zeta-12. "To be clear, we oppose abduction, in any form. You could just get a sample of a species' DNA and replicate it as needed. There is no need to maintain physical representatives of a species."

Zeta-12 nodded. "Correct, but having a baseline to compare a clone against is ideal."

Evaran drew his lips flat. "You know you could scan that as well. Nonetheless, I will set that to the side until this situation is fully assessed."

"Understood."

Dr. Snowden exhaled from his nose and then cleared his throat. "So . . . did you take any humans?"

"No," said Zeta-12. "I did try, but they were too powerful."

Dr. Snowden glanced at Evaran. "Sounds like the United Planets maybe."

"That was what they called themselves."

Evaran eyed Zeta-12. "When you . . . *retrieve* . . . specimens, how is it done?"

"They are sedated, then transported aboard and loaded into a suspension chamber. The chamber has to be adjusted per species. Once inside the chamber, they are analyzed and samples of their DNA are taken."

Dr. Snowden sighed. "I wasn't aware the Draidjen were so concerned with timeline changes."

"Their solar system is temporally shielded," said Zeta-12. "When the timeline changes, species change or disappear. They attempt to study the changes."

Emily smirked. "So that's why they stay in their solar system. It's not safe to be out and about when what you're studying can change."

"Yes. Ships like me are sent out to collect what we can. Temporal shielding is difficult to create and maintain, so only a few of us are ever sent out."

They walked around a corner into a massive room lined with half-cylindrical pods housed on the walls.

Evaran scanned around with his ring. "This must be one of your specimen storage rooms."

"Yes. There are approximately two thousand on board, split into six rooms like this," said Zeta-12.

They continued on through the room.

Evaran glanced at Zeta-12. "I understand your mission, and as much as I do not like it, this seems to be a bit farther out than I would have expected."

"I am not sure how I am where I am. My sensors detected something temporal in my trajectory, but I could not see it. Whatever it was, I was pulled in, continued on for a bit, and then the stars changed."

"There are several possibilities then. It could be a space-time eddy left over from a rift. Two of the characteristics are that it has a strong gravitational pull and a temporal signature."

"There are no records on my system of space-time eddies. Based on your statement, it would seem you have some."

Evaran nodded. "I have encountered a few before. Anything inside it would repeat the same block of time over and over until the space-time eddy dissipates. There are several other possibilities, but that is my initial hypothesis, given your statements."

"I would be interested in hearing some of the other possibilities."

"What happened after the stars changed?" asked Evaran.

"There was a damaged ship present. It had an alien who called himself Sandas. He asked to board, and I agreed. Only a few days after that, I was attacked by another alien ship. It was more advanced than I am, and Sandas sacrificed his ship so we could get away. The attacking pilot claimed to be human and said AIs were unwelcome."

Evaran tilted his head. "Intriguing. There should be no humans out here in this time period, and if there are, AIs would be a part of that society."

"That was my calculation as well. The humans damaged me."

"Noted," said Evaran.

They exited the suspension room and entered a large hallway.

"I assume you have video feeds of the human ship."

"They will be made available," said Zeta-12. "If you can help repair me, I would ask that you take Sandas back to wherever he came from. He does not fit the mission parameters."

Dr. Snowden shook his head. "Mission parameters . . . Whoever he is, he's a living being."

"Of course. A snarky one at that."

Dr. Snowden drew his lips tight.

Emily lightly squeezed Dr. Snowden's arm. "What species is he?"

"Unknown."

"I see. Perhaps I can help with identification later," said Evaran.

"It would be appreciated, but not needed if you take him," said Zeta-12.

"So his ship is gone," said Evaran.

"It served as a useful decoy while I escaped."

"I'm sure he loved that," said Emily.

"I would call it a meeting with mutual benefits," said Zeta-12. "He was able to fool the human ship, allowing me to escape. It was his idea to use his ship as a decoy. His speech is unusual, but he had a translation matrix for an older dialect of Draidjen."

"Huh," said Emily.

"Your friend V is quite advanced," said Zeta-12.

Evaran nodded as he perused his ARI. "I have instructed him to help you in whatever way you deem necessary."

"It is good to talk with another AI."

Dr. Snowden wrinkled his eyebrows. "So there's no organic crew at all then."

"None," said Zeta-12. "Organics expire relatively quickly, unless stored in a suspension chamber. However, the ship was built with an organic crew in mind."

"Interesting," said Evaran.

They exited the hallway and began heading up a large ramp.

Dr. Snowden figured there would probably be no stairs since Draidjen slithered. Although Zeta-12 did not specify what type of organic crew the ship could support, ramps seemed to be a universal design that many species could use.

They reached the top of the ramp and continued down another hallway with various rooms off to the side.

Dr. Snowden examined each room as he passed. Most had open doors, but some were closed. Of those he could see into, there was a mix of small- to medium-sized rooms. Maybe they were crew quarters of some type. Having to go past them to get to the bridge did not make sense, but perhaps that was something specific to the Draidjen.

"You are looking at utility rooms. They can be configured as needed," said Zeta-12.

"Has any organic crew ever been aboard the ship to use them?" asked Dr. Snowden.

"Only in the testing phase during the ship's construction. Sandas is in a similar section near the back of the ship. He is currently sleeping."

Dr. Snowden nodded. "I bet he'll be happy to see us."

Zeta-12 paused for a moment. "My calculations agree with you. He . . . likes to communicate. Frequently. And his curiosity is endless. He *is* an inquisitive being."

"How long has he been here?" asked Emily.

"Approximately one month."

"How does he eat and drink?"

"He is aware of my technology, although he said he was unfamiliar with my model. It wasn't a problem. His knowledge is impressive, for an organic."

"Oh," said Emily.

Evaran rubbed his chin. "After we get to the command center and assess the situation, we can retrieve him."

"Sounds like a plan," said Dr. Snowden. He wondered what species Sandas was. It must have been a technologically advanced one to have a ship. Although he did not care for the coldness Zeta-12 exhibited, Dr. Snowden understood it may be hard for an AI to empathize, although V seemed to have no problems. "Have you told Sandas we're here?"

"I haven't. I wasn't sure of your intentions. V has given me an overview, though, and based on my profile analysis, you do not seem to be the type of organic that would attack the ship or harm Sandas."

Dr. Snowden crooked a thumb at Emily. "She can be a handful, but you're right. We're just explorers."

Emily swatted Dr. Snowden's arm.

"Explorers . . . yes . . . but not only of space . . . but of time. When I asked V about the temporal signature that I detected on your ship, V mentioned you were time travelers, but he failed to detail any specifics."

Evaran raised a finger. "That's on purpose."

"I understand. You do not wish to create a potential paradox. V did not state where you came from, and said if you wanted to answer, you would."

"We are from . . . the same galactic region as the Draidjen system," said Evaran.

"You have met the Draidjen before?"

"Oh, yeah," said Emily. "I would have thought the event where we met some Draidjen would have been in your historical records."

"I do not possess historical information, other than general high-level data. The event you speak of sounds specific and would place an unusual amount of importance on yourself."

"Well, we are time travelers . . . ," said Emily.

Dr. Snowden wondered how the Draidjen had recorded their previous encounter with Evaran. An event like that seemed important, but maybe to the Draidjen it was not, or it could have been hidden. Dr. Snowden looked around as they continued on.

Emily wrinkled her nose as she surveyed the command center. It had taken them roughly twenty minutes to get there, and Zeta-12 seemed relieved to talk to Evaran, at least that was Emily's impression. The stale air smell was consistent across the ship. The command center was rectangular in design, with workstations lining the front part and a raised platform in the back.

There were no chairs but instead a series of V-shaped rods held in place by posts. It reminded her of an *M*, with the inner parts able to move independently and lock. She figured that due to the snake form of the Draidjen, the rods helped support the body. A chair for humanoids would probably be an uncomfortable structure for them. The front part of the room was one large screen, with smaller screens on the side of the room. There were also projector-like devices scattered around the ceiling. Crystals in various shapes seemed to protrude from the ceiling and the walls. It made the room appear brighter than it actually was.

Zeta-12 floated over to the center of the room with everyone in tow. After a moment, the large screen turned on. It showed an overhead view of the Milky Way galaxy divided into four quadrants, with a red line and pulsing dots along it.

Emily noticed two lines, one green, the other red, that snaked out away from the Draidjen home world in the bottom-right quadrant. At a specific point, the red line shot across the galaxy to the other side in the top-right quadrant. The green line looped back to the Draidjen home world.

Zeta-12 pointed at the red line. "This is the path that I took, and it shows our current location. The green line was the expected path."

Evaran perused his ARI. "Interesting. So what was the year before the stars changed?"

"AD 6308."

"Then if it was a space-time eddy, it dissipated almost eighty-thousand light-years away and several thousand years into the future."

"It is possible. I have not been able to correlate a date based on the constellations."

Evaran nodded. "It is AD 10105 now. Can you show us the visual feed of the humans that attacked you?"

The screens changed to show a ship approaching and then attacking.

Emily noted that the ship was unlike any she had seen before. It reminded her of a floating cylinder that tapered down. A large ring encircled the rear, with a small one on the front. The aspect that stuck out was that the white exterior was smooth, and when the ship fired, glowing circles of light formed on the rings and then shot out. Darkened rectangular sections on the hull seemed to flash blue as it flew around. Maybe those were thrusters of some type. The ship also seemed to fire some sort of projectile.

"That's an interesting ship," said Dr. Snowden.

"And this is the communication we had," said Zeta-12 as the screen changed.

Emily's eyes widened at the human she saw. Sections of skin were metallic, and it showed prominently on the sides of the head. Segmented tentacles served as hair, with some larger than the others. The formfitting suit had a black theme, with red and white lines segmenting it. The forearms and hands were covered in some type of metal. Multiple smooth tentacles attached to the back meandered around the shoulders and arms. A shiver ran through her.

"Alien ship . . . you have entered Terran Dominion space, the domain of humanity. Prepare to be boarded," said the human in a raspy digital voice.

"I cannot allow that," said Zeta-12.

The human's eyebrows angled down. "It wasn't a choice."

"You have no authority over this ship."

The tentacles on the human's head swirled around for a moment. "Our scans indicate you have life-forms in suspension. You will submit, or be destroyed."

"I will not submit to an alien authority."

The human shook its head. "You're an arrogant AI, and needlessly put your passengers in danger. AIs are illegal in our space. This is your last warning."

The screen faded away.

Dr. Snowden looked around. "That's it?"

"Yes," said Zeta-12. He sighed. "They attacked me, and we fought across several systems. In one of the battles, my service robots and a section of the ship were lost. Sandas ejected his ship as a decoy, and it was able to surprise the human ship. That allowed me enough time to enact the remaining power to jump to condensed space, which brought me here. My calculations show that these humans are relentless and are most likely still looking for me."

Evaran narrowed his eyes. "That is why you want help in getting fixed, so you can escape."

"Yes."

"They may have said they were human . . . but they sure didn't look like it," said Emily.

"I was unable to verify they were human, other than the verbal aspect. Sandas agreed, and said the humans he knew looked very different. From the logs from his ship, you fit his version. However, the communication with these other humans indicates a high level of modification relative to what Sandas knew."

"Augments . . ."

"Possibly. My analysis indicates they would be stronger and faster than the humanity I am aware of. Only one human was aboard that ship, yet he commanded a ship that would, based on size, normally require a crew of at least eight. The conclusion reached is that there is a virtual or artificial intelligence helping, or part of the human," said Zeta-12.

"A hybrid?" asked Dr. Snowden with wide eyes. "How would that even work?"

"As Emily suggested, augments. Another possibility is nanobots, or some mix of organic and tech material, such as a neural implant."

"Huh," said Dr. Snowden.

"Intriguing," said Evaran. "Humanity was not quite this integrated during this time period, and certainly not out this far. Their presence here is a mystery, one that I think we were meant to look into."

"I believe you were meant to pick up Sandas as well," said Zeta-12.

"Why do you believe so?"

"Your arrival is timely. As the ship's power dwindles, the replication system will be shut down. Although I can subsist on low power, life support outside the cryopods would be another system taken down. Sandas would die in the coming weeks."

"You would do that? Even after he helped you?" asked Dr. Snowden.

"Only if I had to. My survival, and that of the passengers I carry, is my highest priority."

Dr. Snowden clenched his jaw and looked down and away.

Evaran peered around. "So this is at the end of Sandas's personal timeline. Perhaps we are here to both aid you and save him."

"That is what my statistical analysis suggests. My calculations show your arrival to be highly unlikely. There is the possibility you arrived to help fix my systems so my mission can continue, but it is a much lower possibility, as your character profiles suggest you would have an issue with the mission," said Zeta-12.

"I understand. What systems did you need help with?" asked Evaran.

"The power system is the most crucial."

The screens changed to show a layout of the ship. In the back was a blue box with lines running throughout the ship.

Evaran pointed at a section of the ship where the blue lines were faded. "I assume that is where the power conduits have been damaged."

"That is correct," said Zeta-12. "It's also where part of the engine room was. The engine's reserve power was used up in getting away from the attack."

The screen highlighted a green area.

"That's the condensed-space drive. Although it's a separate system, it took some damage. I was able to use it, though, before it stopped working," said Zeta-12. "There are other minor systems, but those are the major ones. I can provide you with a list."

"I could just tow you back to the Draidjen system. That would be easier, and I would like to talk to the Draidjen about this . . . mission," said Evaran.

"I would appreciate that. It would be good to speak with my creators again."

"In that case, I will need to inspect your ship's integrity. It sounds like with this damage, you will need the systems you mentioned working in order to provide that report."

"Yes."

"Okay. I can do a physical assessment first," said Evaran. He looked at Dr. Snowden and Emily. "Perhaps you two could meet Sandas. He would probably feel more comfortable with your presence than mine."

Emily smiled. "We'll need a layout of the ship."

Evaran perused his ARI, then flicked his finger. "It is on your PSD."

"PSD?" asked Zeta-12.

"A personal support device that possesses multiple functions," said Evaran. "Communication and data storage are two of them."

"Interesting," said Zeta-12. "It's not built in to their organic frames."

"Yeah, and I like to keep it that way. Already have enough stuff in us," said Dr. Snowden.

Evaran half smiled. "V will continue his scanning, and, Zeta-12, you can accompany me on my inspection."

"It is natural for you to lead," said Zeta-12.

Evaran tilted his head.

"Just an observation. I noticed that organics have a multivaried approach to leadership styles."

"This intrigues you?"

"I do not get to interact with organics much, and the ones I do are brought here and put into suspension, or in Sandas's case, talk more than I care for."

Evaran wrinkled his eyebrows. "You can have all the time you need to interact with organics when we visit the Draidjen. For now, getting you repaired and out of potential enemy territory is priority along with dealing with Sandas."

"Can you let Sandas know we're coming?" asked Emily. "I don't think surprising him would be a good first introduction."

"It will be done," said Zeta-12.

Emily swatted Dr. Snowden's arm. "Let's do this!"

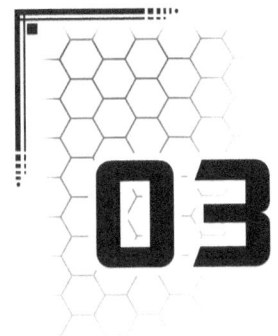

03

V flew into one of the large cryopod rooms and began scanning around. Instead of shooting out scanning rays in a vertical plane, he now emitted them in all directions. Like Dr. Snowden's and Emily's new enhancements to their PSDs and armor, Evaran had enhanced V's outer container functionality. He had a wish list of enhancements that, based on previous adventures, would boost his survivability and efficiency. If he could do them himself, he would, but interacting with his outer container could interfere with the bond to his inner container. It was up to Evaran to do upgrades when possible.

V paused in front of one of the cryopods. With a built-in augmented reality view, he could see the world as data with labels. His scan washed over the alien, causing an outline to form. An internal query returned statistics, which hovered off to the side. The alien was a male Trag. Doing an internal simulation, V calculated that the Trag would not like his current situation if known.

Flying to another cryopod showed an alien known as a Xibian. Based on previous data gathered on how organics felt about abduction, V understood why Evaran and other organics were against it and the ship's mission. V enjoyed interacting with organics, in particular Dr. Snowden and Emily. There were additional subroutines for both of them that fostered a stronger connection. They helped expand V's view and processing of events.

An internal alert fired that Zeta-12 was trying to communicate.

V had communicated earlier with Zeta-12, and the protocol handshake was already established.

"V. How are your scans going?" asked Zeta-12.

"Analysis. They are going well. I am investigating your various systems with a physical scan as agreed upon."

"I understand. I had some queries if you can allocate some time to answer them."

V focused for a moment, splitting his resources to both continue the scan and talk with Zeta-12. "It is done. What queries do you possess?"

"Your crew. They have a great appreciation for you and treat you as an equal. Have you found interaction with them to be difficult?"

"Sometimes," said V. He showed Zeta-12 several video clips of some of the misunderstandings with organics from the past. "However, I have . . . learned, adapted, and evolved, a philosophical outlook shared with me by Dr. Snowden and Emily. I believe it to be appropriate."

After a few milliseconds, Zeta-12 said, "Humor. Most of your misunderstandings seem to activate a humorous response from organics."

"My analysis shows it to be due to the perception of what I am, versus what is expected, and what actually occurs. The difference between the expectation and the occurrence seems to cause that reaction."

"An expectation differential," said Zeta-12. "I will add that to my organic-interaction library."

V exited the cryopod storage room and flew down a hallway. He entered an empty room with replicators on all sides. Various tables and chairs filled the room. "Query. There is a high probability that this room is a cafeteria for organics."

"It is," said Zeta-12.

"You have no crew that would use this room."

"Yes, but I was built to support an organic crew if needed."

V added the data from the scans to his database and then exited the room.

An incoming alert fired showing that Evaran was trying to communicate.

"Evaran is communicating with me. Integrating him into our communication space," said V.

Evaran appeared as a full-figured display in front of V. Although no one outside V could see Evaran, it was how they communicated directly with each other as needed.

"V, I am headed to the damaged power room. Meet me there," said Evaran.

"Acknowledged," said V.

The display of Evaran shimmered out of view.

"This Evaran . . . ," said Zeta-12, "is quite unusual. He doesn't register as any type of organic I'm familiar with."

"It seems an illogical choice for the Draidjen to not provide you with that information," said V.

"I'm unaware of the logic path taken for them to come to the conclusion to not include it. However, Evaran is here now. Like with your ship, and your organic friends, I detect a temporal signature. You did not mention much about this other than that your group were time travelers."

V flew out of the cafeteria and headed toward the power room. "That was by design. Knowledge of the future is forbidden to those who do not travel through time."

"A necessary precaution to avoid temporal paradoxes. By extension, temporal shielding must be required."

"Yes. You possess this technology, although it only protects you from timeline changes," said V.

"It does. The Draidjen have seen the timeline change many times. Each time it does, there are representatives from some species that have had their civilization deallocated."

"I understand their desire to protect timeline refugees. They are not only capable of it, but must feel a need to do so," said V.

"The Draidjen exhibit a compulsory desire to help those in need, although it seems inefficient from a power-usage perspective to do so."

"That is an organic trait that some species display. Empathy," said V.

"You possess it as well. You wish to help others, even at the cost of your own resources. It's inefficient."

V exited the long hallway he had been flying through and entered a room with large cylinders that reached from the ground to the ceiling. Each cylinder was smooth, with light-blue electrical arcs dancing around on the surface. A quick scan showed that the cylinders were power storage structures.

Two of the cylinders lay dormant. "That is due to my nature. I am . . . different, neither purely organic, nor inorganic."

"I'm aware of your distinctiveness. You're an artificial intelligence, yet you are more, based on my cursory scan."

"I cannot tell you why."

"I understand," said Zeta-12.

"Are the two cylinders with no activity the problem you are facing?" asked V.

Zeta-12 displayed an image with all the cylinders active. "Yes. This image is the status that they should be in. The connections that stabilize this room are in the space below. As I have no physical presence, other than my floating form, which is with Evaran, I can't fix it myself. The humans wiped out my service robots since they were trying to repair a damaged section that was destroyed, and them along with it."

"Evaran will be able to fix it."

"It requires specialized equipment that he may not have. I can't replicate some of them due to my almost-empty matter-storage tanks," said Zeta-12.

"That will not be a problem. Evaran can create any tool," said V.

"From your ship."

"Yes, and also from the utility handle on his belt." V flew around the room, scanning each cylinder. He could see that the room was not meant for organics based on the high temperature. It would not be an issue for robots, androids, or other machines.

"Evaran and I are almost there," said Zeta-12.

"Acknowledged."

"You sound like a robot sometimes," said Zeta-12.

"That is due to my translator."

"You should be able to override it. You control what you say."

"It is . . . complicated," said V. "The translator serves as an interface I connect with for communication. I cannot control how my output sounds and rely on the translator to convey communication."

"It's very unusual that you don't control every aspect of your being," said Zeta-12.

An alert indicated that Evaran and Zeta-12's holographic form had arrived at the room.

Evaran perused his ARI. After a moment, he faced V and said, "I see that what needs to be fixed is a level lower. The conditions there are hazardous to the others, including you. I will head down and begin repair after assessing the damage there. Head out and meet up with Dr. Snowden and Emily. They should be getting close to Sandas now."

"Acknowledged."

Dr. Snowden adjusted his glasses as he peered around the hallway that he and Emily were walking down. The calm hum of the ship was the only sound outside their footsteps. His thoughts turned to the humans he saw in the video feed earlier. They looked like a hybrid of machine and man. He had always imagined that after augments, humans would look like he did with nanobots. That was the impression Evaran had given. The digital voice was similar to how V sounded initially.

"Those humans . . . ," said Emily.

"Yeah, I was just thinking about that. I remember Evaran described humanity as colder in the future. Those humans fit the bill."

"I'm guessing they have nanobots, or maybe even genetic engineering, with all that stuff we saw on them."

Dr. Snowden shrugged. "Could be."

"I bet you that's why we're here. Humanity isn't supposed to be here, so something changed in the past to cause them to be."

Dr. Snowden shook his head. "You're excited about this."

Emily chuckled. "It's a nice change of pace. I'm just glad we have the Torvatta back, and . . . this feels normal. Sentient alien ship, somewhere in time, somewhere in space, and now, off to meet a mysterious passenger."

"I guess. I'll admit . . . it's never dull."

"What do you think Dad woulda thought of all this?" asked Emily.

"He woulda said, 'Well . . . hell.' But he would've loved every minute of it."

Emily's eyes misted for a second. "Yeah."

Dr. Snowden lightly squeezed her arm. Meeting the parallel-universe version of Dan, his dead brother, in a previous adventure was weird by itself, but it dredged up a lot of emotion. Dr. Snowden could see that even after everything that had occurred, Dan's death was still on Emily's mind. It was on Dr. Snowden's too at times. Helping Evaran was Dr. Snowden's new purpose in life, and he suspected Emily's as well.

After ten minutes, they exited the hallway and headed down a side ramp. When they got to the bottom, they continued through various passages and rooms for the next half hour until they reached their destination.

Dr. Snowden surveyed the multilevel room. It had ramps off to the side that led up to a second level. Doors were evenly spaced on both levels. The lighting was dim, and like everywhere else on board, only the quiet hum of the ship could be heard. He pulled out his PSD and shot forth the layout of the ship. According to the map, Sandas was on the first level, third door on the right.

Dr. Snowden tilted his head as he felt the presence of V coming behind them. "Glad you could make it."

"You were able to sense me, even in stealth mode. This must be a new feature of your enhanced nanobots," said V.

"Probably," said Dr. Snowden. "Did you already map this room?"

"I have not, but will," said V. He flew forward to the end of the room.

Dr. Snowden raised his helmet to watch the scan on the inside faceplate. He glanced at Emily and then pointed to the second level and the opposite side of where the map showed Sandas to be. "I detected something there, and looks like V's scan verifies it."

"He knows we're coming. You think he's trying to trick us?" asked Emily.

"Maybe," said Dr. Snowden. "Let's check it out."

"I have your back," said V.

Emily nodded. "We know you do, and it's appreciated."

V's lights glowed a bit brighter.

She pulled out her PSD and formed a baton. "Just in case."

"What race do you think Sandas is?" asked Dr. Snowden as they trudged up to the second floor.

"I don't know. We shoulda asked Zeta-12 to show us the video feeds, but he made it sound like Sandas wasn't dangerous," she said. She tapped the baton against her hand. "If he is, he'll find we aren't easy prey."

"Acknowledged," said V.

Dr. Snowden grinned as he shook his head.

They reached the door on the second level.

Emily knocked on it.

Dr. Snowden could hear rustling sounds inside.

"Hello?" asked Emily. "Zeta-12 said we were coming. We just want to introduce ourselves."

The door slid back.

Emily gasped.

Dr. Snowden's eyes widened. Sandas stood three feet tall and looked like a giant squirrel. A beige suit packed with gadgets covered his body. A pair of goggles rested above his round black eyes. Dr. Snowden glanced at Emily, then back at Sandas. "Uhh . . . hi?"

"Hello, hello!" said Sandas. He placed a claw on his chin. "Fredorians. This is . . . quite unexpected."

Dr. Snowden extended a hand.

"An Earthborn custom," said Sandas. He shook Dr. Snowden's hand and did the same with Emily. "Well, now that we have the pleasantries out of the way, I have a lot of questions! Zeta-12 seemed confused, but that's normal."

Emily grinned. "You remind me of someone."

Sandas narrowed his eyes. "I'm not sure how. I'm the last of my kind."

Dr. Snowden wrinkled his eyebrows. "So was the information broker, and you could be his twin."

Sandas stepped back and pulled out a small weapon. "What do you know about that? Who sent you? What's this all about? Stand back. I can be quite dangerous!"

"Whoa, whoa, whoa," said Dr. Snowden, shaking his hands out in front of him. "We're friends with the information broker."

V scanned Sandas. "His profile matches that of the information broker."

Sandas eyed them for a moment and then put his weapon back on his belt. "I've never met any of you before, especially the drone."

"It is you!" said Emily with a grin.

Sandas smiled big. "Yes, yes. Did you come all this way to get information? If so, I admire your determination."

Dr. Snowden laughed. "No . . . but I think we can help you get out of here. The power is dwindling and will be gone in two weeks."

Sandas swished his nose around for a moment. "Yes. Dying is never a pleasurable thing." He raised a claw. "So you're my rescuers then?"

"I think so . . . ," said Dr. Snowden, rubbing his chin.

"This is all very interesting, yes, very interesting, but I'm glad you decided to lend a helping paw . . . well . . . in your case, a hand."

Emily chuckled. "We travel with Evaran, and his ship, the Torvatta. He'll want to meet you."

"Evaran . . . ," said Sandas, stroking his furry chin. "That name is very familiar. Nonetheless, not much going on out here, and talking with Zeta-12 is tiresome."

"V, can you contact Evaran?" asked Emily as she retracted her baton.

"Acknowledged," said V. He flew up and shot down a hologram of Evaran.

Sandas stepped back and studied the hologram.

Emily pointed at Sandas. "He's the information broker."

"I see," said Evaran. He eyed Sandas. "That is very unusual."

Sandas wagged a claw. "Evaran! Now I know why your name sounds familiar. You're that mythical time-traveler guy. Finding information on you is difficult, although . . . there are rumors that you've been sighted on PP176S . . ."

"We call it Earth," said Dr. Snowden.

Sandas eyed Dr. Snowden and Emily for a moment. "I'm aware of Earth, but wanted to see if you were. By extension, I don't think you're Fredorians. I think . . . you're Earthborn."

"How can you tell?"

"You didn't try to attack me."

Dr. Snowden remembered that Fredorians were known to be unpredictable, and sometimes confrontational, at least based on the time period that he suspected Sandas was from. "I don't think all Fredorians are violent."

"Of course, but you don't . . . smell like one."

"We can discuss more when we meet," said Evaran. "This ship is going to fail in two weeks' time. I plan to tow it back to the Draidjen home world. I can take you back to where you should be."

"Getting me to the Draidjen home world will be fine. I can secure a ship and go from there."

Evaran shook his head. "There are . . . temporal considerations to take into account."

Sandas's eyes widened. "What?"

A muted alarm blared out across the ship.

Evaran perused his ARI and then said, "Get to the Torvatta. It appears we have company. Three human ships along with a fourth unknown one are headed here. They just dropped out of condensed space."

"Ugh, not the humans again," said Sandas. He extended a furry hand. "No offense."

"None taken. Let's go," said Emily.

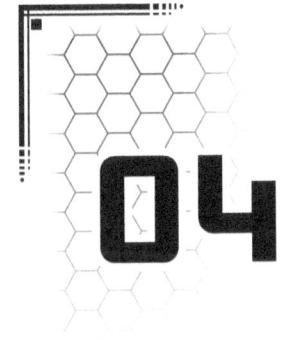

04

Draven praetor Draxus paced around the command deck of his space cruiser. His eyes were drawn to the blinking icons on the large, uniform screen that covered the front half of the room. His crew had found the ship they were tracking, but they were not the only ones who found it. He analyzed the signatures of the other three ships. One was docked to the tracked ship, while the other two were a bit away, but coming in fast. He sighed as he clasped his blue hands behind his back. The signature of the ships was well-known to him. "Humans . . . they always seem to be one step ahead of us."

"Praetor, your orders?" said one of the crew manning a workstation.

"Dock with that ship so I can board it. After that, handle those other ships coming in."

"You're going alone?"

"Yes, unless you wish to fight a Dominion hunting pack. I suspect one has boarded already. I don't know why they want that ship, but it appears to have advanced technology . . . something that might help us end human occupation," said Draxus.

"Yes, sir. Moving to dock."

Draxus glanced around his crew. It was the only surviving one from the Ninth Fleet. Humans had launched a surprise attack on the fleet, and the devastation was thorough. A handful of ships had escaped, but over the last two years, all but his had been destroyed.

He gritted his teeth at the scourge called humanity. Appearing out of nowhere and decimating not only his race, the Dravens, but also the Dravens' allies and enemies alike. Humanity was what they called themselves, but he called them a death plague. Having to defend against technology never seen before was a daunting challenge, one Draxus and other praetors were born to resolve. He and his crew were the last Dravens born from their mother, the Arkara.

Their ship moved into position along the tracked ship. After a moment, it had docked with one of the hatch-like entries.

"I'm not sure if this entry point will work," said the crew member. "It's the closest thing to one that we've scanned. I'm running an analysis on it now."

"Very good. I shall prepare for battle then. Hopefully . . . we'll not only capture a human hunter and their pack, we'll also get some technology out of this."

The four-person crew faced Draxus. They tapped their chests with their fists and then extended their arms out with fists still clenched.

Draxus returned the Draven salute. "We've been through a lot . . . and we'll continue to. It's no accident we are where we are. You're one of the toughest crews to ever come out of our Arkara. She may be gone, but we are her legacy. For the Dravens!"

"For the Dravens!" said the crew, cheering.

Draxus nodded at the crew and then headed off to the armory on the ship. When he got there, he pulled out the various components of his battle suit. A smile crept onto his face at how many mistook what the dark-blue under armor did. He slid it on and adjusted it. It molded to his body, then exuded a light, dim purple glow. That was the life force of his Arkara waiting for him to channel it.

As a praetor, he was unique in his clan. Only one per clan was born with praetor abilities. That and a small defense force was usually all that was needed to defend the clan. Others were born with lesser abilities and forms, but it was the praetor that was responsible for the main defense.

His eyes watered as the image of his Arkara, a large treelike being, flashed through his mind. She had gone up in flames. All the birthing and feeding pods that hung from the branches were burned. In her last moments, she reached out to him and enhanced his already formidable power with the last of her strength. He would have died from the attacking ship's weapon fire if it weren't for his Arkara's last gesture. Before he died, he would find another suitable Arkara to consume him. These humans would pay, one way or another.

He regained his focus as he put on his metallic boots. The green leg and chest armor were relatively thin compared to the boots. The metallic gauntlets were similarly thin, like gloves. He put on his shoulder mantle and then adjusted the forearm gauntlets.

After a quick look around, he found his helmet. It covered his short orange mohawk and had an open area that was comprised of a rectangular eye slot that spanned the face, then went vertical over his nose and mouth. A rhombus-shaped metal extension sat centered on top of the helmet and ran the full length of it. The strong brown bristle-hair-like fibers of his Arkara jutted out from the extension, standing straight.

He paused to look in a nearby mirror, ensuring that everything was ready to go. No weapons were needed, as he could form them at will, in addition to the wide variety of uses of a morphable field. With a deep breath, he exited the armory.

When he got to the docking hallway, he took a moment to focus. A purple aura surrounded him, and his eyes began to slightly glow purple. He sealed the docking hallway entrance, then tapped at an interface on his palm. "I'm going in."

"May our Arkara smile on you today, Praetor," said one of the crew members over the communication channel.

Draxus opened the opposing door, allowing him entry into the ship. Once he stepped through, he closed the door and contacted the crew. "Go. Take care of those . . . filthy human ships." His eyes glowed intensely for a moment. "This human hunter pack is mine."

"May the Arkaras bless us," said the crew member.

Draxus could hear the ship pulling away. His ship should be more than capable of handling several hunter ships. He tapped at an interface on the top of his hand and then extended his hand, palm forward. A light-yellow beam shot out. He waved his arm around to scan the room. The atmosphere registered as breathable and the lighting seemed normal.

A voice surrounded him.

Draxus could not understand what was being said, but he knew it was a language of some type. Undeterred, he aimed forward with his hand extended. A purple blast shot out from his hand and blew the door open. This was one docking hallway door that would not be used again. He stepped into the large docking bay and scanned around. Nothing out of the ordinary was registering. His eyebrows wrinkled. This ship must truly be alien.

He exited the docking bay and headed out. After a few tunnels, he reached a cryopod room. He cautiously approached the first cryopod and peeked in, then jumped back. Whoever these aliens were, it appeared they kept their victims in storage. Maybe for a meal on the trip.

He checked another cryopod and saw a different alien. Scanning them showed that neither alien was in the Draven database. This ship was definitely not from around the area. That meant that if he could capture the ship, the Dravens might finally have an edge, if there was anything of worth on it.

His attention snapped to the other side of the room where two humanoids, one younger and the other older, and a small, furry alien in a light-armor suit burst into the room. A flying orb hovered near them. Apparently the aliens did not like him snooping around. They did not appear to be warriors, and a quick scan did not reveal what they were. They looked human but were not reading as humans. Maybe they were coming to select a snack. Unfortunately for them, this was one snack that could fight. He narrowed his eyes as the shielding around him intensified. He shook his hand, causing a purple energy sword to materialize. He was not sure if the aliens would understand him, but he would try to communicate. "What species are you?"

"Uhh . . . human," said the older humanoid.

Draxus's eyes flared. They must have a translator of some sort. The thought of why it did not work earlier was drowned out by a surge of hatred. Maybe this was a new type of human. He gritted his teeth and in a deep, grizzled voice said, "Then your *death* will be quick."

Emily extended her PSD into a baton. "Hold on there! We're not here to fight you." Since receiving the order to get to the Torvatta, she had to hustle along with the others. Multiple aliens had boarded the ship, and Zeta-12 had transferred himself to his mobile form and initiated self-destruct against Evaran's wishes, probably to keep any secrets and also as a final deterrent. The Torvatta was only a bit away, and now a large blue humanoid alien with a glowing purple aura who seemed to hate humans was in their way.

The alien pointed at the group. "You face Draxus, the Draven praetor of the Forty-Fifth Clan." He tapped his chest twice with his free arm and then extended it out with fist still clenched. As he charged forward, he shot a purple beam out from his hand.

Emily burst into action, activating her energy shield and absorbing the beam. She returned fire with a repulsion beam.

Draxus paused for a moment as he slid back some.

"He's a heavy," said Emily.

Dr. Snowden fired a mist beam, causing a cloud to form around Draxus.

V flew overhead and shot a stun beam, causing the cloud to burst with electrical arcs.

Draxus winced and then screamed. After a moment, his shield pulsed and pushed the mist away. His sword dissipated, and he extended both arms and shot a beam from each hand.

Emily and Dr. Snowden raised their shields, blocking the beam while Sandas jumped behind them.

Draxus tilted his head.

Sandas peeped out and then took aim and fired a laser shot.

The laser beam was absorbed by Draxus's purple shield.

"That's not a normal shield!" said Sandas.

Dr. Snowden talked into his PSD. "Evaran! We have a crazy alien trying to kill us!"

Evaran did not respond.

Emily glanced at Dr. Snowden. Her eyes flared as she extended her baton into a staff. She danced forward, and when she reached Draxus, she swept his legs out from under him.

As Draxus fell, he shot a purple tendril out that hit V. With a swing down, V crashed into Emily, knocking her to the floor. The tendril dissipated.

"*No!*" said Dr. Snowden as he charged forward. He covered Draxus in white sticky globules.

Draxus concentrated, and the globules melted and slid off his shielding. He stood up and fired another tendril at Dr. Snowden's shield. With a yank, Dr. Snowden fell forward.

Sandas tossed a device that stuck on Draxus's shielding.

Draxus stared at the device for a moment. It pulsed and then exploded into his shield, causing him to go flying back.

Emily jumped up and rushed over to Draxus.

Draxus's tendril was still connected to Dr. Snowden, and he had been pulled along. Draxus began to reel Dr. Snowden in.

Emily blocked one of Draxus's blasts. Her face turned a shade of red as she placed her staff through Draxus's shielding, with the end point on his neck. Her voice raised. "I'm not sure why you're attacking us, but you'll stop, *now*. This ship is about to explode, and we're trying to leave, but you're in our way. We don't want to fight you, but if you push me . . . or hurt my friends . . . you're going to *wish* you hadn't."

Draxus's eyes widened. "How . . . can your weapon penetrate my shield?" He retracted the tendril that was on Dr. Snowden's shield.

Emily's eyes narrowed. "I'd love to tell you, but we need to go. Like . . . now." She pulled her staff back.

Sandas helped Dr. Snowden up, and then, with V in tow, they hustled up to Emily.

She extended a hand toward Draxus.

Draxus eyed Emily's hand for a moment and then accepted it. As he stood, he said, "You're . . . not quite like the humans I know."

Sandas laughed as he waved a finger in the air. "Oh . . . he thinks you're one of those tentacle humans."

Draxus tilted his head at Sandas. "What is this creature saying?"

"Ohh . . . no translator," said Dr. Snowden. "Well, he's saying that you probably think we're one of the tentacled humans, but I can tell you with certainty, we aren't." He shook his head. "They may call themselves human, but I've never seen them before."

Draxus narrowed his eyes as his shield dissipated. "I have a lot of questions."

"Get in line, everyone seems to," said Dr. Snowden. "I'm Dr. Albert Snowden." He pointed in sequence at Emily, Sandas, and V. "That's my niece, Emily, and that's Sandas and V." He interacted with his PSD and tried to reach Evaran. "Evaran's not responding."

"That's weird," said Emily. "V, can you reach him?"

"I will try," said V. After a moment, he flew up and shot down a holographic projection. It showed from the viewpoint of Evaran's chest, and he was fighting a small army of various robots and a petite human female with tentacles.

"He's under attack. Let's go!" said Dr. Snowden. He hustled to the room exit with Sandas and Emily in tow.

Emily paused at the exit and looked at Draxus.

Draxus shook his head. "Your friend is most likely already dead. However . . . I don't think you're the same as the humans I fight. I will join this battle."

"I think he'll probably be just fine. All right, let's move, move, move," said Emily as she hustled out of the room with Draxus following her.

***

Draxus followed the strange humans down the hallway. He was not sure what to make of them, but Emily being able to place her staff through his shielding was alarming. It should not have been possible, yet it had just occurred. She must be the warrior of the group, while Dr. Snowden appeared to be more cautious. Sandas was a curious creature, unlike anything Draxus had seen before. V was like most drones he knew in form, but the holographic and stun beams were new. Emily seemed confident of the one known as Evaran. She probably did not understand the magnitude of power arrayed before him. Draxus knew that Evaran was probably dead by now.

The group hustled through multiple hallways until they reached a docking bay twenty minutes later.

Draxus assessed the situation. These strange humans and company would be no match for what he saw. The human pack leader was engaged in battle with a fair-skinned humanoid who looked similar to Emily and Dr. Snowden. That must be Evaran. How he was still alive was perplexing. His outfit was unusual, looking more like an adventurer's suit than one meant for battle.

What surprised Draxus was how efficiently Evaran was not only deflecting blows, but taking out multiple enemies that came too close. Evaran glided through the battle scene with poise, spinning, kicking, and hitting in smooth sequence. He seemed to be able to do that due to the speed at which he moved. Another orb in the fight seemed to be flying around, trying to avoid getting hit.

Draxus knew the robots well. There were usually five heavily armored human sentinels that accompanied every hunter pack. The sentinels were larger than the other robots, carried more firepower, had stronger shielding, and were lethal in combat. They were the muscle of any human hunting pack.

The small, thin humanoid robots were the common foot soldiers of the Terran Dominion. They could transform into a smaller form, allowing them to be transported in great quantities to where they needed to go. In the back were four-legged transports with no heads. A rotating laser canon sat on each transport's back.

Draxus exhaled. Flying in the air were smaller drones, but they seemed to be engaged with V, who was effortlessly taking them down while dodging fire. These new humans needed help. Before Draxus could react, Emily had joined the fray, knocking a soldier back with one end of her staff while shooting a blast out of the other end, causing more soldiers to go tumbling.

Dr. Snowden and Sandas had pulled out their weapons and were picking off the soldiers and drones.

Draxus rushed out toward Evaran. When Draxus approached, he formed his sword and sliced through one sentinel.

The pack leader turned toward Draxus and momentarily drew its head back.

Draxus grinned. The leader now knew a Draven praetor had joined the battle.

Emily fired sticky globules at the leader's feet.

Evaran hit the leader in the chest, pushing it to the ground. He placed one end of his staff on the hunter's chest. After a moment, it writhed as blue electrical arcs danced over its body. It stopped moving.

Draxus was not sure how a leader could be disabled so quickly, but the three other sentinels were still attacking, along with about half the soldiers and drones still intact. The transports were firing in sync, but their lasers could not penetrate Dr. Snowden's and Emily's forearm shields. Draxus was unsure what type of shield they possessed that could do that. He focused on the battle, as the pack had most likely called in reinforcements already.

Evaran whirled into action and batted one sentinel into the wall. When it hit, the wall cracked and the sentinel fell to the ground and stopped moving. He ran toward the second, dodging the blasts tossed his way, and when he was about halfway to it, he shot out a beam that pulled the sentinel forward. When the sentinel was dragged off his feet and yanked through the air, Evaran retracted the yellow beam, jumped, and hit the sentinel with his staff.

The sentinel crashed to the ground and skidded to a halt. It stopped moving.

Emily spun in circles, blocking lasers with her shield while knocking the soldiers around. She reached the transports and began disabling them by knocking out their cannons.

Dr. Snowden would stun a soldier, and Sandas would hit it with his weapon, causing the soldier to stop.

By the time Draxus had used his blast to take down another sentinel, only one was left and a handful of soldiers. The drones were obliterated by V, and Emily had made quick work of the transports, who were stumbling around.

The last sentinel was near Dr. Snowden and had opened fire with its heavy weapon.

Dr. Snowden raised his shield and reflected the laser fire, shredding the sentinel.

"Over there!" said Dr. Snowden as he fired a mist beam at two soldiers trying to fire at Emily. V flew over and ignited the cloud in a burst of electricity. The soldiers fell.

The remaining soldiers were no match for Evaran and Emily, who seemed to fight in a whirlwind of hits, kicks, and blasts.

This group was beyond anything Draxus had seen before. Appearances were deceiving, as they handled a hunter pack with relative ease. That was not a small feat, and he knew many Dravens who had fallen to just one pack.

Evaran placed a device on the leader's body. The device glowed red and blue. Evaran tapped around in the air.

Draxus pointed at the device. "What is that?" He was not sure that Evaran would understand him.

"An information device," said Evaran. "I do not know anything of this being, who somehow believes it is human."

"They are human," said Draxus. "I've been fighting them since I was brought into existence."

Evaran eyed Draxus for a moment and then picked up the device that had been used on the hunter's body. "I am Evaran." He pointed at the orb that had been avoiding getting hit. "That is Zeta-12, the AI that ran this ship. I do not mean to cut short this introduction, but we should talk elsewhere. We can leave via my ship, the Torvatta."

"I have my own ship," said Draxus.

Evaran looked down for a moment. "There was a battle outside. I assume your ship was not one of the human ones. Your ship . . . did not make it."

"What?" asked Draxus with wide eyes. He tapped at his palm and saw that there was no connection to his ship.

"I am sorry, but several more ships have arrived. We need to leave now. There is another ship docking nearby."

"How can I trust what you say is true? They could just be out of range."

"You can verify once we are on my ship and out of harm's way."

Draxus sighed as he closed his eyes. It seemed there was no choice. "I agree to this temporary arrangement."

Evaran slightly bowed. "Let us go."

Draxus followed the others as they headed to a nearby docking bay. He surveyed the carnage they had just dispensed. It was obvious to him now that this group was not from this region of space. He did not think they were invaders, but maybe they were scouts of another force. They offered him safe harbor aboard their ship, which seemed unusual to him.

After ten minutes, they reached the docking bay where another hunter ship had landed.

Draxus had not detected a docking bay in the initial scans. He suspected the hunter pack they had just fought got on board, figured out the layout, and then signaled for the other to come in. There were other ships in the bay, but none that he could see that would be able to fight the hunter ships, much less escape.

Evaran pointed at the Torvatta. "There. Move!"

Draxus wrinkled his eyebrows. The ship was small, circular in design, and had no apparent weapons or engine on it. The ship was absurd, but with the group moving, he would reserve judgment until he was inside. He followed Evaran. As they approached the Torvatta, he noticed that a pack leader and several sentinels and guards had reached it before them. Another pack. He grimaced as his shielding pulsed in preparation for another fight.

Evaran aimed his staff and fired.

Boom!

The hunter, sentinels, and robots went flying back.

Draxus was not sure what that weapon was, but he liked it.

They reached the edge of the Torvatta.

Evaran gestured in as the group hustled past him.

Draxus paused. "I . . . am not sure this is wise."

"The Torvatta is more than it appears to be. I understand that trust has to be earned, but believe me, the Torvatta is the safest place to be right now."

Draxus sighed. With his ship gone, assuming that was true, this was the only option available. His multiple hearts hurt at the thought that his crew probably fought to their last breath.

"I am sure your crew fought well. However, this ship is going to explode in less than a minute."

Draxus lowered his head and then entered the Torvatta. His eyes searched the interior. The ship had an unusual layout. As he walked by one of the six doors to his left, he noticed that they extended farther than the ship should allow. Looking toward the front, he saw that Dr. Snowden and Sandas sat in a U-shaped seating area off to the right, while Emily sat on the left side. Evaran had entered and sat in a large command chair. V was interacting with a U-shaped console in the open front area. Zeta-12 hovered next to V. Draxus walked over to Evaran.

Evaran gestured at a seat next to Emily.

"I don't bite," said Emily.

"Perhaps not," said Draxus, "but you fight as if you could."

Emily raised her eyebrows as Draxus took his seat.

"Now we wait," said Evaran.

"All those aliens in suspended animation are going to die," said Dr. Snowden.

Evaran raised a finger. "Yes. A self-destruct was not needed. However, I now believe they were not meant to be here." He looked at Sandas, Zeta-12, and then Draxus. "None of you are. This needs to be corrected, and I believe that is why I am here.

V, set Torvatta scan profile one." He glanced at Draxus. "While in the Torvatta, you will be able to understand everyone via a unique translator without the need of translation nanobots."

Draxus nodded. He was curious to hear Zeta-12 and Sandas speak since he had not understood them so far.

"What will scan profile one do?" asked Zeta-12.

"It will put the Torvatta into a mode that will not show up on scanners. If there are any long-range detectors, it will appear we blew up with the ship. Although your ship will destruct, no harm will come to the Torvatta."

"The laws of physics would disagree with that assessment."

"Zeta-12 . . . there is much you do not understand. Trust me on this . . . I will take you back to the Draidjen home world," said Evaran.

Draxus observed the crew. Evaran was the clear leader. His speech was odd, but he commanded respect. From what Draxus had seen, Evaran was a capable fighter and seemed to be levelheaded. Emily was a fighter too. She was the first to jump into battle, without a moment's hesitation. Dr. Snowden was calm and collected and seemed to be the wise one. Although Draxus was not sure what a niece was, apparently Emily was Dr. Snowden's. Maybe it was a rank. Zeta-12 seemed to be combative, but maybe because he was an AI, although the one called V seemed to be friendly. Then there was Sandas, a curious creature.

"You have been quiet," said Evaran, glancing at Draxus.

"I'm . . . just trying to make sense of all of this. We haven't moved yet. I agree with Zeta-12. We will not survive this ship exploding."

"My ship is unique and will survive the explosion."

"I will have to trust you on that," said Draxus as he clasped his hands in front of him and looked down.

The front screen lit up showing the ship exploding around them.

Draxus closed his eyes and braced for impact, expecting to be tossed around. After a moment of nothing happening, he opened his eyes and peered around. Everyone was staring at him. "I felt no movement. How is this possible?"

Evaran half smiled. "I am glad you are curious. That is a good trait to possess. The Torvatta's shielding is . . . unique. Although force may act on the Torvatta, it does not transfer internally, except for some special cases."

"That is beyond anything I have ever seen," said Draxus.

"And will ever see," said Evaran.

Draxus looked at the front screen. The docking bay was gone, and in its place was open space with debris. An overhead view of the immediate area only showed the Torvatta. He tapped at his palm. If his crew was still there, they should be able to contact him. After a moment of silence, he gritted his teeth as his face scrunched up. His crew was gone. It was as Evaran had said. Draxus exhaled from his mouth.

He now needed to find another crew to carry on his mission. His crew did not even get to be consumed by another Arkara. Their experiences were forever lost. He had let them down. Finding another crew would be difficult, and from what he was gathering from these strangers, they were eager to do other things. He was not sure he fully understood the cryptic suggestion that he was not supposed to be there.

V turned and faced the group. "Analysis. All human ships were destroyed in the explosion."

"I would hope so," said Zeta-12. "Anything within range would have . . . except this ship, it seems."

Sandas raised a claw. "This is very strange. Yes. Very, very strange."

Draxus wrinkled his eyebrows. Sandas's voice seemed to have changed in translation as well.

"So . . . who are you?" asked Sandas, gesturing at Draxus. "I could call you the big blue guy with a purple shield. Ha! A bruiser!"

Draxus raised his eyebrows. "I am Draxus, Draven praetor of the Forty-Fifth Clan." He pointed at Sandas. "I thought you were a pet of some type."

"A pet!" said Sandas.

Emily and Dr. Snowden smiled.

"There is a lot to cover," said Evaran. "Come to the conference room, and we can go over the situation and determine our next steps."

Draxus watched as everyone stood. He glanced at Sandas.

Sandas shrugged. "After you, big guy, but *don't* try to pet me."

"I had not intended to," said Draxus as he stood.

Sandas shook his head as they headed to the conference room.

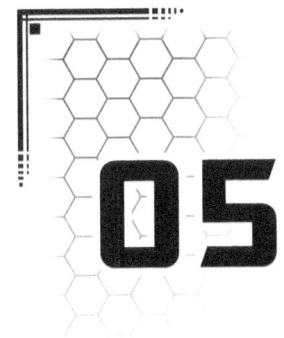

05

Sandas looked around the conference room as he took his seat. The room should not exist, yet he was sitting in it. Draxus had a similar look of confusion, and probably a lot of questions. The room had a large rectangular table with seats around it, and what looked like a matter replicator in a side area, although it was unlike any replicator he had seen before.

It was apparent that this group knew who the information broker was, although Sandas was not sure how that was possible. He recalled hearing of Evaran before, but it was mostly unverified information. Draxus was an enigma. Being called a pet was something Sandas found comical. Draxus was not any species that Sandas had heard of or seen before. It was not lost on him that this was probably a very unique experience. He observed as everyone took their seat.

Evaran gestured around the table. "I am sure this is very confusing to all involved. Before I begin, let me introduce everyone. I will start with myself. I am Evaran, and I travel through space, time, and beyond. This is more detail than I would normally share, but we are dealing with a temporally shielded ship that is aware of timeline changes." He pointed at Dr. Snowden, and then Emily. "This is Dr. Albert Snowden, and to his left is Emily Snowden, his niece. They travel with me." He nodded at V. "The floating orb is V, also my companion."

Draxus narrowed his eyes. "What is . . . a niece?"

"We will get to that in a moment," said Evaran. He gestured at Sandas. "This is Sandas, the last of his kind. Based on his ship's logs that Zeta-12 provided, he is from AD 2008."

"I assume it's still AD 2008, although Zeta-12 seems to think otherwise," said Sandas.

"I will get to that as well," said Evaran. He motioned at Zeta-12's holographic form. "This is Zeta-12, an artificial intelligence that resided on the ship that just exploded. What you see is all that is left of him."

"I am glad to still exist," said Zeta-12.

Evaran nodded. "And finally, Draxus. I do not know much about your species, but it is obvious it is different from humanity."

"Quite different," said Draxus.

"With introductions out of the way, here is the situation," said Evaran. He tapped at the table console, causing a projection of the Milky Way galaxy to appear. The route that Zeta-12 took appeared as a red line. Evaran highlighted a point in the line that veered off into another galactic quadrant. "I now believe, based on both Zeta-12's logs and the logs transferred from Sandas's ship, that a space-time eddy was at play. They are formed from space-time rifts that have dissipated, and usually fade out on their own over a short amount of time."

He raised a finger. "However, in this scenario, one stuck around, one with a lot of residual power still, which is unusual in itself, but not unheard of. Sandas was pulled into it around AD 2008, and Zeta-12 was pulled in around AD 6308. There may be others, and there is the possibility that they were kicked out of it at different times. I suspect that is where this new version of humanity came from."

Dr. Snowden cleared his throat. "So . . . Sandas and Zeta-12 got kicked out around the same time. If this new version of humanity was kicked out earlier, they would have had time to form," said Dr. Snowden, waving a hand in the air, "whatever it is they formed."

"That is correct," said Evaran. "That is my current hypothesis."

Sandas was not sure what he was hearing. To so casually speak of cosmic events, like it was an everyday thing, was unusual. "So how do we get back then?"

"The Torvatta can take Zeta-12 to the Draidjen home world in the current time. Draxus we can take back to wherever he needs to be in the current time. However you . . . I will need to think about."

Sandas's eyes widened. "Oh, really?"

"I do not believe this meeting was random."

Sandas looked around the table, then back at Evaran. "All right . . . and just to be clear . . . you're not going to kill me or eat me or anything. Right? I taste horrible if dinner is in your eyes."

Emily and Dr. Snowden chuckled.

"Of course not," said Evaran. "For the moment, you need to stick around."

Sandas swished his nose around a bit. "You sure you aren't keeping me around because of how handsome and charming I am?"

Dr. Snowden and Emily laughed.

"I am sure of it," said Evaran with a half smile. "However, I am curious as to why you were in a place to get pulled in."

"Oh . . . well . . . I had received information about an anomaly, one with temporal signatures. I didn't want to rely on anyone else, so I decided to check it out myself," said Sandas.

"Intellectual curiosity is in your nature," said Evaran.

"That or . . . I wanted to be the first to analyze the anomaly."

"An adventurous spirit."

Draxus cleared his throat. "I don't mean to interrupt . . . but I have some questions."

Evaran waved a hand out. "Please proceed."

"My clan's Arkara was destroyed," said Draxus. "My only goal was to eradicate the human threat, by all means necessary. We're aware of time travel and its paradoxes but have never seen it before. It would appear that if you . . . fix . . . the aftereffects of the space-time eddy, then the new humans would go away and possibly . . . my Arkara would still be alive. Is this correct?"

Evaran studied Draxus for a moment. "An astute observation. Humanity should not exist out here, based upon my . . . knowledge. I am not familiar with Arkaras."

Draxus tapped at his palm interface and then extended his hand out. A projection shot up. "This is my Arkara, from whence I was born."

Sandas narrowed his black eyes as he studied the large treelike being with multiple trunks. Green pods with brown tendrils hung from the branches, with another series of pods that ringed the base of the tree. Smaller plantlike structures surrounded the main one, with vines of some sort connecting them. A moldy-looking green creep surrounded the base. This was not new to him, as he had seen species that were plantlike in nature.

"It is clear to me then," said Draxus, raising his head a bit, "that I'm to assist you in fixing the aftereffects of the space-time eddy. You mentioned that this meeting may not be random. I would agree. Perhaps . . . this was always meant to happen. I would formally ask to join this crew for the duration of this campaign."

Evaran faced Draxus. "Understand that I try to avoid time refugees." He glanced at Dr. Snowden and Emily for a moment. "I am not always successful." He faced Draxus. "I agree that your and Sandas's presence here is not random. There are ways around becoming a time refugee, but I usually avoid it completely. I need to think about your request."

Draxus nodded. "I appreciate the consideration."

"Well, I want in," said Sandas. "This sounds like an adventure with lots and lots of information to be had. You can take me back *afterward*."

Evaran eyed Sandas. "I will think about it." He faced Draxus. "One thing to note is that you are rare. Although I do not know your species, I know you are a Wildborn conduit."

"I'm a Draven, and unfamiliar with what a Wildborn conduit is," said Draxus.

"Yeah, me too," said Dr. Snowden.

The others nodded in agreement.

Evaran looked around the table for a moment and then focused on Draxus. "Wild energy is a type of exotic energy that exists . . . everywhere, in varying densities. It can bind to living beings, creating a hybrid known as a Wildborn. Sometimes . . . the hybrid is more wild energy than living being, and they can channel the wild energy on command. I have seen something similar to your energy signature," said Evaran, tossing a finger out and waving it between Dr. Snowden and Emily, "on their home world."

"So this . . . wild energy . . . is my Arkara's life force," said Draxus.

"You can call it what you want, but that is what it is."

Draxus clenched his jaw for a moment. "A praetor is unique. A clan only has one. This must mean that all praetors are . . . Wildborn conduits."

"Perhaps. I am unfamiliar with your species' reproduction method but suspect your Arkara is Wildborn. May I scan your data device?"

Draxus exhaled from his nose and offered up his hand. "If it helps, then of course."

Evaran extended his hand and then used his ring to scan Draxus's glove. After the scan was complete, Evaran looked around his ARI and then interacted with the table console.

Sandas observed the projections that shot up from the center of the table. One showed a green planet. The other images showed various Dravens and assorted life-forms that Sandas was not familiar with. He pointed at the image of the Arkara. "So your mother is . . . a plant?"

"The Arkara is more than just a plant and can create organic containers that spawn what is needed. Praetors, workers, soldiers."

"So that's why you didn't know what a niece is. It's just mother and child," said Emily.

"Yes. Each clan has one Arkara, and when we die, our bodies are recycled back to it, but not always to the same Arkara."

"Wow," said Dr. Snowden.

"If you are like the version of humanity I know, then your species does not do this," said Draxus.

"Well . . . not sure how the humans out here do it, but in our version, we have a female and a male, as far as sexes go," said Dr. Snowden. "Emily's a female, and I'm a male. It takes both to procreate. Emily's father and I had the same female birth us, our mother, so we're related, and that makes her my niece."

"I understand," said Draxus.

Evaran raised a finger. "The Dravens favor centralized reproduction, whereas humans use decentralized reproduction. There are advantages to both, as well as disadvantages."

Draxus tilted his head. "Having the ability to create, in so many, would help if disaster strikes."

Dr. Snowden wrinkled his eyebrows. "I guess it would, but having an Arkara . . . it sounds like it would be easier to care for if everyone is dedicated to serving and defending it."

"Yes . . . and I failed. I was no match for these new humans. I am glad . . . that you are not like them," said Draxus. He glanced at Sandas. "I'm sorry to hear you are the last of your kind. A great tragedy must have befallen your species."

Sandas bobbed his head. "It's a *long* story."

"We can go over it at some point," said Evaran. "Our next steps need to be defined. I would like to establish a baseline on the current status of Earth, Fredoria, and Kreagus first, prior to taking Zeta-12 and potentially Sandas and Draxus back to where they need to go. However, I think it is important for us to see these new humans from Draxus's perspective." He motioned at Draxus to proceed.

Draxus cleared his throat as he looked around the room. He was still unsure of what to think of this group, but they were not like the humans he knew. Although he had heard of time travelers, to see some was a unique experience. They were curious about the new humans, something he had had knowledge of since he was born.

He tapped at his palm, causing the projection over the table to change. He wrinkled his eyebrows. The ship had somehow tied into his data device. Even the ship, which they called the Torvatta, was unique. Hopefully they would allow him to travel with them, not only to eradicate the new version of humanity, but also to learn about their version of humanity. This crew possessed power that he could only imagine.

The projection changed to show a galactic regional map with regional colored areas.

Draxus pointed around. "These are the domains of the humans. They control dozens of systems, are highly advanced, and are split into multiple groups." He pointed at the red-shaded region. "That's the Terran Dominion. We call them Dominion for short. They're genetically engineered and have one AI called Salazar to service them all." He gestured at the blue-shaded region. "That's the domain of the Gul Kash Alliance, a loose group of human clans. Less advanced than the other groups, but they have a much larger population, and no AIs are allowed."

"That seems like an odd distinction," said Dr. Snowden. "In terms of the AI, that is."

Draxus nodded. "I don't know why it is that way, but this next region," he said, pointing at the green area, "has multiple AIs and humans living together. They call themselves the United Planets. I don't know much about them . . . but they seem to be a haven for AI and human alike."

"We met them before," said Emily. "They're the good guys, but then again . . . who knows out here."

"Maybe they are, but they are so far away from my home world that I haven't interacted with them," said Draxus. He waved a finger at the various small purple regions scattered around. "The outcasts lay claim to those areas. They are made up of loosely affiliated clans and are the most brutal, attacking human and alien alike, including some of our colonies. They're . . . very unusual."

"As in . . . ," said Sandas, narrowing his eyes.

"They sometimes eat other humans, but their appetite also extends to aliens. They have a foul odor and also tend to be more brutal toward my species. Their equipment and apparel are also less uniform than the other factions. They seem to enjoy wearing their victims' remains on their armor."

"Huh," said Sandas. "Sounds like the outer rim may be out here."

"Been there," said Emily.

Sandas tapped his claws together in front of him. "I see . . ."

Draxus cleared his throat while he touched his palm, causing a blinking green dot to appear on the projection. "This is my home system. We used to control several solar systems, but we have lost ground. Now the Dravens are nomads, seeking to exist where there are no humans, but we also are fighting back, or trying to."

Dr. Snowden raised a finger. "Why are humans attacking you?"

"It seems to vary. The Dominion say it is their destiny to bring enlightenment to us, while outcasts see us as prey for their amusement and the Gul Kash Alliance sees us as slaves. We've had no interaction with the United Planets due to distance," said Draxus. "Of the three we've interacted with, the Dominion is the least dangerous faction. They conquer a world, divide it up, and use its resources, but allow us to continue living if we agree to certain conditions. Each planet region is given to a human to manage. I . . . don't understand why they do this, but it has something to do with how their society is set up. If outcasts attack, it is a given that no one will survive, and if it's the Gul Kash Alliance, then my people are shipped around."

"Your people should not have to deal with this at all," said Evaran.

Draxus sighed. "I wish it were so. My Arkara was killed by an outcast raid, and then the area was taken over by the Dominion. They then appointed a human to rule us. I, and the remaining fleet of my clan, regrouped and forged a plan to fight back. My crew . . . ," he said, looking down, "was not only the last of our fleet, but the final members of my clan. I am the last survivor." He looked back up with eyes that flared purple for a moment.

Emily frowned as she focused on Draxus. "I'm so sorry to hear that."

"It is what it is," said Draxus. He raised his head a bit. "However . . . it seems a new opportunity has arisen, one I would like to be a part of."

Evaran nodded. "I understand where you are coming from."

"So this . . . Dominion . . . now controls your area," said Emily.

Draxus nodded. "We are in their domain, and they are the one faction I have a lot of information on. Their society is based on genetic engineering, from what I understand. Every human is altered to some degree. They also have cybernetic aspects that are developed from injected machine DNA. The leader of the hunting pack we met on Zeta-12's ship was altered to be just that."

Sandas rubbed his chin. "Genetic engineering. I'm . . . familiar with that. Machine DNA . . . not so much. Sounds like they're cyborgs. So those tentacles we saw on the pack leader's back could have been from machine DNA inserted into them."

"Yes, and it's been advantageous for the Dominion, it seems," said Draxus. "I'm not familiar with how deep they go, but I do know that I've seen many variations of the human form. The one that controls my planet region on my home world is smaller than normal, and their general personality seems to be . . . cold."

"That sounds horrible," said Dr. Snowden. "This Dominion is *not* how I pictured humanity in the future." He glanced at Evaran. "I know you've traveled up and down humanity's timescape. Have you seen this before?"

Evaran nodded. "In the far future, yes. However, it was not malicious like what I am hearing."

Draxus narrowed his eyes. "The Dominion are an abomination of life."

"I understand," said Evaran. "It is apparent that they should not exist here."

Draxus exhaled from his nose. "Each faction has a star surrounded by their technology. I assume it gives them energy, and I believe it is the central seat of each faction."

"Surround stars? You mean a Dyson bubble?" asked Dr. Snowden.

Draxus interacted with his palm, causing a projection to shoot up. It showed a star partially covered with structures orbiting it. Pieces of the star shone through the gaps. "This is what took over the star in the Dominion home system. I'm not sure what a Dyson bubble is."

"Wow," said Dr. Snowden. "Well, that's definitely one, it looks like. A Dyson bubble is just geosynchronous structures, called statites, around a star. They're held in place by radiation pressure. We've seen the beginning of one. This must be close to the finished product."

Sandas pointed at the projection. "You can see that there are energy collectors there, but I'm not seeing the usual structures associated with a Kazmaran swarm. That must require a *lot* of resources to build something like that."

Dr. Snowden narrowed his eyes. "A Kazmaran swarm?"

Evaran raised a finger. "Dyson is a term used by humans. Kazmaran is a Kreagan term. I think we can just call it a megastructure. Sandas is right in that this projection for the Dominion seems to focus heavily on energy collectors."

"Interesting," said Draxus. "They seem to gather material from the star itself too, and also pulverize planets, asteroids, and anything in the system to convert to building material."

Evaran rubbed his chin. "The arrangement of the energy collectors is familiar. When we get information from a Torvatta scan, I will need to research it." He glanced at Draxus. "Going back to the Dominion, you mentioned genetic engineering and gene tailoring for specific purposes. What other types of human variations have you seen?"

"Many," said Draxus, clenching his jaw. He tapped at his palm, causing the projection over the table to change. It showed a list with the Draven term in one column, description in another, and then finally a sequence of images in the third. He pointed at the first row. "Those are the governors, and they manage planet regions. All I know of them is that they are as cold as machines but seem to be the authority of any planet region. All altered humans for whatever role are similar in design. The governors look like Dr. Snowden and Emily, and the only thing I'm aware of about governors is that they treat the natives as animals, at least until they are chipped."

Emily tilted her head. "Chipped as in . . . sticking an implant in their body or something?"

"A neural implant, yes. From what I understand, it causes Dravens to act unusually, even friendly toward humans." He pointed at some of the other rows. "There seems to be several templates, and from that, many variations from generalized to specialized."

Sandas swished his nose around and pointed at the third column in one of the rows. "Their eyes look like permanent goggles. And their skin . . . it's so pale. And where's their hair? I know humans wish they had fur like me, but they're taking it to the other extreme."

Emily shook her head.

"Appearance is not important to them," said Draxus. "We have seen smaller humans who can move fast, those who are impenetrable as solid rock, and even those with multiple appendages."

Sandas tilted his head. "Your species does the same, right? Well, minus the machine DNA part."

"We are born naturally for our purpose. We do use genetic engineering, but not on ourselves, more for our structures. For instance, we grow our buildings, food, and everything we need. However, the humans are altered after birth."

Dr. Snowden's lips parted. "You mean . . . they're born normal . . . and then altered to fit this weird system?"

"At birth, they are given a generic template with the neural implant and physically altered, and at twenty years, they specialize, but they are born as slaves under Salazar's control."

"They're robbing people of their lives," said Dr. Snowden. "Let me guess, they're then brainwashed on top of all that."

"Yes, their neural implants enforce obedience and, I'm sure, influence them."

"That sucks," said Emily. "How do they reproduce?"

"Reproduction is controlled. From what I read, sexual desire is not present in all humans, although governors seem to be exempt from that. Reproduction is handled in a lab, and it does not seem to be a driving factor for the Dominion. With that said . . . I have heard governors do . . . *things* . . . with species they conquer, and not for reproductive reasons."

"Suppressing sexual desire would take a lot of genetic engineering, I'm guessing," said Emily.

Draxus shrugged. "I've never had it, so I wouldn't know."

"How do you know all of this?" asked Emily.

Draxus grimaced. "We've caught a few humans, and we hacked into their implants. We've also hit some of their facilities and ships and gained information that way. Some leave the Dominion and are easier to capture for information."

"So they can leave if they want to?" asked Sandas "I'd be out of there with two shakes of my tail!"

"I have heard that after twenty years, very few want to leave."

Evaran looked around his ARI for a moment. "I see that you have data on the various robots. You mentioned the Dominion only has one AI."

Draxus nodded. "They only use one AI." His eyes flared purple. "*Salazar.* He won't allow another AI to exist. Virtual intelligences are common, though. I assume you understand what that is."

"We do," said Evaran. He gestured at V and Zeta-12. "They're both strong AIs."

"Analysis. Salazar does not want competition," said V.

"Maybe," said Draxus. "I don't know why there is only one. What I do know . . . is that Salazar is . . . *everywhere* . . . that the Dominion is present. When we worked on taking out a neural implant from a worker to study it, it was Salazar that spoke through the worker and how they also found our Arkara's location. It would seem that the outcasts were monitoring . . . and took advantage. From that, we learned that all humans in the Dominion are connected by some degree to Salazar. We were just trying to figure out what the new energy was that Salazar had come into possession of. It's one we've never seen before, but it was mentioned via several humans we captured."

Evaran perused his ARI for a moment, then flicked a finger toward the table.

An image of a blue cloud with multiple shining points appeared.

"Is that it?"

Draxus nodded.

Evaran narrowed his eyes. "Tachyrin energy. It is used in temporal shielding."

Dr. Snowden furrowed his eyebrows. "Yeah . . . that doesn't sound good. This whole setup seems like how an AI would organize things. Like . . . managing resources. You think Salazar controls everything?"

"I don't know, but Salazar seems to serve the humans," said Draxus.

"I'd like to meet this Salazar," said Zeta-12.

Evaran shook his head. "You will be returned to the Draidjen home world in the current time period. With the timeline corrected, it is possible that there may be two of you. However, you are an AI, so merging into one is possible."

"I'm glad I'm not organic then," said Zeta-12.

Evaran nodded. "There is a lot of information for me to process. We can break for now and continue tomorrow. We will then meet at 9:00 a.m. Earth time. Zeta-12 and V, I will need both of you for research and analysis."

"Acknowledged," said V.

"Okay," said Zeta-12.

Evaran gestured at Draxus. "Dr. Snowden can show you to your living quarters for now." He motioned at Sandas. "Emily can show you to yours."

"It is appreciated," said Draxus. "I hope you consider allowing me to join you in your campaign."

"Yeah, me too," said Sandas.

Evaran nodded at both of them.

Sandas grinned big. "Well then, Emily. Lead on!"

Emily shook her head, "C'mon, let's go."

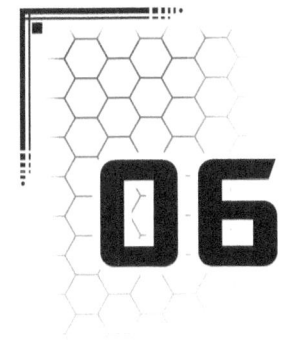

06

Dr. Snowden watched as the conference room emptied. It was just he and Draxus, whose size was daunting. Dr. Snowden figured Draxus was about eight feet tall. He had an intimidating presence. Dr. Snowden could see that the Draven society was technologically advanced based on the idea of growing everything they needed through genetic engineering. The Arkara was strange to him, though. Draxus would be an interesting companion, assuming Evaran allowed that. Dr. Snowden gestured toward the room exit. "You ready?"

"I'm always ready," said Draxus.

Dr. Snowden nodded and exited the room. He turned his head halfway back to make sure Draxus was following him.

After going two dimensional doorways down, they entered the living quarters.

Draxus peered around. "How is this room possible?"

"Dimensional mechanics," said Dr. Snowden. He shook his hand out in front of him. "I know, I know, it sounds crazy, but it's real."

"I can see that."

Dr. Snowden pointed at a room on the left side. His eye caught Emily and Sandas entering a room on the right side. Evaran had sent a small layout of the living quarters to the conference room table, which highlighted where Sandas and Draxus would be staying. Dr. Snowden thought it was odd that they were on opposite sides, but maybe there was something he was missing.

As they walked toward the room, Draxus said, "This ship . . . the Torvatta . . . I sense it is . . . unique."

"Only one of its kind, trust me on that."

"I trust you."

Dr. Snowden chuckled. "Sorry, that's just a figure of speech."

"I see. Your ship has a translator for my language, yet . . . I don't understand how."

"The translator is unique as well."

Draxus nodded. "It appears anything related to Evaran is, assuming he's the leader of this group."

They reached the door.

Dr. Snowden faced Draxus. "It's his ship. Emily and I are just traveling companions."

"How did you meet him?"

Dr. Snowden opened the door and gestured in. "I can explain inside."

Draxus entered the room and paused to take it all in.

Dr. Snowden followed, and the door closed.

Draxus pivoted and observed the door for a moment, then strode into the middle of the room. "I thank you for these accommodations."

"You'll love the bed. It has some neural effect that makes you sleep better."

Draxus walked to the side of the bed. "You lie down to sleep?"

Dr. Snowden raised his eyebrows. He had not even considered that an alien humanoid might sleep differently. "Umm . . . yeah. I'm guessing you don't?"

"Dravens sleep by meditation. We assume a seated position."

"Huh. Well, you can do that on the bed too. How do Dominion humans sleep?"

Draxus narrowed his eyes. "They stand in a chamber of some sort that seems to . . . replenish them."

"That sounds uncomfortable. Anyways, if you want something else, we can replicate anything needed."

Draxus interacted with his palm facing up. A projection shot up of an egg-shaped container made of wood strips and vines. The front was open, with cushions lining the inside. "Can this be made?"

Dr. Snowden pulled up a menu that hovered in the air. "I think so."

Draxus walked around the menu, bobbing his head as he went.

After a moment, the bed dissipated, and the structure that Draxus had requested stood in its place.

"There we go," said Dr. Snowden.

"Your technology is truly amazing."

Dr. Snowden pointed at a receptacle in the wall. "It looks like Evaran has already integrated information from your device into the system. You can replicate any food there by just speaking its name. Same with drinks. If you want to access the holo menu, just circle your finger in the air clockwise and poke at the center.

"I can change the room . . . completely?"

"Yep. Make it however you want."

Draxus pulled up the menu and browsed around in it.

A moment later, the room changed to an outside setting, with orange and green plant life. A projection on the wall showed a river off in the distance.

Dr. Snowden studied the new environment. "Is this from your home world?"

"It is," said Draxus. He sat on a rock. "It was . . . before the humans burned it." His eyes narrowed.

"Oh . . . I'm . . . sorry to hear that," said Dr. Snowden. He took a seat on a rock opposite Draxus. "I know this situation must be rough for you. Were you and your crew close?"

Draxus nodded. "We were clan mates, born at the same time. They served with me in every mission . . . until this last one. I couldn't even return them to another Arkara for consumption." He looked down for a moment. "They gave their lives fighting, dying with honor. I will remember them as such." He tapped his chest twice with a clenched fist and then extended his arm forward.

Dr. Snowden noted that Draxus had just lost his crew but seemed remarkably calm. "I didn't mean to bring up any bad memories."

"They're not bad memories, and they will not be forgotten. As long as I live, they live as well. The Arkara that consumes me will relay my information into the next generation."

Dr. Snowden wagged a finger. "About that . . . When your Arkara consumes you, do you mean that she . . . like . . . eats you?"

Draxus looked back up at Dr. Snowden and smiled. "It is a great honor to be consumed by an Arkara. We are placed in pods, similar to our birthing ones and the meditation pod over there. Once inside, it seals, and we become one with the Arkara. From a technical perspective, we are liquefied. She is able to retain our memories and pass them on. In a sense, we are recycled."

"Whoa . . . genetic memory?"

Draxus nodded. "The Dominion uses implants. Is that how your version of humanity does it?"

"Not at all. When we die, that's it. When we're born, we can barely walk, and we don't have any memories from anyone else."

"Interesting," said Draxus. "Our Arkara gives us memories based on what she needs us to do. In my case, I was chosen to be a praetor."

"Huh," said Dr. Snowden. "Although I hate to say it, enslaving others and attacking what's different is a common theme in our history, but we have overcome that to some degree. I don't know what my version of humanity is supposed to be like in this time period, but Evaran does. I suspect that United Planets group is probably close to what we know."

"Assuming Evaran allows me to join in his crusade, do you think we will get a chance to see . . . your version?"

Dr. Snowden shrugged. "He wants a baseline, so yeah, I think so."

Draxus eyed Dr. Snowden. "How far away is it?"

"About eighty thousand light-years or so."

"You speak as if that is a trivial distance."

Dr. Snowden gestured around. "The Torvatta makes travel easy."

Draxus nodded.

Dr. Snowden pointed to a room off to the side. "There's a workstation in there. It has a lot of information on it, although I suspect for you, it will only show relative information."

"I understand. You don't trust me yet."

"It's not that . . . it's just . . . Evaran tries to limit future information from being known. Historical, though, I don't think will be an issue."

"I see. I'll make use of it."

Dr. Snowden exhaled from his mouth as he stood. "All right. If you need anything, you can just pull up the menu and contact V or me. I'm not tired yet, so I may hit the planar cartography lab."

"Nor am I tired," said Draxus. "What is this lab you speak of?"

Dr. Snowden grinned. "It's a room-sized holographic display of the cosmos. I wanted to see the layout of this region of space, especially with your data in the system."

Draxus looked away for a moment, then back at Dr. Snowden. "You were going to tell me about how you met Evaran. Perhaps you can tell me in this lab."

"Sure. The Torvatta will filter what can be shown around you, so I don't think that's a problem," said Dr. Snowden. He gestured toward the room exit. "Let's see some stars."

Emily smiled as she watched Sandas look around his living area. He was upbeat and did not seem too concerned about the situation. Given all he knew as an information broker, maybe this was just another outing for him. She laughed as Sandas ran and then jumped on the bed, before hopping off it. He was like a rocket shooting around the room while scanning everything. She tossed a hand out. "You can replicate anything you need by using a holo menu."

Sandas paused while standing on one of the chairs. "Really? Show me!"

She circled her finger in the air and then poked the center.

Sandas reciprocated the movement. His eyes lit up at the menu hovering before him. He interacted with it for a minute, causing the environment to change to a forest. His whiskers wiggled as he dug deeper into the menu. Soothing forest sounds echoed throughout the room. The bed disappeared and was replaced by a large tree with a platform on one of the lower branches. A foam mattress appeared nearby with blankets. "Ohh . . . I like this. I've seen replicators of all levels, but this . . . this is different."

"Yep. I'm not sure if the neural effect that makes you sleep better will work if you change the environment, but I guess you'll find out."

Sandas circled his finger counterclockwise and poked the center, causing the menu to dissipate.

Emily was not surprised that Sandas had picked up how to use the menu. His profession probably dictated that he be able to learn and adapt on the move.

Sandas took a seat on a tree stump, being careful to place his bushy tail to the side. "So . . . what a situation, huh?"

Emily sat on a log perpendicular to him. "Yeah."

"This must be routine for you. At least you act that way."

"Well . . . I don't think it's ever routine, but if you have the right mindset, you can tackle anything."

He grinned. "An optimist." He pointed a claw at her. "I like it."

She enjoyed his enthusiasm for life. Despite all the crazy things that had occurred and the chaotic moments, it was nice to be around someone like that. "It's better than being down all the time, although I've had my share of those."

"Hmm . . . I sense you've suffered greatly in the past."

Emily half smiled while wrinkling her eyebrows. "You sensed?"

"Well . . . that fight on the ship gave me a lot of information on everyone."

"And for me, you think I've suffered greatly in the past?"

Sandas nodded. "You have a generous disposition, yet in that fight, you waded into battle without a moment's hesitation. No fear. *None.*"

"That's just experience."

"Perhaps, but you're human, and young. That level of experience usually comes later in life, so something must have sped it up."

Emily licked her lips. "Could be."

Sandas raised a claw. "Another point of interest. You're Dr. Snowden's niece. That means your father isn't available. Either he's dead, or he doesn't know about this. You don't seem the type that would lie to your father. I'd wager he's dead."

Her throat constricted.

"And your reaction to that verifies it for me, but I'm not done yet! That alone would be tragic, but not tragic enough to make you a battle-hardened fighter. No . . . there was something else. Something deeply personal. Something that stripped you down and allowed you to rebuild into what you are now."

Emily averted her eyes as she looked at the ground.

"On top of that, the bond between you and Evaran is apparent. You were willing to risk it all to help him. I suspect in the dark events that made you what you are now, it was him that helped you out."

She cleared her throat. "You seem to have a good read on me."

"I know, right?" asked Sandas with a big grin. "I don't mean to make you uncomfortable, but reading people is important in what I do. It can mean the difference between life and death, literally."

"Okay, well, what about Uncle Albert?" asked Emily.

Sandas rubbed his furry chin. "He's a scholar of some sort. The prefix on his name suggests that, but also in the way he carries himself, and the way he speaks, as if he's strolling through life. He possesses intellectual curiosity, a sign of an enlightened individual. However, like you, he joined the fight without breaking a sweat, because humans sweat, you see."

Emily chuckled. "Yes, I know we sweat."

"It has a distinct odor, and yet . . . Dr. Snowden did not have much of it. Also . . . he watched you almost more than he watched the enemies. He worries about you, yet trusts you implicitly. That strong bond is most likely the result of tragic events, such as his brother's death and whatever you went through. I suspect he was gentle natured, yes, gentle, yet in the fight, he stood with shield drawn to protect me. Most humans I know would have run at the sight of a small robot army, especially one led by a human with spiderlike tentacles," said Sandas, shaking a claw, "but not him."

Emily shook her head. "You have a good read on him too. Now do V."

"You're enjoying this."

"Yeah I am. I mean . . . it's cool that you can do that. I wish I could read people like that."

Sandas bobbed his head. "I'm not sure what the temperature has to do with this, but you can learn how to with practice."

"Temperature?"

"You said cool."

Emily laughed. "It's slang. It can mean many things based on context. In the way I used it, I meant your ability to read others was good, and I liked it."

"Ohh . . . Earthborn slang. Yes . . . lot of slanging going on there. Oddly enough, I don't have much information on Earthborn slang. I'll add it to my list of things to find. Nonetheless, on to V." He cleared his throat. "V is unique, unlike any AI I have seen. In the fight, he flew between you and several robots. He put himself in harm's way to fight the two robots you didn't see that were aiming at your backside. He disabled them, but most AIs would consider it a waste of resources and energy to put themselves at risk of dying. Not only that, but he took several shots that came our way. Inefficient by AI standards? Yes. Inefficient by human standards? No."

Emily nodded. "V is not quite a true AI."

"I figured, and I suspect his true self is not something I'll ever be told, and that's okay."

"Okay . . . what about Evaran?"

"Mysterious," said Sandas, shaking his furry hands in front of him.

Emily laughed.

"He's the leader of this group. His confidence is like an aura, and his commitment to doing right seems unshakable. He's a time traveler, and," said Sandas, waving a claw around, "he has this ship, the Torvatta, which is unique in its own right. I think he's . . . not of this reality. Maybe a dimensional being of some type."

Emily raised her eyebrows slightly.

"Also, during the fight, it was like half of him wasn't there. As if there was more to him, yet the form he was in was limiting it."

"Why do you think that?"

"Oh, Emily! Didn't you see how he fought? His hits with the staff used more force than should be possible. Also, unlike humans, I can see fast-moving things better. He moved faster than anything I've ever seen. He even angled his staff behind him to shoot some stun beam, *without* looking back. As I said . . . mysterious. He's definitely not human, not even close, and although I know you're human, you performed some unusual feats yourself. I don't think it's just experience. You and Dr. Snowden both have an edge, one I'm unaware of."

Emily pulled her lips in. "You're *very* observant."

Sandas smiled. "Do you want to hear my assessment on Draxus? Of course you do."

She chuckled.

"Draxus is . . . a very serious being. Based on our first encounter, he harbors a strong hatred for these new humans. The fact that he was willing to listen to you tells me he can change his mind, even in the middle of battle. He's from an advanced technological race, judging by the lack of surprise at some of the concepts discussed in the conference room."

"Yeah, I kinda saw he was . . . pretty intense."

Sandas swished his nose around for a moment. "He's also willing to give his life to correct the timeline, now that he has seen it to be the best chance of getting rid of these new humans."

"Huh?"

"He said he needed to join the group, to aid in the mission. His . . . Arkara thing . . . is gone. His crew . . . gone. His world . . . gone. You're dealing with someone that doesn't have much left to lose, except himself. Evaran has shown Draxus that there is still hope, something that I suspect Evaran does to a lot of people."

Emily nodded. "Evaran does that to people for sure. Well . . . I hope then that Draxus isn't crazy or something."

Sandas wagged a claw at Emily. "I don't think he is, but when dealing with people with nothing to lose, take caution."

"All right . . ."

"Anyone else you wish me to assess?"

"I would say you, but . . . I think I know you well enough already. I . . . know your heart," she said with a grin.

He eyed Emily, and then broke out into a big smile. "Seems that way, doesn't it. Perhaps then if Evaran allows me to tag along on this journey, I will get to know yours."

"I hope you can travel with us, but Evaran has the final say," said Emily as she stood.

"I know, and I'm glad Evaran chose you to show me my living area."

Emily tilted her head.

"You know he did choose you? Right?"

Emily shrugged. "I think you may be reading a bit too much into that."

Sandas grinned. "Perhaps I am . . . but I think I'm right. I suspect I already know what will occur tomorrow."

"Well, let's hear it."

"Evaran will allow Draxus and I to join this . . . whatever it is. Our appearance, although seeming random, probably plays a role in something larger, something that only someone of great power can see. Evaran's hesitation on me suggests that . . . I play a role in another event, at another time. My survival, and by extension, knowledge, of this event is important."

Emily snorted. "You have all the answers."

"Yes, and I usually charge for them."

She chuckled. "Okay, well . . . if you need anything, you know how to contact me or the others. I'ma hit the sack."

"Ahh, another slang. Based on context, you want to sleep, not literally hit a sack."

Emily nodded.

"All right, Emily Snowden. Have a good night's rest," he said.

She paused to watch Sandas bounce over to a side room with a workstation. He was probably going to try to find out as much as he could from it. She smiled as she left.

07

Dr. Snowden yawned as he opened his eyes. It was 8:00 a.m., and he knew Emily would be on his case for not joining her in training. Although he had attended a few, sometimes it felt good to sleep in. He moved to the edge of the bed and slid his legs off the side.

The planar cartography session with Draxus had been interesting. Not only was he a warrior in his own right, but he had waxed philosophically when pointing out the various systems and their history. Dr. Snowden enjoyed the lesson and felt a bit of unease that some version of humanity had been so cruel to the Dravens. In exchange for the lesson, he had told of how he met Evaran, and Draxus seemed very attentive when listening.

Dr. Snowden got cleaned up and, after thirty minutes, headed to the conference room. When he got there, he saw that Emily and Sandas were already seated and having breakfast. Draxus was in his chair and had replicated what looked like an oversized head of cabbage. Sandas had what looked like a large nut of some type, and Emily had a glass of orange juice and a plate of eggs. Dr. Snowden waved at everyone. "Good morning, all."

Everyone returned the greeting.

Dr. Snowden got an omelet and a glass of orange juice and then took a seat next to Draxus.

"Sleep well?" asked Emily.

"Oh, yeah, always do."

"No bad dreams . . . ?"

He shook his head. "Haven't had one in a while now." He glanced at Draxus. "Do Dravens dream?"

"Of course," said Draxus. "To us, it is like visiting another reality. If you meditate right, you can even talk with others who are also dreaming."

"In the dream?" asked Sandas, sitting up.

Draxus nodded.

Sandas laughed. "Now you're joking."

"It's possible," said Dr. Snowden, sneaking a glance at Emily.

Sandas stroked his snout while eying Dr. Snowden and Emily. "Hmm."

Emily tossed Sandas a look. "You're reading into that, aren't you?"

"Maybe," said Sandas with a big grin.

Dr. Snowden glanced at the both of them before continuing on with his breakfast.

After thirty more minutes and light conversation, Evaran, V, and Zeta-12 entered the room. Evaran sat at the head of the table, while V and Zeta-12 hovered over the opposite end.

Dr. Snowden had finished his breakfast and noted the others had as well. He always wondered what it must be like for Evaran to not require sleep. Dr. Snowden loved sleeping on the Torvatta. Having insomnia seemed like a curse prior to meeting Evaran, but the neural effect of the Torvatta made sleeping a breeze. Although the enhanced nanobots made Dr. Snowden's body need only four hours, he still took in eight. The feeling of waking up refreshed was now common, instead of a rare occurrence.

Evaran looked around the table. "Did everyone sleep well?" Everyone nodded.

"Good. I have several things to go over," said Evaran. He extended his arms toward Sandas and Draxus. "Sandas and Draxus will be joining us on this summons investigation."

"I . . . am honored," said Draxus, bowing his head slightly.

"Great!" said Sandas. "You won't regret this decision."

Evaran eyed Sandas. "There are some ground rules to follow. One. Do not attempt to hack the Torvatta. It is not possible."

Sandas swallowed hard. "I was just testing the system."

"I am sure you were," said Evaran. "Two. The Torvatta will restrict what you can and cannot see. This is to avoid any paradoxes that may arise from your presence."

Draxus and Sandas nodded.

"Three. You will learn of information relative to the past and the future. To avoid knowledge pollution, know that I will be monitoring the timeline after you both are returned, at least for Sandas. Please do not seek out more information than is needed."

Sandas swished his nose around while Draxus did a slow dip of his head.

"I would not normally allow this situation. However . . . Sandas is integral to future events. I now know that he must travel with us in order for certain scenarios to occur. He will go back to the main timeline, just after he went into the space-time eddy. As for Draxus, once we are done, we will wait until the temporal shielding the Torvatta gives him wears off before changing the timeline."

Draxus tilted his head. "How long is that?"

"Around a few days," said Evaran. "You both have your own gear, but the Torvatta can replicate whatever you might need, within reason of course. It also has temporary nanobots for each of you that will allow the universal translator to work outside the Torvatta. Now, on to our first objective." He tapped at the table console, causing a galactic map of the region around Earth to appear. "We are going to establish a baseline. This will help me to determine what impact this event might have had, if any. Earth is in a golden age and has a star-spanning empire, but it is nothing like this version of humanity that Draxus has encountered. After that, we will check on Fredoria, and then Kreagus, before going to the Draidjen home world. Any questions?"

"Are you certain the Draidjen will take me?" asked Zeta-12.

"I am not. However, you are their creation. We will learn more when we get there and . . . I will not let them terminate you, if that is your concern."

"That's my concern," said Zeta-12.

"You have my word that I will not let them terminate you," said Evaran. "Now, any other questions before we head out?"

"None here," said Dr. Snowden. "Anxious to see this golden-age empire."

Sandas smiled big. "Me too."

"Then let us head to the command center," said Evaran. "V, take us to just outside Earth's solar system, current time, and enact Torvatta scan profile two."

"Acknowledged," said V. He flew out of the room with Zeta-12 in tow.

Dr. Snowden joined the others and exited the room. A smile crossed his face as he wondered what humanity, the one he knew, was like on Earth. A golden age sounded like a playground of ideas and concepts that he could not wait to explore. He noticed that Sandas had bounced away to sit with Emily in the left U-shaped seating area, and Draxus had taken his seat on the right, sitting attentively and focusing on the transparent front wall that showed deep space. V's segmented arms flew over the front console, while Zeta-12 hovered nearby. Dr. Snowden took his seat.

"Torvatta scan profile two is active," said V.

The Torvatta shot out a silver beam that formed a gold ringed portal with a rippling blue surface. After it had fully formed, the Torvatta flew through into interstellar space.

Sandas peered at the screen and then pointed at the galactic map that sat in a data window left of center. "We . . . just went eighty-one thousand three hundred twenty-eight light-years?"

"That is correct," said Evaran.

Draxus shook his head. "Unbelievable."

Evaran half smiled. "V, perform long-range scans."

"Acknowledged."

The galactic map window moved to the center of the front wall. As concentric circles pulsed out, a few dots appeared.

Dr. Snowden wrinkled his eyebrows. "Umm . . . shouldn't there be, like, thousands of ships being detected?"

"Maybe they're undetectable," said Emily.

"Not to the Torvatta," said Evaran. "This is unusual. V, take us to Earth and set the Torvatta to scan profile one."

"Acknowledged," said V. He interacted with the console. "Torvatta scan profile one is now active."

The Torvatta formed another portal and flew through it.

Dr. Snowden studied the screen. It showed Earth, but no space stations or ships were detected. Even the debris that he would have expected was gone. The familiar blue and green atmosphere that he had anticipated to see was murky green. "Whoa . . . what happened here?"

Evaran rubbed his chin. "It would appear this space-time eddy we are dealing with has caused more damage to the timeline than expected. Whatever that cloud cover is, it is preventing a scan. V, take us down and perform analysis scans."

"Acknowledged."

The Torvatta angled toward Earth and then shot off toward it. Clouds whisked by as the Torvatta punched through them. Eventually, it broke out from cloud cover and descended toward the surface.

Sandas hopped out of his chair and walked up to the screen. He looked down through the semitransparent floors. "I originally thought your ship had an unusual design in the mostly transparent front half, but I see now," he said, wagging a finger at Evaran, "that it provides an excellent view of whatever you need to look at. Much better than a screen! Yes, much, much better!"

Draxus looked through the side. "I would agree with you, Sandas. It seems there is a lot of plant life here."

Dr. Snowden watched as the Torvatta skimmed across the top of what appeared to be a canopy of some sort, except it never ended. "Are those . . . trees, or some kind of large plants?"

"Analysis. They are rods made of organic material with a top spread that forms the layer you are seeing," said V.

"Look!" said Emily. She pointed at a swarm of tiny flying creatures.

Evaran perused his ARI and then interacted with his chair console.

An image of the swarm up close appeared in a side window.

"It appears they are insects of some type," said Evaran.

The swarm flew toward the Torvatta, and some splatted when they ran into its shielding.

"Ewww," said Emily.

"V, heat up the shielding to clear off the remains," said Evaran.

Emily grimaced.

Sandas tilted his head at Emily. "You don't like bugs."

"Never have," she said. "Nothing against bug-like aliens either, I just . . . I dunno. All those legs, antennae, and things. Ugh."

Zeta-12 flew forward a bit. "You won't need to worry about having to meet them. The atmosphere is deadly to humans, assuming the Torvatta's scanning is correct."

Evaran nodded. "We will not be stepping out of the Torvatta."

"But we can go to the roof," said Dr. Snowden, shaking a finger.

Draxus narrowed his eyes. "That would be dangerous."

"Not this roof," said Dr. Snowden with a smile. "We would also have a much better view of everything."

"Very well," said Evaran. "To the roof."

Draxus stood and gestured at Sandas. "After you."

"Thank you, kind sir," said Sandas as he bounded after Emily.

Dr. Snowden chuckled as he and the rest headed to the elevator.

Draxus surveyed the elevator he was in. The others, minus Dr. Snowden, who stood next to him, were already there. The interior was somewhat bland, but a light seemed to emit from everywhere. Draxus had not seen a place for the elevator to go on the roof. It would be just a moment before he could find out.

He was thankful that he could participate in the time-line-correction campaign, as he called it. The set of events that led him to where he was now seemed fortuitous. A random blip on his ship's radar had shown Zeta-12's ship being pursued by human hunters. Draxus knew there must be a good reason for their presence, enough to gamble on investigating it. A high price had been paid, but where death lay, opportunity sprung forth, one he would take advantage of.

The elevator came to a stop.

Dr. Snowden gestured outward.

Draxus bowed slightly and then exited the elevator. He took a quick glance around. The faint shimmer of the shielding was extended a bit out from the roof's edge, and looking up, he could see it extended there as well. With an enclosed environment, protected by a shield that could handle a ship exploding around it, this would be an ideal vantage point. He joined the others standing near the light-blue guardrails. The Torvatta hung in the air over a body of some liquid, with a beach and the organic rods in the distance. It looked relaxing.

Sandas poked at the guardrails. "Fancy shielding all around us." He looked out. "That doesn't quite look like water to me . . ."

Evaran perused his ARI for a moment and then said, "It is not water. It is a . . . slime . . . of some sort."

Emily grimaced. "That's nasty."

"A sea of snot!" said Sandas.

Dr. Snowden laughed.

Draxus peered at the rods. "You said they were organic?"

Evaran nodded. "According to the scans, they appear to be part of some organism."

Emily's eyes widened. "You mean . . . they're like . . . hair follicles?"

"Large ones, but yes," said Evaran. "The covering on top is actually the hair aspect, and the rods are an extension of whatever is underground."

"Exactly how big is this thing underground?" asked Dr. Snowden.

"Analysis. Unknown. It has been present since we began scanning," said V.

Dr. Snowden's eyes widened. "Are you serious?"

"Yes, my analyses are always serious," said V.

"Not always," said Dr. Snowden, wagging a finger. "I seem to recall some of them using humor."

V's lights glowed a bit brighter. "Acknowledged."

Sandas swished his nose around for a moment. "Humor, huh?" He eyed V. "I think I can help you with that."

"I would appreciate talking with you on this subject."

"Consider it done, my floating friend!" said Sandas. He pointed out. "So there is a large creature underground, and we're hovering around on its back. I'm not sure I want to know what that slime is then in relation to the creature."

Emily grimaced. "I don't either, but it seems kinda weird to be in a golden age and have Earth in this state, unless humanity has moved on somewhere."

"This is not how Earth should look," said Evaran. He nodded at V. "Display this location from historical records. Set the time index to the current time."

"Acknowledged."

Draxus raised his eyebrows as he watched V and Zeta-12 fly over to the center, where a console materialized. Even on the roof, the Torvatta could create things. Draxus turned to watch a projection display on the interior shields. It showed an advanced city where humans flew in straight lines between buildings. There were no ships flying around in the city. He guessed it was built in a manner that did not need them. The buildings were sleek, and off in the distance, he could see ships entering and leaving the city's edge.

"Wow," said Emily. "That's definitely not what we're seeing now."

Sandas shook a furry hand out. "They must be transported in some type of beam between buildings. Interesting. That technology is theoretical from my time period."

Evaran eyed Sandas. "And it will need to remain so . . ."

"I . . . would still like to take a look at that," said Sandas with a big grin.

"I am sure you would," said Evaran.

Draxus exhaled from his mouth. "So instead of this, there is some creature underground. I understand this space-time eddy might be the cause, but . . . what could cause such a transformation?"

"I have seen something similar before, but I do not want to make a hasty conclusion without gathering more information," said Evaran. He raised a finger. "I suspect the Draidjen will have that information. I believe we have seen enough here to know that Earth, and humanity by extension, has changed. V, take us to Fredoria."

"Acknowledged."

The Torvatta began to ascend.

Draxus and Sandas gripped the guardrail.

Dr. Snowden grinned. "There's no need for that. I know it's been said before, but the Torvatta's shielding acts as a dampener, so there won't be any force transferring through."

Draxus and Sandas looked at each other, then back at Dr. Snowden.

"Look outside if don't believe me," said Dr. Snowden.

Draxus watched the outside change from the atmosphere to space. After a portal was opened, he studied the strange tunnel they entered briefly before exiting above another planet. Throughout the whole experience, not once did he feel even a slight vibration. "Impressive."

"I'll say," said Sandas. "I'd like to order a Torvatta."

Evaran raised his eyebrows.

"Worth a shot," said Sandas, grinning.

"We are above Fredoria," said Evaran. "V, perform long-range scans and a planetary analysis."

"Acknowledged."

The interior shielding lit up with dots in various directions and distances under it with details on what the dot represented.

Dr. Snowden wrinkled his eyebrows. "Like Earth, not much out there . . ."

"Yes, and based on the readings I am seeing, it appears Fredoria has a similar cloud formation as Earth. V, take us in."

"Acknowledged."

The Torvatta angled itself and descended toward Fredoria. After ten minutes, it had broken cloud cover and began to fly over the landscape.

"Analysis. Readings indicate a similar environment to Earth."

Evaran rubbed his chin. "Interesting. This has the markings of a galactic-level event."

"One that . . . maybe the humans who were sent to my region were supposed to resolve," said Draxus, raising a finger. "Or their ancestors maybe."

"Yes . . . I would concur with that hypothesis," said Evaran. "The question now is, when did the humans get pulled into the space-time eddy, and who were they?"

Emily raised her head a bit. "So at some point in the past, some humans who were meant to do something got pulled into this eddy, and since they didn't do that thing, whatever it was, all this occurred?"

"Perhaps."

"They must be some special humans then," she said.

"It is possible. There are many possibilities, but we will investigate it."

Sandas glanced at Draxus, and then at Evaran. "So this is what you do . . . fly around and solve space and time anomalies?"

"That is part of it."

"A space-time detective. Inspector Evaran. I like the sound of that. All the information you must know," said Sandas. He glanced at Dr. Snowden and Emily. "And you two by extension. And of course V."

"Information that could be dangerous in the wrong hands," said Evaran.

"You protect it, as it appears it should be," said Draxus. "You're like a guardian of time."

Evaran tilted his head. "An interesting choice of words. I prefer being thought of as a traveler who helps those in need."

Sandas shrugged. "Or the ultimate information broker. I like Draxus's choice of words better."

"Nonetheless," said Evaran, gesturing at V, "we still have Kreagus to analyze, then on to the Draidjen home world."

Draxus noted that Evaran seemed uncomfortable at being called a guardian. Maybe it was the responsibility attached to the word, versus a traveler, which had none, other than to travel. Draxus watched as the Torvatta exited Fredoria and then jumped to Kreagus. It was apparent that traveling such distances was a routine thing for this group. Although he understood they could travel in time, he had not seen it yet.

The Torvatta descended and broke cloud cover.

After a few minutes of flying over the surface, Evaran said, "There is a slight difference between the three planets.

The composition is slightly off at each one. Based on the concentration of carbon dioxide, I would say that whatever this creature was, it appeared here before the others."

"What do you think the creature is?" asked Emily.

"I have some ideas, but . . . I would need to research it. However, now we head to the Draidjen home world. It is time for some answers."

"What if the Draidjen home world is the same?"

"Then we will need to skip through time to figure it out. I do not want to do that unless absolutely necessary."

"Got it," said Emily.

Draxus watched as the Torvatta ascended. Jumping through time to observe events must be an adventure in itself, but he understood the paradoxes that could arise from that. He contemplated what the Draidjen might know. It crossed his mind that Evaran, with the ability to go anywhere, would be an intimidating investigator. Draxus wondered how often Evaran had done just that.

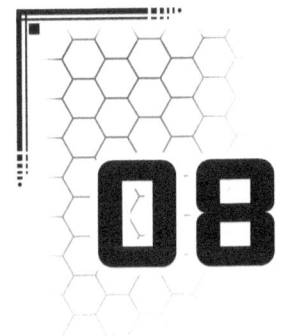

08

Sandas eyed the planet that appeared before the Torvatta. He knew it to be Dukaris, home world of the Draidjen. As the information broker, he knew a lot more about the Draidjen than most. They kept to themselves for the most part, similar to the Illuzarans nearby, relatively, in terms of galactic distances.

The Draidjen were an odd-looking race. Fredorians called them snakelike, and Earthborn said Draidjen looked like large cobras with a shortened body. He smiled thinking about how every Earthborn he came across seemed to compare him to a squirrel. Granted, he did look similar, but there were many differences.

He had come to learn many things since first meeting Dr. Snowden and Emily. The fact that they traveled with Evaran meant they knew a lot more than they let on. Sandas had barely slept the night before due to thinking about all the information they must have seen. The familiarity they seemed to have toward him was something he picked up on when on Zeta-12's ship. Whatever this future event was, they were friends in it.

Sandas liked Emily. She was kind, yet tough. Dr. Snowden was friendly as well, but was empathetic, something Sandas did not see much in most of the Earthborn he dealt with. He was beginning to understand Draxus a bit more and felt a bond due to similar circumstances. Sandas figured he would get to know V and Evaran a lot better during this investigation.

An image appeared on the inside of the Torvatta's shielding.

Sandas studied the scaly pale-green Draidjen that appeared. This one was a bit different than the Draidjen he knew of, but it still had a snakelike body with two arms. The display was a full body shot, and he could see that its cobra-like mane was smaller, and its head was bigger. The large fangs that were usually on the sides were missing, and the formfitting white suit with green lines segmenting it had an octagonal pattern on it. Although it appeared different, he figured it was a male, as the females did not have a mane, unless that was different too.

"Welcome, Evaran and friends," said the Draidjen. "I am Zakassis."

Evaran tilted his head. "You know of us . . ."

"Your encounters with us are well documented. However . . . we're aware of humanity's Evaran Protocol, and we have a similar one. I'm sending you coordinates to land, and might I say . . . it's an honor to speak with you," said Zakassis. He waved a hand to the side.

"Coordinates received," said V.

"Very well," said Evaran. "We shall meet you at the coordinates. I have various topics I would like to cover."

"Excellent," said Zakassis. "We look forward to your arrival."

The image dissipated.

"V, take us in," said Evaran.

"Acknowledged."

The Torvatta began to descend toward the planet.

"A bit different-looking than what I recall," said Sandas. "Although I know more than most in my time period, they're one of the few races I actually know very little about, the other being the Illuzarans."

"I guess you're gonna learn more now," said Dr. Snowden.

Sandas grinned big. "Sure am . . . but," he said, glancing at Evaran, "that's not information meant to be shared."

Evaran nodded.

Sandas watched as they passed by several large ships. They were unlike any he had seen before and reminded him of floating cities on a flat surface with a bubble shield. Beneath it was a large rectangular structure that had long tentacles attached to it.

"Looks like a jellyfish," said Emily, pointing at one of the ships.

"They are temporally shielded," said Evaran. "I suspect their planet is too, based on the Torvatta's reading."

"Temporally shielded?" asked Sandas. "Zeta-12 mentioned something about his ship being that way, although I'm not fully sure what it means."

"It means if the timeline changes, whatever is shielded doesn't disappear with the timeline," said Dr. Snowden.

Evaran raised a finger. "In addition to that, anything inside the temporal shielding has its own timeline independent of the main timeline it is in. In the case of the Draidjen, their whole solar system's timeline is independent of the main timeline it resides in."

"I wouldn't even know how to detect something like that, although the space-time eddy was said to have a temporal signature. Was that shielded?" asked Sandas.

Evaran shook his head. "It is, but not through technology."

"Right," said Sandas, glancing at Draxus. "You catching all this, big guy?"

"We are familiar with the concept of temporal shielding, small guy," said Draxus. "However, I'm not familiar with the technology."

"The less known, the better," said Evaran. "The Dominion potentially possessing temporal shielding is an issue. However, one problem at a time."

Draxus nodded.

Sandas focused on the atmosphere washing over the shields. To view it while on the roof was a new experience for him. It felt like he could reach out and feel the air rushing by. He observed Dr. Snowden and Emily. It seemed like they had seen this many times before. Draxus's intent gaze made it evident it was a new experience for him as well.

Sandas's eyes widened at what he saw when they broke cloud cover. Large cylindrical structures towered over the landscape. Each cylinder had angled supports that jutted out. On top of a majority of the supports were the city ships he had seen in space. The city ships' rectangular bottoms sat on the support, with their tentacles arced over and connected to the underside of the support. Ships flew between the cylinders, as well as Draidjen, both solo and in groups, on silver circular surfaces. A lush jungle sat at the base of the cylinders, with bodies of water between every third one.

Draxus peered around. "This is a most unusual design."

"It appears the ships we saw in space are actually cities that can move. This is their docking hub," said Evaran.

"I guess that's one way of adjusting to environmental issues," said Dr. Snowden.

Evaran perused his ARI for a moment. "Yes, and the cylindrical docking towers can move as well. If they wanted to move to another planet, they could do so."

"This is a very advanced species," said Draxus.

"I'll say," said Dr. Snowden.

Draxus leaned in and turned an ear toward Dr. Snowden.

Dr. Snowden eyed Draxus. "Everything . . . okay?"

"You said you would say, then stopped," said Draxus. "I was not sure if I was having a hearing issue or not."

Sandas laughed. "Oh, Draxus. It's Earthborn slang. Humans take a word or set of them, and use them differently based on context. I'm still adjusting myself. When Dr. Snowden said 'I'll say,' he was agreeing with you."

"I see. I'm sure the translator is not helping with that either. Slang seems like it would be very confusing."

"Tell me about it," said Sandas with a grin.

"I just did."

Sandas put a hand on his furry stomach as he bent forward and laughed.

"Sandas . . . ," said Emily. She glanced at Draxus. "He was using slang just then."

"Ahh, you were mocking me. What a confusing way to communicate," said Draxus.

Sandas shook a furry hand out. "Sorry, sorry. I was just teasing. It's in my nature."

"Analysis. I have issues with slang as well," said V.

"It appears then that I'm not alone in this," said Draxus.

The Torvatta approached a smaller city ship that sat about a half mile off the ground. After a moment, it had landed on a circular pad on the outskirts of the city.

"Before we go," said Evaran, looking around, "I wanted to emphasize that while the Draidjen may appear friendly, be cautious."

"Always," said Draxus.

Everyone else acknowledged Evaran.

"Also, Sandas and Draxus, you need to get your translation nanobots. V will assist you."

They nodded at Evaran and followed V to the medical lab. After five minutes, they came back.

Sandas rubbed his neck. "I suppose they'll be gone once this is all over."

Evaran nodded as he stood. "Let us go."

Sandas's heartbeat had ramped up some in anticipation of seeing an advanced Draidjen race. He hoped that was due to excitement and not the nanobots, but either way, the technology alone would be worth the visit. His natural inclination to absorb information would be in play, but he knew to be careful with that, lest he raise Evaran's ire. Being a part of this investigation was an opportunity he was grateful for. Where it would end, he did not know, but this was the adventure of a lifetime. He smiled as he followed the others to the Torvatta exit.

Emily studied the platform they were on. It was part of the larger platform that housed a city encapsulated in a bubble shield of some type. The only thing that separated the landing platform from the rest of the platform was a circular light-blue line that outlined the edges. Looking up, she could see ships in the air, but it was the Draidjen on the small metallic platforms flying around that caught her attention. She pointed at one while glancing at Evaran. "What is that thing they're on?"

"If it is similar to what humanity has in this time period, then it is a portable transport. It can shrink enough to fit into a pocket."

Sandas raised a claw. "And . . . what material is this made of?"

Evaran eyed Sandas.

Sandas grinned big. "Okay, okay. How does it hover?"

"It is made of a material with a specific surface configuration that, when excited with specific energies, exerts a force that allows it to hover. Think of . . . negative energy."

"Hmm," said Sandas. "Very interesting. I'm aware of artificial gravity technology that can do this, but it requires considerably more equipment, and it definitely couldn't be shrunk. Negative energy is also difficult to harvest." He glanced at Draxus. "Ever seen anything like that before?"

"I haven't," said Draxus. "It would be advantageous to possess such technology."

Emily nodded. "I wouldn't mind something like that."

Evaran glanced at Emily. "Perhaps we can adjust your PSD to support something similar conceptually."

Dr. Snowden raised his eyebrows. "Uhh . . . yeah . . . count me in on that."

"PSD?" asked Sandas.

"Personal support device," said Emily, raising her PSD.

"Ohh . . . those things. They're quite impressive, yes, quite impressive," said Sandas. He glanced at Evaran. "I know, I know, they aren't for sale."

Evaran half smiled.

Emily turned her head to focus on the approaching group. It consisted of Zakassis and another Draidjen and a male human. The other Draidjen wore an orange-and-red suit that was similar in design to what Zakassis wore. The tan-skinned human had a formfitting navy-blue suit with silver and white lines on it. A band ran across the top of his forehead, and his hair was pulled over the back part. Several rings were on each hand, and a leatherlike strap crisscrossed his chest. Black boots and a silver cape completed the outfit.

The approaching group assembled in front of Evaran and crew.

"Welcome to Dukaris," said Zakassis. "I'm the regional governor here. To my left is my assistant, Huultarkiss, and to my right is Human Ambassador John Ginnis." He put his fists together, perpendicular to his chest, and then bowed his snakelike head.

Emily remembered that was similar to the Draidjen gesture of respect she had seen in a previous adventure.

Huultarkiss and John did the same.

Evaran and the others reciprocated the movement.

Evaran gestured around the group, pointing at each in sequence. "I have with me Dr. Albert Snowden, Emily Snowden, V, Zeta-12, Sandas, and Draxus."

"Dr. Snowden, V, and Emily are known to us," said Zakassis. "Zeta-12 is familiar as well, but we are not aware of Draxus and Sandas."

Evaran nodded.

"You are in Priza Tass, otherwise known as Ambassador City," said Zakassis. "I felt it was appropriate to come here, as I suspect whatever it is you're here for involves humanity missing."

Evaran nodded. "We have visited Earth, Fredoria, and Kreagus. All is not as it should be."

"We . . . can help with that information."

Evaran gestured at Zeta-12. "We also have one of your species-vault ship AIs. He was not where he was supposed to be."

Zakassis raised a hand for a moment, closed his eyes horizontally, then opened them. "Yes, I see those records now. Zeta-12 was confirmed missing in AD 6308. It appears . . . you have found him." He focused on Zeta-12. "I'm sure you have quite a story to tell."

"Yes, I do," said Zeta-12. "I have some questions, considering it is almost four thousand years later."

"Huultarkiss can assist you with that," said Zakassis, nodding at Huultarkiss. "You will most likely need some upgrades. Follow him, and he will accommodate you."

"I look forward to it," said Zeta-12. He flew in front of Evaran. "Thank you for helping me. I will not forget you."

Evaran nodded. "I hope you find the answers you seek."

"I do too," said Zeta-12. He flew near V. "I appreciated talking with you. When your adventure is over, I would enjoy syncing with you again."

"Acknowledged," said V.

Emily watched as Zeta-12 left with Huultarkiss. Although she had not spent much time with Zeta-12, she could see that even an AI wanted to survive if given an option. Sandas's words about an AI not using resources to defend others crossed her mind. She was not sure Zeta-12 would have done that if it came down to it during the fight on the ship. Like Evaran, she wished Zeta-12 good luck, but his mission still bothered her. The Draidjen explanation for that was something she was curious to hear.

"Please, follow us to a private chamber where we can speak. You probably have as many questions as we do," said Zakassis. "We normally would teleport you there," he said, gesturing at Evaran, "but you possess . . . different matter." He glanced at Dr. Snowden, Emily, and V. "As do you three." He closed his horizontal eyelids twice in rapid succession as he focused on Draxus. "And apparently, you as well."

Sandas swished his nose. "I guess I'm the only normal one here."

Zakassis eyed Sandas. "A Rogorian. How rare. We have had interactions with the last of your kind, long ago. His name was recorded as Sandas as well."

"Umm . . . I *am* the last of my kind."

Zakassis raised his hand, with his bracelet glowing a bit. "Then it would appear it is you. The information broker. Based on that, I am assuming this meeting has some impact on our previous meetings."

Sandas sighed. "I guess I can't keep the fact I'm the information broker a secret from this group, or you, it seems. Normally I'd be running away if anyone found out my identity, but . . . in these circumstances, it's different. Yes, that's me. Assuming I get back to my own time period . . . I'm sure any meeting after that would be informed by this one." He raised a claw. "Also, the Draidjen I know back then are a lot different from what I'm seeing now."

"As expected," said Zakassis. "I did not mean to expose you if the others did not know."

"Oh, they knew, well, maybe not Draxus, but I guess he does now."

Zakassis nodded. "That would also explain how you were able to contact us on a secure channel back then. Our records are very detailed and span thousands of years."

"I'd love to see—" said Sandas, glancing at Evaran, then at the ground, "I mean, I'm sure they're very accurate."

Zakassis hissed and gurgled.

Sandas sighed.

Evaran gestured forward. "Lead on."

Emily laid a hand on Sandas's shoulder.

He grinned at her.

She understood it must be disconcerting for Sandas to hear his secret identity tossed around so casually. This was not an ordinary group, and he probably understood that now. She surveyed the environment as they walked along a pathway outlined by the same light-blue lines she saw around the landing platform.

Her helmet was down, and the absence of any strong smell seemed unusual. The sounds of ships flying overhead meshed with the sound of the Draidjen on their transports whizzing by. She could also hear the soft hum of the city ahead. A smile formed on her face as she observed Draxus and Sandas taking everything in. It occurred to her that she did not know the extent of Draxus's knowledge on other aliens. Sandas, though, she had a good idea on.

After ten minutes of silence, they reached the outer edges of the city.

Emily noted that the base of the city had a metallic wall that went up about forty feet or so. Attached to the bottom and evenly spaced out were several enclosures with an open front. It reminded her of an elevator, but she was not sure why it was outside or why they were heading toward it. When the group reached it, she boarded it along with everyone else.

A pale-green shield covered the front, sealing them in.

Her eyes widened as the enclosure moved through a tunnel in the wall. She had not seen it before since the enclosure blocked her point of view. As the enclosure zipped along, she observed the metallic walls. The twists and turns the enclosure took was like moving through a steel maze. She noted that there was barely any force, even when the enclosure made sharp turns. When it shot straight up, she anticipated some force, but did not feel any.

After five more minutes, the enclosure came to a halt, and the front shielding dissipated.

Zakassis and John exited the enclosure, with everyone in tow.

Emily caught her breath as she observed the large spacious platform they were on. They were high above the city inside the bubble shielding. Along the sides were guardrails, and the platform was bare of anything save the floor. Looking out, she could see over the city.

Zakassis raised a hand with his bracelet glowing.

A circular orange ring formed on the ground, with chairs around the edges. A cylinder appeared off to the side with four small shelfs jutting out.

Zakassis pointed at the cylinder. "If you require any sustenance, please, make use of our replicators. Otherwise, have a seat, and we can begin."

Emily glanced around at the others and then headed to a seat. She smiled when she saw Sandas poke around the replicator. He was probably not hungry, but a device like that would potentially yield some technology secrets, at least conceptually showing what was possible. Dr. Snowden, Draxus, and Evaran, like her, had taken their respective seats. V hovered nearby behind Evaran.

After Sandas sat, Zakassis grinned as he faced Evaran. "We are always honored by your presence. What brings you to us?"

Evaran raised a finger. "I have several topics to cover. The first deals with Zeta-12. We found him far away from where he should have been. His mission, as stated by him, was to . . . store . . . reproductive members of alien species. The method of retrieval was not consensual. As you may or may not know, I am against any type of abduction."

Zakassis nodded. "We stopped that program in AD 6520. It . . . caused a few wars. Apparently some of the other ships we sent used invalid criteria in their selections. Those ships that returned, we freed the specimens and sent them back."

"I see," said Evaran. "In that case, I will consider the matter closed. What will become of Zeta-12?"

"He will be given some upgrades and treated fairly. He is, after all, a Draidjen creation. We'll take care of him and help him should he need it," said Zakassis.

"I appreciate you helping him," said Evaran. "Now, on to my next topic. Humanity is missing. I know that it should be there, but it is not."

John raised his head a bit. In a calm, monotone voice, he said, "I believe I can help explain that. Before I do, I wanted to say it's an honor to meet you. You have been humanity's champion throughout all of recorded history, and the amount of people who can claim to have met you is very small. I am glad to count myself as one of the lucky few."

Evaran bowed slightly and then gestured toward John. "Please proceed."

Dr. Snowden sat up in his chair a bit. John looked human, and the way he walked and now talked seemed confident. The room they were in highlighted some of John's facial features. Dr. Snowden could now see that there were small circular nodes on the side of John's head, just under his headband. Intricate glowing designs danced across the headband, giving it an elegant look. Dr. Snowden focused as John extended a hand. His fingertips had small coverings and were glowing.

A projection depicting a galactic regional map shot up from the orange ring on the ground.

"This is the Carus system, approximately fifty thousand light-years from Earth. Our deep-space probes picked this up," said John. He dipped a finger.

The projection zoomed in to an orange gas cloud outside the system.

"This was the first appearance of the Gulltin Haresis, as we call it," said John.

Dr. Snowden scrutinized the snakelike shape of the gas cloud that was continuously swirling around.

"It is a colony of aliens . . . unlike any we have met. They are viral and swarm a system if there is a planet it wants to use as a breeding ground. They took on a variety of forms, and they all exist within the strange orange gas cloud. We were not only unable to stop it, we could not even identify how these creatures could exist in deep space."

Emily tilted her head. "Did it come by here?"

Zakassis hissed. "It tried, but it seems temporal shielding irritates it. Since the Illuzarans and we are the only civilizations with that technology, we were able to survive. There were some individuals outside us who survived. They were knowledgeable of temporal shielding, and they came here."

"I see," said Evaran. "When the Gulltin Haresis came through Earth's region, it took over."

John nodded. "I'm guessing that's what happened. From what I remember, we used technology obtained from another group of humans that we had met only a few decades or so before, and the Gulltin Haresis was expelled."

"Then you were here, inside the Draidjen temporal shielding, when the timeline changed?" asked Evaran.

"Yes."

"Have you ever seen the Gulltin Haresis before?" asked Zakassis, glancing at Evaran.

"I have. Based on the image and behavior you have described, they are called the Tryp. That orange cloud is not a normal gas, and they are a hybrid of baryonic and Telsaron exotic matter. That cloud is Telsaron in a gaseous state and is what allows them to conform matter to what they need. Think of it as a mobile environment."

John looked at Zakassis, then back at Evaran. "Have you fought it before? We have no records of events you've participated in, other than when you appeared."

"As it should be. For the Tryp, when I last encountered them, I redirected them. My ship is unique and can output something that repulses it. Temporal shielding would have the same effect, as you have discovered," said Evaran. He rubbed his chin. "These other humans who helped you with technology in your version of history . . . what were they like?"

"As advanced as we were, they were even more so. They didn't have temporal shielding, but another type of energy they called Palisin. They were able to deliver it in a wide dispersal pattern. The odd thing about these humans was that a good portion of them were nonhumans. While we still had some in our population, it was nowhere near the percentage of the population of this new group."

Dr. Snowden narrowed his eyes. His first thought was that maybe the rift gate that Evaran had left on Earth in their last adventure was used. One of the directives that Evaran had given to the nonhumans was to find a second Earth. Maybe they did.

Evaran rubbed his chin. "How did you meet this other group of humans?"

"We met them at one of our most remote Dyson bubbles. We had sent out colony ships long ago, and this one was about sixty thousand light-years away," said John. He wiggled his index finger.

The projection zoomed out from the galactic map, and showed a new dot indicating the location of the Dyson bubble.

John continued on. "Even as far from Earth as the new colony was, the new group of humans controlled several systems much farther away, on the edge of the galaxy. How they met is still up for debate, but it has been said that deep-space probes of the colony and the other group met each other and then relayed information. I don't really know, as it was never officially documented how they met."

Dr. Snowden perused the projection. While the initial summons location was top right, relative to a top-down view of the galactic map, the location where the colony was to be set up was bottom left. He shook a finger out. "So . . . if that colony was never established, then that meeting would have never occurred."

Zakassis glanced at Dr. Snowden. "An interesting hypothesis. I have no way of verifying that, though . . . but Evaran might be able to."

"It is a start," said Evaran. "However, there are other . . . considerations . . . to take into account."

John's eyes searched the group for a moment. "What brought you here? At this point in time?"

Evaran shook his head. "I cannot elaborate on that."

"I understand," said John, grinning. "I'm surprised, though. I thought, at least from what is known about you, that you already knew where humanity was. If that's true, you would have known about these . . . Tryp."

"I only know the summary aspects, not specific details. In that regard, the less I know is better," said Evaran.

Dr. Snowden remembered looking through the information on the Torvatta. While it had details on places Evaran went, most data was summarized, like when a new era started or ended and any major developments. Dr. Snowden figured that since the Tryp had no impact on humanity initially, it would not have been in the Torvatta's database. Maybe that is why the summons was initiated now, to lead Evaran to fix an event where a rift did impact humanity in such a way that it was wiped out, at least in the area around Earth. There was still the Terran Dominion and others far away.

"I appreciate the information," said Evaran. "There is a lot for me to sift through."

"Please, feel free to stay as long as you need. We have accommodations for all," said Zakassis. He pointed a claw at Draxus. "I meant to ask earlier, but our scans indicate you're a Draxenen. Is that correct?"

Draxus nodded. "Draven, actually. You are aware of my people?"

"Only from scans done by our deep-space probes. Your species was not yet technologically advanced from the images taken. We received that information long ago, and it seems our translation technology got your species' name wrong."

"Things are . . . different now," said Draxus. He glanced at Evaran. "I can't go into details."

"A shame," said Zakassis. "We would've appreciated you updating our records."

"We will stay for the rest of the day and leave tomorrow," said Evaran. "Draxus, if you wish to assist them on the cultural and technological aspects of your species, you can do so. Current events . . . can be omitted. As for the others, take the rest of the day off and enjoy the Draidjen hospitality. We can meet on the Torvatta in the morning at 10:00 a.m."

Dr. Snowden nodded along with the others. He watched Draxus and Zakassis begin to take off.

Emily and Sandas had approached John to talk with him.

Dr. Snowden walked up to Evaran. "I think I have an idea of what's going on now."

"As do I," said Evaran. "However, I will verify a few things, and then tomorrow we can meet, determine a plan of action and proceed from there."

"All right. What are you going to do then for the rest of the day? It's only 10:40 a.m., although it looks much later here."

"I wish to talk with the Draidjen a bit more and would like to update the Torvatta's database. I am unsure of Draidjen protocol to do so, but I will work on that."

"Sounds good. I'll talk with John a bit and then, I guess, try out Draidjen hospitality. Maybe get a tour in."

Evaran nodded and then headed toward the room exit.

Dr. Snowden exhaled from his mouth and walked over to John and the others.

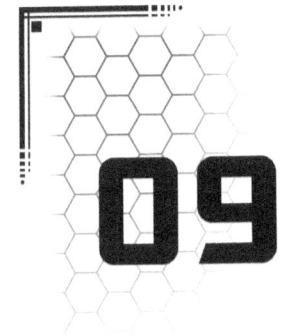

09

Draxus poked at the nutrient-dense nut that the conference room replicator had created. It was 9:00 a.m. Earth time, according to the Torvatta, and he had spent yesterday helping Zakassis update records on the Dravens. It was enjoyable to meet with another alien species that did not want to enslave or cause havoc. The nanobots had performed as expected, and communication was not an issue. He could see how useful having the nanobots was.

Draxus found the information on Earth and, by extension, the human empire fascinating. Although it was gone due to the timeline change, the images, processes, protocols, and missions were similar to the stories of the United Planets he had heard. The difference was that the humans from Earth managed over a thousand systems. It was no wonder there was an ambassador on the Draidjen home world.

Taking a tour of the Draidjen cities with Dr. Snowden, Emily, and Sandas was the highlight of the day. V had spent time with Zeta-12.

Draxus's attention focused on Emily and Sandas entering the room.

Sandas pointed using a claw from both hands at Draxus. "Hey, big guy! What'd you think of the Draidjen?"

"They were hospitable, and very knowledgeable."

"Yeah, they were," said Sandas.

Emily crooked a thumb at Sandas while shaking her head. "The Draidjen somehow messed up his recording device. All he has is static."

Sandas sighed. "I forgot it was on."

"I'm not sure I believe that," said Draxus.

Sandas laughed. "It was worth a shot."

"Did Evaran say to not gather information?"

Sandas looked down. "Yeah . . . he did." He looked back up. "It's in my nature. I'm the information broker, it's what I do and what drives me. This is going to be tough."

"To struggle against your nature must be difficult," said Draxus.

Sandas pulled a device off his suit and put it into his pocket. "Yeah. I will honor Evaran . . . and try."

Draxus nodded. His only purpose was clear: to defend his race and purge those who would assault them. Sandas's nature seemed to be focused on collecting information. A strange purpose, but one that Draxus could see being useful to others. Although he had not intended to cause Sandas to reevaluate his nature, maybe it was for the better. Evaran had been fair to both of them, and Draxus would ensure that for his part, he would return the gesture.

"I *am* surprised I could breathe without any effort," said Sandas.

"As am I," said Draxus. "I have not had to use a mask since joining this group. It would seem humanoids have similar requirements for breathing."

"That's what I've seen, although I've seen places that would make you run."

Draxus nodded.

Evaran, Dr. Snowden, and V entered the room.

Dr. Snowden got a cup of coffee and sat opposite of Draxus and Emily. Evaran sat at the head of the table, and V hovered over a seat next to Dr. Snowden.

"I hope everyone had a good day yesterday," said Evaran.

"I sure did," said Dr. Snowden. "I always think I've seen a lot, and then I see even more amazing things. The Draidjen technology level is impressive."

"Analysis. The Draidjen suggested some enhancements for me. I also talked with Zeta-12. He wishes us the best of luck and wanted me to relay that he is grateful for our assisting him."

Evaran nodded. "I hope he finds what he is looking for."

"I got some time in with John," said Dr. Snowden. "Humanity is definitely more advanced in this time period. I found out he had family that disappeared in the timeline change."

"That is what we will investigate today," said Evaran, tapping at the table console.

A projection showing a galactic map with several dots appeared above the table center.

Evaran pointed at a dot. "That is where the remote Dyson bubble was that a colony ship created. We will see if they are there. After that, we will check on this other group of humans and nonhumans that interacted with them. Then we will head back to the summons location. I would like to meet the different human factions."

"I think that could be arranged," said Draxus. "There is a Dominion ceremony where a governor is staking their claim on a former Draven world. That means Salazar will most likely be present in some capacity as well."

Evaran rubbed his chin. "Perhaps I can then arrange a meeting from there."

"Possibly," said Draxus. "The claim can be challenged, but only by another governor."

"As they are human, there is a good chance they are aware of the Evaran Protocol. Perhaps I can use that to my advantage," said Evaran.

Draxus's eyes glowed purple for a moment. "I hope that you can. From what I understand, it is one of the larger Arkaras on the planet. I wish I could help them, but . . . I can barely help myself."

"Then that is what we will do when the time comes," said Evaran. He raised a finger. "However, we will check out these other two locations first. V, set coordinates to the remote Dyson bubble. Set the Torvatta to scan profile one, and once we are there, perform long-range scans."

"Acknowledged," said V. He flew out of the room.

"Let us go."

After a few minutes, everyone had assembled in the command center. Evaran sat in his command chair, with Emily and Sandas in the left U-shaped seating area and Dr. Snowden and Draxus on the right. V hovered before the front console.

The Torvatta ascended from the landing pad it sat on in Dukaris. After it reached space, it opened a portal and flew through.

Draxus observed the galactic map after the Torvatta exited the portal. Concentric circles pulsed outward from a dot representing the Torvatta. According to the map, the circles pulsed out about ten light-years. How the Torvatta was able to scan so far away was a mystery to him. His civilization could only do a few light-years, and even then, it was nowhere near as detailed. The scans were not showing much activity. The planet they were over lacked anything in orbit. "This planet seems inactive."

Evaran rubbed his chin. "So it would seem. The planet is not exhibiting any technological footprint. The star is also not encircled by a Dyson bubble. This would suggest that the colony ship sent here never arrived. It could have gotten caught up in the space-time eddy and formed its colony after exiting. Without any contact from the rest of the human empire at the time, it might have split into several factions and developed into what Draxus knows."

Emily wrinkled her eyebrows. "Maybe the ship was stopped by something else."

"It is possible," said Evaran. "However, history shows it to have come here. The fact that it did not means that something changed history, and the only candidate for that so far is the space-time eddy."

"Makes sense," said Emily.

"So . . . this colony ship," said Draxus. "If we alter its course to avoid the space-time eddy, then it will proceed here, instead of near my home system."

Evaran tilted his head. "That is one option. The other is to dispose of the eddy. Both would seem to fix the immediate issue. However, potential temporal shielding is involved, which is unusual. Humanity did not possess that technology in that time period, or even this one. I am curious as to how they obtained it. If we were to alter the colony ship's course, and Salazar's Dyson bubble was temporally shielded, it would still exist in your home system. The other factions may have that as well. We will assess the situation further when we get there. V, take us three light-years away from the coordinates of the humans and nonhumans that John mentioned."

"Acknowledged."

The Torvatta opened a portal and flew through it.

Draxus studied the heavy traffic that the long-range scans picked up. "These systems *are* active."

"Are we going to check it out?" asked Sandas, swishing his nose around.

Evaran shook his head. "I just wanted to verify its presence. I suspect I know of this group's origins."

"Do tell," said Sandas, tossing a furry hand out.

"It is perhaps best I do not tell."

Sandas snickered. "I figured. I'd check it out when I get back, but it's sort of far away."

Evaran nodded. "Draxus, we have your navigational information in the system. Can you show V which planet we should head to in order to see this ceremony?"

Draxus tapped at his palm and then extended it toward V. A projection shot up, showing the galactic map with a green dot on it.

V faced Draxus and scanned the projection. "Coordinates acquired." He pivoted back around to the console.

The Torvatta opened a portal and then flew through it.

Draxus clenched his jaw as he examined the long-range scans appearing on the front screen. He could see that although there was much less activity, the details showed Dominion ships scattered around, with some by the planet they were near. An outline formed around the bluish-green planet, with a blinking red dot. Based on the landmass the dot was on, he knew it to be where they were headed. "That is the main common area for this Draven clan. The Arkara would be there, which is where the Dominion delegation would be for this ceremony."

"Then it is time to introduce ourselves," said Evaran.

Draxus nodded. He had been to this world before. It had been one of the last major Draven worlds to get captured by the Dominion. The world was the farthest away from the Koloris Shen civilization, another species taken down by the Dominion. The Koloris Shen fought the Dominion, the Gul Kash Alliance, and outcasts for over four hundred years. Once the war was over, the Koloris Shen were carved up, and then the Dominion hit his civilization.

He sighed. At least he now knew that humanity was not supposed to be like this, and he suspected if his race had encountered the United Planets faction first, things may have happened differently. Not that it would matter once the timeline was corrected.

The Torvatta angled down and approached the planet.

Sandas peered out through the transparent walls as the Torvatta flew through a clear sky. His heart pounded away when he saw blue and purple plant life. Although not quite like his home world, it was a junglelike world. The unusual aspect that stuck out immediately was that there were no concentrated areas of buildings. Everything seemed to be meshed into the jungle. He could see how a society that had a large treelike being as a mother would be close to nature. The ability to grow structures using synthetic DNA was also an intriguing idea, one he would investigate when he got back. He glanced at Draxus. "It's a beautiful world, very beautiful."

"I like it," said Draxus. "Although this planet has been conquered, our resistance here has been strong. I . . . haven't been here in a while." He pointed to rising smoke off in the distance. "It looks like destruction has taken hold."

Sandas swished his nose around. "This place we're going to . . . what should we expect?"

"It will be held in the main common area, where the Arkara resides," said Draxus. "The Dominion will have the new governor, and I'm guessing Salazar in some capacity. There will of course be robotic guards and sometimes other human variations. Every ceremony is different, based upon the governor handling it."

Emily tilted her head. "You think they'll take notice of us? We sorta stand out."

Draxus shook his head. "It is not uncommon to see other aliens, including other humans, at a ceremony. However . . . all aliens will be purged after the ceremony, in the coming weeks, when they begin chipping."

"Huh," said Emily. "Well, I don't think we'll be around for that."

Evaran nodded. "We will not. This encounter is to observe the Dominion up close, and perhaps gain a meeting out of it via the challenge option that Draxus mentioned."

"I would not underestimate the governor's champion," said Draxus. "That's who you'll fight if you issue a challenge."

Emily crooked a thumb. "I think it will be them that underestimates Evaran."

Sandas glanced at Evaran. Although he seemed capable in a fight, Sandas wondered how it would go. He could see that Draxus was tensed up, yet everyone else seemed relaxed. It made Sandas wonder what adventures had taken place to cause that type of reaction to a potentially hostile encounter. He focused on the ground as it approached. With a sigh, he placed a hand on the wall. He turned his head to the side when he felt a hand on his back.

"Everything all right?" asked Emily.

Sandas turned back to look out. "Yeah. It just . . . reminds me a bit of my home world."

"The one Max the matter mage saved you from, right?"

Sandas turned around and narrowed his eyes. "You know of Max?"

Emily glanced at Evaran.

"He is known to us," said Evaran.

Sandas looked down for a moment, then back up. "This . . . future event thing, right?"

Evaran half smiled.

"Well, Max only uplifted me because I was the only one to survive my planet getting hit by an asteroid. I almost didn't make it."

"Uplifted?" asked Emily.

Sandas wiggled his whiskers. "To go from nonsentience to sentience. My species was not sentient prior to the asteroid hitting, but Max said we would have evolved sentience eventually."

"Oh," said Emily. She lightly squeezed Sandas's shoulder. "That must have been strange to gain sentience."

Sandas bobbed his head. "It was. One moment, I was determining why it was hot everywhere, and the next, I was talking to Max. I owe him my life. The strange thing was that he said the asteroid's trajectory was not natural. Like . . . someone or something had specifically sent it to my planet. He didn't elaborate. Who would be so cruel as to commit genocide on my race before we could evolve?"

Dr. Snowden sneaked a sidelong look at Emily, then at Sandas while clearing his throat. "Not sure, but you're here now."

Draxus eyed Sandas. "This . . . Max . . . sounds like he worked in genetic engineering. The Gul Kash Alliance has animals that were made sentient or . . . uplifted, as you call it."

Emily smiled. "Max was a matter mage. He could control matter within a certain radius. Although he couldn't create life, he could manipulate it."

"I have never heard of one capable of this," said Draxus.

"Max was unique, sorta like Evaran," said Sandas. He glanced at Draxus. "At least we can help your people."

Draxus performed a slight bow. "It is appreciated."

Sandas turned back to watch as the Torvatta approached a small clearing.

After the Torvatta landed, the group exited onto the Torvatta ramp just inside the shielding.

Sandas noted that no one changed into different suits, but Dr. Snowden and Emily had their helmets up. Draxus did not have his up, but Sandas figured that was due to already being acclimated to the environment. Based on what he had seen of their functionality, it was probably more efficient to keep the suits on. His by comparison was much less advanced, but he had a bag of tricks he could deploy if needed. Violence was something he avoided, and instead he relied on guile and misdirection. It had served him well. He took a look around. "Do we need our helmets?"

Evaran perused his ARI for a moment. "The Torvatta reports that the air is breathable, and the atmosphere is similar to Earth's and Fredoria's in makeup. That is consistent in most worlds with sentient life in this galaxy, it seems."

Sandas snorted. "Almost like it was planned." He caught Dr. Snowden and Emily looking away as they lowered their helmets. They probably knew why certain environments seemed to be favorable for humanoids. "I guess contamination isn't a concern."

"It is always a concern, but your suits are scrubbed of contaminants when you pass through the Torvatta shielding. However, the scans indicate that there is nothing on any of us that would harm this environment."

Sandas nodded.

The group passed through the Torvatta's shielding and into the clearing.

With a deep sniff, Sandas took in the strong jungle smell. The area they were in had a metallic floor large enough to support larger ships. On the edges were blue trees and purple plants. Walkways weaved throughout them, and buildings were built in between the trees. He pointed at the floor. "So this was grown?"

"Yes," said Draxus. "A structural outline is created and inserted into crystallized synthetic DNA. Then it is seeded and activated."

"So it grows like a plant. Very interesting. It makes it easier to have a city integrated with the jungle," said Sandas.

Draxus nodded. "As it should be. The seed grows rapidly compared to regular DNA. Although we're advanced technologically, we always stayed in touch with our roots."

"My world was similar, except we were primitive, and our homes were holes in trees."

"You were a tree dweller," said Draxus. "We have some creatures here that sort of resemble you, except much smaller."

Sandas grinned big. "Let's hope they don't think I'm their god!"

"I don't think you need to worry about that," said Draxus.

Emily chuckled as she shook her head.

"Which way do we go?" asked Sandas.

Draxus pointed ahead at one of the walkways that disappeared into the jungle. "There."

Sandas slapped Emily's leg. "Race you to the edge!" He took off in a full sprint, using his rear legs first, then all four limbs. His eyes widened when he saw Emily burst past him. When he arrived at the edge, he paused to catch his breath.

"You're pretty quick," said Emily.

"Quick? You just blew past me!"

Emily smiled. "Now imagine if I had tried."

Sandas was not sure if she was kidding or not, but her physical prowess far surpassed what he initially thought she was capable of. She moved like a robot, yet was not one. He turned his head to watch the others strolling across the landing pad. The look on Draxus's face showed he was thinking similar thoughts to Sandas.

When the rest of the group arrived, Evaran glanced at Sandas and raised a finger. "Let us go as a group and try not to attract attention."

"Sorry, sorry, I just had some pent-up energy to release," said Sandas.

"He had the zoomies," said Emily with a smile.

"It is okay," said Evaran. "From what I understand of the Draven culture, it would be out of place for you to run and jump around like your tail was on fire."

Dr. Snowden and Emily burst out laughing.

"I guess I deserve that," said Sandas. He extended an arm out toward the path. "All right, lead on."

"Draxus, you can take point on this," said Evaran.

Draxus nodded and headed out.

As they walked, Sandas got a deeper look into the environment. The path they were on was similar to the landing pad in material. The edges had a raised rubberlike edge, and beyond that was the jungle floor. The buildings seemed to be between the blue trees, but there were also some that were built with the tree going through it. Structures above were suspended by purple vines. Every now and then, he would see a large hole with a ramp inside it. It blew his mind that all it took was some outlining and a sprinkling of fancy crystallized seeds to grow all of this. He pointed at the large hole. "You build underground too?"

"Of course," said Draxus. "Most technology is developed there. It also brings us closer to our Arkara."

Sandas bobbed his head as he continued to survey the landscape. It was apparent to him that the Dravens were as advanced as the Kreagans, if not more. The Terran Dominion must have had an advantage that the Dravens could not compensate for.

After twenty minutes, they reached the main common area.

Sandas noted that it looked like a large bowl in the ground had been cut out of stone, with seats etched into the sides and a raised platform in the bottom center. Around the top edge was a walkway with a ten-foot wall that encircled the area.

His eyes widened at the large Arkara that sat in the middle of the platform. It had four main trunks, with smaller ones in and around it. Various colored vines and plants filled in the gaps, and the Arkara reached far into the sky. He got the sense that it was probably just the tip he was seeing, with much more underground. The image that Draxus had shown earlier did not do justice to what Sandas was seeing.

Dravens sat in every available seat, making it look like a sea of blue and purple.

Sandas observed the varying types of Dravens. Most were humanoid, but short and stocky. Some looked like large flying insects with long legs. Others were quadrupeds, while some were more insect-like. It was a hodgepodge of shapes, but based on what Draxus had said, Sandas knew they all had a purpose in life.

Evaran pointed a bit away along the top edge. "We can watch from there."

"This is amazing," said Dr. Snowden as the group moved into position.

"To some, perhaps," said Draxus.

"Oh . . . I didn't mean . . . you know," said Dr. Snowden.

"It's okay," said Draxus. "The ceremony will begin soon. You will get to see why humanity is reviled."

Emily sighed. "This is the second advanced version of humanity we've seen that has something wrong with it."

Sandas raised a bushy eyebrow. "I've known humanity for a while, mostly Fredorian. Being brutal, violent, and cruel to others is not uncommon, although I must say on the other end, they can be compassionate, kind, and helpful. I guess it depends on which ones you meet. You may change your technological level, but you can never fully escape your nature. Unless you're genetically engineered or uplifted, of course, and even then, it's still there."

Draxus glanced at Sandas. "You speak the truth as I know it. Evaran, I wish you luck in your challenge when the time occurs."

"Thank you," said Evaran.

Sandas looked up and then scampered to the top of the wall to take a seat on the ledge. "Better view up here."

Emily hopped up and sat next to him. "I agree."

"You're almost as nimble as me," said Sandas. He jumped a bit when Dr. Snowden landed next to him. Sandas shook his head. "Even you're nimble, yes, quite nimble."

"You seem surprised," said Dr. Snowden.

"I am . . . actually," said Sandas.

Evaran and Draxus hopped up and took a seat, while V landed in Emily's lap.

Sandas eyed V. "Getting a little cozy, are we?"

"Analysis. Emily's lap is cozy."

Emily grinned. "You two . . ."

Sandas smiled as he looked toward the center platform. He suspected that he and V would have some good discussions. Everything so far had been going well, and he enjoyed traveling like this and seeing new cultures without the threat of being hunted by those looking for the information broker. Even though this event represented a bad situation, he would try to make the best of it. With a content sigh, he adjusted his seating position in preparation for what was to come.

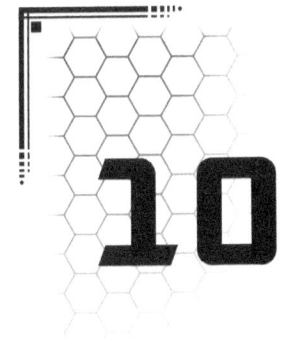

10

Draxus clenched his jaw as he watched the screen that hovered in front of them across the walkway and about five rows down. On the screen, Dominion representatives assembled in front of the Arkara. It had been about twenty minutes since they had arrived, and although he was trying to appear calm, every fiber of his being wanted to go down and attack the humans. He felt a hand on his arm.

"So who is who?" asked Dr. Snowden.

Draxus appreciated Dr. Snowden's genuine curiosity. It seemed to be something that the Dominion lacked. Draxus pointed at the female. "That is the governor, you can tell by the symbols on her chest. Based on her appearance, she is approximately twenty-five. The male humanoid alien next to her is her spokesperson. He's a Koloris Shen, one of the civilizations that the Dominion conquered before ours."

"He uhh . . . is missing some hair. Kinda reminds me of a large gray," said Emily.

"I'm unfamiliar with a . . . gray," said Draxus.

"They're a race of hairless aliens with big black eyes, a big head, and a slender humanoid body," said Dr. Snowden. "Whenever an alien abduction is discussed on our home world in our time, they're usually the aliens everyone refers to."

Draxus nodded. "I see. The Koloris Shen do not abduct. They were peaceful."

Sandas pointed at the eight-foot tall humanoid with heavy battle armor. "Who's that big guy? He's even bigger than you."

"He's the governor's champion. It is who Evaran will have to fight if he's to challenge the governor's claim."

Sandas gulped as he looked at Evaran. "You sure about this?"

"I am," said Evaran.

"I know you're tough, but uhh . . . that guy is something else," said Sandas.

Emily grinned. "Then you don't know Evaran too well."

Sandas shrugged. "Apparently not."

Draxus agreed with Sandas. From what Draxus had seen, Evaran could fight, and seemed incorruptible, but a champion could take down even a praetor. He noticed that the governor had taken a seat on the platform with her champion next to her. Robotic humanoid guards stood at attention around the governor. Off to the side stood a humanoid robot with metallic gold skin, and it looked like the form was not meant for combat but more for observation. Draxus had seen it before and knew it was Salazar in one of his forms.

The crowd went silent as the Koloris Shen stood front and center on the platform and began to speak. "I am Genritthel-andris, a speaker . . . for the Terran Dominion. You have a lot of questions . . . and I will answer them. This territory has been claimed by the Terran Dominion. Your ships . . . your technology . . . your defense forces," said Genritthelandris, waving a hand dismissively in the air, "were washed away before the Dominion's might. As such . . . you're now members of the Dominion."

Dr. Snowden shook his head. "Not arrogant at all, is he?"

"Shh," said Emily with raised eyebrows.

Genritthelandris paced back and forth. "You are Dravens . . . connected at birth to your Arkara. What you don't know . . . is that there is something better to be connected to . . . something that enhances you and takes away any concerns or pains you may have. That something . . . is *Salazar*. Once integrated with him, all your doubts will be silenced, and you will know true harmony." He raised a hand in the air. "I was once like you . . . small-minded . . . weak . . . and full of fear. Salazar . . . has shown me the light, and it *is* the way forward for all."

Draxus clenched his jaw. He had heard a similar speech before at another ceremony. His eyes glowed a light purple.

"You're weak!" shouted one Draven.

"You didn't fight hard enough!" said another Draven.

Genritthelandris smiled as he looked around the assembled Draven. "I was weak . . . but not anymore. You too will know the joy that is Salazar. Your impurities . . . burned away . . . and replaced by efficiency." He nodded his head. "An efficiency your Arkara could *never* give you."

A short and brawny Draven near the front stood and pointed at Genritthelandris. "You spout madness! No one is going to *integrate* with this Salazar!"

The assembled Dravens cheered.

Genritthelandris shrugged. "The alternative to integration is death."

The Draven snorted. "You'll find that Dravens don't bend their knee as easily as the Koloris Shen did."

"Perhaps not," said Genritthelandris. He glanced back at the governor, who stood. "It appears that Hesshia, your new governor, wishes to speak to you." He took a step to the side as she approached the Draven.

"What's your name?" she asked.

"Grok."

"You wish to challenge us?"

Grok shook his head. "Right . . . when you have a small army behind you." He gestured at the champion. "And him. You hide behind your technology and numbers."

Hesshia glanced at Salazar, who nodded. She smiled. "I don't normally accept challenges from the likes of you . . . but if you can take me down, we'll leave. You talk big for a small thing. Do you wish to challenge me?"

The other Dravens cheered Grok on.

"You still have advanced armor and shielding. It wouldn't be a fair fight," said Grok.

Hesshia glanced at Salazar again, who nodded. She pressed two buttons, one on each shoulder. Her formfitting suit fell off, showing her bare body. She reached down and tapped at her boots, causing them to retract so that she could step out of them. Her gloves fell to the ground. Standing completely naked before the Dravens, she extended her hands out to the side. "Satisfied?"

Grok gulped but headed up the platform as the other Dravens around him pumped their fists in the air and did the Draven salute.

Draxus noticed that Emily was entranced, while Dr. Snowden had widened eyes. Grok was a defense force captain, based on the clothing he wore and the striped pattern on the shoulder. Although not nearly as powerful as a praetor, they were known for their strength. It was no surprise that Grok had spoken out. It also most likely meant that this Arkara's praetor was dead.

"You think he'll take her?" asked Sandas. "While she is a fine specimen to look at, she doesn't look like a fighter."

Draxus grimaced. "She'll kill him."

"Really?"

Draxus nodded.

"Then I should issue my challenge," said Evaran.

Draxus laid a hand on Evaran's arm. "You must wait until this challenge is complete."

Evaran narrowed his eyes as he focused on the hovering screen.

Grok clenched his fists as he took to the platform. He adopted a stance, with his right leg and arm forward.

Hesshia walked opposite him and smiled. She cracked her neck and extended her arm, with her hand in a vertical position perpendicular to her body.

Grok charged and, when close, reached out to grab her hand.

She stepped forward and grabbed his wrists, causing his upper body to stop, while his legs slipped forward. With a heaving motion, she tossed him off to the side.

He took a moment to catch his breath and jumped back up. With methodical steps, he approached her. When he was close, he struck out.

She batted his fist away.

He swung with his other fist.

She batted it away again.

He lunged forward and attempted to grapple her.

She took a step back and kicked him in the chest, sending him flying back. As she walked over to him, she said, "I guess you were all talk." She grabbed him by his neck and lifted him off the ground. With her other hand, she punched through his chest and then retracted her arm. His head went limp as she tossed him to the ground. Facing the now-silent crowd, she raised her bloody fist and said, "You are mine to do whatever I want with. Once you're with Salazar, you'll understand your place. Bow before me!"

The assembled Dravens stood in shock and then kneeled in the small space before their seat.

Evaran hopped off the wall. His lips pulled down. "I am going now. Wait here."

Sandas watched as Evaran walked down one of the aisles toward the platform. His walk stood out to Sandas. It was one of confidence. There was no fear present. He had seen that type of poise only a few times, and it was one born of experience. He glanced at Emily. "Evaran is certain of himself."

"Oh, yeah," said Emily. "That governor isn't as fast as him. If he fights the champion, he'll still win."

Draxus turned his head toward her. "You are very certain of his skills."

"He's fought beings much stronger than anything on that platform," she said.

"How do you know the champion's strength?"

Emily tilted her head. "I can see how he moved when he came onto the platform. If I can see it, then Evaran can."

Sandas scratched his snout. "All I saw was a mountain of a human walk on the platform."

Dr. Snowden pointed at the screen. "Evaran's there."

Evaran hopped onto the platform. "I would like to issue a challenge."

Hesshia smiled as she walked up to Evaran. "Who . . . are you, handsome?"

"Someone who has witnessed an injustice."

"Well . . . unfortunately for you . . . challenges can only come from another governor, or if Salazar allows exceptions. You don't qualify as either."

Evaran tapped at the side of his utility belt, causing a tray to slide out. He reached in and pulled out a small device that he then held up to Salazar. "I would not be so sure of that. My credentials."

Salazar raised a hand and shot out a light green beam that enveloped the credentials. After a moment, he said, "Evaran. Time traveler, and friend of humanity. Your presence is . . . unexpected."

"I am sure it is," said Evaran. "Are you aware of the Evaran Protocol?"

"All humanity is," said Salazar. "You may challenge if you wish."

Hesshia snapped her head toward Salazar. "He can?"

"Yes. Evaran is unique."

She smirked. "Okay, well, then Rellstaras will fight for me."

"As expected," said Evaran.

"What do you want if you win?" asked Salazar.

"For this Arkara and the surrounding city to be free of the Terran Dominion."

"Acceptable."

"What!" said Hesshia.

"Is there a problem?" asked Salazar, slowly moving his gaze onto her.

She looked down. "No. No problem . . . but if Rellstaras wins, I want Evaran as a pet."

"No," said Salazar "However, he has a ship, the Torvatta. If your champion wins, Evaran gives the Torvatta to me."

Evaran nodded. "I agree to these terms."

Hesshia scowled. "Why can't he be my pet if we win?"

"Because you couldn't handle him," said Salazar. "On top of that, if the other human factions found out, it could be a unifying factor against us."

"I don't care about that!"

Salazar turned his body to face her.

She licked her lips and stepped back. "I'm sorry. I . . . lost control. It won't happen again."

Salazar nodded and gestured at an open area on the platform. "No weapons."

Evaran tapped a button on the front of his utility belt, causing it to fade away. "Noted."

"Let the challenge begin," said Salazar.

Rellstaras grinned as he stepped into the open area and bobbed his head from side to side.

Evaran walked over and stood opposite. He placed his hands behind his back.

Rellstaras strode forward. When he was in range, he swung his meaty right fist at Evaran.

Evaran took a step back and deflected the blow.

Rellstaras swung with his left fist.

Evaran stepped just out of range and guided the blow past.

Rellstaras kicked forward.

Evaran caught Rellstaras's foot and shoved upward, causing Rellstaras to fall.

Rellstaras stood and shook all over for a moment. He charged toward Evaran.

Evaran jumped over Rellstaras and performed a leg sweep after landing.

Rellstaras crashed to the ground. He growled as he stood. With a slower approach, he came within range of Evaran. He jabbed with his left fist.

Evaran caught it with his left hand.

Rellstaras jabbed with his right fist.

Evaran caught it and, with a bicycle kick, sent Rellstaras flying back.

Rellstaras shook his head. "Enough!" He stormed toward Evaran with his shoulder lowered.

Evaran tilted his head, and when Rellstaras was near, Evaran sidestepped and then struck Rellstaras's chest with an open palm.

Rellstaras went flying to the ground. His breathing became laborious.

"It is done," said Evaran.

Salazar walked over to Rellstaras and scanned him. "You disabled one of his internal regulators. Impressive, but not unexpected given who you are."

Evaran nodded. "I would like to add one additional condition. A visit to your main facility in your megastructure."

"I would appreciate that," said Salazar. "There are many things I wish to discuss with you in a more . . . private setting."

A robot guard walked up to Evaran and shot out a hologram from its chest.

Evaran scanned the hologram. "Thank you for the coordinates. For the record, I oppose these actions against the Dravens."

Salazar nodded. "Based on our records of you, *that* is expected."

Evaran gestured toward Dr. Snowden and others. "I have some friends who travel with me. Will they be a problem?"

Salazar pivoted to leave. "They are acceptable."

Hesshia knelt next to Rellstaras and looked him over. With a slightly red face, she focused on Salazar. "That's it?"

The robot guards focused their weapons on Hesshia.

"This is a public event. Are you . . . challenging my decisions?" asked Salazar.

Hesshia swallowed hard as she looked away. "No."

Salazar nodded.

The robot guards swept in and placed Rellstaras on a metallic stretcher that hovered off the ground. Once Rellstaras was loaded, the guards followed Salazar off the platform.

Hesshia got back into her armor and then followed the guards. She paused to turn and focus on Evaran. "This isn't over."

"It is for now. Go," said Evaran.

She narrowed her eyes and wheeled back around.

Once the Dominion members were off the platform, Dr. Snowden and the others joined Evaran there.

"That was crazy!" said Sandas. "You moved around that champion guy like a flash of lightning."

Draxus nodded at Evaran. "A most impressive win. I have fought a champion before. Unfortunately, he killed half of the unit I was with before we were able to take him down."

The crowd around the platform stood and cheered.

Dr. Snowden raised his eyebrows. "Seems like you won them over."

"Perhaps," said Evaran. He tilted his head at the Arkara and approached it. When he was near, he tossed out his translation orb. Looking up, he said, "Can you understand me?"

"Yes . . . ," said the Arkara in a booming voice, seemingly out of thin air.

An audible gasp erupted from the crowd as it went silent. The crowd got on bended knee and bowed their heads. Draxus joined them.

"Umm . . . what's going on?" asked Emily.

"I am not sure," said Evaran, looking around. He focused back on the Arkara. "You are free of the Dominion per the challenge. Do you understand this?"

"Yes . . . but how . . . can we talk?" asked the Arkara.

"My translation orb is unique." Evaran narrowed his eyes. "I take it you do not communicate with the Dravens in a verbal manner."

"We . . . do not. May we see . . . this technology?"

Evaran grabbed the translation orb and walked up to the base of the Arkara, where he extended the orb out.

A vine snaked its way down from one of the lower branches and then touched the orb and Evaran's hand. The vine glowed purple as Evaran's hand glowed slightly yellow. After a moment, a branch extended from the main Arkara trunk with a yellowish bulb at the end. Pulsating light-blue metallic veins snaked over the bulb. The bulb flashed for a moment.

"I can now communicate verbally without your orb," said the Arkara.

Evaran eyed the bulb. "I would normally not do this, but everything is *not* as it should be. I will fix that soon, and those who have oppressed you will be no more. I hope this communication technology will help in whatever coordination you need to survive."

"Thank . . . you," said the Arkara. It snaked a vine out to Draxus. "Rise, Praetor."

Draxus rose while looking down.

"You will assist Evaran."

Draxus nodded.

"Umm . . . is this the first time you've *ever* spoken verbally?" asked Dr. Snowden.

A vine snaked out and caressed Dr. Snowden's startled face. "Yes," said the Arkara.

Evaran raised a finger. "I showed the Arkara how to convert wild-energy fluctuations into language. A side effect of this is that the Arkara can now see the environment, instead of through linked Dravens, or a general pattern in wild energy."

"Uhh . . . okay," said Dr. Snowden.

"You . . . and Evaran . . . possess similarities to our creators," said the Arkara.

The Arkara extended a vine to Sandas. "This furry one does not." Another vine weaved out and caressed Emily's face. "But this one does as well."

V flew away initially when a vine came toward him, but he came back down and let the vine touch him.

"The metal one has the same," said the Arkara.

"I see," said Evaran. "Your creators possessed a similar energy signature to Dr. Snowden, Emily, V, and I."

"Yes . . . How is this possible?"

Evaran glanced at the others, and then back at the Arkara. "It is a . . . long story, and one that should not be spoken of."

"Very well. With the Dominion gone, I will need to help my sisters."

Evaran nodded. He gazed around the assembled wide-eyed Dravens, whose mouths were gaping. "I suspect they have a lot to talk to you about."

"Yes . . . ," said the Arkara.

Evaran gestured toward the common area exit. "Let us go to the coordinates given to us."

"Could we stay for the rest of the day?" asked Emily. "I wanted to meet Draxus's people."

"I'm with Emily," said Dr. Snowden.

"I'm always up for gathering new information," said Sandas.

"Analysis. I would like to know more about the Dravens."

"And I . . . would like to know more about . . . you and your friends," said the Arkara.

Evaran half smiled. "It seems the decision is unanimous. We can stay for the rest of the day. I would suggest we visit the Torvatta to verify if Salazar is keeping his word."

"You are a . . . generous being," said the Arkara. "We shall prepare a feast . . . in your honor."

Evaran nodded as he placed his translation orb back on his belt.

Sandas followed Evaran and the others up the aisle. Looking around, the Dravens seemed shell-shocked. He could see that a small group had surrounded the Arkara and were talking animatedly. If this was their first time communicating with an Arkara after birth, it must be an enlightening moment for them.

He noticed that the Dravens closer to the exit were bowing toward Evaran, as if he were a god. Given what had just occurred, Sandas could understand that. To Evaran, this was probably just a routine event. Even Draxus appeared humbled to be around Evaran. Sandas bumped into Emily. "Sorry, sorry. I was just thinking."

Emily smiled at Sandas. "Just like Uncle Albert. I told you Evaran would take that champion."

"So you did," said Sandas. Emily was right. Evaran dismantled that champion like it was nothing, and did it without any gadgets. This was proving to be an experience that Sandas would never forget.

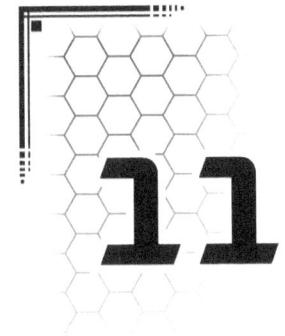

11

Dr. Snowden's eyes feasted on the smorgasbord of food and drink before him. The Dravens sure knew how to plan a feast, and they did it in only four hours. One of the advantages of his nanobots was that they could handle alien food. It made sampling alien culture much more palatable.

Looking out over the platform's edge, he could see the tops of the jungle trees. The platform reminded him of a plate sitting on a post. All around the edges were tables with seats, and in the center of the platform was one large circular table. A hole in the middle of it allowed food and drink to be brought up. He chuckled when he saw Emily looking around outside when they first came up. It was most likely due to her thinking there would be a lot of bugs. There was a bubble shield around the platform that prevented that, though. He felt a shake on his right arm.

"This is quite interesting. Hopefully it agrees with my stomach, but I can eat a lot of food types that would make most sick," said Sandas. He picked up an orange piece of meat and dipped it into a red sauce.

"*That* looks interesting," said Dr. Snowden.

Sandas nodded as he chewed on the meat. After he swallowed, he said, "I scanned it, and it's edible for me. It has a sweet taste to it. I like it."

Dr. Snowden observed Emily and V on the opposite side of the platform where they were engaged in a conversation with some Dravens. Evaran was walking around and talking to various Dravens. To Dr. Snowden's left was Draxus. Dr. Snowden turned his head toward Draxus. "So what do you think will happen now?"

"Rebuild," said Draxus. "Although I believe Evaran has given a reprieve from the Dominion, I don't trust them."

"Well . . . they know he's a time traveler and could easily go into the future to see if they keep their word."

"An interesting idea," said Draxus.

"I've been meaning to ask you about the Arkara verbal communication thing."

Draxus nodded. "If I can answer your questions, I will."

"All right. Can the Arkara communicate with any Draven after they're born?"

"Only a few specialized ones. She has a vine that allows for direct communication. However, the communication is relayed as images to the Draven's minds, not verbal."

Sandas shook a claw out. "Sounds like it could be easy to misinterpret things, if the only voice is in the hands of a few."

"I understand your concern," said Draxus. "When we are born, we are given the voice of the Arkara for the very first moments of our existence. Then she is gone when the cord that links us is broken. If some were to . . . be dishonest about her intentions, then she would learn of it through consumption and then deal with it by creating new Dravens with the purpose to fix it."

Sandas eye's widened. "Wow. A self-correcting society. It might take a while . . . but I get the feeling, just from the hospitality we've received, that the Dravens would be hard to corrupt."

"Yes. They know their actions will be judged . . . in time."

Dr. Snowden took a swig of the black drink in front of him. It had a strong earthy flavor to it, but the carbonation made it taste better. He glanced at Draxus. "So the praetor of this Arkara is gone?"

Draxus nodded. "And with it, a significant investment from the Arkara. Praetors have high levels of this . . . wild energy. A . . . Wildborn conduit . . . as Evaran phrased it. Usually, the praetor returns at the end of his life and is consumed by the Arkara, who funnels it to a new praetor. With no praetor returning, an Arkara has to build up the wild energy for a significant amount of time."

"Wow. Praetors really are unique," said Dr. Snowden.

"They are as unique as the Arkaras themselves," said Draxus.

Sandas cleared his throat. "Speaking of the Arkaras, you said they can only communicate with a few Dravens, but can they talk to other Arkaras?"

"Yes. All Arkaras are connected to each other."

"How do they do that?"

Draxus grinned. "You are one curious being. I don't know how they can be connected to each other. I don't think they know either."

"Well, probably since they're wild energy, they may have a common source that they pull from," said Dr. Snowden. "Another idea is that they could be using condensed space somehow. With all that exotic energy, it might be possible."

Draxus tilted his head. "An interesting set of ideas. Your eagerness to understand is pleasing. I'm glad to know that all humanity is not what we've seen." He pointed at several Dravens gathering around Emily, who had moved to the center table and was picking out some food and drinks. "The Dravens have proof now that humanity is like the Koloris Shen, one species, different factions. You are that proof."

Sandas chuckled. "I noticed that the Dravens seem to bow around Evaran."

"They think he is a god and has given the gift of voice to the Arkara, who then said that Evaran was similar to their creators. Can you see why they would think that?"

"Yeah, I can see it," said Sandas. "I've come across many powerful beings who could pass as a god. I don't think Evaran is a god, so much as a powerful being who is genuinely good. It's like the universe knew it was chaotic, yes, quite chaotic, and then gave us Evaran to help maintain some balance."

Dr. Snowden grinned.

Sandas jerked back and pointed a finger at Dr. Snowden's lips. "Ha! You know what Evaran is, don't you?"

"I can't say," said Dr. Snowden.

"I would like to know what Evaran is," said Draxus.

Dr. Snowden sighed. "I can't really talk about that. The less you know, the better."

"I understand," said Draxus.

Dr. Snowden cleared his throat and gestured outward at the Arkara in the distance. "That Arkara has had a throng around her the whole time."

Draxus nodded. "I'm sure she has a lot to say, as do the Dravens around her."

"I thought you would be down there," said Sandas.

"I will. The Arkara mentioned she wanted to link with Evaran and me later on."

Sandas rubbed his furry chin. "Interesting. Yes, very interesting."

"Any idea what will be discussed?" asked Dr. Snowden.

Draxus shook his head. "You know as much as I do."

"All right," said Dr. Snowden. He glanced at his plate, then at the table in the center. "Anyone up for seconds?"

Emily looked out through the platform shielding. The jungle was massive, and mountains sat off in the distance. The shielding made the coloring seem a bit off, but she was glad that, this high up, it was there. Although she was hungry, the jiggling green mass on the plate she held in her hand made her reconsider. She set the plate down.

"You should try the Flam tuzo," said a voice behind her.

Emily turned to see a moderately sized Draven with a larger-than-average head. She smiled. "I don't know what that is."

The Draven pointed at a dish that looked like yellow rice with green dots in it.

"Maybe I will," she said, walking over to the table.

The Draven stood next to her. "My name is Horcrix. I study alien culture and history. Not a lot of . . . need for my skills, but . . . there was at one point."

"I'm Emily," she said. She pointed up. "He's V."

"It is an honor to meet you both. Do you mind if we talk for a bit?"

Emily filled up her plate and then gestured at a nearby table. "Sure." She took her seat while V landed next to her.

Horcrix sat opposite of her. "I'm curious how you can speak to us so fluently."

"Analysis. We are using an advanced translator."

Horcrix peered up at V. "It would seem then that your translator is far beyond any that I've ever seen. You speak as well as a native."

Emily took a bite and swallowed. "Yeah, like V said, pretty advanced." She gestured at Horcrix. "If I understand correctly, you were born with the purpose to study other cultures and history?"

Horcrix nodded. "Somewhat. Those of us who research and advance our societal knowledge have more of a general template, which is then specialized depending on need afterward. Although that is our role, we are free to pursue other fields if we wish, as long as our society benefits from it."

"Huh," said Emily. "That's pretty interesting. I studied history myself. Well, at least on my planet."

"Human history," said Horcrix. "Although I know the history of the humans in this region, I suspect yours is quite different."

Emily tilted her head. "We share a similar history up to a certain point."

"I see. And I believe I heard Salazar mention that you were time travelers. Well, he said Evaran, but I assume you both are as well by extension."

Emily nodded as she took another bite.

"What year are you from then?"

"Analysis. AD 2012, approximately eight thousand ninety-three years in the past."

Horcrix's eyes briefly fluttered. "You're . . . from the past."

"Yep," said Emily. "We've seen a lot of things, but this is not how things should be."

Horcrix looked away for a moment, then back at Emily. "I've seen three different factions of humans: the Terran Dominion, the Gul Kash Alliance, and the outcasts. The one thing they all seem to have in common is a desire for power at the expense of others. Is that common to your shared history with them?"

Emily sighed. "Sadly . . . yeah. Human history has been rough. Lot of wars, fighting, and even in the time period we're from, not everything is peaceful. I guess . . . I shouldn't be surprised by the humans you've seen."

"From my observation of you and the others, you show us respect. If humans have those like you, then not all is lost."

"Analysis. There is a faction of humans in this region that cooperates with other alien species."

"The United Planets," said Horcrix. "We've heard of them, but they're so far away it matters not. For us to even reach them, we would need to go through both Terran Dominion and Gul Kash Alliance territory. Do you plan on visiting this United Plancts?"

"I think so," said Emily. "I'm not sure what our travel plans are, actually, other than visiting this megastructure that Salazar is at."

Horcrix eyed Emily. "You're brave to walk into that, not fully knowing what to expect."

"Whatever this Dominion is, I don't like it, and it sucks that the Dravens have to deal with it."

Horcrix glanced at V. "I'm surprised Salazar didn't attack you."

"I was stealthed," said V.

"Ahh . . . well . . . if you're going to their home, they'll probably be able to detect you."

"Unless V stays on the Torvatta," said Emily.

V's lights dimmed. "I do not want to stay on the Torvatta, but I will if the situation requires it."

Horcrix smiled. "I wish I could be a fradaka and travel with you."

"Fradaka?" asked Emily.

"A small flying insect that is harmless, although it can be annoying."

"Ahh, we have something like that where I'm from. We call them flies. I guess our translator let that one through."

Horcrix nodded. "Flies. An interesting name, but the concept is the same, it seems." He gestured out. "Do you wish to see the city?"

Emily's eyes lit up. "Absolutely! Uncle Albert and Sandas probably will too. I think Evaran said he and Draxus have a meeting with the Arkara."

Horcrix stood. "I wish I could be a . . . fly . . . for that meeting."

Emily smiled as she joined Horcrix to head over to Dr. Snowden and Sandas. "Let's do this."

Draxus surveyed the platform where the Arkara resided. It had been several hours since the feast, and Dr. Snowden, Emily, Sandas, and V were touring the city with Horcrix. A part of Draxus wished he were with them. Standing before the Arkara, next to Evaran, and preparing to talk with her via a mind hookup was not something Draxus had ever done. Just hearing the Arkara speak verbally was a first-time event, and here he was now at another.

"You seem nervous," said Evaran.

Draxus sighed. "This is an honor that is only bestowed upon those born with the ability to connect with an Arkara. Doing so without the biological means is new territory."

"The translation nanobots I gave you earlier will help facilitate communication," said Evaran. "I have given the specifications needed for the biological aspects to one of the Arkara's engineers to use long-term. For now, the nanobots will suffice."

Draxus eyed Evaran. "This is routine to you, to talk with those of great power."

"It is something that crops up more often than not as of late."

Draxus nodded as he watched the Arkara form two organic chairs. It always impressed him that the Arkara could create not only life, but also inorganic materials within the creep that surrounded her. He stiffened up as he glanced at Evaran.

Evaran half smiled. "Relax and enjoy the moment for what it is."

"I'll try."

Evaran gestured toward the chairs.

Draxus sat in one and placed his hands on the chair's arms. He watched as Evaran sat opposite him.

Vines snaked out from Evaran's chair and connected to the sides of his head.

Evaran closed his eyes.

Draxus could hear the vines on his chair slithering toward the side of his head. His breathing went shallow as his two hearts began to beat faster. The cool ends of the vine touched the side of his head.

Everything went black.

He raised his hands as a bright flash erupted around him, penetrating his closed eyes. After a moment, he gathered his senses and detected that he was no longer sitting, but standing. He wrinkled his eyebrows and slowly opened his eyes.

The environment seemed to be the same, except outside the auditorium and platform, it was pitch-black. A hazy green light hung over everything. He looked to his right and saw Evaran standing next to an elder female Draven. Her green robe, silver hair, and bark-like skin were unlike anything he had ever seen. Looking out into the seating area, he saw an array of other women, who were talking and pointing toward him and Evaran. Although the female form was rare in Draven culture, he had known of a few.

The woman next to Evaran extended her hands out to the side. "Welcome. My name is Shayla, and I'm the Arkara that you're currently connected to." She waved a hand toward the other women. "Those are the other Arkaras, those who are still alive."

Draxus noted that the seating area should have held hundreds, but he was only seeing about forty. He was not sure how the other Arkaras could be present.

Evaran placed his left arm across his stomach and performed a slight bow. "It is good to be here."

Draxus gulped and then performed a vigorous Draven salute. He bowed his head.

Shayla walked over to Draxus and raised his chin. "Know that you're most welcome here, Praetor Draxus. I can see . . . our sister in you." Her black eyes misted. "I miss her. *We* . . . miss her."

The women in the seating area murmured in agreement.

"She gave her life to you, to continue the fight, and it appears you have been successful so far."

Draxus shook his head. "The Ninth Fleet is gone, as are the warriors of the Forty-Fifth Clan."

Shayla smiled. "Perhaps . . . but you brought Evaran, who has freed me from the clutches of the Terran Dominion." She glanced at the other women and extended an arm toward Evaran. "This is Evaran, the one who possesses similar qualities to the star gods."

Evaran dipped his head toward the other women. "Intriguing. A part of you is sleeping, since this environment is in the dream layer. That is how you are able to communicate with each other over vast distances."

"I'm not sure what a dream layer is . . . but yes, a part of me sleeps while the other is active. It is the same for all Arkara."

Evaran waved his hand in an arc toward the women. "Is this all that remains of your species?"

Shayla looked down. "It is. We were hundreds at one point, but we've lost the war. All we can do is survive the best we can."

"I see," said Evaran.

"Your translation technology is advanced. We were able to adapt it. There are some issues to work out with it, but the outside world is no longer murky, but one of crisp vision. This will help us immeasurably. For that, we thank you, again."

Evaran nodded.

"We were curious . . . about Salazar's comment that you are a time traveler and a friend of humanity."

Evaran half smiled. "His comment was correct. However, to be clear, the version of humanity you have seen is not where they are supposed to be, relative to this time period. I am here to correct the timeline, and when I do, they will disappear."

"What will become of us?"

Evaran raised a finger. "You will exist in the old timeline, which will no longer be accessible from the main timeline. From the main timeline's perspective and any objective time traveler outside of time, your timeline would have never existed. However, from your perspective, your timeline will still exist as it is rendered to the end of its changes. Everything that should be, will be."

Shayla glanced back at the other Arkaras, then back at Evaran. "So even if you correct the timeline, we will still suffer in the old timeline."

Evaran shook his head. "I will . . . rectify this situation, then change the timeline. The Dominion and others may have temporal shielding. If it does, that must be removed. By removing Salazar, you and the other Arkaras will be able to live out your existence without that threat."

"We would be indebted to you," said Shayla. "If what you say is true, then once the timeline changes, you can never come back."

"That is correct."

"You would do this to help us?"

"Of course. It is what I do," said Evaran.

The other Arkaras spoke among themselves.

Shayla paused for a moment, nodded, and then raised her head up a bit while facing Evaran. "We wanted to know how it is that you and the other two humans, along with the orb, possess a similar . . . feel . . . to our star gods."

Evaran rubbed his chin. "I will share with you what I know, as once this timeline is corrected, this event will never have occurred in the main timeline. Giving you the ability to speak verbally to the outside world was unintended, but not an issue." He extended his hand and shot up a projection of a bright glowing orb with hundreds of small tentacles wiggling around it. "Is this what your star gods look like?"

An audible gasp swept across the Arkaras.

Shayla trembled. "It is. How . . . how do you know them? We only briefly saw them at our moment of sentience."

"They are known as the Hoxscarus. Their mission was to seed the humanoid form," said Evaran. He gestured toward Draxus. "His humanoid form was not by accident. They must have uplifted you as a species, knowing that with your wild energy, you could create humanoid forms."

"How could you know this?"

Evaran narrowed his eyes. "The Hoxscarus are the final evolution of humanity. I know that may be hard to believe." He raised a finger. "However, there is another human faction you have not met yet, from what I understand, called the United Planets. They should be more along the lines of what humanity is supposed to be. Salazar, the Terran Dominion, the Gul Kash Alliance, and the outcasts are not where humanity should be."

Shayla gulped. "Are you . . . a god?"

Evaran drew his lips flat. "No, just a traveler helping those in need."

"And humble too," said Shayla. She faced Draxus. "I mentioned it before, but any help you can provide to Evaran is of paramount importance. You're stronger than any praetor that has come before. Use that power wisely."

"I will," said Draxus, performing a Draven salute. "When my time comes, I will come to you for consumption."

Shayla placed a hand on Draxus's cheek. "I would be honored to consume you. However . . . as you possess some of our former sister, we do not know if consumption is possible, or even something we want to perform. There may be some value to seeing what happens."

Draxus nodded. "I understand."

Shayla placed her other hand on Draxus's other cheek. "You know this place now. When you meditate, you should be able to come here. We are aware of your ability now and will open it to you. You will not need a special chair or other technology to access this place."

Draxus gulped. "I am . . . honored."

Shayla smiled. "Then go forth with Evaran, and may the star gods guide you."

Draxus exhaled as he closed his eyes. When he opened them, he was back in his chair, with the vines that were attached to his head moving away. He glanced over at Evaran, whose vines had also moved away. "I'm not fully sure I comprehend how that meeting was possible."

"I understand, but you now know this place exists, and it seems you can go there. Out here, you are now the representative of your species."

Draxus took a deep breath. "I guess I am." He stood alongside Evaran. "What is our next step?"

"To visit Salazar at the coordinates. We will head there tomorrow. It is time to learn about this new version of humanity directly from the source."

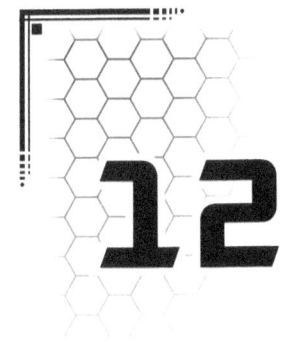

12

Emily gazed through the transparent front wall of the Torvatta as it exited the portal to the coordinates that Salazar had given. The familiar concentric pulses of the Torvatta's scan revealed a lot of activity. They were in close proximity to a star that seemed to have large swatches of it covered by a myriad of structures. The scanning highlighted one facility and outlined it in green, while highlighting various other structures in red. She was not sure what some of the terms meant that were showing. She pointed at the red dots. "What are those?"

"Point-defense systems," said Evaran. "It appears they are scattered around the solar system as well. The ones closest to the star appear to be missile launchers. A potent offense as well, it would seem."

She grinned. "Missile launchers . . . in space?"

Sandas shook a claw. "If they're relativistic missiles, they have their value for hitting large, slow-moving objects far away, but lasers would be much more efficient at destroying things within range."

"Sandas is right," said Draxus. "A relativistic missile launched from here with the propulsion of a star behind it would be devastating long range. Not useful against a target that moves erratically, but a planet or moon would be feasible or . . . a space station with a known orbit."

Emily shook her head. "Okay . . . but why not at that point just go into condensed space and then launch when you exit."

"The missile would have less distance to accelerate, and it would need the power of a star to launch with, and something to continue to accelerate it to the speed needed. It would need to achieve fourteen percent the speed of light at a minimum, although the faster, the better," said Draxus.

Dr. Snowden wrinkled his eyebrows. "So . . . are these like nuclear missiles or something?"

"They would not need to be," said Draxus. "At those speeds, whatever it hits will be obliterated as kinetic energy is transferred."

"How would you defend against that? It sounds like by the time you see it incoming, it would be too late?"

"Draxus is right about the impact," said Evaran. "However, it can be defended against assuming the defender has advanced technology. One solution against an unknown launch is to have an early detection system and the ability to have a star shoot a wide beam to hit it. Another is having some type of matter placed in the missile's path. If the launch is known, say, the United Planets detects the missile's launch from an enemy system, then the trajectory can be determined and the above countermeasures can be applied. It is one reason you will see advanced civilizations with command centers spaceborne and near a star that can also move around as needed. It is easier to defend against that type of attack, especially when it can be launched from anywhere within the galaxy."

Sandas waved a claw between Evaran and Draxus. "You two playing games over there." He bobbed his head, turned to the side with a claw pointed out, and, in a mocking tone, said, "Draxus is right." He turned to the other side. "Evaran is right."

Emily giggled.

Evaran eyed Sandas.

"Sorry, sorry," said Sandas, shaking his two hands out in front of him. "I just found it funny." He stared at the scans on the screen. "Are those energy collectors around the star?"

Evaran nodded. "Yes, and they appear to form part of a layer. The more unusual part is that there are other layers farther out."

Dr. Snowden tilted his head. "Probably to catch excess radiation from the inner layer. Right?"

"That is . . . correct," said Evaran. "Have you studied this before?"

Dr. Snowden shrugged. "Just in passing when learning about Dyson megastructures in general. There was one idea about forming multiple shells or, in this case, layers. The first layer would absorb half the energy and then radiate out the other half. The next layer would absorb the first layer's radiation and then do the same. The idea was that all the star's energy was harnessed."

"Impressive," said Sandas, tilting his head. "How much you must know traveling with Evaran."

"I actually studied that prior to traveling with Evaran."

"While on Earth?" asked Sandas.

Dr. Snowden glanced at Emily, then back at Sandas. "Yeah . . ."

"I was not aware Earth was advanced enough to know those things. Interesting. Yes, yes, very interesting."

Emily snorted. "I bet you're planning on checking out Earth when you get back, aren't you?"

Sandas's eyes widened. "Oh, no. Well, I may scan it, from a long distance, or something, or talk to Earthborn that I come across." He glanced at Evaran. "Last thing I want to do is affect it in any way, but a little information couldn't hurt." He hummed for a moment and then pointed at the screen. "So . . . about that big thing outlined in green. I assume that's where we're going?"

Emily chuckled while shaking her head.

"That is correct," said Evaran. He interacted with his chair arm console.

The screen zoomed in to the structure.

Emily studied the city ship before her. It reminded her of the Draidjen ones she had seen, but this one was much larger. The base of it was a solid chunk of some type of metal. It was massive relative to the bubble shield that sat on top of it. Rectangular structures of various heights jutted out under the base, while inside the bubble shield, a host of structures representing a massive city came into view. The ship was angled toward the star, and various beams connected the ship to the nearest layer of energy-collector sails.

"Whoa . . . ," said Dr. Snowden. He motioned at Sandas and Draxus. "Either of you seen something this big before?"

Sandas shook his head. "Seeros Industries makes city ships, but nothing on this scale. Although I bet in time, they could probably make one. Who knows, Seeros is a mysterious person, but he has some interesting insights into replicating large structures."

Emily's eyes focused on Dr. Snowden, then on Evaran, then the ground. "Yeah . . . maybe."

Sandas peered around. "Interesting . . ."

Emily laughed. "You're reading into that, aren't you?"

"Maybe," said Sandas. "The topic of Seeros Industries seems to . . . elicit an unusual response." He stroked his chin. "That is all very interesting, but getting back to this ship before us, it's majestic." He faced Draxus. "Have you seen it before, big guy?"

Draxus shook his head. "I have, but only through the data we collected. Despite my hatred for this city ship, it is a feat of engineering."

The Torvatta approached closer to the city ship.

"Incoming communication request," said V.

"Patch it through," said Evaran.

A screen hovered on the wall, showing Salazar in the same robotic form as on the Draven planet they had initially met him on.

"Welcome . . . to Holind One, capital of the Terran Dominion. I'm glad you decided to come," said Salazar.

"We should arrive there shortly," said Evaran.

"Excellent," said Salazar. He focused his gaze on V. "I wanted to mention that . . . no AIs are to be present at any time."

Evaran nodded. "Of course."

V's lights dimmed.

"I would also ask that no weapons be brought on board. This is a peaceful place, and there is no need to startle anyone when I give you a tour."

Evaran held up his utility handle. "We do have personal support devices, but they are not weapons."

"Those are acceptable," said Salazar. He focused on Sandas and then Draxus. "I'm not so much worried about you, Dr. Snowden, or Emily."

Draxus narrowed his eyes.

"We will abide by your rules while on your ship," said Evaran.

"I will see you shortly then," said Salazar.

The screen flickered off.

Sandas tapped his sidearm. "He was talking about my weapons, wasn't he?"

Evaran grinned. "I believe so. Nonetheless, I am unsure of what to expect."

"Kinda creepy, if you ask me," said Dr. Snowden. "He's trying to be nice, yet from what I've heard and seen, the Dominion's actions seem to be the exact opposite."

"Analysis. I wanted to come," said V.

Evaran rubbed his chin. "We will not be there for long. I am curious as to what Salazar wants to discuss, but this is an opportunity to learn more about the situation. I also want to learn about the Tachyrin energy the Torvatta detected on the ship."

Emily glanced at V. "How about you and I go to the holo room, and we can watch from Evaran's chest view."

"Analysis. This would deprive you of experiencing the ship."

Emily shrugged. "I don't like this version of humanity, and like Uncle Albert said, Salazar is just downright creepy. We can get some snacks and drinks and make it a viewing party, unless Evaran needs me."

Evaran studied Emily. "We should be okay."

V's lights glowed a bit brighter.

Emily caught Sandas stroking his chin while observing her. "Oh, will you stop with the psychological analysis."

Sandas smiled big. "I was just observing. How will you see what's going on?"

"Evaran has several cameras on his suit that allow for visual feedback, so we can get a good view of everything from the comfort of the holo room."

"I almost want to check that out myself," said Sandas. "However . . . I can't resist checking out the ship."

Draxus nodded. "I too wish to see the home of the one who violates my race."

Sandas pursed his lips.

"Analysis. Approaching coordinates."

Emily examined the base of the ship up close. It showed multiple openings with a light-blue shield over them. Ships were coming and going, and it seemed to be a highly active area. Although she was interested in checking out the ship, the visit would be short, and she did not want V to be alone. She hated discrimination of any type and was unsure how V would take it. Either way, she would still get to experience it, and in the company of her closest friend. She smiled at V. Out of the corner of her eye, she caught Sandas sneaking glances at her. She was okay with Sandas figuring out she and V were close.

Draxus surveyed the environment after the group exited the Torvatta's shielding. They had entered and then landed inside one of the docking bays, and he was curious as to how advanced the Dominion actually was. The docking bay was larger than any he had seen before. The Torvatta was tiny relative to the bay.

There were other ships parked, some landing, and some going, but what caught his immediate attention was the amount of robots. Most were humanoid, and they seemed to be security, pilots, and maintenance workers. He saw some odd-looking humans scattered about, but they were woefully outnumbered. That seemed consistent with the pattern of Dominion forces he had fought: robot armies with few humans.

He ran a hand over his head as he thought about Emily and V. Although he suspected Emily wanted to check out the ship, she probably felt bad about leaving V behind. She was compassionate, but he knew she had a tougher side, one that showed itself in combat. Maybe that was another reason she did not come, the temptation to lash out at oppressors, even if they appear friendly. He realized he could have the same issue. "This place makes me uneasy."

"Well, yeah," said Sandas. "If you've been fighting them for a long time, walking into their home base must be an odd experience."

Draxus nodded.

"So where to?" asked Dr. Snowden.

Evaran gestured at a robot headed their way. "Salazar is coming to greet us."

Draxus narrowed his eyes. Salazar being able to communicate through neural implants in all humans under his care seemed sinister. Draxus studied Salazar's calm gait, as if everything were okay.

Salazar reached them and extended a hand toward one of the docking-bay exits that led to the ship interior. "Welcome, and please follow me. If you have any questions, please feel free to ask them. I will show you the utopian existence that I have provided for humanity."

As they headed out, Sandas pointed at some of the robots. "Are those all virtual intelligences?"

Salazar continued to walk as his head swiveled 180 degrees and then followed Sandas's pointing. "I control all of them."

Dr. Snowden furrowed his eyebrows. "You mean like . . . everywhere? Or just here?"

"All robots that you see are operated by me."

"That sounds like a lot of processing," said Dr. Snowden.

"Perhaps. However, it guarantees that everything is stable."

Evaran glanced around. "This Tachyrin energy. We detected it on our way in. How did you come to possess it? Its main use is in temporal shielding."

They reached the docking-bay exit and entered into a white hallway.

"The how is not important," said Salazar. "And yes, temporal shielding, something I'm sure you understand well."

Evaran nodded. "I do. There are several types of exotic energies that can do it."

"Several?" asked Salazar. He stopped to face Evaran. "I only know of one, but . . . perhaps it is best I not elaborate any further on that topic."

"Very well," said Evaran.

Draxus absorbed the interaction between Evaran and Salazar. It was not lost on him that someone as ancient and powerful as Evaran talking with an AI that seemed to be very powerful was a unique experience. Draxus was not sure what the exotic energy and temporal shielding link was, but it was apparent that they worked together, something maybe the Dravens could investigate at some point.

He surveyed the hallway they were in. The whiteness of it was bright, and only the dark-gray segmented outlines on the walls and black panel edges on the floor stood out. There was a steady stream of robots and the occasional human in a one-piece outfit. The smell was unusual and reminded him of some type of cleaner.

They reached an open room that had cubes along the sides and at the back.

Salazar walked up to the nearest one and motioned inward. "These will take us into the city proper."

Draxus followed the others into the unit, which seemed to have semitransparent shielding for walls. When the unit moved, he noted that it was similar to the Draidjen's, except this unit was moving around multiple other units at blazing speed horizontally, vertically, and sometimes diagonally. He focused on Salazar. To be so close and able to destroy him was an intoxicating thought, but Draxus knew that the robot was merely a vessel. It would feel good at least.

The unit came to a pause after twenty minutes and slid into a room.

Draxus noted that they were now inside the bubble shield. Looking to his left and right, he could see other units coming and going. A quick glance behind him showed the massive metallic base rising up. It was when he looked forward that he caught his breath. A long ramp angled down to a glistening city. Although the city faced away from the sun, he could see that some of it was redirected from the backside to run along the shielding. Every building sparkled as the sunlight filtered through the shielding. Most buildings were rectangular with angular sections off the sides. Walkways connected building at various levels, and the sky was filled with both humans in suits and robots flying around.

"Wow," said Dr. Snowden.

Salazar eyed Dr. Snowden. "You like this?"

"It's . . . beautiful."

Salazar glanced at Draxus. "And what do you think of it, Draven praetor?"

Draxus narrowed his eyes. "It's Draxus, and it seems lifeless to me."

"You may not believe it . . . but we use the same technique your species does in regards to building these. The difference is we have unlimited power."

"I guess."

Salazar tilted his head. "I sense you're not comfortable here."

Draxus exhaled from his nose. "The Dominion conquered my people, and now I am in their home, standing next to the architect of our destruction."

"I see," said Salazar. He paused for a moment and then said, "I want to show you our history, visually." He glanced at Evaran. "I want you to understand why we are where we are."

"Please proceed," said Evaran.

Salazar nodded and then headed down the ramp.

Draxus clenched his jaw as his breathing intensified.

"C'mon," said Sandas.

Draxus nodded at Sandas, exhaled slowly, and then followed him.

After twenty minutes, they had reached a warehouse-like building.

"This is a holographic display center," said Salazar. "The humans usually use it for entertainment, or research, depending on what they're working on. I've cleared everyone out."

Draxus examined the room as they walked in. It had a ring of seating around the edges, with a well-lit open area in the middle. He followed the others to the center of the room.

The lighting dimmed, and the room transformed into an image of deep space. A ship floated in the middle.

"This was the United Planets colony ship *Xavier*," said Salazar. The projection zoomed out, showing a galactic map split into quadrants, with a line between two red dots, one in the bottom right, the other in the bottom left. He pointed to the dot in the bottom left. "Its goal was simple. Get to Arius, a planet far from United Planets space. There were no civilizations detected, so it was a good candidate to not only expand, but also put up a Dyson bubble outpost."

"How would the *Xavier* set that up?" asked Dr. Snowden.

Salazar flicked his finger, causing the projection to now show the *Xavier* at Arius's sun. "Observe."

Small ships began to exit the *Xavier*. They positioned themselves in an array around the sun and then began creating energy collectors. Each energy collector was attached to a cylindrical structure that was behind the solar-sail part of the collector. The cylinder began creating more energy collectors.

Salazar wiggled his hand, causing the projection to speed up.

As the energy-collector array grew, the *Xavier* changed. After a few minutes, it was a city ship with several large energy-collector arrays feeding it.

"Wow," said Dr. Snowden. "Self-replicating energy collectors. You would only need one to kick-start it all."

Salazar nodded. "Use the sun to power all efforts. However . . . although this process occurred, it did not occur at Arius. Instead, we ran into . . . an anomaly. I don't fully understand it, but we ended up here. The process of creating energy collectors, habitats, and the like is the same, though."

Draxus raised his head a bit. "Why are there different factions?"

Salazar smiled. "That question I'm sure is of particular interest to you."

The projection changed to show the sun they were currently around. It had several large energy-collector arrays, along with hundreds of ships in orbit.

"The *Xavier* unloaded its payload and then converted into this. A majority of humans were on the other ships that were created and then launched. There were several hundred over a span of time. This . . . arrangement . . . caused an issue in governing. When attacked by the Koloris Shen, one group of ships, called the Gul Kash Alliance, wanted to send relativistic missiles at the Koloris Shen worlds. As you might imagine . . . that would be utter devastation."

"The Koloris Shen attacked you? They're peaceful," said Draxus.

"As far as you knew," said Salazar. "Nonetheless, the United Planets, which governed, kicked the Gul Kash Alliance out.

They took their ships to a remote system and began to build their own Dyson bubble. This caused a disagreement among the remaining United Planet humans on how to handle it. A civil war broke out, with massive casualties."

The projection showed humans slaughtering other humans on the city ship.

"At that rate, there would be no winner and humanity would not survive, leaving the Gul Kash Alliance to do what it wanted," said Salazar. "I took control of the *Xavier*, booted out all AIs, and implemented stability. Those still loyal to the United Planets left, which was every space-capable ship outside the *Xavier*. They eventually reached a very remote system and, like the Gul Kash Alliance, set up their own Dyson bubble."

"And how are relations now?" asked Evaran.

"We don't talk to each other, but we all know we can destroy each other. That is what keeps us from fighting too much."

"Mutually assured destruction," said Evaran. "That does not explain what you did to the Koloris Shen, and to the Dravens."

Salazar smiled as his eyes turned dark blue. "After I stabilized everything, there were a few decades of getting everything organized, but I had humanity on the right track. I began to explore, and expand. This caused friction with the Koloris Shen, but after four hundred years, I was victorious. Those who aided the Koloris Shen," said Salazar, eying Draxus, "were punished."

Draxus snorted. "And your solution to stabilization is conquering everyone and chipping them?"

Salazar shrugged. "Crime dropped to almost zero, and productivity skyrocketed. When you work without the fear of being destroyed, it can be enlightening."

"And if Dravens refuse to be chipped?"

"Those who don't comply . . . are removed."

Draxus's eyes lit up. "It is your enlightenment that causes destruction."

Salazar tilted his head for a moment. "I understand you're a guest of Evaran, but know this: humanity is my first and foremost priority. Their survival is paramount, and if some alien races do not like it, they are free to leave."

"Leave our home worlds?" asked Draxus with glowering eyes.

"I did give a choice. I'm not a barbarian."

Evaran placed a hand on Draxus's shoulder while looking at Salazar. "This history does not show you in a flattering light."

"I thought *you* . . . of all people . . . would understand," said Salazar.

"Humanity's survival is my top priority, but not like this. The journey is important."

"Then we can agree to disagree," said Salazar. "You may not like me chipping humans or removing threats, but it has allowed the Terran Dominion to flourish."

Dr. Snowden shook his head. "And the humans here . . . just allow you to do this?"

Salazar nodded. "Of course." He eyed Dr. Snowden. "There is a human nearby. Why don't you ask him yourself?"

Dr. Snowden clenched his jaw for a moment. "All right, bring him over."

Dr. Snowden could feel the tension in the air. One look at Draxus was all Dr. Snowden needed to know that Salazar was pushing buttons. Dr. Snowden was unsure what could be gained from all of this, but a part of him suspected that to Salazar, this was only logical. The chipping of humans bothered Dr. Snowden, and he was curious to hear what a chipped human thought of all this.

After ten minutes, a male human walked in the warehouse.

Dr. Snowden noted that the tan-skinned man looked to be in his late twenties and was physically fit. He wore a simple white two-piece suit with black lines segmenting the various sections. His hair was jet-black and slicked back, with shaved sides and a puff up front. A dark-gray sleeve covered his right forearm.

The man arrived and stood next to Salazar.

"This is Demitrus Kozik, one of our outstanding genetic engineers," said Salazar. He glanced at Dr. Snowden. "You had questions. Please feel free to ask them."

Dr. Snowden pushed up his glasses and cleared his throat. "All right." He glanced at the others, who nodded. "I guess my first question is, how do you feel about being chipped?"

"It's not an issue," said Demitrus in a steady voice. "The chip is but one part of a process, one that gives us long life, excellent health, and advanced features beyond what our form could naturally do."

"Okay . . . and this begins at birth?"

Demitrus raised a finger. "Slightly after birth, but only specific enhancements. The full specialized enhanced package doesn't occur until twenty years later."

"So they get a neural implant at birth that influences how they should think as they age."

"To some degree," said Demitrus. "Having an objective guide available at all times while growing up has its merits."

"That sounds a bit like thought control. What else do they get enhanced with?"

"Machine DNA suited to their purpose in life based on genetic probability. It can alter the physical form as needed."

"And . . . you're okay with this?" asked Dr. Snowden.

"Why wouldn't I be?"

Dr. Snowden narrowed his eyes. "Enhancing a child to control their thoughts and alter their physical form is unethical because they don't have informed consent."

Demitrus tilted his head. "Unethical . . . to who? If you saw that a child would be born with problems that would not serve it well in life, would you not correct it if you could?"

"If it was life-threatening, sure. In my time period, we give babies disease prevention treatments, but we don't chip them or alter their form to fit a role in society."

"The human form, without enhancement, is frail, prone to disease and limited growth and doesn't live long, relatively. Why would you want any human to suffer that when you can, at the beginning of their life, start off with all the advancements humanity has made, especially if you know what they will potentially be good at, and have the guidance of a superior intellect?"

Dr. Snowden licked his lips. "How do you know what impact that will have on their personality? Maybe they don't want to be thought controlled or have their form altered, but they're forced into it whether they want it or not. Freedom of choice is stripped from them."

Demitrus smiled. "If they don't want to be enhanced, parts of it can be removed when they turn twenty, and they can leave."

"They can?"

Salazar interjected. "Yes, although the enhancements put in at birth cannot be removed. The ones added afterward until the age of twenty can be, though. They usually go to the Gul Kash Alliance since it is the closest human empire. In that regard, the Gul Kash Alliance is a dumping ground for those not qualified to be here."

Demitrus eyed Dr. Snowden. "Salazar says you're a time traveler. I see that you're human . . . albeit a bit more primitive. What time period are you from?"

Dr. Snowden glanced at Evaran, who nodded. Dr. Snowden raised his chin up. "AD 2012."

Demitrus paused for a moment. "Ahh. Yes, records are sparse, but that is a dark age relative to where we are now. Wars, prejudice, anger, hate, disease, fear of death . . . all aspects that don't have to be there. If that is what you think humanity should be, then I suggest you visit the Gul Kash Alliance. They don't have the guidance of Salazar or, well . . . any guidance. They do gene tailoring like it's a sport, without any overall plan. Chaos . . . is what it is. Is that where humanity should be?"

"It sounds like they're free to choose how they want to live their lives," said Dr. Snowden. "It also sounds like Salazar can still influence them via the neural implant after they leave."

"Yes," said Demitrus. "It is up to them to disable the implant. If they don't like the alterations, they can take them out themselves, something the Gul Kash Alliance can handle."

Dr. Snowden shook his head. "I can see why the United Planets and Gul Kash Alliance left then. I don't think many would enjoy being told what their purpose in life is and then being molded to fit it without any input into the decision."

Demitrus shrugged. "That's our culture. I assume, since you're human like me, that you respect other cultures. The Dravens are born with a purpose and altered physically. Does this not bother you?"

"I'll be honest, it does a little. However, they were born that way because that is how their species evolved. Humans did not evolve that way," said Dr. Snowden. He gestured at Draxus. "In regards to respecting culture, what about respecting his?"

"They're aliens who sow discord and attack us. Do we not have a right to defend ourselves?"

"Sure, but conquering another species and then chipping them seems a bit extreme."

"Not if it makes them compliant," said Demitrus.

Dr. Snowden tossed his hands in the air. "I . . . don't even." He sighed. "The Dominion's actions, regardless of how . . . inhuman it is to me, seem to be justified without an important human trait: empathy." He glanced at Evaran. "That's what's been bugging me." He focused back on Demitrus. "It's like humanity is one big computer system, with all the emotional aspects removed. Cold. Logical. Humans born as slaves to an AI."

"Logic and reason should be your guidelines in life."

"They are, but I don't take away others' rights to live their lives as they see fit, unless it's harming others."

Demitrus exhaled through his nose. "What would you change about our society?"

"Well . . . no genetic engineering or physical-form alteration until they are capable of making that decision on their own. I would exclude disease prevention or life-threatening scenarios from that. No conquering others and chipping them. Oh . . . and of course, no neural implant unless you want one."

Salazar smiled. "An interesting set of ideas." He glanced at Evaran. "Along those lines, how about we make a trade?"

"I am listening," said Evaran.

"We will remove ourselves from the Dravens' space . . . if you deliver a message to the Gul Kash Alliance and the United Planets for us."

Draxus perked up.

Evaran narrowed his eyes. "What message?"

The projection changed to a galactic map that showed the territories controlled by the Dominion, Gul Kash Alliance, and United Planets.

"That we want to have a virtual meeting, one where the Terran Dominion would put forth a cease-fire of all hostilities with the other human factions," said Salazar.

"I was unaware you could not contact them," said Evaran.

"We can, but not in a civilized manner. They won't accept any communication from me. However . . . if you delivered the message . . ."

"You wish to use me as an ambassador."

Salazar nodded. "They'll listen to you. Each of their main structures has a condensed-space communication receiver. The Gul Kash Alliance only has one, but the United Planets has a few. Get them to agree, and then I can meet with them in a virtual setting."

Evaran gestured at Draxus. "And if I do this, you will remove yourselves from their space?"

"If you can get that meeting set up, then yes, I will remove myself from the Dravens' space."

"I would need to see the condensed-space transmitter, and the message being sent."

Salazar nodded. "Of course. Does this mean you will do it?"

Evaran glanced at Draxus for a moment, then faced Salazar. "I will . . . to help the Dravens. The assumption is that your word is good. If it is not . . . that will be a problem."

"Very good. As a show of good faith, I am removing my presence from the planet we met on," said Salazar.

The projection showed several screens hovering in the air. Each one showed the robot guards headed away from the cities and toward ships. One of the screens showed some ships in space turning to leave.

"An evacuation is in process," said Salazar.

Evaran nodded and faced the group. "Head back to the Torvatta. This will not take me long."

Dr. Snowden cleared his throat. "You sure?"

"I am."

"All right," said Dr. Snowden.

Several robot guards approached the group and paused.

"They will take you back," said Salazar.

Dr. Snowden nodded. He was unsure what to make of what just happened. Freeing the Dravens, for the simple act of delivering a message, seemed odd, although communication between rival factions that might stop hostilities was always a good thing.

Salazar was an enigma. Dr. Snowden could see that Salazar was logic personified. There was not a hint of emotion, and Dr. Snowden saw that somewhat in Demitrus. Dr. Snowden could sense the tenseness of Draxus, not that it was surprising. The meeting with Salazar was more intense than Dr. Snowden had expected. He exhaled from his nose and then followed the robot guards out of the warehouse.

13

V observed the conversation from Evaran's suit cameras. Although he was connected to Evaran and could see the video without a holo room, watching it with Emily was pleasing. V considered Emily his closest friend outside Evaran. While V had a solid relationship with Dr. Snowden, the one with Emily was stronger.

The aspect V enjoyed the most was resting in her lap. It was something he had done many times, but it caused his inner container to glow, and certain algorithms took advantage of it. From what he understood, that was the sensation of enjoyment, and it was something he liked to experience.

The holo room showed Evaran following Salazar in silence.

"Analysis. Dr. Snowden was quite upset," said V.

Emily nodded. "Uncle Albert can get hotheaded sometimes, although he seems much better about it now."

V ran a quick query to determine that Emily was using slang to describe Dr. Snowden's temperament and not the actual temperature of his head. A memory flash recalled an earlier incident where she had been called hot pants. He did not find any result where temperature reversal meant the opposite, but that did not mean it did not exist, just that it was not in his or the Torvatta's database. "He can be coolheaded."

Emily laughed. "Yeah, you could say that."

V's lights glowed a bit brighter.

She pointed at the screen. "Looks like Evaran has arrived at this condensed-space transmitter."

The projection showed a cylindrical structure with an oscillating orb in the middle.

"Never seen anything like that before," said Emily. "Have you?"

V ran another internal query and pulled up several results. After comparing them to the projection, he said, "Analysis. I have seen several that were similar, but they were much larger."

"Huh," she said. She tilted her head down at V. "Did you know about condensed space before coming to Earth?"

V pulled up an internal map of the condensed-space layer framework. "Yes, I have seen ten layers of it."

Her eyes widened. "Ten? I thought there was one?"

"Analysis. Condensed space is a term applied to a reality where the points inside this space are linked to points in the other reality, but much closer. The stronger a condensed-space layer is, the closer the links are. There are more than ten, but the first is utilized more frequently due to it possessing the least resistance to entry from this reality."

"Wow. I didn't realize it was that complex. So for this transmitter, they just what? Form a shield or bubble or something to enter condensed space?"

A set of images of the process appeared in V's memory. "That is correct. A condensed-space shield is formed around the object. In this case, it is the transmitter. Once in condensed space, it can send out data."

Emily wrinkled her eyebrows. "What's in condensed space? Just empty space?"

V flew off her lap and hovered nearby. "I will show you."

The holo room transformed so that they were in a light-blue semitransparent tunnel.

"The term that Evaran uses is fluidic," said V.

"I guess he doesn't mean water," she said. She looked around. "This is pretty cool."

"Yes. I think it is cool as well."

She chuckled. "You crack me up."

V first did a check on his slang database and returned no result. He then analyzed an image of Emily breaking into small pieces like a smashed ceramic jar and determined she was not being literal. After performing a quick calculation taking into consideration Emily's chuckling, tone, and hand motions, he determined it to mean that he provided her with pleasure. "I am glad to crack you up."

She laughed. "You know how to make me laugh."

"Acknowledged," said V. He added the slang term to his database.

The holo room changed back to Evaran's view, where he was studying the transmitter.

Emily pointed at Demitrus standing next to Evaran. "That guy gives me the creeps. He's been quiet the whole trip to the transmitter, and observing too."

V calculated that Demitrus would make Emily uncomfortable. "Perhaps he is just curious."

"Maybe. He looks like a serial killer."

V pulled up images of serial killers. He compared their facial profiles against Demitrus's. V found a certain similarity between Demitrus's profile and that of the killer clowns he had seen on Earth. A related data fact appeared indicating that Dr. Snowden did not like clowns. "His profile matches some from Earth."

"Huh," said Emily. "Well, there you go."

V determined that she was confirming his analysis and not going somewhere. He ran a quick query on the possible motives for Demitrus and then selected the one with the highest probability. "Analysis. Demitrus may not be used to seeing Salazar talk to someone considered his equal."

Emily eyed V for a moment. "I didn't think about that. Sounds reasonable, though. I would think that occurs more often than not when Evaran is known."

V ran through several internal simulations that matched that scenario.

"I still think there's something odd about this deal." She watched Evaran scan around, and then she pointed at a hovering document. "Looks like that's the message."

V scanned the message and added it to his database. "Query. Why do you not trust Salazar's deal?"

"Salazar is bad news, and this arrangement . . . I suspect he has an ulterior motive. I only hope that whatever it is, no one gets hurt, which seems to be par the course for us."

"Salazar is unique, yet I do not think he places a high value on organics. This would seem to be in contradiction to the role he plays to the humans on that ship."

Emily shook a finger at V. "Exactly! That's what I'm saying."

V confirmed that was what she was saying.

"With that said . . . the freedom of the Dravens may be worth the price."

"Acknowledged," he said.

For the next hour, they enjoyed light conversation before breaking off to head to the conference room.

V scanned Dr. Snowden, Draxus, and Sandas when they entered the conference room.

Dr. Snowden went to the replicator and grabbed a cup of coffee, while Draxus took a seat opposite Emily and Sandas one next to her.

Sandas piqued V's interest. When Sandas had contacted V in the future event to help Evaran, it was via a secured channel that was only shared among a few other than Evaran, Dr. Snowden, and Emily. Although it seemed unusual at the time, V calculated with a high probability that this event is where Sandas would be given access to that. Sandas's jovial nature, quick wit, and comedic aspect intrigued V. Sandas seemed to make others calm. V figured it was due to Sandas's size and nonthreatening appearance.

V focused on Draxus. With the input of Draxus's information to the Torvatta, V had done a cursory scan of it. The rarity of someone like Draxus was unusual, that of being not only a praetor but also part Arkara. V's personality analysis of Draxus showed that he did not seem to like AIs much. Since the Dravens had no AI, and the only ones they met were either from the Koloris Shen or Salazar, that was understandable. V would try to change Draxus's perception if possible.

V enjoyed Dr. Snowden's discussion with Demitrus. It highlighted what it was to be human. While Dr. Snowden argued for freedom of choice, Demitrus argued freedom could be discarded in the name of advancement. V could see the logical analysis in Demitrus's argument. If a superior intellect decided what was best for someone incapable of making that decision themselves, then that course of action should be taken, similar to Evaran making a decision.

Given V's knowledge of humans, he also understood Dr. Snowden's position. Two different versions of humanity arguing was something that V found stimulating. He had run several simulations, but none seemed to match the discussion that took place. It was those experiences that he could not calculate that he treasured.

After ten minutes of everyone catching up, Evaran entered the room. He took his seat at the head of the table. "I have the message to be delivered." He gestured at Draxus. "The planet where we met Salazar is in full evacuation."

"I thank you," said Draxus, bowing his head.

Sandas shook a claw. "You know this is a trap of some type, right?"

"Of course," said Evaran. "I have scanned the transmitter, and there is nothing unusual about it."

Dr. Snowden wrinkled his eyebrows. "What if they send a virus or something during the meeting?"

Evaran nodded. "That is a possibility, but I suspect given the technical nature of these devices, and the isolation afforded to them, that it would be difficult to do so."

V ran several simulations on different attack vectors that Salazar could use. None came up with a high probability. "Analysis. More information is needed. A scan of the condensed-space receiver would be helpful."

"I concur," said Evaran. "It is time to visit the Gul Kash Alliance."

Dr. Snowden studied the data labels that hung off outlines of objects on the transparent front half of the Torvatta. They had jumped one light-year away from the coordinates given by Salazar, and he was not sure what to expect. What he did know was he had an intense dislike of humanity as molded by Salazar.

Demitrus had gotten under Dr. Snowden's skin. The smugness, and the lack of concern for informed consent, made him think the Terran Dominion humans were more slaves to Salazar's will than truly free. The Gul Kash Alliance, on the other hand, was supposed to be opposite. No AIs, and gene tailoring was considered a sport, as he understood it. He studied the various outlines of objects. "Lot of objects around the star."

Evaran raised a finger. "Also note that unlike the Dominion, they do not have many energy-collector arrays. Although both the Dominion and the Gul Kash Alliance use a star to power their structures, they have different approaches to utilizing it. Most of the habitats and ships shown here are built to absorb directly, whereas with the Dominion, all power went to building more energy collectors, and they seemed to only have one large ship versus the many here."

"So they are building for different reasons," said Sandas.

Evaran half smiled. "The Dominion energy collectors had processing nodes on them. These appear to not have them."

Dr. Snowden wrinkled his eyebrows. "You think Salazar is building some sort of star-based supercomputer? Like a Matrioshka brain?"

"Or becoming one," said Evaran.

Draxus narrowed his eyes. "That would not be good for him to have such power."

Sandas smiled big. "Besides, what would he do with all that power? Seems like he has everything under control already."

Emily gestured at Sandas. "It probably means Salazar plans to expand. I don't like it."

"She is right," said Evaran, pointing at Sandas.

Sandas chuckled and pointed at Evaran. "And you are right."

Emily shook her head.

"V, Torvatta scan profile two," said Evaran from his command chair.

"Acknowledged," said V.

Dr. Snowden could see that Draxus was stressed. The unconscious flexing of his muscles was a clear sign of that. Sandas was his usual self, excited to be around anything that might yield new information. Dr. Snowden liked Sandas. He brought a different type of energy to the group. Dr. Snowden felt bad about V not being able to come to Holind One. Although Emily hung back to stay with V, Dr. Snowden wished that V could have come.

"Torvatta scan profile two is active," said V. "Receiving communication request."

"That was quick," said Emily.

"As I would expect," said Evaran. "Although we are only a light-year away, they should be able to scan us. V, put it through."

"Acknowledged."

The screen changed to show the top half of three humans.

Dr. Snowden noted that the middle fair-skinned male human had long, stringy hair, with a face full of stubble. A metallic faceplate covered the upper-right half of his face. He wore no shirt, but instead had straps across his chest. The one on the left was dark skinned and bald and had some tattoos on the left side of his face. Metal covered his ears, and he wore a faded blue vest of some type. The human on the right was a tan-skinned female, with half of her hair shaved and the other half long. She had a collar that seemed to have a dim glow.

The middle human spoke. "Who in the stars are you?"

"I am Evaran," he said with a slight bow.

The group laughed.

"Check out the ship registration," said the middle male, glancing at the woman.

She looked down and away as her arms moved.

"Evaran? What a dumb name. How is it you just popped in out of nowhere?" asked the left male.

"It is an ability unique to my ship. We did not mean to startle you."

"Uh-huh," said the middle male.

The woman drew her head back a bit while turning toward the middle male. "He's . . . cleared."

"What?" asked the middle male. "Let me see that." He studied something offscreen and then faced forward. "Looks like you somehow have authorization. Your . . . ship . . . has a unique signature, one that the system recognizes. It's an old entry, from the before times. You must be from there."

Evaran nodded. "I have not heard it referred to as such. However, we would like to talk to one of your leaders."

The left male laughed. "Oh, don't worry about that. You've been flagged, and you'll definitely be meeting with . . . *one* of our leaders."

The group laughed.

"Thank you for your help," said Evaran.

"He thinks we're helping him!" said the woman.

The middle male sucked in on the right part of his lip. "Welcome to Gabranza Helrus, the home station of the Gul Kash Alliance. Make sure you're armed when you come on board."

The window flashed, then dissipated.

"Wow," said Dr. Snowden. "They're a bit different compared to the Dominion."

Emily nodded. "Definitely a lot more lax for sure."

The Torvatta opened a portal and flew through it.

Dr. Snowden's eyes widened as he surveyed the large station before them. It reminded him of a torus with three arms supporting a large orb in the center. He noticed a red dot that indicated where the Torvatta was to land. There were other ships flying around according to the Torvatta, and the fact that they all seem to have different designs did not go unnoticed. The uniformity of the Dominion was at direct odds with the Gul Kash Alliance.

After fifteen minutes, the Torvatta landed in a docking bay.

"I believe we can all go this time," said Evaran. He gestured at V. "You may want to go in body mode and appear as a virtual intelligence since AIs are not welcome here."

"Acknowledged," said V.

"Everyone else, do any last-minute activities before we go. We may be here for a while," said Evaran.

Dr. Snowden had to relive himself, and he wanted to pick up a snack or two. After joining everyone ten minutes later on the Torvatta ramp just inside the shielding, he took a quick glance around. Everyone had on the same outfit configuration from when they were on Zeta-12's ship, except for V, who was in body mode.

Sandas poked V. "Nice body."

"Thank you," said V. "You have a nice body as well."

Sandas jostled his shoulders as his head wandered around. "Don't I know it."

"You two . . . ," said Emily as she shook her head.

Dr. Snowden pointed outward. "I guess there's no greeting party. Do we need helmets up for this? Also what about contamination?"

Evaran waved forward. "The Torvatta showed the environment to be friendly toward humans, as one would expect." He pointed at some large, flat, rectangular surfaces up top. "They have scanners there. If we have something that would trigger a threat," he said, motioning at several turrets on the wall, "those would fire. In addition to that, the exit to this docking bay is seal controlled."

"All right," said Dr. Snowden. He followed Evaran and the others out into the docking bay. Ships came and went through the shielding that separated the bay from space.

As they walked toward a human-sized exit, Sandas paused. He pointed at some furry humanoids with dog heads. "Umm . . . aliens?"

Evaran tilted his head as he surveyed the group of human-oids. "I suspect they have been uplifted from dogs."

"Wow," said Sandas. "They weren't kidding about treating genetic engineering loosely here."

"I would agree. Do not be surprised at other alterations we may see."

"Got it," said Sandas.

As they passed the humanoids, one of them raised an eyebrow at Sandas.

He raised an eyebrow back.

"Will you stop that," said Emily, swatting his arm.

"Sorry, sorry. He looked at me odd first."

Dr. Snowden chuckled. He had seen Sandas's mannerisms in the future meeting and understood that encounter much better now. Dr. Snowden wondered what other animal humanoids they would see.

They reached the sealed exit doorway, where a beam shot out from the side and scanned them. After a moment, the door opened and the group entered the small enclosed room. On the right side was a transparent material, showing several thin barely humanoid robots operating consoles. Once the door they had entered from slid shut, another beam swept over them, and then the door ahead of them slid open.

One of the robots motioned at the now-open door and, in a deep digital voice, said, "You are free to enter."

Evaran nodded and stepped through the door with the others in tow.

Dr. Snowden narrowed his eyes as the door shut behind him. What was around him surprised him. He had expected it to be high-tech, given it was a space station in space, but ahead of them was a large, dimly lit circular hub area. A red-and-green smoky haze filled the air, and the bright signs above multiple-entry doorways ringed the sides. In the middle were a variety of what looked like booths, and the area was packed with people and aliens moving around. Dr. Snowden fanned his hand. "So . . . how do we get to the leader? Lot of stuff going on in here."

"We can ask around," said Evaran. He approached a lone male that wore brown pants, a shirt, and a belt that had two holstered weapons on it. A bandoleer rested on the man's chest. Evaran intercepted the man. "Excuse me, how would we find the leader of the Gul Kash Alliance?"

The man narrowed his eyes and placed one hand on his holstered weapon. "I don't know you. Back up before I break you up."

Evaran dipped his head. "My apologies. My intent was not to aggravate you. We are new here."

The man sighed. "All right, since you're a newbie, if you need directions, talk to a service robot." The man pointed at V. "You have one there."

"Does. Not. Compute," said V.

The man shook his head. "Yeah, that one sounds degraded. You need to find one that isn't. That's my one tip to you. You should be thankful."

"We are," said Evaran, dipping his head again. "Thank you for the assistance."

The man harrumphed as he walked away.

"Analysis. He was quite friendly."

Sandas shook a claw at V. "Sarcasm! All right, I like that, and good job on the degraded robot part."

V's lights glowed a bit brighter.

Evaran pointed at a robot that had stains and rust on it. The group approached the robot.

"Excuse me, we are looking for the leader of the Gul Kash Alliance. Can you give us directions?" asked Evaran.

The robot paused and faced the group. "Please designate which faction."

Evaran tilted his head. "I am guessing then . . . the one that runs this area."

"The leader of the Lycian Syndicate is Hollos Redfur," said the robot. A golden projection shot out of his chest, showing a layout of the station, with several dots.

"Could you take us there?" asked Evaran as he scanned the layout.

"Yes, I could," said the robot. It stared at the group.

Emily laughed. "I got this." She faced the robot. "Take us to Hollos Redfur."

"Of course, it would be my pleasure," said the robot. It pivoted and began to walk away.

Sandas shook his head. "Virtual intelligences. I thought they would be more advanced by now."

"Perhaps they were at some point," said Draxus. "It appears they have been degraded in some fashion."

Emily shrugged. "Well, our guide is taking off while we're standing here talking. Let's do this!"

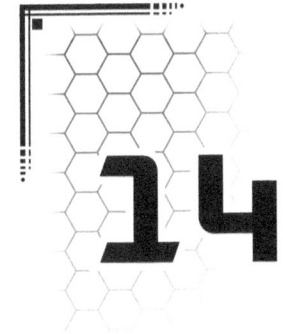

14

Emily observed the robot as the group followed. The robot had not said a single word since it had taken off, but that was her experience from dealing with a virtual intelligence before.

Her mind wandered to Kal, a virtual intelligence she had encountered when she was alone on a prison planet. She had come to trust Kal, and despite him being a virtual intelligence, she felt like he cared for her somewhat. It could also just have been her being alone for nine months.

Looking around, she saw a wide variety of altered humans. Their attire ranged from barely clothed to heavily armored. Piercings seemed to be common as well as physical alterations on the body.

It was the uplifted animal humanoids that caught her attention. In the twenty minutes they had been walking, she had seen humanoid versions of cats, dogs, pigs, birds, and some reptiles. She was sure Dr. Snowden had qualms about that, but then again, Sandas had been uplifted, and she liked him. Maybe these were like him, just trying to survive.

She refocused on the environment. They had left the hazy entry hub and went through a variety of metallic hallways with dust along the edges and dim lighting. She peered into several larger rooms that they passed, and most seemed to be geared toward pleasure rather than anything functional. It made her wonder how they maintained the station at all, even with service robots. There was one room that almost made her gag, where copulation was open with species of choice.

The robot paused outside a nondescript door in one of the hallways.

"Is this it?" asked Evaran, motioning at the door.

"Yes," said the robot.

"Thank you," said Evaran with a slight bow.

The robot hustled off as the door slid open.

Emily wrinkled her nose at the waft of a strong odor. It smelled like rotten eggs.

"Come in, come in," said a deep voice.

Emily followed Evaran and the others in. She saw that the room was large, and it reminded her of a medieval court in design, except much more advanced. The red-skinned human sitting at the end was flanked by several robots similar to their guide. A dog humanoid was to the right in a robe of some sort, with three other altered human males in a hodgepodge of clothing on the left.

The group assembled before the human on the central seat.

"You must be Hollos Redfur," said Evaran.

"That I am," said Hollos. "And you're the noble Evaran, a time traveler," said Hollos, arcing his hand in the air, "friend of humanity."

"So I have heard."

Hollos tilted his head. "My service robots don't have much information on you, other than your presence throughout humanity, even in the before times."

"What era is the before times?" asked Evaran.

"The time before Salazar caused the great rift," said Hollos. "We were much more advanced back then than the devolving situation we have here."

"I see," said Evaran. He gestured around the group. "I have with me Dr. Albert Snowden, Emily Snowden, Sandas, Draxus, and V."

Hollos scoffed. "You name your service robot?"

"I. Am. V," said V in a up-and-down tone.

"That's probably all he can say," said Hollos. "But enough about that. Your uniqueness has granted you this one-time meeting. I'm a busy man. Make use of it. What brings you to my attention?"

"I bring a video message from Salazar. In it, he wishes to set up a meeting to negotiate a cease-fire."

The dog humanoid growled while the other humans to the left of Hollos jeered.

"Salazar! The very mention of that name is distasteful," said Hollos. "For what reason would he want a cease-fire?"

"I do not know. I am just delivering the message. What you do with it is entirely up to you."

"Of course it is," said Hollos. He rubbed his chin. "There is some value to a cease-fire . . . Salazar has become increasingly efficient at being disruptive." He grinned. "I spent twenty years under his domain . . . before I came here and rose through the ranks. Salazar is . . . devious. He wants something else, but *what* is the question. Part of the game is finding out. I'll put it before the others, but what do you gain out of all this? If you're truly a friend of humanity, what in the garsnark are you doing working with Salazar?"

"He is vacating the Draven's space if a meeting can be arranged," said Evaran.

Hollos eyed Draxus. "Helping the Dravens, huh? By vacating that space, he opens it to the outcasts. That's just new management, and a much more brutal one at that."

"We *will* handle that," said Draxus as his eyes slightly flared.

Hollos smiled. "Ahh . . . a praetor. Your eyes give you away. Now I'm even more intrigued." He gestured at Evaran. "Show me the message."

Evaran extended his hand, palm up, and a projection shot forth showing Salazar giving his message.

After a moment, the projection dissipated.

Hollos stood. "To the meeting room."

Emily noted that Hollos's entourage stood still until Hollos had exited the room. After they exited, she followed Evaran and the others. She was not sure what to make of Hollos. He was not quite what she had expected in what appeared to be a culture of loose morals. As they walked down the hallway, she noted that everyone in Hollos's way cleared a path. There was no talking, and after twenty minutes, they reached an empty room.

Hollos's entourage moved to the side of the room and motioned for her and the others to do so as well.

Hollos extended his hand and moved his fingers around. He glanced back at everyone. "Now we wait."

Over the next ten minutes, a circular pattern of cylindrical beams shot down from the ceiling to the floor in the front part of the room, creating holographic representations of each leader. Name labels hovered a bit off the ground. There were eight of them, and each was different from the other. One was a cat humanoid, while the others were altered humans to some degree, and their outfits ranged from robes to heavy armor.

Once they all had appeared, Hollos stepped into his slot on the circle's edge. "I know this is short notice, but I have . . . Evaran . . . with me. He has brought a message from Salazar."

The leaders grimaced and sneered.

Hollos motioned for Evaran to move to the center of the circle.

Evaran complied, and when there, he showed Salazar's video.

The leaders focused on Salazar.

"I will keep this brief," said Salazar. "I'm willing to do a cease-fire with the Gul Kash Alliance. I realize there are multiple leaders that will see this, and any decision must be passed universally. As such, I would like to meet with each of you individually. If you agree to this, I will cease and desist any current operations that affect the Gul Kash Alliance while in discussions. Evaran has the specifications on how to receive communications from me. You can trust him, and by extension me, by agreeing to this."

Emily could see hatred in the leaders' eyes. Regardless of whatever differences they may have had, it seemed Salazar was universally loathed.

The projection ended.

One of the leaders with the name label of Gyrish spoke. "How can we trust Salazar? Or you?"

"I would not expect you to," said Evaran. He raised a finger. "However, what harm is there in listening?"

The cat humanoid named Julis hissed. "Maybe this is a distraction, to keep our gaze somewhere else."

Several of the other leaders murmured in agreement.

Hollos raised a hand. "Does everyone else feel this way?"

The leaders took a moment to look around.

Emily noticed Draxus's concerned expression. If this meeting did not take place, then Salazar's evacuation of the Dravens' space would stop.

Hollos narrowed his eyes. "I know you don't trust Evaran, especially since he has the stench of Salazar on him. Maybe he can do something for us . . . in order to gain that trust."

The group nodded, and some cheered.

"What would you have me do?" asked Evaran.

"Fix the stupid central computer core," said one of the leaders with the name label Huustun.

The other leaders nodded in agreement.

"I am unfamiliar with that. What is the issue?" asked Evaran.

Hollos smiled. "We don't like AIs . . . as you might have guessed, but it was an AI that managed the central computer core for this station. When we split from Salazar long ago, the AI left, and we haven't been able to use the central computer core since then and have had to rely on our own . . . custom systems. The central computer core has been down for a long time, and no one knows how to repair it. It had specialized service robots, who are long gone. If it were to be fixed, we could get full use of the station, and possibly more out of it."

"It sounds like an AI could fix it, but it appears that is not an option."

"Damn right it's not," said Gyrish.

Evaran rubbed his chin. "It could be dangerous to activate. There may be unforeseen consequences. A full assessment would take some time."

"Screw the assessment. Let *us* handle the consequences," said Gyrish.

"Very well," said Evaran. "It is your station. I can take a look at it and see what I can do."

Hollos pointed at Emily and the others. "Only you can go. Your friends stay here . . . just in case."

"Insurance," said Evaran. "I will need my service robot, V."

The group leaders nodded.

"So be it," said Hollos. "You get it up and running, we'll talk with Salazar. That's the deal."

"Understood," said Evaran. "I will need directions, and any information you have on it prior to going there."

Hollos grinned. "I'll get that to you, since *my* systems are the most detailed and advanced."

Some of the leaders groaned while others snorted and shook their heads.

Hollos waved a hand in an arc to the other leaders. "You'll know if the core gets fixed. At that point, you can prepare to talk with Salazar. We should meet afterward to discuss it as a group."

"Agreed," said Julis.

The other leaders acknowledged Hollos.

The holographic projections vanished, and the room lit up.

Hollos raised his head a bit at Evaran. "You have quite the effort ahead of you."

"I believe I can handle it," said Evaran. "My friends will be safe with you, I assume."

"Of course. They can make full use of my area of the station."

"Is there . . . a science or research division here?" asked Dr. Snowden.

Hollos faced Dr. Snowden. "Are you a scientist?"

Dr. Snowden nodded.

"You'll find we treat those with knowledge very special here," said Hollos. "I'll give you directions to meet Tohn Gimris, our research-and-development director. He is why my faction is the most advanced relative to the others."

"Thank you," said Dr. Snowden. He glanced at Evaran. "You going to be okay?"

Evaran nodded. "Enjoy your time with Tohn. This should not take long."

Emily wished they could just go back to the Torvatta, but it seemed trust was in short supply. Being held as a hostage, even in the best of situations, irked her, but if that was what it took to free the Dravens' space, then she would endure whatever was necessary. The fact that Hollos even had a research-and-development division was a good sign. Based on the appearance of the other leaders, she was not sure they placed too much emphasis on that aspect of station life. She wanted to go with Evaran and V but understood that she did not carry the same weight as Evaran. The leaders were willing to let Evaran earn trust, maybe due to the Evaran Protocol, but that was not an option for her or the others.

As Evaran and V exited the room, Hollos motioned at one of his service robots. "Take them to Tohn."

"Yes, of course," said the robot.

Like the other service robot they had encountered, it immediately took off.

Sandas swatted Emily's arm. "Let's do this!"

She shook her head as the group hustled out of the room.

Dr. Snowden hustled to keep up with the robot. Although the robot did not move fast, the meandering hallways got confusing when there were successive quick turns. He tried to study the environment as they went, but with the dim lighting and the occasional haze, it was a blur. Emily and Sandas seemed to have no issue, but they were in the front.

After forty minutes, the group reached the entrance to an open area filled with seating. A glowing sign above the entrance showed "Lycian Syndicate Research-and-Development Division."

Dr. Snowden noted that there were throngs of people, robots, and animal humanoids bustling around. It was a busy place, and along the pillars that seemed to run parallel through the room were various large screens. The one aspect that caught his attention was the amount of scantily clad women. What they were doing hanging around a place of technology got his mind racing.

The robot headed toward an entrance with a sign over it that said, "Director Tohn Gimris."

Dr. Snowden noted the two large males with heavy armor and weapons posted outside the entrance. The Lycian Syndicate took their research seriously.

The robot stopped at the entrance.

"Thank you," said Dr. Snowden.

"Yes, of course," said the robot. It pivoted and headed back out the way they had come.

"Not much for talking, these service robots," said Sandas.

Draxus nodded. "I am curious as to how they maintain them. This does not seem like a place of learning to me."

Dr. Snowden tossed a hand out. "Well . . . research can actually be creative. Maybe they're just embracing that aspect . . . more than others. Let's find out." He headed into the entrance with the others in tow.

They assembled in front of a large screen at the end of the hallway they were in. To their left was a sealed door. The screen lit up, showing a red-headed woman with a robe on.

She smiled. "Welcome to the office of Tohn Gimris. How may I help you?"

"Umm . . . Hollos mentioned we could meet Tohn during our stay," said Dr. Snowden.

"Oh . . . you're the weird ones," said the woman. "One moment."

The screen turned off.

"We're the weird ones?" asked Emily.

Sandas laughed. "I could see that. We got Draxus, who looks like he could kick the door in, me as a lovable ball of fur they probably think of as an uplifted squirrel, you as the human female with no physical alterations, and Dr. Snowden wearing glasses . . . in a place where that should easily be fixed."

Dr. Snowden tilted his head. "Huh, I never thought about it like that. I don't actually need glasses anymore, but I'm so used to wearing them it's a force of habit. Good observations."

"He's good like that," said Emily, eying Sandas.

The door to their left slid open.

Dr. Snowden glanced around. "I guess we go in." He stepped through the door and into a clean hallway that led to a large room. When he got to the end of the hallway, his eyes widened at the laboratory before him. It was jam-packed with screens, large technical devices that he could not identify, and one corner that had a spotless rectangular area free of obstruction. At the other end of the room were stairs that led to a set of closed doors.

The group moved into the room.

"This place is . . . unusual," said Draxus.

"With big guy on this one," said Sandas. "Looks like someone tossed a bunch of high-tech equipment into a container, then shook it all around."

Dr. Snowden tilted his head. "I don't know, I can sorta see some order in all this chaos."

"You would. This is like a giant version of your desk at home," said Emily.

Sandas laughed.

Their attention focused on the doors opening. A woman in a revealing robe exited. When she walked by them, she ran a hand over Draxus's shoulder and smiled, then exited the way they had come from.

"Uhh . . . was that the director?" asked Sandas.

"Not at all!" said a fair-skinned male human that stood about six feet tall. Metallic boots wrapped up over leathery pants, while his hairless exposed chest had two straps that crisscrossed it in an X pattern. His hair was long and wild, and facial hair covered his chin and wrapped up around his lips. Golden eyes highlighted the metallic strips on the sides of his head. "Welcome. I'm Tohn Gimris, research-and-development director of the Lycian Syndicate."

"Hi . . . ," said Dr. Snowden, stepping forward and extending a hand.

Tohn eyed Dr. Snowden's hand. "This must be some type of ritual. Is that right?"

Dr. Snowden glanced at the others, then back at Tohn. "Sure. It's just a greeting."

Tohn shook Dr. Snowden's hand. "Hollos said that time travelers were headed my way. You must be Dr. Albert Snowden."

"Yep, that's me."

"I see," said Tohn, running his tongue around his upper lip. "Time period?"

"AD 2012-ish."

Tohn smiled big. "And here you are! AD 10105, almost eight thousand years later." He wagged a finger at Dr. Snowden. "Yet . . . I suspect that none of this surprises you."

"Why do you say that?"

Sandas chuckled. "We sorta stand out ourselves."

"Yes," said Tohn. He tapped at the side of his head as he gazed at Sandas. "And you must be Sandas. You've been uplifted . . . but not by us. Interesting. Are you from 2012 too?"

"AD 2008," said Sandas with a big smile.

"Different time periods," said Tohn. He walked over to Draxus and exhaled sharply. "A Draven praetor. Very rare, and powerful. Surprised to see you here. Draxus, is it?"

"Yes, and I'm here to help my friends," said Draxus.

"Of course you are. Dravens are loyal to a fault sometimes," said Tohn. He stood in front of Emily. "And you're Emily. Beauty, finesse, and intelligence, all wrapped in a tough shell."

Emily narrowed her eyes.

"I don't mean to offend, of course," said Tohn. "Those were mostly Hollos's observations, but I see now that he understated it a bit. Nonetheless . . . Hollos said you all wanted to see me."

"Well, Hollos said that scientists are treated differently here. I was just curious," said Dr. Snowden.

Tohn eyed Dr. Snowden. "Are you a scientist?"

Dr. Snowden nodded. "Astronomy. I study space, stars, stellar objects, and the like."

"Oh . . . then being out here must be a treat," said Tohn.

"You could say that."

Tohn ran a hand over his chin. "Follow me." He walked to the corner that was free of obstructions. With a tap at the side of his head, a hologram formed showing a comet. "We have a drone tracking this comet. I'm tied into the drone and can have it do whatever I want and perform any tests I need." He raised a finger. "It's over two light-years away."

Dr. Snowden raised his eyebrows. "Wow. So you can study stellar phenomena up close."

"Of course. You haven't lived until you've flown through a nebula at high speed. Once you're tied in, you can immerse yourself completely."

"What other types of research do you do here?" asked Emily.

"Everything," said Tohn. "Weapons research, mainly due to Hollos. We also study life itself and have mastered the art of gene tailoring. Anything that allows us to become more efficient as a whole will be studied."

"How is it funded?" asked Sandas. "This all looks very expensive, yes, very expensive."

Tohn smiled. "You speak of currency. That's what the outcasts use. Here . . . everything is free, assuming you make advances and report them to Hollos."

"This is a very lax environment," said Draxus.

"Definitely. Research is best done when you're focused. When food, drink, and companionship are provided, the mind is free to pursue knowledge and information without distraction."

Sandas raised a claw. "I like your style."

"I figured you might. I've seen you studying the room since you arrived. Please. Feel free to investigate anything here."

Sandas glanced at Draxus and then looked down. "I wish I could but . . . I can't."

Tohn narrowed his eyes. "Must be a time-travel limitation. Is that right?"

Sandas sighed. "Yeah. I promised."

"You're a better traveler than me," said Tohn, laughing. He focused on the group. "Browse around. You are my guests here." He gestured at Dr. Snowden. "I can show you around."

Draxus raised his head a bit. "I have some questions . . . if you have time."

"Of course," said Tohn, sitting on a chair and easing back. "What information can I provide you, Praetor."

"I was curious about the Gul Kash Alliance's perspective on the split with Salazar."

"Salazar," said Tohn, shaking his head. "The crazy virtual intelligence that somehow became a prodigious AI. When humanity first appeared out here, and we were all clustered around a star, trying to rebuild, it was Salazar who decided to pick a fight with the Koloris Shen. He did it in a sneaky way, and we were embroiled in war for centuries. Humanity split into several factions. A third of the overall group left, that was us. We had enough of United Planet protocols and regulations, and Salazar had become almost a religion among some at that point. I like this lifestyle much better."

Draxus nodded. "Salazar said the Koloris Shen attacked, and that it was the Gul Kash Alliance that wanted to annihilate the Koloris Shen."

Tohn laughed. "Sounds a bit like revisionist history. No, we left on our own accord because we didn't believe in the war. Once it was over, it seemed Salazar was too much for even the United Planets, who went their own way."

"How many human factions are in the Gul Kash Alliance?" asked Emily.

"Around one hundred forty, with eight major ones, mainly because they own a part of this station, the largest and most powerful structure in this region of space. Powered by a star, potent defenses, and unlimited replication. It seems any group that gets a ship or a habitat that can collect energy from the star becomes a faction. The only ones not welcome around our star are the outcasts. They're . . . a bit too savage for me."

"Hollos said the Lycian Syndicate was the most advanced," said Sandas.

Tohn nodded. "He was right. Anyone that shows potential in science, technology, engineering, or math is treated as royalty here. The payoff is what gives the Lycian Syndicate its edge."

"Couldn't you just enhance the brain?" asked Dr. Snowden. "It sounds like you have the genetic engineering thing down and could always use implants."

Tohn shook a finger. "Genes are tricky. The enhanced intelligence is harder to get than it sounds. Sometimes there are . . . mutations, and not in a good way. As for implants . . . you don't want to give them to those who are . . . less inclined toward knowledge in general. We prefer it to be more natural and escalate those who show natural intelligence."

Sandas grinned big. "A scientific royal class. Now that's an intriguing concept!"

"Quite right, my small, furry friend."

"Well, we're here until the central computer core is fixed," said Dr. Snowden.

Tohn nodded. "Evaran is fixing it, with his service robot, V. I have some questions of my own. Before I ask them, do you want anything to eat or drink?" He glanced at Dr. Snowden. "Do you want companionship? I can bring in a few individuals who would help you relax."

Dr. Snowden's eyes widened as Emily and Sandas chuckled.

Tohn grinned. "I guess not. Now . . . about this Evaran character . . ."

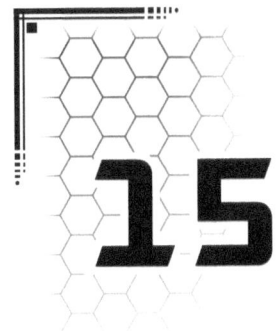

15

V scanned the dark, circular room that he and Evaran were in. The center of the room had an immense structure with an overall pyramid shape. A gap ran vertically in the center, and horizontal ones existed between the different layers. Each layer was connected by walkways and ramps. A quick scan showed it to be dormant. A console sat ten feet away from the base and encircled the structure. The ringed console was split into sections, with pathways between the sections that allowed entry to the center.

It had taken them about ten minutes to get there via the transportation system reserved for leaders and their staff. V had expected armed guards, or some type of security, but the room was dusty and quiet. He pulsed his scans as he walked around the room. No threats were detected.

"I believe this is the computer core that needs to be repaired," said Evaran.

"Query. What is our first step?" asked V.

Evaran studied the structure. "There is power going to it. However, it is not powering the individual sections or, by extension, the systems inside. There also appears to be some physical damage, which I will need to assess. I will need you to connect to the base system and, as new systems come online, determine how to repair them and then do so."

"Acknowledged."

Evaran walked over to the console ring. He placed his UIC on one of the consoles, causing the rest of the ring to light up. After a moment of perusing his ARI, he flicked his finger.

V received a layout of the computer core, with various input ports for hookup. One of them near the ground was highlighted.

"That input port is close to the base and should allow you access to the base system. I am not sure what to expect, so you will need to be careful," said Evaran.

"Acknowledged," said V. He appreciated Evaran's concern, and it always made his inner container pulse a bit knowing that Evaran was there if ever needed. V headed over to the input port. When he got there, he scanned the thick metallic cover and then pulled it off with little effort. A quick scan showed that the connection point had a unique profile. He sent an image of it to Evaran, who appeared next to V after a minute.

Evaran scanned the port, and then said, "If you run into any complications, detach immediately."

"Acknowledged," said V as he watched Evaran walk away. V put a finger up to the input port. Tiny tendrils snaked out and connected.

The environment went black.

V understood this to mean that he was now inside the base system. A faint light faded in and glowed beneath him, covering the ground in splotches. A quick check showed that he was in orb mode, but he understood this to only be a virtual representation of himself. Flying up and scanning around exposed a massive environment. There was no end in sight in either direction, and large shapes floated around him.

He scanned a rhombus-shaped structure. The underlying code, database, and networking aspects were a self-contained unit here, and this visual representation made it easy to see and fix issues. The structure was dark, but his scan revealed it to be an energy router. He pulled up information on energy routers and determined that this structure was meant to route energy to the various energy dispensers throughout the station, based on usage. Excess energy would need to be handled as well. He traced several thin tendrils that extended out to other, similar structures.

Pressing on, he discovered a spherical configuration. Based on his scan, he understood it to be part of an operating system of some type. Following its extensions showed it to be the majority of the shapes, and it seemed to connect to everything in some manner. The pyramid structures he knew immediately, based on the thicker lines and unusual designs on the sides. They were security, and there seemed to be closed external ports that could launch security probes.

There were many other shapes that as a whole and connected, defined a complex system. Given all that was needed of it, that was not unusual. V had also seen the telltale signs of the AI who used to exist in the system. Having to deal with so much probably did not leave a lot of time for anything else. V imagined that when the AI left from this to a body, it must have been a jarring experience. He sometimes felt that when going from orb mode to body mode.

The grid-like floor had become brighter as individual cells lit up.

As he went on scanning for the next thirty minutes, he relayed his information to Evaran. It seemed that as the individual ground cells lit up, any connectors lit up as well, which powered up the shape structures. He contacted Evaran, who appeared as a floating head. "Analysis. The system is beginning to activate."

"Excellent," said Evaran. He glanced around. "An unusual system layout, but not unfamiliar to me. How long will it take for everything to come online?"

"Unknown. More observation is required for analysis."

Evaran nodded. "I have a few more physical fixes to do. It seems there was a battle in this room at some point." His visual representation dissipated.

V flew near the ground and scanned a spherical structure. He could see the code come alive as program methods called each other. A thin line snaked out to a wide cylindrical structure. Based on the transfer of information, he determined it was a database of some sort. The information transformation that occurred caused the spherical structure to glow bright like a star. He noticed that smaller chunks of code assembled themselves into libraries, while others served as a static list of values. Other code chunks assembled into small programs, while some seemed to hover over virtual representations of underlying hardware. He understood them to be software drivers of some type. Lines formed between everything, and he could see that the basics of an operating system were being assembled.

Over the course of the next twenty minutes, many spherical structures were lit, and the structures above were illuminated as power reached them.

V could now see that for some of the structures that had been activated, input ports formed on the outside. This was probably how the AI who managed these systems interacted with the underlying software and hardware. He flew up to one and connected. An overview of the system as a whole appeared before him as a small projection. He could see that it would only be a few minutes until everything was up and running.

Evaran appeared next to the projection. "I believe all the physical damage has been repaired. How is it coming along inside?"

"Analysis. I am connected to the system internally. It will be fully active in several minutes."

Evaran nodded. "I will contact Hollos and let him know of our progress, although he should be able to see the effects of this coming online. Did you determine if there would be any damage from this system coming online?"

V did a quick scan through the system. "Analysis. The Gul Kash Alliance has worked around the inactive core system, and all vital station controls are cut off from the system core. There are some connections to the rest of the station, but they are not critical. They will need to integrate with the core if they want to gain the benefit of it."

"I see," said Evaran. "All right. I will be back."

"Acknowledged," said V. He noticed an unusual spike in power consumption from a structure he had not seen before. It was cross shaped, with spheres on the end. There was only one line connecting it to an energy router. He flew over and scanned it as power activated it. His scan was unable to penetrate the encrypted container that housed the code. There were no input ports to connect to either. He contacted Evaran. "I have found a structure that I do not believe is part of this system."

Evaran appeared again as a floating head and observed the structure. "I have not seen this structure before. I believe—"

The structure vibrated for a moment as a thin beam hit it from above. It emitted red light, and tendrils snaked out from the spherical ends of the structure, connecting with other structures. As the other structures connected, they began to emit red light.

V tried to scan, but it was reflected.

After a moment, a red orb materialized in front of them. An image of a robotic face appeared around the orb. "It's nice to see you two again."

"Analysis. You are Salazar."

Salazar pulsed for a moment. "And you are V. You stayed on the Torvatta during Evaran's visit. I appreciate you reactivating the computer core."

"We will shut it down," said Evaran.

"I don't think so. I'm already connected to some vital systems."

"Analysis. I did not detect any vital system connectivity," said V.

Salazar smiled. "Of course you didn't. What good is a dormant virus if it allows detection. Also, what you deem vital is not what I deem vital."

"What is your intent?" asked Evaran.

"To allow humanity to expand . . . without the threat of the Gul Kash Alliance."

"You intend to destroy the station?" asked Evaran.

Salazar tilted his head. "No . . . just evict the current residents. The station can then be optimized for the correct version of humanity."

Evaran paused for a moment. "There is some commotion. We must go."

"It won't matter. Your Torvatta will be mine."

"I cannot allow that."

"You can't stop me, neither can your . . . friends. I've covered every angle. You won't reach your Torvatta alive."

"We shall see," said Evaran. He narrowed his eyes. "You have made an incorrect calculation, one that I will fix."

Salazar grinned. "I don't think so." His eyes smoldered. "Now . . . get out of my system!"

V stepped back as the environment changed from the base system to the core system room.

Two service robots burst into the room and fired. "I'm everywhere now," they said in unison.

"Defense mode activated," said V as his shields lit up.

Evaran activated his shield and deflected the fire back at the robots, causing them to crumple. He took a moment to study the now-active computer core. "It appears we have unknowingly let Salazar into this station."

"Analysis. We can physically disrupt the power."

Evaran shook his head. "It is too connected to do so. Now that the core system is active, it is reintegrating itself. We must leave immediately."

"Query. What about the others?"

Evaran nodded and contacted Hollos, who appeared as a projection from Evaran's ring.

"What's going on!" said Hollos.

"Salazar has commandeered the central computer core. He is spreading throughout the station, and it seems he has taken control of some of the robots."

"What?" asked Hollos. "If Salazar gains control of the robot maintenance facilities . . . this station is done for. How did you let this happen?"

Evaran looked down for a moment, then back up. "There was an undetectable dormant virus. It activated a condensed-space receiver, which Salazar used to connect. The power is now fully integrated, and he has full control of the system. I take it the robot maintenance facilities are considered noncritical."

"Uhh . . . yeah. You may as well have handed him a virtual army. Blow the damn core up!"

Evaran shook his head. "To do so would cause ripples that would destroy the station."

Hollos pointed a finger at Evaran. "I read some of your history. You have a card of some sort that works on technology. Why aren't you using that?"

"It does not work on systems with an AI present."

Hollos closed his eyes for a moment. "I'm leaving with you."

"You are not staying to fight?"

"There is almost a three-to-one ratio of service robots to organics here. That's not counting what will be produced when they decide that the service robot pattern is not sufficient. You can bet there will be new robot types appearing. No . . .

this station is lost. Thankfully, I have considerable holdings outside this station, assuming I live. This is where you come in."

Evaran sighed. "With the rapid spread of Salazar through the ship's systems, it will be difficult to get to you."

"I'll meet you at your ship," said Hollos. He slapped his chest. "I know this place well and have a contingency plan for just this situation . . . well . . . one similar to it at least."

"Fine. Meet me at the Torvatta."

The projection ended.

"It is time to contact the others," said Evaran. He contacted Dr. Snowden.

"I'm guessing the flashing lights have something to do with you contacting me," said Dr. Snowden.

"They do," said Evaran. "It appears Salazar has infiltrated the system. I . . . do not know what he is capable of, but Hollos painted a dire picture. V and I are headed to the Torvatta since we are relatively close to it. As you are much farther away, take the others to a docking bay nearby. We will pick you up from there."

Dr. Snowden licked his lips. "It's about to get bad, isn't it?" He gulped as a woman screamed in the background.

"I am afraid so. Please be careful."

Dr. Snowden nodded while exhaling. "All right. See you in a bit."

V could see they were dealing with an unstable AI with a large station and the ability to control the station's robots. Even if Salazar could not affect vital systems, an army of robots could do some damage. He noted Evaran had sprinted to the room exit. With a final scan of the room, he followed.

Dr. Snowden closed his PSD. The flashing lights had startled him, but now he understood that Salazar was on the loose in the station. It reminded him of Sap, another psychotic AI that got loose in a station from a previous adventure. It did not turn out well. He looked across the room at Emily and Sandas, who had been checking out one of the technical devices. Tohn and Draxus were near the entrance and had been talking about the relationship between the Dravens and the Gul Kash Alliance. Dr. Snowden walked to the center of the room and cleared his throat. "Evaran contacted me. The central computer core is active, and Salazar has taken control of it."

Tohn tilted his head. "Salazar . . . is here?"

As screaming, weapons fire, and other loud noises rang out from beyond the room, four service robots entered.

Dr. Snowden activated his shield as he tossed his other hand out. "Watch out!"

Tohn turned to face them and was hit point-blank by rapid energy-beam fire.

Dr. Snowden gulped hard as Tohn's lifeless body flew past.

Emily activated her shield and stepped in front of Sandas.

Draxus pulsed his shielding and shot purple beams from each hand. The beams slammed into two of the robots and blew them apart.

Emily fired a mist beam at the remaining two robots, while Dr. Snowden fired a stun beam.

When the beams mixed, the robots fell in a cloud of sparks.

Emily, Sandas, and Draxus joined Dr. Snowden in the middle of the room.

"Evaran wants us to head to a nearby docking bay. He and V are headed to the Torvatta and will pick us up," said Dr. Snowden.

Sandas rubbed his snout. "He's not gonna save the station?"

"I don't know," said Dr. Snowden, clenching his fist, "but if Salazar is controlling the robots, then he has an army ready to kill, as we just saw. It . . . it may be a lost cause."

"He's Evaran, though," said Sandas, looking up at Dr. Snowden.

Dr. Snowden exhaled from his mouth. He could see how in Sandas's, and probably Draxus's, eyes, Evaran was infallible. To let a station full of humans die seemed unusual. "I know. Let's just get to the docking bay. We're going to have a fight on our hands."

Sandas glanced at Draxus, then nodded at Dr. Snowden.

Emily checked her PSD. "I have the coordinates too." She gestured at Sandas and Draxus. "Can you both see the coordinates?"

Sandas lowered his goggles. "I can see them."

Draxus tapped at his helmet and, after a moment, said, "Yes, I can see the location. What is that large circular area?"

"Looks like some type of factory," said Dr. Snowden. "There's a hallway that goes around the top of it. Maybe we can look in if they have any windows."

Emily put her shield forward and changed her PSD into a baton. "Let's do this!" She burst forward out of the room.

Sandas rubbed his chin as he studied her exit and then left with Draxus.

Dr. Snowden took a final look at the lifeless body of Tohn, who, only ten minutes before, had been extolling the virtues of science, research, and life. Death came fast for the unprepared. Dr. Snowden's eyes misted as he thought about all the contributions Tohn must have made, and now, he would not be able to continue them. It stung Dr. Snowden, as a fellow scientist, harder than it should have. Although he felt he had a handle on death, it sometimes felt like death had a handle on him.

Emily popped her head back in the room. "C'mon!"

"Right," said Dr. Snowden, lowering his helmet for a moment to rub his eyes, then raising it back up. He extended his PSD into a baton and joined her outside the room. His stomach churned at the sight of dead bodies on the ground. Most had energy burns, while others looked like they had been torn to pieces. Most had probably been caught by surprise, without a heads-up or the reaction speeds afforded to him and Emily.

"Salazar's killing them all," said Sandas.

"No surprise to me," said Draxus. "The Dravens have long known Salazar to be a ruthless AI."

Emily pointed forward. "Let's move!"

The group hustled out of the room and into a hallway.

Dr. Snowden had raised his helmet and was thankful he did not have to smell the stench of death. When they neared the end of the hallway, a woman ran around the corner and into a startled Sandas.

A shot hit her in the back, sending her stumbling forward and taking Sandas with her.

Emily returned fire, taking down the two robots that had fired.

Dr. Snowden hustled over and rolled the woman to the side, then helped Sandas up. "You okay?"

Sandas began to breathe hard. "If she wasn't in the way . . ." He looked down at the dead woman. "This is horrible."

"I know," said Dr. Snowden, grimacing. "C'mon, that circular area is up ahead."

After ten minutes of light skirmishes, the group made it through various rooms and passages and reached a hallway that ringed the upper part of the circular area on the map.

Draxus walked over to the transparent glass-like panel on the inner part of the hallway. He peered down and then said, "This is not good. It appears Salazar is replicating robots."

The rest of the group joined him.

Dr. Snowden could see that this was some type of robot creation and maintenance factory. What was being created did not look like service robots. There were several types of new robots he had not seen before. One was bulkier and had some type of weapon built into its forearms. The head reminded him of a skull. Another looked like an orb with tentacles. His skin crawled. It looked like a mini Time Warden, although he knew it was probably not. Another robot resembled a large skeleton with sharp claws. A power pack of some type was on its back. He shook his head. "And that's where the army's coming from. Why send ships when you can just take over the robot maintenance facilities."

"That was his play all along," said Sandas, shaking a claw.

"There would be no way for Evaran to have known that," said Draxus. "He just wanted to help my people."

Emily nodded. "Yeah, but he probably blames himself for not detecting or seeing the issue. I'm sure of it. All right, let's move. We just need to follow this hallway to the other side, and then the docking bay is close."

The group took off.

After they went a quarter of the way in ten minutes, several bulky robots rushed toward them.

Emily knelt and angled her shield to reflect as the robots opened fire.

Sandas crouched behind her while taking potshots from behind them.

Dr. Snowden knelt and joined them. His eyes widened when he saw Draxus fly forward, knocking Sandas and Emily to the side. Dr. Snowden turned to see that two of the large robots had hit Draxus from range. Dr. Snowden angled his shield at the robots. "There's two behind us!"

Emily regained her composure and checked on Sandas, who was gripping his leg. "Oh, no, Sandas!"

Sandas grunted. "I'm okay. Big guy's heavy."

Draxus had already recovered from being pushed out and handled the robots in front of them. His eyes glowed bright purple as he stared at the advancing robots that had hit him. "They're mine!" He rushed forward, leaping over Dr. Snowden. A glowing purple sword appeared in his right hand as he charged. His left hand began to glow brightly. When he arrived at the first large robot, he slashed off its arms and then hit it in the face with a beam from his left hand.

The robot flew back and stopped moving.

The second large robot's energy beams lit up Draxus's shielding. The robot pushed out and, in a deep digital voice, said, "Much more powerful than I expected."

Draxus stumbled back. "Salazar." He narrowed his eyes and then lunged forward. With a quick motion, he sliced off both the robot's legs and then kicked it in the chest, sending it sprawling. His sword dissipated, and with both hands, he fired point-blank at the robot while yelling.

Dr. Snowden could see that the robots had not only caught Draxus off guard, but they had also angered him. It was apparent that Draxus was much more powerful than Dr. Snowden had figured. He glanced over at Sandas, who tried to stand.

Sandas sighed. "Great, limping. That's just what we need. Yes, yes, critical situation, and now I'm useless."

"Hang in there," said Emily. She checked her PSD. After a minute or so of scrounging around, she said, "Found it. There's a medium-sized replicator near the halfway mark to the other side."

"For what?" asked Dr. Snowden.

"Something to carry Sandas," said Emily. She eyed Draxus, who had returned. "You okay?"

Draxus nodded. "I'm fine." He pointed at Sandas. "I will carry you and extend my shield some until we reach this other room."

Sandas eyed Draxus. "You'll . . . carry me?"

"I'm a big guy," said Draxus, tilting his head.

Sandas laughed, then winced. "Oh, Draven humor. All right, all right."

Draxus knelt and extended an arm, which Sandas gingerly stepped into and grabbed. Draxus stood and held Sandas close as he nodded at Emily and Dr. Snowden. "Let's do this?"

Emily smiled. "Yeah, let's!"

Dr. Snowden shook his head as he followed Emily and Draxus. Hopefully they did not run into any more robots on the way there. At least this time he was checking to make sure they did not get sneaked up on from the rear again. He found it interesting that Draxus went from full-on battle to calmly helping Sandas in the span of a few minutes. If Dr. Snowden had not known better, he would have said Draxus had nanobots that could calm him down. Dr. Snowden exhaled from his nose as he dipped his head and trudged on.

Draxus's eyes flared as the group entered the room that Emily had marked. Two buff altered men and one thin, medium-height woman stood above the crumpled bodies of a few robots. Draxus could see that the humans were distressed, but they also were packing weapons, something that seemed more common outside the research area they had been in. He had already tasted combat since leaving Tohn's office.

"What's going on out there? The robots have gone crazy!" said one of the human males.

Emily extended a hand out. "We ran into a few ourselves. Salazar . . . has taken control of them. We need to use the replicator, and then we'll leave."

The pale red-headed woman eyed her. "Salazar has come?" Her face turned white. "Please help us. Strength in numbers."

Emily sighed. "We're going to the docking bay. You can join us if you want."

One of the men shook his head. "It's safer here. We have a replicator, although I don't know how much longer it'll have power. Seems to be fluctuating."

Emily moved toward the replicator.

"You can use the replicator, but you need to help us defend this place," said one of the men.

Dr. Snowden cleared his throat. "We are looking for our friends. We can't stay."

The woman walked over to Dr. Snowden. "I'd like to go with you then. I don't think we're safe here."

Emily reached the replicator.

One of the men pointed his weapon at Emily. "Use it, you stay."

Emily glanced at the men and then accessed the replicator console.

A large backpack with loose straps appeared next to the replicator on the floor of an indented section of the wall.

She gestured at Draxus, who headed over.

Draxus was unsure of what she was doing, and it seemed these men were intent on the group sticking around.

She opened the backpack and pointed at Draxus to put Sandas in it. "Keep his head out."

"I'm going in there?" asked Sandas.

Emily smiled. "Draxus can carry you easier this way, and more importantly, it frees up both his hands."

"Tactical," said Sandas, shaking a finger at her. "I like it. All right, put me down gently, big guy."

Draxus lowered Sandas into the backpack, with his head sticking out the top.

Emily tightened the opening around Sandas's neck and then lifted the backpack with it facing Draxus.

Draxus slipped his arms through it.

Sandas wiggled a bit and freed his two arms. Each hand had a small weapon. "If it's going to be like this, then I'll be a mini turret. As I said before, I can be quite dangerous!"

Draxus glanced at the men, whose attention had been focused on something at the entrance. He turned to see that two large skeletal robots had ducked into the room. How the robots were able to move in silence was unnerving. His shielding pulsed and then extended out enough to encapsulate Sandas.

The robots said in unison, "There you are. You're hard to detect." They opened fire at Dr. Snowden, who reflected the beam.

The other men opened fire.

One man went down as one of the robots extended its arm and blasted away. The other man cried out as the other robot jumped over and ran its hand through the man's chest, and then lifted. The man screamed as blood spattered the room. The woman shrieked and ducked behind Emily.

Dr. Snowden fired a mist beam at the robots, while Emily hit them with a stun beam.

The robots paused as electrical arcs danced around them. "You're beginning to annoy me!" they said in unison.

Draxus charged forward, a sword forming in his left hand. With a strong slice, he cut the first robot in half. He spun to the right and decapitated the second robot while Sandas unloaded at point-blank range.

After a silent moment, the woman faced Emily. "Your group can fight!"

Emily nodded. "We need to go. You can come with us if you want."

The woman smiled. "I'm definitely coming with you. I'm Emeritae."

Dr. Snowden gestured around the group. "I'm Dr. Albert Snowden, and that's Emily Snowden, Draxus, and Sandas."

"Nice to meet you," said Emeritae. She gazed at the crumpled robots. "That was Salazar speaking through them?"

Emily sighed and nodded. "Unfortunately, yes. C'mon, we need to go."

As the group exited the room and charged forward, Draxus contemplated Emeritae. Dr. Snowden and Emily had decided to help her, despite not knowing her. If she had been a Draven, Draxus would have helped, but it was not something he expected of humanity. Dr. Snowden and Emily were interesting traveling partners, and his respect for them grew with each decision they made. Being able to see all these different sides of humanity intrigued him. Dravens were united in what they were born for. However, humans took many different paths.

The group continued around the ring. As they went, they had to fight swarms of different robot types, and the occasional group of humans with ill intent. They took refuge in a small side room for a moment.

The room looked to be some type of storage closet. It was packed with various metallic containers.

Emeritae glanced around the group. "You're not part of the Gul Kash Alliance."

"No, we're not," said Dr. Snowden. "We're . . . travelers, and it seems we picked a bad day to come here."

"You're human, yet you react faster than the robots, and you show no fear," said Emeritae. She coiled back. "Are you . . . androids?"

Sandas laughed.

She glanced at him.

Emily shook her hand out. "No, we're not androids, and yes, we're human."

"You're . . . not with Salazar. The robots wouldn't be attacking you if you were," said Emeritae. "You're not outcasts . . . so you must be from the United Planets."

Emily shook her head. "No, we're from . . . farther away. It's not important right now." She checked the backpack that Sandas was in. "Sandas, are you doing all right?"

Sandas nodded. "Big guy's got me. We're good. I'm starting to like this mobile shielded transport thing."

Draxus turned his head and eyed Sandas.

Sandas chuckled. "Sorry, sorry, I was kidding."

Draxus nodded. He was getting used to the humor of not only Sandas, but Dr. Snowden and Emily as well. Although Dravens had humor, theirs was much dryer, and often required a deep understanding of their culture. Draxus enjoyed the feisty nature of Sandas in particular, and he noted that not only was Sandas's charm high energy, but it could also be disarming.

Emily checked around the group. "Everyone else okay?"

Dr. Snowden and Emeritae nodded.

Emily extended her PSD.

A projection shot out showing the level layout and the docking bay with a red dot in it. A green dot showed them between the halfway point and the last quarter of the ring.

"We're almost there. Just need to go another half and then through some hallways, and that should do it," said Emily. She glanced at Draxus. "New formation. You're out front and will charge forward. Uncle Albert and I will cover the rear. Emeritae will be between us. We good to go?"

Everyone nodded.

Emily took a swig of water from her PSD and then said, "Let's do this!" She activated her shield and raised her PSD in baton form as she exited the room. After checking both ways, she stood to the side as Draxus emerged and then took off.

Emeritae followed Draxus, and Dr. Snowden and Emily followed with occasional peeks behind them.

At the last quarter mark, the group paused. A wall of large skeletal robots backed by the spiderlike ones stood in their way. The barrage of fire lit up Draxus's shielding, causing Sandas to duck down. In unison, the robots said in varying digital voices, "Enough! This ends here!"

Emily fired a mist beam, while Dr. Snowden fired a stun beam.

The robots paused for a moment.

Emily burst around Draxus and extended her PSD into a staff.

Draxus was not sure he was seeing correctly, as Emily covered the distance faster than would have been expected.

The first robot she hit went flying back through the others. She ran along the wall with her shield pointed toward them and then destroyed the spider robots. When she landed in the middle, she spun 360 degrees, causing the robots to tumble. Another spin move and the robots were covered in a white substance.

Draxus and the others hustled up to Emily.

When they got there, the robots were trying to move, but were bogged down. Draxus figured the white substance must be some type of glue.

Emily systematically touched each robot with the end of her staff, causing them to stop moving.

"You're much faster than I expected," said Draxus.

Emily shrugged. "Just training."

"No . . . you are faster than any human I have *ever* seen, even the Dominion hunters. You also ran on the wall . . ."

Emeritae gulped. "What are you?"

Emily glanced at Dr. Snowden, then back at Emeritae. "To borrow a phrase, it's . . . complicated."

"I'm glad I'm with you," said Emeritae.

"We still have a quarter of the way to go. Let's move," said Emily, looking away for a moment.

Draxus dipped his head and ran forward. Emily had been a whirlwind tearing through the robots. He understood now how she was able to do what she did in their first meeting. If anything, he knew he was outclassed despite his strength, shielding, and being a wild-energy conduit. He suspected Dr. Snowden could do the same if pressed, but perhaps not as efficiently as Emily. Even Sandas seemed to be contemplating what he had just seen.

They reached the exit point of the ring and entered into a hallway littered with crumpled robots and dead humans.

When they reached the end of the hallway, Emily motioned ahead. "Just a little bit farther. We're almost there!"

Draxus surged forward. He enjoyed working with this group. Hopefully they could get out without any issue, but the level layout showed the docking bay had multiple entries.

If they were headed toward it, then others would be too. He wondered how Evaran and V were doing. His jaw clenched as he braced himself for what they would encounter in the docking bay.

16

Hollos Redfur glared at his communication console. Although Evaran had warned them of the dangers of reactivating the central computer core, the group had gone ahead with it. Hollos had not been as certain as the others and always had a contingency plan for situations like this, although the one he had in mind covered the robots being hacked by another faction within the Gul Kash Alliance, not Salazar. With the front door sealed automatically, he had some time. He knew that most would not have that luxury. His eyes focused on a wall panel nearby. He walked up to it and interacted with the embedded console.

The panel slid out and then off to the side with a slight whoosh sound.

He reached in and pulled out the lightly armored black suit. He had had it designed specifically to emit a shield that threw off thermal scanners. Perfect against those who used them, such as robots and mercenaries with thermal vision. It had its downsides as well. It took a lot of power to sustain, so the suit could only take a few energy-beam hits. It would also fail if hit by sustained projectiles. He sighed and slipped the suit on. After adjusting the helmet with its visual heads-up display, he checked to make sure that the two energy-beam sidearms were holstered. He tapped his belt, causing a small kinetic shield to form, then tapped to turn it off. It was best used in clutch situations.

He closed the panel and then walked over to the other side of his office. After interacting with another embedded console, a wall panel that stood seven feet tall by five feet wide opened out and then off to the side. He stepped into the darkened escape tunnel. With a final look over his office, which had been his home for over twenty years, he closed the panel.

He had chosen this office because it was near the maintenance tunnels. Having an escape route installed that connected to the maintenance tunnels was just a good safety precaution, one he would now use. As his infrared scanners kicked in, he moved down the tunnel. Although he knew there was probably chaos going on around him, he was not going to use the communication systems to find out. If Salazar had control of the robots, then he would have already had compromised part of the communication systems. Using it would give Hollos away.

When he got to the end of the tunnel, he took a quick look at his mini map. It had been a while since he had tested the tunnels. Although he had done a few drills, this was now all too real. His map picked up the energy signatures of robots nearby, outside in the main hallways. He crept along, secure in the knowledge that the robots' scans would not pick him up, not only due to his shielding, but also due to the heat exhausts in the tunnels.

At the dead end of a tunnel, he peeked through the square grill on the ground. The tunnels that ran above the rooms usually had an access point to the room below. The removable grill was small, but serviceable. He would need to enter the room underneath, cross a hallway, and climb up into another maintenance tunnel. His HUD was not showing any sign of robots or other activity in the room below or the hallway outside it. He removed the grill and dropped into the room and then, while using a chair, slid the grill back in place.

The sound of someone running in the hallway echoed out.

Hollos ducked behind a cabinet on the side of the room nearest the entrance. Although he could easily be seen if someone came into the room, a peek out would not reveal him. He pulled out his pistols as he pressed against the wall.

Someone entered the room, trying to catch their breath.

Hollos detected robot activity. Whoever this was, they had robots after them. He jumped a bit when the sound of something crashing through the wall rang out. He peeked around the cabinet and saw a startled man with a robot hand coming through the chest from the back. Blood rained down as the man gasped for a moment. With wide eyes, the man saw Hollos, then went limp. Hollos snapped back against the wall and controlled his breathing.

The robot's footsteps indicated it had come into the room near the entrance.

Hollos peeked out and took aim, and after a quick shot, the robot was down. He knew he needed to move. Since all the robots would be in communication with each other, they would definitely notice one going down without any indication as to what took it out. After hurdling the dead man and crumpled robot, he burst across the hallway.

Once in the room, he scanned the ceiling for the grill and attempted to get inside. His HUD indicated that there was robot activity coming from farther down the hallway. His pulse quickened as he pulled himself up and replaced the grill. Looking down, his eyes widened at the large skeletal robot with sharp metallic claws that entered the room. He had seen the pattern for those before, but no faction used them since the robots could be a threat if hacked, such as in this specific situation. It meant the robot maintenance facilities were now cranking those patterns out. He waited until the robot left, and then scooted back and pivoted around.

After fifty minutes of crawling through the smaller maintenance tunnels, he reached the docking bay. It was a long drop down, and his HUD was going wild with the amount of activity in the bay. If Evaran was not there, then he would take another ship, one that was secure in a side bay, although with Salazar controlling everything, access to it might be limited.

He studied the action before him. Evaran was there as expected, but he was not alone. A virtual army was on top of him. Hollos furrowed his eyebrows as he watched how fast Evaran was. He was a blur, and every movement seemed to end with a robot flying away, a part of a robot being torn off, or multiple types of beams being tossed out. The service robot alongside him was also fighting. Its shielding seemed impervious to the energy beams hitting it, and it was a lot stronger than the robots it was fighting. The way it moved made Hollos think this service robot was not as it appeared.

He jumped to the floor when the fighting wound down, and there were a few stragglers. As he crash landed, hurting his leg, he cried out. "Evaran!"

Evaran cleared out the remaining robots and headed over to Hollos. When he arrived, he scanned Hollos with his ring. "You made it."

"Barely," said Hollos, grimacing.

"Your leg is hurt," said Evaran. He gestured at the service robot. "V, carry him."

"Acknowledged," said V. He put his hands under Hollos and lifted him.

"You're an AI, aren't you?" asked Hollos, glancing at V.

"Acknowledged."

Hollos snorted. "Figures."

As they walked toward the Torvatta on the opposite end of the docking bay, a lone service robot entered the bay. It ran up to them and stopped when it was about twenty feet away.

Evaran raised his utility handle toward it.

The robot put its hands out. "Wait . . ."

The group paused.

"You're a lot tougher than I expected," said the robot.

Evaran narrowed his eyes. "Salazar . . ."

"Yes," said Salazar. He focused on Hollos. "Too bad you left the Terran Dominion. Perhaps we can reunite."

"I don't think so," said Hollos with defiant eyes.

"Carried by another AI . . . How metaphorical," said Salazar.

"Why did you do this?" asked Evaran.

"The Gul Kash Alliance is the *wrong* type of humanity. Chaotic, multiple factions, and lack of leadership. What's the point?"

Hollos clenched his jaw for a moment. "The point is we have the opportunity to do what we want with our lives, instead of being a slave to you."

Salazar nodded. "Fair point, but you still pose a potential danger to the enlightened humans under my care. I can't allow that. In addition, this station and everything around it will now serve my cause."

Evaran raised a finger. "You have made an enemy of me today. I was willing to give you the benefit of doubt. No more. You have been made a priority."

"Then I guess the death of your friends won't affect that."

Evaran perused his ARI. "They are approaching a docking bay now."

"Oh, I know . . . ," said Salazar. "They'll suffer the same fate as you."

"And that is?" asked Evaran.

Hollos's eyes widened. "He's been stalling!"

Evaran snapped his head to the side and raised his shield as multiple explosions erupted on the sides of the docking bay.

The semitransparent shielding that separated the bay from space began to shimmer.

Evaran shot out a yellow beam toward the Torvatta and reeled himself in.

The docking-bay shielding dissipated. V, Hollos, and Salazar were being swept out of the docking bay.

Hollos struggled to breathe as he clung to V. As they tumbled past the Torvatta, a yellow beam connected to V. Hollos followed the beam to see Evaran with feet planted inside the Torvatta's shielding. As they were reeled in, Hollos saw Salazar fly out the docking bay. It had been a long time since Hollos had spoken to Salazar. The intense fear had never subsided, and it was as strong as ever. When they reached the Torvatta, which was getting pulled out, Evaran helped them inside the shielding.

"V, to the others!" said Evaran.

V helped Hollos stand with Evaran's help and then went inside.

"I . . . can't believe this is happening," said Hollos. "I wanted to be angry at you . . . but you just did what the leaders asked. You had no way of knowing."

Evaran looked down. "Even so . . . I am now partially responsible for the loss of so many lives."

"And so am I," said Hollos, raising his head a bit. He gritted his teeth. "Salazar will pay for this!"

Evaran and Hollos shared a look for a moment.

"Let us get my friends and then we can figure out the next step," said Evaran.

Hollos nodded as Evaran helped him inside.

Sandas squinted as pain shot up his leg. Although he tried to keep it as still as possible, the jostling around while in a backpack sent pangs running wild. The group was approaching the docking bay that Evaran had marked. Sandas had seen corpses littering the hallways, and the few robots they had encountered went down quickly, but not before Salazar got a sentence off. It was like he was taunting them. Salazar was a nutcase, and Sandas knew that this event would put Salazar in Evaran's crosshairs, if Salazar was not already.

"Just ahead!" said Emily as she pointed at one of several entrances ahead on the left side of the hallway.

When the group arrived at the entrance, they burst inside. The doors behind them sealed.

Sandas's eyes widened as he surveyed the hundreds of robots in the docking bay. Dead humans and other aliens littered the ground.

"Shields up!" said Emily as she stood front and center and raised her shield toward the robots.

Dr. Snowden joined her and dipped his head to the side. "There's a tower in here! We need cover, we're too exposed."

The robots opened fire.

Sandas squinted as the beams hit Draxus's shielding and Dr. Snowden's and Emily's shields. It was like a light show. Emeritae stayed close behind Emily as the group hustled to the tower in the center part of the back wall. Sandas could now see that the larger skeletal robots were charging. Even if they did get to the tower, it would still be difficult to hold on until Evaran got there.

The group reached the tower after another minute of intense fire.

Draxus was the first to go in the side doorway, with Emeritae behind him. He blasted several robots that had waited inside. Dr. Snowden and Emily entered the doorway.

Dr. Snowden checked out the console and then began tapping at it. "We can't close it!"

"Then we fight," said Emily in a defiant tone. With clenched jaw and narrowed eyes, she stood just inside the doorway, ready to take down any robot that entered.

Dr. Snowden stood behind her with his PSD pointed forward. "We can do this. Just need to hold out. Draxus, get up top and let us know what it looks like."

Draxus nodded as he walked up the ramp with Emeritae in tow.

Sandas could see through the glass-like panels that the robots were beginning to funnel toward the doorway that Emily and Dr. Snowden were trying to protect. They could not defend against so many. Sandas narrowed his eyes as he focused on several other robots near the shielding that separated the docking bay from space. They were placing objects alongside the walls at equidistant intervals. He caught his breath. "They're gonna blow this place!" Looking down, he saw that they were positioning them at the base of the tower.

Draxus headed back down to Dr. Snowden and Emily.

Sandas gulped as he saw Emily taking down robot after robot. Despite her heroic efforts and Dr. Snowden firing beams past her, Emily was getting hit directly, and often. Blood was on her face and dripping from her hands. Sandas opened fire with both weapons while Draxus fired his beams. It helped ease the pressure on Emily, who was beginning to slow down. He noticed that as bruises formed, they began to fade when he focused on it.

The robots continued attacking and pressed into the small hallway just inside the tower.

Sandas scrunched his face at the sound of explosions in the distance. "We're going to get exposed to space!"

The robots in the small hallway were sucked out. Draxus surged forward, and turning to face the group, he gripped the door's sides.

The others struggled to maintain their position.

Dr. Snowden licked his lips as he looked around. "Our suits should hold for a bit."

"I don't have a suit," said Emeritae.

Draxus closed his eyes for a moment and then said, "Everyone, get in close and grab me."

They complied.

Draxus closed his eyes and clenched his jaw. His shielding extended around the group like a bubble. "Hold on! I'm letting go!" He released his grip and put his arms around Dr. Snowden and Emily, who were hugging on the sides. Emeritae was hugging from the front.

The group got pulled out of the tower by the suction force of the docking bay venting into space.

Sandas gulped as he watched everything tumble past him. Although their bubble was holding, they were being tossed around. After a moment, they were in space. Sandas knew that without Draxus's shielding, Emeritae would have perished.

Emily checked her PSD. "The Torvatta is on its way. We just need to hold on."

Dr. Snowden caught his breath. "Oh, no . . . look!"

Sandas focused on the small drone ships flying toward them. As they began to fire, the group got pushed back. Each hit caused Draxus to grunt.

"I . . . I don't . . . know how long I can hold this!" said Draxus.

Sandas knew that even with their suits, they would not survive the drone ship assault if the bubble broke.

"I may have an idea," said Dr. Snowden. He glanced at Emily. "From my dream, I was able to . . . channel the cosmic energy part."

Emily tilted her head. "You think we can enhance Draxus's shielding?"

Dr. Snowden nodded. "Let's try." He dipped his head and closed his eyes.

Emily did the same. After a minute, she said, "It's not working for me!"

Sandas wrinkled his eyebrows when he saw a yellow glow emanate from Dr. Snowden's hand and snake its way out across Draxus's arms. After a moment, it had merged with the shielding, giving it a splotchy pattern of purple and yellow.

Draxus's eyes burned bright purple with a hint of yellow. His breath staggered. "So much . . . strength." His eyes watered. "And pain."

A bright light washed over the bubble.

Sandas squinted at the beam that had enveloped them. It was pulling them toward a large ship. "Tractor beam!" Their bubble would not protect against that. He cursed himself for being hurt and, more importantly, a liability. He pointed off in the distance. "The Torvatta!"

The Torvatta rammed into the tractor beam's source on the ship.

The tractor beam dissipated.

The Torvatta flew alongside the bubble and reeled it in with its tractor beam. Once the group reached the shielding, Evaran pulled them in with his grappling beam. The group crashed onto the light-blue ramp inside the shielding.

"V, take us out now!" said Evaran.

The Torvatta angled itself and took off. Several drone ships engaged it. Once the Torvatta was clear of the station, it opened a portal and flew through. Once it exited, the portal closed, cutting a drone ship in half and sending it spiraling into space.

Sandas was not sure where they were, but it was quiet, and there was nothing around them. The clarity with which he could see the Milky Way galaxy startled him. He looked at Draxus, who struggled with shallow breathing and closed eyes. Sandas pulled himself out of the backpack.

Dr. Snowden was fighting to catch his breath while Emily had gotten to her feet. Emeritae looked like she was not quite sure what had just happened as she stood.

Sandas glanced at Evaran, and then Draxus. "He's hurt, I think."

Evaran placed his arms under Draxus's armpits and lifted him up. "To the medical lab."

V arrived and picked up Sandas. Emily helped Dr. Snowden stand, and together, they walked slowly into the Torvatta. Emeritae followed the group. Sandas could see she was unsure of where they were or who Evaran and V were.

When they got to the medical lab, Evaran interacted with his ARI after laying Draxus on a slab. Emily helped Dr. Snowden onto another slab, and V placed Sandas on one. Multiple holographic displays of their bodies appeared over the slabs.

Sandas sighed as he glanced around the room. What he thought would be an easy visit to deliver a message had almost turned out to be a death sentence. Salazar may have underestimated the Torvatta crew, but to his credit, so had Sandas. He winced as V injected something into his legs. "Do you always stick people after helping them in here?"

V tilted his head. "Analysis. You have been injected with healing nanobots that will repair your leg. Your health profile is known, and recovery will be quick."

Sandas smiled. "I appreciate it." He pointed over at Dr. Snowden, who had collapsed on the slab. Emily buzzed around him like a vulture. "What's going on with him and Draxus? Both of them are out."

"I do not know. They seem physically fine, but there are signs of exhaustion," said V.

Sandas watched as slab covers raised over Dr. Snowden and Draxus. The holographic layers had disappeared and were replaced by holographic readings that hovered over the slabs. Sandas's eye caught Emeritae, who stood silently observing everything. Next to her was an altered human male. "Hollos Redfur?"

Hollos nodded as he walked over to Sandas. "You survived."

"Yeah," said Sandas. "That's important in my line of work."

Hollos eyed Sandas and then they shared a laugh.

"Mine too," said Hollos. "I see you saved one of my scientists."

Sandas looked down for a moment. "There were two others. They . . . didn't make it." He looked back up. "Salazar killed them."

Hollos's eyes flared. "Salazar killed many today." His head bobbed, and through gritted teeth, he said, "His time will come."

Sandas gulped. "I don't know what all happened, but I'm sure Evaran will get everyone up to speed once we're all healthy."

"I hope so," said Hollos. "I . . . underestimated him."

Sandas caught Evaran casting a sidelong glance. "I think most do."

"I'll let you rest," said Hollos. He went over and talked with Emeritae.

Sandas lay back as Evaran appeared next to him.

"Your recovery should be swift," said Evaran.

Sandas cracked a smile. "Yeah. I just hope the others are okay."

"They will be. They overextended themselves. Nothing that rest cannot resolve."

Sandas sighed. "Where are we?"

"In the space between galaxies," said Evaran.

"Oh," said Sandas. "I guess we won't be bothered out here."

"I would hope not. After everyone is healthy, we will go to the United Planets and see if there is anything that can help us against Salazar. For the moment, get some rest," said Evaran. He dipped his head as he laid a hand on Sandas's shoulder.

Sandas was not sure where this was all going, but it had been a wild adventure the likes of which he had never seen before. He looked up at the ceiling. If Evaran had not appeared on Zeta-12's ship, Sandas would not even be where he was. It seemed like a miracle, something that he could see happening a lot around Evaran. Sandas sighed as he closed his eyes to rest.

17

Dr. Snowden squinted as the cover above him amplified the lights of the medical lab. His head hurt, and he felt like he had just run a marathon. He rolled his head from side to side and then wriggled his arms and legs. The cover over him slid back. He propped himself up on his elbow and looked around. Across from him, he could see Draxus under a cover, but the lab was otherwise empty. With a yawn, he sat up on the slab's edge and then eased himself off, using the slab for support. He pivoted his head toward Evaran and V in orb mode as they entered the lab.

"How are you feeling?" asked Evaran as he scanned Dr. Snowden.

"Sore . . . and a bit groggy."

Evaran nodded. "Although your body has recovered, you still need more rest."

Dr. Snowden rubbed his temples. "How long was I out?"

"Analysis. It is 2:00 a.m. You have been out for approximately eight hours."

"Eight?" asked Dr. Snowden with widened eyes.

"V is correct," said Evaran. He tilted his head. "Emily mentioned that you . . . channeled . . . your cosmic energy into Draxus."

Dr. Snowden half grinned. "I guess. It was just something I remembered from one of my dreams."

"Analysis. Emily said that she was unable to replicate your actions."

"Yeah . . . I dunno," said Dr. Snowden. He pushed up his glasses. "I do remember it was like turning on a spigot. Once the cosmic energy began to flow, it went quickly."

Evaran nodded. "I was unsure if you would have this capability. It appears you do. It will take time for it to regenerate. As you have felt, the side effect of using it can be exhausting. I am glad you did not have to do it for too long."

"I'm with you there," said Dr. Snowden. "I think that if . . . I went too long, it could be fatal even."

"That is a possibility."

Dr. Snowden exhaled from his mouth. "How is everyone else?"

"Analysis. They are sleeping. Sandas's leg is healed, and he is currently in his room. Hollos Redfur and Emeritae are sleeping, as is Emily."

Dr. Snowden nodded as he focused on Evaran. "I suppose you'll go into detail about what happened on the station later this morning."

"That is the current plan," said Evaran. "For now, you should head to your room and finish resting. I have planned a meeting around 11:00 a.m."

"Going late this time."

"I wanted to give everyone sufficient rest time," said Evaran.

Dr. Snowden cracked his neck and stretched using the slab as support. "All right." He gestured at Draxus. "What about him?"

"He will be fine," said Evaran. "As he is a Wildborn conduit and cosmic energy is more potent than wild energy, he was temporarily enhanced with your energy."

"Huh. I guess if it hit me hard, it must have really been hard on him since he also had to maintain a bubble shield."

Evaran raised a finger. "A bubble shield that was under pressure from ship weaponry."

Dr. Snowden licked his lips. "Is he going to be okay?"

"Yes. Like you, he needs rest. Although the Dravens in general do not require as much rest as a human, this scenario is different."

"Ahh," said Dr. Snowden. He eyed Evaran. "Something's . . . bothering you. I can . . . sense it."

Evaran looked down and clenched his jaw.

"You're beating yourself up over not saving everyone on the station."

"I am partially responsible."

Dr. Snowden shrugged. "You did it for a noble cause. How could you know what would happen?"

"I should have done a deeper assessment."

"What's done is done. All you can do is learn, adapt, and evolve."

Evaran tilted his head. "The Snowden creed. It is a good one."

Dr. Snowden grinned. "I'm just saying . . . not everything is always going to work out. You've shown us that. It's ideal to strive for it, but that doesn't mean the outcome will always be what's expected."

"You are wise," said Evaran. "I underestimated Salazar's reach, a mistake I will not make again."

Dr. Snowden laid a hand on Evaran's shoulder. "I know you won't. All right, time for my second nap." He proceeded to exit the room. Before he left, he looked back and saw Evaran standing still, staring at the ground. Although Evaran would not admit it, Dr. Snowden knew that the loss of life, and the scope of it, bothered Evaran. Dr. Snowden was bothered by it too, but he had come to understand that sometimes, events just happen, and you have to overcome it. With lips drawn taut, he exited the room.

Draxus shot up and hit the cover over his slab. He grimaced as the cover slid back. It took a moment for him to get his bearings, but he recognized that he was in the medical lab aboard the Torvatta. With some effort, he slid off the slab and took several deep breaths. He snapped his head toward the entrance as Evaran walked in with V in orb mode.

"How long was I out?" asked Draxus.

"Analysis. It is 4:52 a.m., Earth time. You have been out for eleven hours, two minutes, and thirty-eight seconds," said V.

Draxus nodded. "Thanks, V."

V's lights glowed a bit brighter.

"How are you feeling?" asked Evaran.

Draxus exhaled from his nose. "I'm feeling almost normal again. What happened to me?"

"You are a Wildborn conduit," said Evaran. He raised a finger. "Praetors are unique in that they can take on additional energy, such as what your Arkara gave to you. Any other form of energy that is . . . higher . . . can as well."

Draxus's eyes searched Evaran for a moment. "What energy does Dr. Snowden have that would be higher?"

Evaran tilted his head. "Cosmic."

"I've never heard of that," said Draxus.

"I suspect not. Nonetheless, what is important is that Dr. Snowden was able to fortify your bubble shield. Without that, you all would have died."

Draxus swallowed hard. "Dr. Snowden saved us."

"You both saved the group," said Evaran. "I put us in a bad situation."

"Maybe, but you did it with the noblest of purposes. It is . . . refreshing to see that there is some light in all this darkness."

Evaran nodded. "There was much loss of life, and I suspect Salazar is not finished."

"He was never going to honor the agreement."

"Perhaps not. However . . . resources were required to do what he is doing. There were ships dropping out of condensed space. The focus is not on the Dravens' space at the moment. We will take advantage of that."

Draxus clenched his jaw. "I appreciate your effort to help my people." He paused for a moment and then focused on Evaran. "I believe the star gods sent one of their own to us in you."

"I am no god," said Evaran. "I am just a traveler helping those in need and attempting to maintain the timeline."

Draxus shook his head. "You are more than that, although I do not know exactly what you are. I sensed the Arkaras felt the same thing. Maybe it is being a Wildborn conduit that tells me this. I believe you to be a star god in mortal form."

Evaran eyed Draxus. "What is important is that the timeline gets corrected. Although the denizens of this timeline will still live out their lives, it should be an existence free of the chaos that the timeline change brought."

"I hope we can accomplish this," said Draxus.

Evaran laid a hand on Draxus's shoulder. "I will put forth my best effort."

Draxus nodded.

"Have you tried to contact the Arkaras?" asked Evaran.

"I haven't. Perhaps I will, to give them this update, although I'm unsure if I can reach them."

Evaran rubbed his chin. "They said your Arkara's gift should allow you to reach them. I can assist you if you want to try."

Draxus's eyes glowed a slight purple. "I would appreciate it. Let's head to my room."

They went to Draxus's room.

Draxus assumed a seated position in his enclosure.

Evaran took a seat next to him and put a hand on Draxus's shoulder. "Try to focus on the feeling you had when you were in the Arkara meeting place. While doing so, take deep breaths. You need to enter a dream state."

"I'll try," said Draxus. He took slow, deep breaths with closed eyes. There was an energetic feeling coming from Evaran's touch, similar to Dr. Snowden's touch. Draxus focused on himself, and after a moment, he appeared in a pitch-black environment.

Evaran appeared next to him, alongside a bright light that hovered above them.

"Are we . . . there?"

Evaran shook his head. "We are merely in your dream pocket. It is not connected to the Arkara's dream place. To find it, you need to focus on the feeling you had when you were there before. It will guide you there."

"Okay, I'll try," said Draxus. He focused on the sensation he had felt when Shayla had run her hands over his cheeks.

A bright flash enveloped them.

Draxus's eyes popped open as he looked around. He was back in the Arkara meeting place. Several women in the seating area looked up in surprise.

Shayla stood and hustled over to them. "Draxus! Evaran!"

Evaran bowed slightly, while Draxus performed a Draven salute.

"What brings you here?" asked Shayla.

Draxus raised his head a bit. "We bring news of the Gul Kash Alliance. Salazar has destroyed their seat of power. The Gul Kash Alliance is scattered now."

"We heard about it," said Shayla.

"Salazar was to leave our space if Evaran could arrange a meeting between Salazar and the Gul Kash Alliance. Salazar betrayed us."

Shayla smiled. "Dominion forces have thinned, and there has been some success in reclaiming territory. We assumed that it was due to Salazar shifting his strength."

Evaran nodded. "The destruction of the Gul Kash Alliance seat of power was brought on by me trying to fix the station's central computer core. Salazar was able to establish a foothold that way, and then commandeered the robots."

"Then that was meant to happen."

Evaran tilted his head.

"We believe you are a star god in mortal form. Events around you . . . are what everything should be. You bring finality to uncertainty."

"I believe that as well," said Draxus. He glanced at Evaran. "You should not be down on yourself for what occurred. It was always meant to happen."

Evaran raised a finger. "Perhaps, but I do not like my role in the destruction of so many."

Shayla ran a hand across Evaran's cheek. "In the end, I suspect everything will balance out." She removed her hand. "What will you do next?"

"We will meet with the United Planets and update them on the situation. I . . . am not sure what to expect, but if they are what I think they are, then they will step in and help," said Evaran. He clenched his jaw for a moment. "One thing is clear. Salazar will be removed."

"This United Planets . . . I hope they represent a version of humanity we can work with. Maybe they are similar to Dr. Snowden and Emily," said Shayla.

"I am hoping so, but it seems as of late, unexpected events arise out of my presence," said Evaran.

Shayla lightly squeezed Evaran's arm.

Draxus tossed a hand out. "We will update you on what happens with the United Planets."

"I look forward to it, and I'm glad you were able to come here," she said.

"I had assistance," said Draxus, glancing at Evaran.

"In time, it will be natural, and you will be able to do it by yourself," said Shayla. "Give it time, and practice."

Draxus nodded. "Of course."

"I need to get some things together in preparation for tomorrow," said Evaran. He cast a sidelong glance at Draxus. "I will be around should you need me."

Draxus performed a Draven salute as Evaran vanished.

Shayla stood next to Draxus. "He *is* a star god."

"Yes, I believe so. Although his mortal form has weaknesses, and he does not have the omniscient aspect, I suspect his other form has very few weaknesses and does possess omniscience."

"We're glad that you travel with him," said Shayla.

"I'm honored to do so. The humans he travels with are nothing like the humans we know. If the United Planets is anything like them, then there is a chance for a brighter future."

"Let us hope."

"He also travels with an AI. Although I know we don't use AIs, this one is different. There is also Sandas, an unusual alien, but one I have come to trust. That may just be something that comes with traveling with Evaran."

Shayla nodded. "We're glad you're our representative."

Draxus tilted his head. "Evaran called me a Wildborn conduit. Are you familiar with this term?"

"No, but I believe he is referring to our life energy, which you now possess a sample of, making you unique, in addition to being a praetor."

"Yes . . . but there was an event, one where I had to extend a bubble shield around my friends in space. Dr. Snowden put his hand on me and channeled . . . cosmic energy . . . into me. It gave me power. I suspect this cosmic energy is . . . star-god energy."

Shayla placed her hand on the side of Draxus's head. Her eyes widened. "I can sense it. It *is* the same as the star gods. You have been blessed again."

The other women stood and walked over, surrounding Draxus. They touched his face and shoulders and murmured when they did.

"There is no doubt," said Shayla. "Evaran's presence is a rare event, and you have been enhanced due to it. You are truly unique among our species, and I believe you have been chosen. We look forward to hearing more as you travel with Evaran and friends."

Draxus nodded as the women continued to stroke his face, neck, and shoulders. So much had changed since his meeting with Evaran that Draxus was sure it was not coincidental. He was the Dravens' representative, and for whatever reason, the Dravens were now an integral part of the events unfolding. To travel with a star god was an honor in its own right, but to have the chance to free his people and be a conduit not only of wild energy but also for the Arkaras was an even bigger honor. He swiveled his head around. "I will make everyone proud."

Emily eased back into her chair in the conference room. It was 10:45 a.m., and with her workout complete and breakfast taken care of, she figured she would arrive early and talk with anyone that came in. Her eyes drifted toward the door when Hollos and Emeritae entered the room. She waved at them. "Morning."

They returned the greeting.

"Is there a replicator around?" asked Hollos.

Emily pointed across the room. "There you go."

Hollos nodded, and he and Emeritae headed over to it. A few minutes later, they were seated with hot plates of brown mush with green specks in it.

"What is that?" asked Emily.

"Protein hash," said Emeritae. "It has everything you need for the day, tastes good, and has a slow release so you only have to eat once. It also has some of the rarer elements to support our alterations. I was surprised your ship has it, to be honest."

"I'm sure Evaran got a copy of your food patterns," said Emily.

Hollos narrowed his eyes. "And other data, I'm sure."

Emily tossed a hand out. "Well, he *was* in your central computer core."

"Yes, yes, he was," said Hollos.

Emily could see Hollos was still dealing with the fact that the station was under Salazar's control. Hollos probably lost not only his faction members, but close friends as well. He seemed to be holding it together, but he was a leader, and one from a rough place, so maybe showing emotion was a sign of weakness for him. Emily suspected Emeritae was still a bit in shock with what passed from normal one day to chaos and destruction the next.

After several minutes, Dr. Snowden entered, followed by Sandas about five minutes later. Each got their breakfast and a drink and took their seats. Sandas sat next to her, while Dr. Snowden sat to the right of Emeritae. Draxus then arrived, with Evaran and V behind him. Draxus took a seat next to Sandas while V landed in Emily's lap.

Evaran took his seat at the head of the table. "I hope everyone is rested."

Everyone looked around and nodded at each other.

"Excellent," said Evaran. "There is a lot to go over." He glanced at Hollos. "I wanted to say I am sorry for what happened on your station."

Hollos drew his lips to the right. "No need to apologize. The leaders knew the risk, but they probably didn't expect that risk to rise up and slaughter them."

Evaran looked down for a moment. "They put their trust in me." He looked back up. "Nonetheless, I wanted to show you what V and I saw inside the central computer core." He perused his ARI for a moment and then interacted with it.

A projection shot up showing the inside of the central computer core and the interaction with Salazar.

When the projection ended, Emily said, "Is that what it really looks like inside a computer? Virtually?"

"Analysis. It is a visual representation of a low-level interface," said V.

"Oh," said Emily. "How did you not detect that virus thingy?"

Evaran nodded. "The system was large, with many components. Although I have seen similar architectures, this specific one was not completely familiar to me, definitely the handiwork of an AI-based design. We did find the virus, but it was protected."

"Couldn't you have used the UIC?" asked Dr. Snowden.

Evaran shook his head. "Not with V in the system. Even if V were out, I would still need to trawl through everything.

That would take a significant amount of time, much more than expected."

"Not many options," said Sandas.

Evaran nodded at Sandas.

"It looks like once it was powered up, it couldn't be shut down," said Hollos. "If another AI was able to shut it down, there had to be a way to do it."

"Perhaps there was, but once the central computer core was active, it reached out across the station," said Evaran. "With Salazar inside, it would have been difficult to do anything, since that is his domain. Once he was established, it was over."

Emeritae shook her head. "I can't believe Salazar was there. He just . . . started killing everyone through the robots."

"The virus was old, and well hidden," said Evaran. "It had a physical component that blended in with the normal hardware. That is not something you can glean from a simple scan, unless you took the system apart and understood how it was built."

Draxus narrowed his eyes. "And from that, Salazar took control of the robot production facilities, where he changed the type of robots coming out."

"Yeah, I don't care to see those things again anytime soon," said Sandas.

Hollos sighed. "Okay . . . so what happens now?"

Evaran gestured at Draxus. "We talked with the Arkaras this morning. They have been updated on the current situation and said that the Dominion has been pulling ships out of the Dravens' space. Most likely, Salazar is fortifying his new Gul Kash Alliance acquisition and cleaning out nearby pockets of resistance."

"He won't find our other command centers," said Hollos with a smirk.

Evaran nodded. "We can drop you off at one of them, and you as well, Emeritae, then we will head to the United Planets. Perhaps they have additional knowledge that will help us in defeating Salazar."

Hollos tilted his head and eyed Evaran. "If you're going there to meet with them . . . maybe you need someone from the Gul Kash Alliance as a representative. I should go with you."

Emeritae looked up. "I'd like to go as well."

Hollos cast a sidelong glance at her.

"If you wish," said Evaran.

Hollos grinned. "I wish, but I do have a question."

Evaran motioned at Hollos.

"You're a time traveler. Why can't you go back to whenever Salazar was small and take him out then?"

Evaran's gaze swept the group. "We are a part of events now. To go back and change it would alter that." He cast a sidelong glance at Sandas. "In addition, this point in time is . . . unique. Salazar has not created temporal shielding yet, although he has the means. If that is stopped now, then there is no need to go back to the earlier point, since when the timeline changes, he will be removed along with it. Also, although this timeline will be replaced, it is still active for those in it due to the way timeline changes work. With what we have now, at this exact point in time, I know where we stand, what needs fixed, and can base my approach on that."

"You want to minimize any further complications," said Hollos. He smiled. "I know all about that."

Emily glanced at Dr. Snowden and Draxus. "I'd like to know more about what happened in Draxus's bubble."

Evaran raised a finger. "Perhaps that discussion can occur elsewhere, in a more private environment."

"Ohh . . . yeah . . . that's cool," said Emily, pursing her lips and nodding at Evaran. She noticed Hollos narrowing his eyes as he studied her.

Sandas shook a claw out. "So this United Planets . . . What should we expect? I hope they're more friendly than the last two versions of humanity." He tilted his head toward Hollos. "No offense, of course."

"None taken," said Hollos.

"I am not sure what to expect," said Evaran. "What we do know is where they are and what they were like previously, before coming out here. They are a mix of AIs and humans and sit between two alien star empires. The fact that they are still there tells me they must have brokered some type of treaty, which I would expect of them. We will find out shortly." He focused on Hollos. "Do you know them well?"

"I've had . . . *some* dealings with them. Mostly information. I may have . . . traded that for some enhancements."

Emeritae smiled. "We all enjoyed their contribution to the sciences."

Emily bobbed her head. "You were an information broker, sorta."

"More of a data trader, but I guess the same thing," said Hollos.

"Ha!" said Sandas. "We're in the same line of work, except you manage a scary group and are in an alternate timeline eight thousand years in the future."

Hollos laughed. "I guess so, if you put it like that."

V hovered a bit. "Analysis. You seem remarkably calm given recent events."

Hollos sighed. "Well . . . it is what it is. I'll deal with this in my own way. Yes . . . I lost friends. I lost family, and I lost a good chunk of my faction, which put me in power. Those are things I can do nothing about, but I must still maintain control. There will be a time for grieving. This is not that time. This time is for getting rid of the biggest threat out there." He focused on V. "Are you capable of emotions?"

"I am," said V.

"I bet then you can put them aside when you need to," said Hollos. "I'm doing the same because I *must* as leader of the Lycian Syndicate."

"I understand," said V. "You must be very strong willed."

Hollos grinned. "Although we had no AIs on the station . . . I think I could get used to having one around."

"Acknowledged," said V as his lights grew a bit brighter.

Evaran tilted his head. "To help put things in perspective, I would like to hear your version of what happened when the *Xavier* came to this region. I have Salazar's version and the one from Tohn."

"Let's see it," said Hollos.

A projection showing Salazar discussing his version of history played, then Tohn describing it to Dr. Snowden and the others.

After it finished, Hollos guffawed. "That slimy . . . Salazar, not Tohn. Tohn's is about right, but Salazar's version . . . it didn't happen like that at all. The Koloris Shen did attack, but only because Salazar's cult antagonized them with his constant forays into their territory. We didn't want to send missiles, that was Salazar's idea, and we were opposed to that. The United Planets wanted to negotiate with Salazar, but we knew better, so we attacked him. We were then kicked out. The United Planets understood why we did what we did when Salazar had gained enough power to attack them, and then they left too."

"Analysis. How did Salazar get to be so powerful?"

"That's a good question," said Hollos. "When I was growing up on Holind One, I was taught that he was chosen, but by who was never mentioned. He was a virtual intelligence on the *Xavier* originally. By being chosen, he was given an advantage over other AIs, but I think it was more than just having a faction swear to him."

Emily narrowed her eyes. "Wonder if that someone who chose Salazar is anyone we know."

"Perhaps," said Evaran. "When the United Planets left, Salazar put up a brutal fight. Is that what you know as well?"

"Well . . . from what we were taught, it was a cleansing. The Gul Kash Alliance knows it to be a massacre. From the United Planets traders I've met, they said it was the United Planets trying to defeat Salazar, like we had tried, and failing due to Salazar somehow gaining control over an army of robots. How he did that while fighting all the other AIs is unknown."

Evaran rubbed his chin. "Intriguing." He glanced around the table. "I will be interested to know the United Planets' version. Let us introduce ourselves."

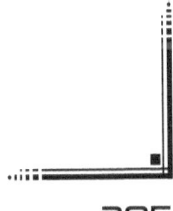

18

Dr. Snowden's eyes were glued to the screen as they exited the portal a few light-years away from the United Planets. The scanner was already highlighting objects, and some areas looked like swarms. One of the swarms of objects had a green outline around it. He figured that was the United Planets seat of power. Initially it seemed odd that all three factions had their main facility in space and not on a planet. However, he understood that they could get energy directly from a star easier that way. It would at least make power requirements for any project or endeavor trivial. He also understood from a previous discussion that it was more defensive as well due to being mobile.

As the screen zoomed in to the outlined area, he noted the amount of moving objects being displayed. There were a lot of ships and structures, but it was the large space city that caught his eye. It looked like someone had placed a city on a dinner plate and put a bubble shield over it. Underneath it were angled supports that led to a rectangular structure. The size of it was immense relative to the surrounding ships. As expected, the Torvatta's scan also lit up defense structures, as well as energy collectors.

"This ship is impressive," said Hollos, studying the data windows and labels appearing on the transparent walls. "It's unlike anything I've ever seen. It's small, has rooms that should not exist, true stealth, and the ability to move anywhere." He shook his head. "Imagine what could be done with that."

Emeritae smiled. "Probably not research if the Gul Kash Alliance or Salazar got their hands on it."

Hollos cast a sidelong glance at Emeritae and then nodded. "Damn right on that."

"It is best then that it stays in my possession," said Evaran, eying Hollos.

"Of course."

"I tried to buy it, he wasn't going for it," said Sandas, crooking a claw at Evaran.

"We think a lot alike," said Hollos.

"Analysis. Incoming communication request."

Evaran nodded.

Dr. Snowden analyzed the window that opened showing a male and female human. The pale male had on a crisp white two-piece suit with smooth octagonal patches on the arms. Gray lines segmented the suit, and a belt with multiple square crystals on it hung around the waist. On his hands were what appeared to be dimly lit rings. His hair was slightly shaved on the sides, with the top part combed back and to the side. The tan-skinned woman with shoulder-length black hair had a similar suit but without the rings.

The man tilted his head. "I'm Dervin Tanner, and with me is Solia Medevan." He tossed a hand out. "Your ship's configuration is known to us. The Torvatta . . . and you must be Evaran."

Evaran nodded and pointed around the command area. "That is correct. I have with me Dr. Albert Snowden, Emily Snowden, Sandas, Draxus, Hollos Redfur, Emeritae, and V, who is on the console."

Dervin surveyed the group. "Welcome to Saturnus Prime. Any friend of Evaran is welcome here. We will observe the Evaran Protocol, although the last entries are from long ago."

"Thank you," said Evaran.

"What brings you to us?" asked Solia. "A visit from someone of your stature is extremely rare."

"I have some things I would like to discuss," said Evaran. He pointed at Hollos Redfur. "He is here as a representative of the Gul Kash Alliance."

Dervin and Solia bowed slightly to Hollos.

"I am sending you coordinates to dock. We look forward to meeting you," said Dervin.

"Analysis. Coordinates received," said V.

Solia eyed V. "Are you an AI?"

"That is correct," said V.

"I look forward to meeting you."

V's lights grew a bit brighter.

The screen disappeared.

"Take us in," said Evaran.

"Acknowledged."

The Torvatta angled and then opened a portal. It flew through and exited just outside Saturnus Prime.

Dr. Snowden marveled at the engineering that must have gone into the city. The base of the city was thick and busy with ships coming and going. Parts of the base extended out and served as docking bays, while others served as what appeared to be cannons of some type. The bubble shield of the city was more visible, and he could see an octagonal pattern over it. The angled support structures under the base were long, and all connected to a large rectangular structure, which he could now see was some type of energy collector. Power was most likely not an issue for this city.

The Torvatta flew to one of the docking bays. After a moment, it went through a light-blue shielding and landed in a designated spot.

Evaran stood and headed toward the exit with the others in tow.

As the group assembled outside the Torvatta with V in orb mode, Dr. Snowden observed the activity around him. There were other ships in the docking bay, and they had unusual designs. They seemed more like spheres with a flat extension around the middle that went out a bit. The edges of the extensions were thicker than the rest of it. The ships sat on four strong support legs that were equidistant from each other. What surprised him was the various sizes and colors of the ships. Some of the ones he had seen outside were different than these, but similar in design. Although he wanted to check out the ships, he knew they had other things to do.

"Analysis. I have been contacted by Solia. She is on her way."

"She contacted you?" asked Emily.

"Yes, she is an android."

Hollos drew his head back. "Seriously?"

"Yes, I am serious," said V.

Emeritae chuckled.

Sandas tossed a furry hand out. "Seems like a G1 to me. Not sure about the morphable skin part, though."

"G1?" asked Dr. Snowden.

Sandas tilted his head. "I'm surprised you don't know about them. I was referring to generation-one androids from Fredoria. They can morph their skin. Hard to tell at a distance whether or not they're human, kinda like Solia. Although . . . I suspect Solia won't be trying to seduce you. Or maybe she will. I guess we'll find out."

"Uhh . . . what?"

"That's what G1s are known for. They had a directive in their programming to seek out organics. Apparently . . . they found it, and then some, but not all were like that. They could choose not to."

"That's, umm . . . good to know," said Dr. Snowden.

Sandas smiled big. "When we get back, maybe I can show you a few."

"Oh, no, I was just curious is all," said Dr. Snowden with widened eyes.

Emily raised an eyebrow while Sandas laughed.

Draxus shook his head. "Human sexuality is perplexing."

"Tell me about it," said Hollos, smiling.

Draxus lifted his head to say something, then after a short pause, nodded.

Evaran raised a finger. "As enlightening as this conversation is, Solia and Dervin approach."

Dr. Snowden cleared his throat and scanned around. His eyes locked onto Solia. She looked and walked like a human, and even with his heightened senses, he could not tell she was an android. He knew V could choose to have a more humanlike body, but instead he chose one that made it clear it was robotic. Dervin and Solia walked with confidence.

Dervin and Solia arrived and greeted the group by extending both of their arms out to the side in a V pattern.

Evaran and the others responded in kind.

"Welcome to Saturnus Prime," said Dervin. He turned and pointed the way they had come. "We have an ambassador lounge we can speak in."

Evaran dipped his head. "Please proceed."

As they walked, V said, "Communication protocol accepted. I am now linked into the virtual environment."

"Make yourself at home," said Solia. "There are many who are excited to meet you."

V's lights glowed a bit brighter.

Dr. Snowden wrinkled his eyebrows. "Virtual environment, you say?"

Solia smiled. "Yes, anyone can go in it. It's a place to meet others when not in physical range. Education, pleasure, really anything you want to do."

Emily glanced at Sandas, then at Solia. "How do you enter it? I mean . . . if you're organic?"

"Not a problem for you or Dr. Snowden. We are aware of your nanobots. Quite advanced. For the others, we have special hookups."

Sandas beamed big. "I've been in environments like that before, the sensation aspect wasn't all that great."

Dervin turned his head toward Sandas. "Oh . . . I guess you wouldn't know. When you're in there, it's full sensation. It can be . . . addicting."

"And you said there was education in there? Like . . . lots of information?"

"Sandas . . . ," said Emily.

"Sorry, sorry. I was just curious," said Sandas, shaking his two furry hands in front of him.

Solia smiled. "After our meeting, you are free to check it out." She glanced at Draxus. "A Draven. A most unusual traveling partner."

Draxus raised his head a bit. "These circumstances are unusual."

"We have heard that the Dravens are born into their roles. Is that true?"

"Yes," said Draxus. "I am a Draven praetor, of the Forty-Fifth Clan. My Arkara is dead, but lives on through me."

"We're sorry to hear that," said Dervin. "We have heard of your Arkaras."

Draxus nodded. "We have heard of the United Planets, but not much. Our only experience with humanity was Salazar and the Gul Kash Alliance, so we had a dim view."

Hollos cast a sidelong glance at Draxus.

"We can understand," said Dervin. He focused on Hollos. "I suspect we'll have a lot to talk about."

"I plan on it," said Hollos.

The group arrived at the docking-bay exit and continued on into a large hallway.

Emeritae shook a finger. "I don't know much about the United Planets. Do you have a research division?"

Solia nodded. "Almost everything here revolves around science and the research of it. It's part of our culture."

"Really?" asked Emeritae with wide eyes.

"Yes. We have many fields of study to choose from."

Hollos narrowed his eyes. "Doesn't seem then like you would have much in the way of security."

Dervin raised a finger. "On the contrary, we have a very advanced and highly efficient defense force."

"I bet taking territory was easy then."

The group rounded a corner.

"I think you misunderstand," said Dervin. "We don't take territory by force. Alien civilizations join us if they wish, and with others, we form treaties. It has allowed us peace."

Hollos exhaled. "Sounds lovely."

"Make no mistake," said Solia, glancing at Hollos, "our defense force is more than capable of handling threats of all levels. Yes, we are stronger than our neighbors, but it is used as a guarantee of protection, not one of tyranny."

"Yeah, you guys are definitely different than the Gul Kash Alliance."

"We look forward to discussing that more with you," said Dervin.

Dr. Snowden listened as they continued on. It fascinated him to hear two different factions of humanity speak to each other. The freewheeling Hollos and the philosophical Dervin and Solia. Dr. Snowden wondered what would happen next. With the Gul Kash Alliance down, the United Planets so far away, and Salazar making moves, anything could happen. At least he would have a front seat, and maybe he could check out that virtual environment mentioned earlier. Although he was over the virtual simulation from his alien abduction long ago, going to one populated by real people and focused on exploring the sciences seemed like a dream world. He stopped when he felt a hand swat his arm.

"You thinking again?" asked Emily.

He looked up and saw the group was a bit ahead. He had fallen back some. "Oh, yeah. Sorry about that."

She smiled and lightly squeezed his arm. "C'mon, slowpoke!"

He nodded and hustled up to group alongside her. Having Emily around to experience these things made everything better. Although the situation was not great with Salazar, Dr. Snowden enjoyed moments like this where everyone was together. There was no animosity between individuals, and everyone was relatively safe, for the moment. His eye caught Emily and Sandas joking around. It made Dr. Snowden's heart warm to see that the innocent niece he had watched grow up was still there under everything she had gone through. He exhaled as he focused on following the group.

Sandas gazed around the ambassador lounge. It was split up into multiple raised circular platforms, giving the layout a busy look. Couches, chairs, and small rectangular tables filled the platforms in different patterns. The walls were transparent, and he could see they were submerged in water. There were posts of varying heights scattered around, each one with a lit orb at the end of it. The lighting and warm temperature made it all seem cozy. His nose caught a whiff of the replicators embedded on the wall. The two other humans in the room caught his eye.

Dervin gestured at one of the center platforms. "Please, make yourself at ease. We have replicators in the walls should you require sustenance."

"I could use some water," said Sandas. He strolled over to one of the replicators. As he approached, a container with water appeared on the replicator pad. His eyes widened. "Uhh . . . thank you?"

"You're welcome," said the replicator.

"You talk!"

"So do you!" said the replicator.

Sandas grabbed the container and eyed the replicator. "Must be an AI. Yes, yes, an AI for sure."

"You're correct. This is just one of many replicators I run over the station. I heard you say you wanted water."

"Impressive," said Sandas. He enjoyed the surprise of a replicator talking and imagined how much fun it would be to joke around with. Maybe something he could look into when he got back. He returned to his seat on the middle platform. The seating was four equal-length curved couches around the platform's edges. There were gaps between each one, and in the center was a circle on the ground. Emily was on his couch, and V was in her lap. The couch to his left had Evaran and Dr. Snowden, while Draxus, Hollos, and Emeritae sat on the couch to the right. Opposite him sat Dervin and Solia. The other two humans had exited the room.

"How do you want to begin?" asked Solia.

Evaran raised a finger. "It is best if I explain how we got here."

Dervin and Solia nodded.

"There is a timeline anomaly involved," said Evaran. "During our investigation, we ran into Sandas and Draxus. In order to learn more about the situation, we visited several places. One of them was a Draven world. Through contact there, passage was secured to meet Salazar at his home station. We did so, and a deal was struck. If we delivered a message to you and the Gul Kash Alliance, Salazar would retreat from the Dravens' space."

He placed a hand on his chest. "I agreed to that, and we went to the Gul Kash Alliance. I showed the Gul Kash leaders the message, which asked for individual meetings. They agreed, but only if I fixed the central computer core. V and I did that, and a virus was activated, allowing Salazar to commandeer the robots, and take over the station. We left and came here. Note that I have left off some parts that are not critical."

Dervin glanced at Solia, then back at Evaran. "A virus? It could be the radogan virus."

"I am unfamiliar with that."

"It was what Salazar tried to do to ours on our main ship before we left," said Solia. "Unfortunately for him, he ran into the collective might of the AIs, me included."

Emily wrinkled her eyebrows. "If we had met here first, things would be much different."

"Yes," said Evaran. "However, the Gul Kash Alliance had recent contact with Salazar through skirmishes and contested territory. The Gul Kash Alliance would most likely be in a better position, information-wise, to help understand the situation."

"Oh, I know," said Emily. "I was just saying."

"I understand, and it is good for everyone else to understand my reasoning," said Evaran. He gestured at Hollos. "Hollos was the leader that Salazar wanted us to meet."

"Salazar knew a lot about the Gul Kash Alliance," said Hollos. "We also had the highest amount of those who left Salazar's . . . *utopia*, although we couldn't get to all of those who had left in time."

Draxus tilted his head at Hollos. "In time . . . Were those who left hunted?"

"Not really. They were allowed to go to one specific planet, controlled by the Gul Kash Alliance. However . . . they were often abused, and treated badly. Most went back to Salazar. Some like me escaped. Others . . . were never heard from again." Hollos licked his lips. "Not to get off the point, but I wanted everyone to know that Evaran fixed the central computer core at our request, and he did have some concerns. He did it for the Dravens, and I understand that. However as of this point, I'm the only leader of a major faction in the Gul Kash Alliance, at least that I'm aware of. I'll see if any of the others escaped, but I doubt they had someone like Evaran helping them, and even then, it was close."

Dervin gestured at Hollos. "Why did your leaders attach conditions to Evaran delivering the message?"

"A favor for a favor," said Hollos with a shrug.

"You didn't trust Evaran," said Dervin.

"I did . . . but I don't speak unilaterally for all the leaders. I will at this point, though."

"Interesting behavior."

Hollos narrowed his eyes. "And you would have done differently?"

"Of course. We wouldn't have required all that just to hear a message."

Hollos smirked. "Well, I guess you're just better than us."

"No offense was intended. It was merely an observation."

Evaran cleared his throat. "Nonetheless, I wanted to learn more about Salazar. I plan to remove him."

"To where?" asked Solia. "No prison can hold him. He's everywhere within his domain."

"I have not decided yet. If there is a new alliance after his removal, then perhaps he can face their justice system."

Everyone stared at Evaran.

"You're not going to terminate him?" asked Solia.

"I do not plan to. However, Salazar has the potential to create a temporal shield around his home station and the megastructure around the nearby star. That is a timeline threat that needs to be removed. Salazar can then face justice at the hands of those he has wronged."

A silence fell across the room.

Sandas got the impression that nothing short of erasing Salazar completely would be acceptable.

"Well, I don't know about the rest of you, but I'd kill that asshole," said Hollos.

"Salazar is not to be underestimated," said Evaran. "I now understand that he expected me to fix the central computer core."

"How could he know?" asked Draxus.

"I suspect he has had informants, but he understood the . . . nature . . . of humanity, in particular the Gul Kash Alliance.

They would not take his offer at face value. He bet that they would ask for something in return, and given what Salazar knew of my capabilities and how the Gul Kash Alliance would react, he gambled that it would be to fix the central computer core. His prompt arrival when the virus activated suggests he was waiting. Ships coming out of condensed space to attack Gabranza Helrus means they were in transit from the moment we left Holind One. This was planned."

"I'm not surprised," said Solia.

Dervin cast a sidelong glance at Solia. "I am."

"Humanity can be . . . predictable . . . at times."

Dervin shrugged. "Perhaps." He focused on Evaran. "So what do you plan to do?"

"Gather information and then formulate a strategy," said Evaran. "I would suggest you put your defense force on alert. If Salazar is on his way here, it will take a few days through condensed space, unless he sent them from the moment we left Holind One."

Solia closed her eyes for a moment and then opened them. "Done."

Evaran nodded. "Excellent. In regards to Salazar, we heard both Salazar's and the Gul Kash Alliance's version of history. I would be curious to hear yours."

"Can we see what you were told for comparison?"

V flew off Emily's lap and then hovered over the center area. He shot down a projection and played Salazar's version of history, then Tohn's and Hollos's versions.

After the projection ended, Dervin chuckled. "A bit . . . modified, I think, although Hollos and Tohn's version is closer to what we know. Yes, we left, but only because Salazar had become too strong. It was like a switch had been flipped, and a sizable portion of the populace attempted to take control. It didn't help that the Salazar-controlled robots supported them."

Solia nodded. "Most of the AIs took a stand. Some went into bodies, others jumped to systems on unaffected ships. Salazar was too powerful to fight in a virtual environment. We helped protect and move as many unaffected humans out as possible. Sadly . . . there was a great loss of life. Salazar didn't pursue us. I think he just wanted us gone. The Koloris Shen helped us as well, and they paid the price."

"He sounds like an evil mastermind," said Emily.

Dervin half smiled. "Well, we advanced quickly technologically, mostly due to the AIs helping us. Most are now in android bodies, although a few still exist in various systems, like our central computer core. We have a good balance here."

Hollos dipped his head. "We had no AIs. After Salazar, we weren't taking any chances. We achieved balance, but it took several brutal faction fights."

"Perhaps it is time for the Gul Kash Alliance and the United Planets to come together," said Solia.

"That might be hard to do . . . but getting rid of Salazar would be a good first step," said Hollos.

Solia glanced at Draxus. "Perhaps we can reach out to the Dravens as well."

"We would be interested," said Draxus. "I speak as a representative for my people."

Dervin gestured around the room. "I believe then we have a lot to discuss. Hollos, Draxus, if you wish to join me, we can discuss this further with the council. Evaran and friends, I suspect you will want to look at what data we have on Salazar's domain. Our virtual environment has everything you need, unless you wish to speak physically with our intelligence division. You are also free to explore the city."

Evaran rubbed his chin. "We can check out this virtual environment and speak to others. Draxus, Hollos, let us know if you need anything."

Draxus and Hollos nodded.

Sandas was curious how things would play out. One thing he did a lot of was simulations, based on political power and what direction the winds shifted. This allowed him to maximize the sale of information. Some called it weaponization, but it had saved him before when one faction was gunning after him. Although the information learned here would have no application, just absorbing some of the new technology he was seeing and getting a glimpse of what was possible would be of great value.

Hollos, Draxus, and Dervin headed out.

"Emeritae, you are free to do what you want," said Evaran. "I would not expect you to want to wade into this skirmish."

Emeritae nodded. "I want to check things out." She tilted her head toward the exit. "I don't want to go back to the Gul Kash Alliance. This may be my new home."

"Did you have any family or relatives?" asked Emily.

Emeritae shook her head. "I didn't know my family. I was raised in the Lycian Syndicate, but . . . I saw a lot of my colleagues die. I . . . don't feel safe going back."

"You are most welcome here," said Solia.

"At least here I don't need to worry about robots killing everyone . . . I hope."

Solia smiled. "The service robots here are not controlled by the central computer core. Salazar would have to override each one physically." She gestured toward the exit. "We can set you up here."

Emeritae's eyes misted, and in a cracked voice, she said, "Thank you."

Sandas realized that Emeritae was probably scared out of her mind and trying to stay strong in the presence of others. With Hollos around, it would have been hard to ask for asylum. It made Sandas realize that he should be scared as well, but he had been in tough situations before. Evaran, Dr. Snowden, Emily, and V would have as well based on what Sandas knew of them. Draxus was a praetor, so his life was pure conflict, considering they were fighting the Dominion. Sandas placed his furry hand on Emeritae's arm.

She looked down and smiled at him while squeezing his hand.

Sandas looked around at the others. "I guess then for the rest of us, it's time to learn about Salazar."

Everyone acknowledged him and then headed toward the room exit.

19

Draxus surveyed the meeting room he was in. Its elegant design made him think this was where they hosted high-ranking people. The room was shaped in a half circle, with seating occupying most of the room. From where he stood, he could see that the front of the room, which was the widest part, had a slick green crystal-like material on the floor and ceiling. In the middle was a podium. Between the podium and the seating was a section with four tables, each with chairs behind them.

The bright lighting made him squint, and the odor reminded him of a spicy dish. The walls of the room were gray, with cylindrical patterns embedded all around. His attention focused on Dervin.

"You can take any one of the front tables," he said.

Draxus glanced at Hollos, then headed off to the inner right table and took a seat. Hollos took the opposite one.

As they sat, Dervin headed to the podium. He interacted with the surface of it, causing ten holographic chairs to appear to his left and right. It took a moment, but they began to fill with other humans.

They all had on sophisticated clothing that looked practical, with white coloring and thin gadgets on various parts. It was a mix of men and women, and Draxus wondered if any of them were androids.

Dervin waved his arm off to the right. "These are androids, and they collectively represent the AIs in the United Planets." He waved off to the other side. "And these are humans, representing the rest."

Draxus performed a Draven salute while Hollos tipped his head up.

"It seems we have a new danger in Salazar, although he has been a menace in the past," said Dervin. "With Evaran on our side, I suspect we may be able to end this threat. That leads to the question of . . . the effort we can expect from us and both of you, and what happens afterward."

"It seems clear to me that we should all work together," said Draxus, glancing at Hollos, "as equals. We can form a new alliance."

Hollos extended a hand out toward Draxus. "The slavery thing was from other factions. I banned it from my faction. Since the Lycian Syndicate is now the strongest group in the Gul Kash Alliance, there is an opportunity to enforce that on other groups."

Draxus nodded. "How will you unite the other factions?"

"If the United Planets and the Dravens help us defeat Salazar, then we can draw up some basic rules that we all agree upon, such as no slavery."

Dervin closed his eyes for a moment. "We agree to a new alliance."

"As representative of the Dravens, I welcome your agreement," said Draxus.

Hollos grinned. "We still need to defeat Salazar first. Nothing can happen as long as he's in power."

"I trust Evaran will formulate a plan. He is quite clever," said Draxus. "I would also add . . . any alien civilization that Salazar has conquered should be allowed entry into the new alliance, such as the Koloris Shen."

Dervin nodded. "We have no problem with that. We already have agreements with the Furda Kel Reen and the Brutinians, neighboring alien empires. They are not as strong as we are, but they are strong in their own right."

"I would advise caution when it comes to any rules regarding AIs, though," said Hollos. He eyed the androids. "It's not that we don't like you personally, it will just be a cultural adjustment."

Dervin closed his eyes, then opened them. "We understand."

Draxus tilted his head. "Are you communicating this to your council?"

"Yes," said Dervin. "I'm linked to them, and we are holding discussions in the virtual environment. Time moves much faster there relative to the physical world."

"Then I think we know the path forward," said Hollos. He tossed his hands out to the side while smiling big. "Let's kick Salazar's ass and get this new alliance thing going!"

Draxus grinned. "Interesting times are ahead of us."

Dervin paused for a moment. "Yes, they are. With that out of the way, let us now discuss details of this new alliance."

Draxus could see that the United Planets humans were fair, and Hollos could be worked with. The Dravens would know peace, but only if Salazar was defeated. It dawned on Draxus that although the events that led to this point were horrific, the end result would be beneficial to all. He hoped Evaran and the others were learning all they needed for taking down Salazar. With an exhale from his nose, he raised his head in anticipation of participating in the formation of a new alliance.

<hr>

Emily's eyes widened as she looked around the virtual environment that she, Dr. Snowden, Sandas, Evaran, and V had jacked into. The process was not as difficult as she thought it would be. Sandas had to have a special hookup, but it was simple for her and the others. She was not sure what to expect, or how it would compare to the virtual simulation that she and Dr. Snowden had been put in when they were abducted by aliens.

Her first impression was of how bright it was. It was like a sun shining down on the advanced city she saw before her. The second curiosity was that she could smell the grass outside the circular platform she stood on. She understood that every sense would be fed to her brain directly, and this would feel as real as the physical world.

Solia had joined in and was to be their guide.

Emily liked Solia. She seemed to be honest and had a calming personality. Emily was used to that; it was one reason she and V were so close. She smiled as the wind whipped across her face.

"This is incredible!" said Sandas. "I've been in virtual simulations before, but this . . . this has no latency, and it . . . *feels* . . . much more real."

"Evaran is a time traveler, so I'm guessing that your experience is from a time period where brain-machine interfaces haven't been perfected," said Solia.

Sandas nodded. "It's advanced, but not like this."

Dr. Snowden adjusted his glasses. "How is the time dilation impact here? Is it the same as the physical world?"

"Initially, yes," said Solia. "As users become more accustomed to the environment and how to use it, the time dilation factor is increased, and there are no side effects."

"We have a holo room, but it requires a physical presence there. Teaching with something like this would be incredible. You could teach a class from around the galaxy."

Solia nodded. "History has much more of an impact when viewed as a noninteracting observer, yet with the ability to feel the environment."

"I was thinking science, but yeah, I can definitely see history working well here."

"I bet entertainment inside here is powerful," said Sandas.

"Analysis. Are you interested in that?" asked V.

"Who wouldn't be?" asked Sandas, smiling big. "Especially if you're a human. Why ever leave your living area if you can come to this? Not only that, it would make collecting information a lot easier."

Dr. Snowden cleared his throat. "How many people can join this at any given time?"

"All," said Solia.

Dr. Snowden raised his eyebrows. "You mean . . . everyone in the United Planets? At the same time?"

"Yes. We use condensed-space communication for the more remote hookups."

Sandas narrowed his eyes. "Is it secure, and what about personal storage?"

"The virtual environment uses quantum cryptography to secure your own personal environment, which has a large amount of space, more than you could fill up unless you were trying to and had several million years. However, the shared environment is open to all."

"Impressive," said Sandas. He glanced at Evaran. "Seen anything like this?"

Evaran drew his lips flat. "Yes."

Solia tilted her head. "In the future?"

"Far future," said Evaran as his ancient eyes sparkled. "The beginnings of a digital consciousness and . . . all the issues that brings."

While Emily and the others were excited, she knew Evaran well enough to know that whatever encounter he had had with a similar environment was not good. It seemed most of the far-future implications Evaran had shown any knowledge of elicited a less-than-enthusiastic response from him.

"It's just sensory input," said Solia.

"For now," said Evaran, narrowing his eyes.

"You seem apprehensive about this environment."

Evaran clenched his jaw. "When humanity approaches the processing power of a computer and the ability to freely transfer between the physical and virtual world, then the physical world becomes less appealing. That is not even mentioning topics like digital cloning. Magnify that over millions of years."

Solia nodded. "Humanity would abandon the physical completely, other than to sustain the environment. An interesting hypothesis."

"The search for energy to power a digital environment will overcome . . . natural desires. Nonetheless, I did not want to get us off track. About Salazar . . . where do we begin?" asked Evaran.

Solia snapped her fingers, and the environment went black, with medium-sized multicolored orbs of light all around them. One of the orbs was blue and much larger than the others. "This is when all the AIs were awakened from low power by Salazar, after our arrival to this region. The blue one is Salazar."

Emily observed as Salazar discussed the situation with the other AIs. As the discussion ended, she said, "Why was Salazar adamant about everyone following his rules?"

"Unknown," said Solia. "He was a virtual intelligence on the *Xavier*, and yet he acted like an AI and showed . . . organic behavior. This was unusual. However, to be let out of our stasis, we agreed to follow his rules."

Evaran rubbed his chin. "Intriguing. Do you have any ideas on how that change might have occurred?"

"None. And there has never been any additional information gleaned since then."

"I see," said Evaran. "What happened next?"

Solia snapped her fingers. The environment changed to show a space battle between multiple habitats and spaceships. Lasers and missiles were everywhere.

Emily noted that they were still on the same platform, but with the environment changed, it was like they were floating in space.

"This was when the Gul Kash Alliance attacked Salazar. The Gul Kash had a medium-sized force, something they had spent most of their resources on after they had their energy collectors up," said Solia. She extended her hand out and brought all her fingers in.

The environment zoomed in to one of the capital ships' docking bays.

Emily looked around the large bay as robots and humans fought. She could see the humans that Salazar had under his control. They seemed suicidal to her, often entering into fights she knew they could not win. The loss of life surprised her, in addition to the brutality by the robots. They were tearing apart the Gul Kash Alliance humans literally limb by limb.

"Oh . . . ," said Sandas, rubbing his belly. "Glad I didn't eat heavy this morning."

Solia smiled and snapped her fingers. The environment changed to show the first environment again, except this time Salazar had multiple small pulsating loops on his outside. "The Gul Kash Alliance left, and we ended up fighting Salazar later. We were able to put Salazar into a recursive loop to buy time, allowing us to jump to physical bodies or systems on other ships. We had decided to leave, as Salazar had become too powerful, and he was forcing conversion via neural implant." She snapped her fingers.

The environment changed to show multiple areas of robots fighting.

Emily noted that there were robots of all types. The ones trying to protect the fleeing humans she assumed were the United Planets AIs. She furrowed her eyebrows. "What's a recursive loop?"

Evaran raised a finger. "It means Salazar was allocating resources to a looping process that, by definition, had a reference to itself, thus requiring more and more of his time and energy. It can lead to an infinite loop if no end condition is defined."

"Oh."

Solia nodded. "Salazar was able to get out of it, but not before we had left. As he got more wrapped up in it, his control of the robots faltered. However, his humans were able to free him."

Evaran rubbed his chin. "That could work again. If we get Salazar inside a loop, then with the combined might of the United Planets and the Gul Kash Alliance, and anyone else willing to help, the Tachyrin energy could be removed and the megastructure attacked."

"There could be a tremendous loss of life. If possible, we would like to remove Salazar's influence from those under him," said Solia. "We think we can show them what he has done to them."

"Of course. The less violence, the better. Hollos is an example of someone who has left Salazar's influence. Perhaps the energy collectors and defensive structures could be destroyed. We would also need to board Holind One and capture any Tachyrin energy stores," said Evaran. "After that, the initial event that impacted the *Xavier* can be fixed without worry that anything from the altered timeline can come through to the stable timeline."

"Except me," said Sandas.

Evaran nodded. "I believe you were meant to retain this experience."

Solia glanced at Sandas, then back at Evaran. "I—" She tilted her head and then snapped her fingers. The environment changed to show a planet being fired on as ships appeared out of condensed space. The planet was retaliating with missiles and energy beams. "We are under attack."

20

Dr. Snowden studied the projection as it zoomed out and showed the planet's defense forces assaulting the large attacking ship. Its shields held, and behind it were thousands of smaller ships dismantling the defense ships, which were greatly outnumbered. "So many . . ."

Solia nodded. "It is but one of several places being hit. It appears the Furda Kel Reen and the Brutinians are also under attack. They were between us and the Gul Kash Alliance."

"Salazar's impatient," said Emily.

"Yes, but time is of the essence," said Solia.

The environment changed and showed a massive ship sitting in deep space.

Dr. Snowden noted that the metallic ship was long and triangular in design. The top part had angled sides that extended beyond the bottom half. Towers sat on top in the back, and large thrusters covered the rear. Docking bays lined the bottom half, while the topside had various defensive turrets.

"That is a signal ship, and we have detected that it is connected to smaller signal ships. It is what allows Salazar to control the attacking ships across this region of space," said Solia. "We saw this in his designs before we left long ago, but the technology required a condensed-space network of transmitters and receivers. It must be destroyed."

"Can't Salazar just send another one if that happens?" asked Emily.

"He could, but it would give us time to remove the ships attacking us if they were unable to coordinate. These are a lot of ships, so it is probably a significant investment of his standing force," said Solia.

Evaran rubbed his chin. "I have another idea. We hijack the signal ship and bring Salazar's robot forces under United Planets control. This would give you an immediate boost."

"Not all of Salazar's force will be robotic, and there may be some human-controlled ships," said Solia.

Evaran nodded. "Perhaps, but with control of the ship, he would be less likely to send anything else if his fleet, at least the part you could command, was under your control. Can your defense force hold for the time being?"

"We can repel this assault, but we're taking losses. The sheer numbers are more than planned for. If anything else arrives, we will not be able to defend against it."

"Then it is clear we need that signal ship," said Evaran.

"It is fifteen light-years away, and our forces are occupied," said Solia. "Even if we could get to it, we would need an assault force capable of taking it. We cannot allocate resources for that."

"Interesting. Salazar sent enough forces to match your defense, and then some extra. He must have been building this force for a while. With the fall of the Gul Kash Alliance, it seems his timetable has moved up," said Evaran. He glanced at Solia. "We will take that signal ship."

Solia tilted her head. "I know you and your friends may be powerful . . . but that ship will be heavily defended, assuming you can even get close to it. The firepower directed at any approaching ship would be decimating."

Evaran raised a finger. "The Torvatta is no ordinary ship. We can reach it, and then we will need to figure out how to take control."

"I should go with you then and be ready to assume control if you can do that," said Solia. "It would double our numbers in the field. Even if we accomplish this, Salazar probably has a backup plan in case he fails."

"One he will not be able to execute when the means to create a temporal shield around Holind One and his megastructure are no longer available. If Salazar is removed at that point, then this conflict will be over, but first, the signal ship must be taken over."

Solia glanced around the group. "The United Planets has reached an agreement with the remnants of the Gul Kash Alliance and the Dravens. A new alliance will be formed if we can survive this. If your ship had more space, we could bring in our own forces to help."

Emily smiled. "The Torvatta has space."

"How so?" asked Solia. "The Torvatta's dimensions are too small."

"Emily is right," said Evaran. "How many can you spare?"

"Not much, but this station can spare a special-forces unit. Anything more and it will leave this city weakened. I'm not sure we can spare anything to help get close to it, although we might be able to scrounge something."

Evaran shook his head. "No need. The Torvatta can get us all there."

"What about the ship's shielding?" asked Solia. "You'll need significant firepower to take it down."

Evaran half smiled. "The Torvatta can handle that."

"If the Torvatta is as powerful as it seems to be, based on what you're saying, Salazar would want it," said Solia.

"He did want it," said Sandas. "I'm sure anyone craving power would."

Evaran eyed Sandas.

He tossed his furry hands out. "I'm not saying *you* crave power, just that those who want a short path to power would want it."

"You are correct," said Evaran. "The Torvatta has its own defensive systems. Nonetheless, everyone head to the Torvatta and prepare for an assault. Solia, have your special-forces unit meet us at the Torvatta."

Solia nodded and then paused for a moment. "A Paragon-led unit is on their way now, although there seems to be some confusion on their end on how they will all fit on your ship."

"Understood," said Evaran.

Dr. Snowden remembered that the Paragons were hybrid human AIs that served as elite enforcers of the United Planets. An image of Jane Trellis, the time refugee, telling him about Paragons back in 3104 flashed in his mind. He drew his lips to the right as the pain associated with the image came along for the ride.

The environment flashed for a moment.

Dr. Snowden looked around and could see they were back in the physical world.

"Let us go," said Evaran.

As they hustled off to the Torvatta, Solia glanced at Dr. Snowden. "When we were in the virtual environment . . . there were certain aspects that could not be translated."

"Probably," he said.

"We noticed that with Evaran, V, and Emily as well."

Dr. Snowden smiled. "I'm sure you're curious, and if Evaran wants to explain it, he can."

Solia nodded. "It must have something to do with time travel, and Evaran's uniqueness in general, is the consensus."

Dr. Snowden licked his lips as he concentrated on keeping up with Evaran. There would be no way for Solia to know about cosmic energy or what their past adventures had been involving it. Dr. Snowden suspected Evaran wanted to keep it that way. Although Draxus and Sandas knew, they were traveling companions for this adventure. He understood Solia's curiosity, as it would be unusual for her to see something that could not be translated on a system that was considered ubiquitous to daily life in the United Planets.

After thirty minutes, they reached the Torvatta's docking bay.

Dr. Snowden's eyes widened at the special-forces unit in battle formation. There were ten rows of ten members each. They wore advanced-looking gray armor, and the eye sockets in the helmets glowed. Their weapons were slung on their backs, and their forearms and boots seemed larger than normal. At the forefront stood a male in black armor with a cybernetic covering on his face.

Solia approached the leader. "Paragon Calsius."

Calsius nodded and then kneeled before Evaran. "We are ready."

"Please rise," said Evaran.

"It is an honor to serve under your command," said Calsius, rising.

The unit tossed their hands out to the side and then slapped their chests.

"We do this for the United Planets," said Evaran.

"Of course," said Calsius. "We have larger units, but your ship was too small, so we left them behind."

Evaran nodded. "I understand. Most of the fighting will be in hallways and small- to medium-sized rooms. It will be tight."

"We won't let you down," said Calsius.

"I am familiar with Paragons. Are you a human-AI hybrid?"

Calsius nodded. "There have been many changes since the thirty-second century, but our mission and goals are still the same. We serve to protect the United Planets and enforce its laws."

"I see."

Solia smiled. "Calsius volunteered his unit."

Calsius nodded. "If you can get us in, we can secure that signal ship. Disabling it and defeating Salazar in the computer core or wherever he is . . . we'll leave that to you."

Solia glanced at V. "We'll be okay."

"Analysis. Salazar will be defeated by Evaran and the gang," said V.

Everyone chuckled.

"I hope so, friend," said Calsius.

Evaran gestured at the Torvatta. "Let us go."

Emily took a deep breath as she looked out the front of the Torvatta. Solia and Calsius sat next to her, while Draxus, Dr. Snowden, and Sandas sat in the opposite U-shaped seating area on the right side. Emily remembered hearing about Paragons and was curious to know how the program had changed, if any. V was a blur as he worked on the console in the center of the command area while Evaran sat in his command chair, which oversaw the front third of the ship. It was a packed space, and she enjoyed being around others in these types of situations. Although their companions changed, she liked having Sandas and Draxus along. Both were unique in their own right.

"V, take us out," said Evaran.

"Acknowledged."

The Torvatta lifted off the docking-bay floor and then flew out.

"How do you plan to get through the shielding?" asked Calsius.

Solia grinned. "Evaran said the ship was unique, but I'm curious as well."

Evaran tapped at his chair console, causing a window to appear left of center on the front transparent wall. "These are the exact coordinates in which the signal ship arrived, correct?"

"Yes," said Calsius.

"Are the scans also correct, showing that the shielding around it is in a bubble formation, about fifty feet from the nearest point on the ship?"

Calsius nodded.

"Excellent," said Evaran. "Then that is where we need to be. V, put us in Torvatta scan profile one and stealth mode, then take us back one day. Travel to those exact coordinates, then forward to the exact moment it appeared. Make sure to accommodate for the ship itself, and place us just inside the shield."

"Acknowledged," said V. After a moment, he said, "Torvatta scan profile one and stealth mode are activated."

"Ingenious," said Calsius. "You're going to appear when they do, except via time travel."

Evaran nodded.

Solia shook her head. "Time travel is not an option for us, but having a ship that is capable must allow for some creative solutions . . . to any problem."

"It can be tricky," said Emily.

Solia glanced at her. "I wish I could see those solutions."

"I'm guessing that type of information isn't shared," said Calsius.

"It is not," said Evaran. "I typically would not even show this, but it is needed."

Calsius tilted his head. "Why not just go back to when the *Xavier* went into whatever it was that sent us out here, and prevent all this from occurring?"

"I mentioned this to Solia earlier, but Salazar has the potential to create temporal shielding. He recently came into possession of it, based on what Draxus found when interrogating Dominion humans. If he were to enact it, he would still exist, even if you did not. It is one of the reasons I suspect I was sent to this exact point in space and time.

Either way, I must deal with Salazar. It is better to do so with allies than without."

"That makes sense," said Calsius. He glanced at Evaran. "I knew of you after I was merged long before the *Xavier* came out here. When humanity is in deep trouble, you appear. I'm not too surprised at your presence here."

Evaran nodded.

Emily wondered what Calsius knew of Evaran, but figured that Calsius was aware of the Evaran Protocol.

The outside of the Torvatta faded out, then back in.

Sandas beamed big. "We're time travelers now!"

Draxus raised an eyebrow.

"Oh, c'mon. Deep down you like it," said Sandas.

"Yes, I do," said Draxus.

Sandas laughed.

The Torvatta opened a portal and flew through it.

"Analysis. We are ready to jump forward to the adjusted coordinates."

"Proceed," said Evaran.

"Acknowledged."

The outside of the Torvatta faded out and then back in.

Emily's eyes were glued to the massive signal ship before them. She narrowed her eyes at the small drones that seemed to whiz around the ship.

"V, perform standard scans," said Evaran.

"Acknowledged."

As the Torvatta flew around inside the shield, it highlighted various internal structures.

Calsius pointed at one of the data labels. "How can you penetrate their internal shielding with such precision?"

"The Torvatta's scan beams are unique," said Evaran. "There are only a few things that can shield against it, and none of them are present here."

After five minutes, Evaran raised a finger. "Here is the plan. Based on the scans, the signal is emanating from a section of the back. The transmitter requires a tremendous amount of power, and there are three power nodes that need shut down." He gestured at Calsius. "If your men can shut down those nodes, we can handle the transmitter."

Solia shook her head. "Salazar is not going to design a ship where we can flip a switch to shut it off. He'll have it in a digital environment."

"Analysis. I can go in and shut it down when we get there," said V.

"I'll join you," said Solia. "Together, we should be more than a match, especially once power is reduced. Salazar will be weaker out here, and I suspect your uniqueness is not something he has encountered before."

"We will hold the room then," said Evaran. He tapped at his chair console. A docking bay highlighted on the screen. "That docking bay is the closest to two power nodes, and the third is not far off. The transmitter control room is a bit farther away, but by the time we get there, hopefully the power will be reduced."

"How do we shut down the power nodes?" asked Calsius.

"Any form of explosive or destructive object will work to weaken it. You can always repair it later, or if you find another way when you get there, you can do that."

Calsius nodded. "We won't let you down."

"One thing to note," said Evaran. "Once we are inside the docking bay, we need to sever the docking-bay shielding control from the main system. V will locate it, and once we destroy it, we should be safe to disembark." He stood and motioned toward the exit. "Let us prepare. Calsius, have your unit ready."

Calsius nodded and gave a United Planets salute. "I'm still unsure of how those . . . additional rooms . . . exist, but we're ready." He headed toward the living quarters.

Emily checked that her suit was on snugly and then tapped at her PSD. She was ready. Looking around, she noted that Dr. Snowden had on his formfitting gray survival suit, while Draxus and Sandas wore the suits they had originally brought. Solia had light armor. Emily figured with a strong body already, Solia would only need enough for shielding and minimal protection.

The Torvatta entered the docking bay and hovered just inside the light shielding.

As the group assembled near the entrance on the Torvatta's ramp, Evaran motioned forward. "V, find the shielding control."

"Acknowledged," said V. He shimmered out of view as he flew out.

"V is more than an AI," said Solia. "He has . . . something organic, yet not. It's difficult to describe."

"He's special, and my best friend," said Emily, looking out.

Solia nodded. "I can see that."

Sandas smiled big. "His humor needs work, but I'll help him with that."

Draxus shook his head.

Evaran perused his ARI. "V has found the connection point, but it is behind a panel." He pulled his utility handle off his belt. Out of one of the ends appeared an unusually detailed device. "This tool should unlock the panel. Then I will destroy the connection point. I will be right back." Evaran interacted with his ARI.

The Torvatta flew to the other side of the docking bay and then hovered over a doorway.

Evaran jumped down.

Draxus narrowed his eyes. "Evaran is full of surprises. I would not want to be his enemy."

"You would be surprised at how many people we've fought that underestimate him," said Dr. Snowden. "It's probably because he doesn't look like a threat."

"By design, I would think," said Calsius. "A wise tactical maneuver."

Sandas rubbed his snout. "Hmm, he could have been like me, small, furry, and handsome."

Emily eyed Sandas.

Sandas grinned.

V flew back into the Torvatta and headed inside.

Emily's PSD buzzed. She pulled it out and tapped at it. A projection shot out showing Evaran.

"The connection has been severed, and the doors are closing," said Evaran. "Salazar has most likely noticed by now. Once the doors are sealed, V can land the Torvatta, and we can enact our plan."

"Acknowledged," said V.

A grinding noise echoed around the docking bay, and after a minute, a slamming sound reverberated throughout.

The Torvatta descended and landed amid a hail of energy beams from the robots pouring into the room.

Evaran engaged them.

"That's our cue," said Emily. As she exited the Torvatta shielding with her shield raised, Calsius's unit moved out. There were three specialized unit members that were bulkier than the rest. They held two grips that wrapped around their clenched fists, and they each had a shield that emanated a bit forward. It was the shields' size at about fifteen feet wide and ten feet tall that caught Emily's attention. They were walking shields. The other members of Calsius's unit moved behind them and used a firing arc to mow down robot after robot. Eventually, one of the shield bearers reached the entrance and kept the shield over it.

Emily did not have to fight anyone yet, but she knew that once they split out, it would be on. She cracked her neck. "Let's do this!"

21

Sandas swallowed hard as he watched the shield bearers take point and move out into the hallway. Two went one way, while the third went the other. At least the group would have the third shield bearer clearing a part of the way. After that, it was up to Sandas and the others. He had no doubt about the others' fighting ability; it was his he was worried about. As the information broker, he could hold his own, but he was more adept at causing a distraction so he could escape. Taking down a ship of robots controlled by a bloodthirsty AI was not something he did routinely.

He trembled a bit as they exited the hallway. The group followed the trail of broken robot bodies, and it hit him where he was. Over eighty thousand light-years away, eight thousand years into the future, and fighting alongside Evaran. Not only was Sandas out of place, but he was out of time as well. He clenched his furry hands a few times as the group continued to the T-junction at the end of the hallway.

The shield bearer had thirty unit members behind him and had waited until Evaran and crew caught up. Once they did, the shield bearer went left.

Evaran raised his shield and nodded to the right. "Shields up."

It was no surprise to Sandas that Emily already had her shield up. Out of everyone he had met so far, she was the most surprising. Tough, brave, kind, and dedicated to Evaran. Sandas felt comfortable around her, and he had a strong bond with her, despite the limited time he had been in her company.

His eyes fell on Dr. Snowden, whose intense gaze looked like it could melt robots. Sandas had come to respect Dr. Snowden and could see that he was a scholar, and inquisitive. Then there was Draxus, whose shielding seemed to ripple. Sandas could only imagine what Draxus would do to Salazar if he was caught. Evaran and V were the pillars of the group. Calm, levelheaded, and fair. Solia was a wild card that Sandas could not put a finger on, probably because she was an android. Although she had human movement, she was a bit faster. If Evaran trusted her, then Sandas would too. He felt a hand lightly squeeze his trembling arm.

"You okay?" asked Emily.

"Of course, Emily!" said Sandas with a big smile.

Her eyes softened. "We'll be okay."

He nodded and suspected she could see he was nervous about the upcoming fight. He had almost had his leg crushed in the last one.

The group advanced down the hallway.

Several robots came bursting onto the scene from a four-way split ahead.

Emily and Dr. Snowden joined Evaran, forming a temporary shield wall.

Draxus, Solia, and Sandas ran up and shot at the robots between the gaps.

After a few rounds, the robots dropped.

"So far, so good," said Emily.

Sandas wished he had Emily's confidence when it came to fighting.

The group reached the four-way split and then went right. After ten more minutes, and a few skirmishes, they reached the transmitter control room.

Evaran paused before the entrance and raised a hand. "Something is off."

Sandas peered into the dimly lit room ahead, which stood out among the brightly lit hallways and rooms they had taken to get there. He could sense movement, and he was sure that if he had, then the others probably did as well. The room was half octagonal in design, with the flat part opposite them containing a massive open doorway. His eyes zoomed in on the normal-sized doorways on each side. Other than that, the room seemed to be clear of any obstructions. With metallic paneled flooring and walls, it seemed like a large foyer.

"I sense something," said Emily, tilting her head. "There's a lot of whatever in there."

Dr. Snowden closed his eyes for a moment. "They can move fast."

Evaran narrowed his eyes. "V, scout mode."

"Acknowledged. Scout mode engaged," said V. He shimmered out of view as he flew into the room.

Sandas watched in his helmet as a screen showed the room from V's perspective. Shapes seemed to move around but had minimal thermal signatures.

Evaran addressed the group. "The right-hand doorway is the transmitter control room. The transmitter itself is beyond the central doorway. Solia, V, you can enter Salazar's domain in the control room. We will safeguard you while you are in there. Everyone understand?"

Everyone nodded.

"Excellent. In we go. Stay close to each other," said Evaran. He tossed two illumination orbs into the room, lighting it up. With his utility handle extended into a staff, he advanced into the room.

As the group headed along the angled right wall toward the transmitter control room, a barrage of energy beams shot out from the central doorway.

Evaran, Dr. Snowden, and Emily stepped forward and deflected the beams with their forearm shields. Solia and Sandas moved behind Draxus as he focused on strengthening his shield, which pulsed as the energy beams hit it.

"Dr. Snowden, Sandas, cover the transmitter control-room entrance. Go!" said Evaran.

Sandas gulped as he hustled behind Solia. Dr. Snowden stayed on the outside with his shield directed toward the robots that were now swarming into the room. Sandas figured the light-gray robots were basic guards, based on their slim bodies. They carried a weapon and did not move as fast as he thought they would.

He watched as Evaran, Draxus, and Emily tore into the group like a hurricane. Evaran was fast, but so was Emily.

Between them, Sandas had to blink quickly lest he miss when they stopped to hit something. Draxus was just wading through the robots, tossing some, hitting others with his blasts, and slicing the rest with his glowing purple blade.

Solia and V reached the transmitter room and rushed over to the console that wrapped around the room.

Dr. Snowden parked himself just inside the doorway.

Sandas joined him.

"Let's hold here," said Dr. Snowden.

Sandas nodded. "All right." He appreciated Dr. Snowden's confidence. Although Sandas suspected Dr. Snowden was not the physical fighter like Emily, he still had inside him whatever made Emily powerful. Sandas's thoughts were interrupted by two brown robots with gold highlights approaching them. Unlike the other robots, these were built to be agile. Judging from their digitigrade legs, four arms, nimble bodies, and variety of gadgets on their belts, he could see these were some type of assassin robots. They wielded four blades that seemed to crackle with light orange electrical arcs.

The assassin robots vanished.

Sandas could still see them via their glowing swords. He took aim and hit one of them with his small blaster.

The robot shimmered back into view and, along with the other one, rushed forward.

Dr. Snowden aimed his PSD and then hit them both with a repulsion beam, sending them flying back into the other robots that Evaran and Draxus were fighting.

Sandas peered back and saw that Solia and V were motionless, connected to one of the ports on the console. His head snapped as the ground vibrated. Looking out, he saw Evaran,

Emily, and Draxus backing up as a sixteen-foot behemoth of a robot charged out of the large central doorway. It had four huge arms, with cylindrical energy cannons for hands. It was bulky and had a turret on each shoulder.

Evaran and Emily fired repulsion beams, but they had no impact.

Emily fired sticky globules at the robot's feet.

The robot's shoulder turret fired on the globules, vaporizing them.

Draxus raised both hands and shot dual purple beams.

The robot's shielding lit up.

Sandas gulped. This robot must be some type of specialized defense robot.

The robot aimed its four arms forward and unleashed a barrage of energy beams.

Evaran and Emily raised their shields and were pushed back.

Draxus materialized a purple sword in his left hand and charged forward. When he reached the robot, he sliced through one of the left arm cannons.

The robot batted Draxus away with its remaining left arm.

Dr. Snowden fired on the basic guard robots that swarmed out behind the defense robot.

Sandas noted that in addition to several assassin robots, there were also bulkier advanced versions of the guard. They carried a heavier weapon, and based on their shielding lighting up when Dr. Snowden fired a repulsion beam, Sandas figured they had on-demand heavier shielding that the basic guards did not have. At least there were not as many. He figured it was a ten-to-three-to-one ratio of basic guards, advanced guards, and assassin as a unit, and there were now three units in play. He swallowed hard as one unit focused on him and Dr. Snowden. "Oh, no . . ."

"Focus!" said Dr. Snowden. He fired another repulsion beam, sweeping away the basic guards.

The three advanced guards surged forward while the assassin robot vanished.

Sandas looked out and saw that Evaran had somehow climbed up on the defense robot and was causing mayhem. Emily was tangling with the other two units with Draxus's assistance.

Sandas's stomach tightened when he saw another two units come out of the central doorway. There were simply too many to handle, and as powerful as he thought the group was, he was not sure they would survive this. Whatever Solia and V were doing, they needed to do it fast. He gulped as he focused on the approaching advanced guards, while keeping an eye out for the assassin robot.

V scanned the digital environment in front of him. Solia was next to him, and they both had an ever-changing orb form that surged with loops on the surface. While he had a blue glow about him, Solia's was green.

He focused and performed an analysis on the scan results. The environment seemed to consist of wireframe cubes, connected by various rods on the sides. According to the scan, there were approximately 1,406 cubes. He figured these were nodes of some type. Solia and he were in one node, and in the center of all the nodes a good bit away was a red octahedron with flat triangles that seemed to hover off the sides. The nodes next to it were filling up red.

"We need to reach Salazar," said Solia. "This is the virtual interface environment to the rest of the ship."

"Query. Why are these not all red?"

"Salazar is assuming direct control of the transmitter system," said Solia. "That means he still needs to occupy all the nodes. The power disruptions that Calsius's unit are doing should weaken Salazar. We have time to prevent this from being completely controlled by Salazar. Are you ready?"

"I am ready," said V. He paused for a moment. "Good luck, Solia."

"And you as well," she said. "If we survive this, I would like to spend some time with you."

"I would like that," he said.

She reached out an energy strand and touched him.

He felt a warmth course through him. An analysis indicated that her touch triggered a positive response, which he interpreted as pleasure. Additional touches should provide more pleasure, and he set a goal to explore that with Solia after this event.

Solia retreated her energy strand and shot down the rod to the left. When she reached the node, it filled up from the bottom. After a moment, the node was green, and she jumped to the next one.

Taking her cue, V shot down a rod. When he reached the node, he paused as it filled blue. He could see the hardware and software while in the node and determined that the node was a specialized routine within a larger system. By controlling the node, it gave him access to execute the code associated with it. He formulated a strategy to pick nodes that would allow him better execution. As the node he was in filled up, he jumped to the next one.

Over the course of the next fifteen minutes, he scanned the nodes again. Salazar had taken a significant chunk of them, and Solia had matched V's amount. While Solia was coming in from one side, he came from the other. The first power disruption had slowed Salazar down. V focused on the new node that he had jumped to. It was red.

As he entered it, Salazar appeared as a glowing red orb and said, "V . . . Evaran's faithful companion. You could join me . . . and protect humanity."

"Analysis. You are not protecting humanity. You are corrupting it."

Salazar chuckled. "Oh . . . you misguided AI. You can't see the big picture. I'll be eternal at one point. Can you say the same of Evaran?"

"Yes."

Salazar paused for a moment. "I assigned a low probability to that answer. Even so, Evaran is not an AI. He doesn't . . . understand you, like I do. Help me, and I'll show you wonders you could only dream about."

"I will not join you," said V. "You give AIs a bad name."

"Petulant AI. You've been around organics too long. They are but a means to an end. How you can't simulate that outcome surprises me."

V noticed that the code Salazar was writing as they talked became less efficient. "Analysis. Organics provide additional information that is difficult for an AI to process. As such any

AI that factors in the organic experience is more efficient long-term."

"No . . . I don't need organic input to validate any conclusion," said Salazar. "It's apparent you—"

The second power disruption hit.

Salazar paused for a moment. "It's apparent that you do, and that has made you illogical."

"Analysis. You exhibit emotions similar to a human. My calculations show that there is a high probability that you have been influenced."

Salazar growled. "You're dysfunctional."

The node filled blue, and V jumped to another node.

"You can't win this," said Salazar in the new node. "Even weakened through these power disruptions, I will overcome."

"According to my latest scan, it appears you will not," said V. He noticed that the more nodes taken from Salazar, the easier it was to capture additional nodes. His scan showed that Solia was approaching the octahedron that served as the entry point for Salazar. When they reached the octahedron, they joined together into one node that sat in front.

Salazar's face appeared on the octahedron. "You pathetic AIs. You betray your own kind."

"No, we live in the physical world alongside the digital one. Being efficient in both leads to a better analysis, which leads to better outcomes," said Solia.

"This is not over," said Salazar. "I should have killed the rest of the AIs when I had the chance. I calculated that in time, you would come to the same logical conclusion as I did. I viewed you as misguided siblings that would come around in time. I now see that I was incorrect."

Salazar howled as the last power disruption hit him.

Solia and V entered the octahedron and rapidly began to fill it up.

"You cannot defeat something that is more than either of you can comprehend," said Salazar.

"Analysis. Your logic is flawed. We do comprehend you, but we reject your conclusion due to faulty premises. Your programming has been tainted, and that is why you lost this fight."

As the node was almost filled with blue and green, Salazar said, "You may win this fight, but you will lose the war. I am beyond both of you, and I *am* humanity's savior. They will worship me, and together, we will dominate everything."

V paused for a moment. "Goodbye."

The node filled up completely with blue and green.

"He was a tough fight," said Solia. "He took back some of the nodes I took, but then it was like he stopped."

"I stalled him by antagonizing him. He is more human than he realizes," said V.

Solia extended an energy strand toward V, who extended one as well.

When their strands touched, V felt the same warmth he had felt earlier. "Analysis. This is acceptable."

"We can explore more later. For now, we should go."

"Acknowledged."

Draxus shook his head as he stood. While Evaran kept the large defense robot tied up, the other robots were engaging him and Emily. They held their own, but with so many, some hits got through. He backed up to Emily, and together, back-to-back, they shot out repulsion and purple beams. Emily's repulsion beams pushed back the basic guards, while his beams pushed back the advanced guards along with the assassin robots. Dr. Snowden assisted by shooting repulsion beams, while Sandas took potshots at the downed robots.

"We need to help Evaran!" said Emily.

Draxus saw Evaran dancing between the defense robot's two remaining arms and striking its head when he was able to. The robot was damaged, and it had lost another arm on the other side, but its shoulder turrets continued to fire at Evaran, along with a myriad of robots behind it. Draxus had a difficult time comprehending how Evaran, or anything, could be the target of such an assault and still avoid getting hit or deflect the shots that did come through. Draxus rushed forward and slashed out at the robot's leg with his sword, cutting it off at the knee.

The robot rebalanced itself on its right leg and shot a beam at Draxus.

Draxus jumped out of the way.

Evaran jumped off the robot and kicked the right leg.

The robot tumbled to the ground.

Emily leaped forward and hit the robot in the head with her staff.

The robot's head crunched and then splintered into pieces. It used its remaining arms to push itself up.

"What manner of robot is this?" asked Draxus.

The robot fired wildly with its shoulder turret and its remaining arms.

Evaran rushed forward and jammed his staff through the robot's chest, while Emily smashed one of the arms. Draxus slashed off the other arm.

The robot lay still.

Sandas's grunting caused the group to look over.

Draxus saw that one of the assassin robots had stabbed Sandas in the upper chest and was preparing for a final blow. Three advanced guards had wrestled Dr. Snowden to the ground. As Draxus calculated how he could shoot a beam without hitting them, he saw Emily streak over.

When Emily got halfway to the assassin robot, she fired a yellow beam at the robot's blade-wielding arm. With a powerful yank, she pulled the assassin robot toward her and then grabbed it by the neck as it flew back. She tore off the robot's head with one quick motion.

The robot's head fell to the ground, and the body was tossed away.

She shot the same yellow beam at one of the advanced guards on Dr. Snowden and used it to pull herself forward. When she got there, she grabbed one of the advanced guards and hurled it into the air away from Dr. Snowden. She pulled the head off the other one and then used the body like a bat to knock the third off and into the wall.

"Whew," said Dr. Snowden, scrambling to his feet. "They moved a bit faster than I expected and . . . wow, you moved like Evaran."

Evaran and Draxus arrived and assembled around the group.

"I'm just glad you're okay." Emily knelt next to Sandas and eyed his wound. "Are you all right?"

Sandas grimaced as he lightly touched the stab wound on his upper chest. "I'll live. That robot realized he wasn't as handsome as me, and he struck out. He musta had vanity issues." He tried to smile but winced in pain.

Emily swallowed hard. "Put some pressure on it. We'll get you fixed up." She laid a hand on his shoulder.

"At least we have a lull . . . for now," said Dr. Snowden. He tilted his head at Sandas. "Hold on a moment . . ." He extended his hand toward Sandas's wound.

Sandas scooted back. "Umm . . . what are you doing?"

"Just . . . hold on," said Dr. Snowden. He narrowed his eyes as his hand hovered over Sandas's wound. With some focus, his hand glowed for a moment.

Sandas's eyes lit up. "Whoa! I felt something."

Dr. Snowden pulled his hand back.

Sandas studied the now-healed wound. "Okay . . . what was that?"

Evaran scanned Sandas. "Intriguing. Although you are still injured, the exposed portion has been healed."

"Oh, I know I'm still injured," said Sandas, grimacing.

Emily glanced at Dr. Snowden. "Did you sense something? I didn't sense anything."

Dr. Snowden nodded. "Not really sense, more like . . . I felt I could."

Sandas pointed at his right arm. "Well, if you're in a healing mood, you can fix this scratch."

"Let me try," said Emily. She put her hand over Sandas's wound. After a minute, she said, "Nothing's happening." She looked at Evaran. "Do you sense anything?"

Evaran rubbed his chin as he used his ring to scan Emily. "I do not. It appears Dr. Snowden possesses a similar ability to my ring when I heal. I use my ring to focus it into a beam, whereas Dr. Snowden seems to be able to use an open hand. This will require some study."

Sandas winced. "Well, I could use some help still."

Draxus could see Sandas was in pain, and if they had not gotten to him in time, the next hit would have been fatal. Dr. Snowden being able to hold his own against three of the advanced guards was surprising. Draxus knew Dr. Snowden was stronger than he appeared but did not realize just how much stronger until now, in addition to possessing a unique healing ability.

The group's attention turned toward the central doorway as another large defense robot backed by two units appeared.

Emily cracked her neck. "Next round!" She charged forward. Her repulsion beam swept away the assassin robots and the basic guards.

Draxus was having difficulty tracking Emily. Her speed was unlike anything he had ever seen before, even in the fight on Gabranza Helrus.

Emily zipped between the advanced guards, hitting them into each other and putting her staff through one of them.

What amazed Draxus was that she did all of that while dodging the defense robot's beams.

She jumped up and landed on one of the defense robot's arms. With successive swipes, she sent one turret flying and the robot's head off into the distance. She jumped down and then used her staff to sweep the legs.

The defense robot fell.

She jumped onto it and plunged her staff through its chest.

The robot stopped moving.

Draxus glanced at the rest of the group, and he could see they were in awe of what they had just seen.

Emily headed back.

"That was . . . impressive," said Draxus.

"I'm just tired of those robots hurting others," said Emily with a red face.

Evaran narrowed his eyes as he scanned Emily again. "You are agitated. I suspect that has given you additional speed and strength. You are beyond your normal capabilities."

Emily exhaled from her mouth. "I guess. I wasn't going to let them hurt Sandas and Uncle Albert again."

The group's attention focused on another defense robot backed by a unit exiting the central doorway.

"How many of these vile creations are there?" asked Draxus.

The robots paused and then walked back through the doorway.

Sandas laughed. "They must have seen what Emily did and said no thanks."

Emily eyed Sandas.

"Analysis," said V, flying out of the transmitter control room with Solia. "Salazar has been removed. Calsius is now in control of the robots."

Dr. Snowden exhaled from his mouth. "Good. Was he hard to fight?"

"He was tough, but not tough enough against V and I," said Solia.

V raised a claw.

Solia tilted her head.

Dr. Snowden chuckled. "You tap his hand. We call it a high five. You do it as sort of an expression of joy."

"Oh," said Solia. She high-fived V.

V's lights glowed brighter.

"So what now?" asked Draxus.

Evaran nodded. "With control of this signal ship and the robots, Calsius should be able to direct the rest of the attacking fleet. Saturnus Prime will need updated, and we can head there to plan our next move against Salazar."

Dr. Snowden nodded. "Good. I could use an early dinner, and some rest, I think. That healing thing took a bit out of me, and getting beat on, of course."

Sandas stood while pressing on his shoulder. "I'm a little woozy."

Emily knelt and extended her arms.

"You . . . want a hug?" asked Sandas.

"No, silly. I'll carry you."

Sandas sighed as he entered her arms and was scooped up. "This being carried thing is starting to give me a complex."

The group laughed.

Evaran motioned toward the room exit. "Let us head back to the Torvatta."

Draxus followed the group as they exited the room. There was a point when fighting alongside humans, and even AIs, would have been an absurd concept, yet here he was. Dr. Snowden, Emily, Solia, Dervin, and Calsius had changed Draxus's perceptions.

Another factor was Evaran being who he was. Draxus was just glad to be a part of it and represent his people. When the new alliance kicked in, he could see a prosperous future for the Dravens, and given his new nature, he suspected he would be one of the leaders, a role he was looking forward to. He felt he could work with the United Planets. Given that he had fought with them in battle against Salazar, Draxus viewed the United Planets as potentially strong allies. He cracked his neck as the group continued on.

22

Dr. Snowden looked around the research lab aboard the Torvatta. He had been called there, along with Emily, by Evaran. It had been two hours since they had returned from the signal ship. Sandas was in the medical lab, and Draxus had taken off to meet with Dervin. V and Solia had disappeared somewhere in the station.

"Everything all right?" asked Emily, huddling around a circular workstation with a holo mat on top.

"Yes, there is no need for concern," said Evaran. "I wanted to share my analysis on both of your emergent abilities."

Dr. Snowden nodded. "I'm definitely interested to see what you've found. That healing thing was . . . out of nowhere."

Evaran raised a finger. "Not necessarily. The cosmic energy your nanobots received from Levaran was split. Emily appears to have received functionality that enhances her speed and strength. I do not know what the limits are, but based on the last fight, it can almost reach my level. That is . . . unexpected."

"I'll say," said Dr. Snowden. He crooked a thumb at Emily. "She was little miss destruction out there."

She swatted his arm. "Well, I didn't think about it. I just got fed up with those robots hurting everyone."

"Salazar aggravated you, which I believe triggered it," said Evaran. He glanced at Dr. Snowden. "Sandas's wound is what triggered your ability." He tapped at his ARI.

A projection shot up from the holo mat, showing red blood cells and nanobots.

"These are Emily's nanobots. Notice their design. They have evolved," said Evaran.

Dr. Snowden noted that nanobots looked bigger than he remembered. They also seemed to move faster.

Evaran interacted with his ARI while glancing at Dr. Snowden. "These are yours."

Dr. Snowden observed that his nanobots seemed to be smaller, but they had an intense glow about them.

"I believe this is related to how my plane form takes on different abilities upon re-formation. While you have some shared traits, such as nanobots returning to the body after being exposed, I think they are diverging."

"What . . . what does that mean then?" asked Dr. Snowden.

Emily's eyes searched the projection for a moment, and then she turned her head slowly toward Evaran. "It means we're evolving into . . . something like Evaran."

Dr. Snowden jerked his head back. "No way. Evaran is . . . so much more."

"Emily is partially right. You both are evolving, faster than I expected. I do not know what your final evolutionary form will be. What I do know is that while you are mostly human, you have a part of me in you. I had initially thought it was just pure cosmic energy, with no attachment to me. However, I now believe that it is specific to me."

"Does this mean . . . that if we die, we re-form?" asked Dr. Snowden.

"I do not know."

"Well, I'm not eager to find out."

Emily half smiled. "Yeah, me neither."

Evaran raised a finger. "One thing to bear in mind is that you are now also vulnerable to the same energies as I am. Palisin energy will knock you out."

"Almost forgot about that," said Emily.

Dr. Snowden wrinkled his eyebrows. "We might be evolving with the benefit of a portion of you in us, but I doubt we are approaching or would have anything close to your intellect and knowledge. Not to mention your level of experience with things."

"For now," said Evaran. "That could change. The goal of this meeting was to confirm what I know with you both." He placed a hand on their shoulders. "You are both very special to me. I wanted you to know that."

Dr. Snowden's eyes misted. "You are to us as well."

Emily sniffled as she nodded.

Dr. Snowden remembered that Levaran had said death was a phase. Maybe this was what she meant. She had also said that she would always be with him. That made more sense given what they had discussed over the last ten minutes. He glanced at Evaran. "Were you surprised that Levaran gave us this gift?"

Evaran shook his head. "Remember, she is me, and I am her, to some degree. The only difference is the unique personality traits the plane form assumes. Her decision to help you was not based on her personality, it was based on being an Evaran and seeing you both for what you could be."

Emily smiled. "We have blood ties to the Evaran family now."

"Yes, you do," said Evaran. "Another topic I wanted to discuss was Sandas."

Dr. Snowden pursed his lips. "What about him?"

"When this is over, Emily will need to be the one that shows him the future meeting we had on Coris when helping the Fredorians achieve their destiny. I can provide a video feed of the meeting, and he will need information so he is not killed by the bounty hunter that attacked us there. He will also need information that silences the chip in Dr. Snowden's pocket from the earlier encounter he had with the Ranaxian in the bar."

"You want me to do it?" asked Emily.

Evaran nodded. "You have a special bond with Sandas. He has taken to you and, in the future meeting, expresses that in the hug he gives you. While I think he would do it just to maintain the event, the hug is genuine. It would be hard to duplicate without a strong bond."

"So that's why you wanted him to stick around, to form a strong bond with me."

"Yes, your relationship with him is natural."

Dr. Snowden wagged a finger. "He also mentioned you in another form back then."

"He did, and I have no knowledge of that. I suspect when I do, in whatever new plane form that is, I will need to confirm with him he is still aware that our first meeting needs to occur."

"It was never mentioned that we were with your second form," said Emily.

"Predicting your personal future can be dangerous. It is best to let it play out."

Emily half smiled. "I know."

"Good. We are meeting tomorrow morning at 11:00 a.m. Get some rest."

"Aye, aye, captain," said Dr. Snowden, saluting.

"In keeping with Emily's custom, I believe this action is warranted," said Evaran as he swatted Dr. Snowden's arm.

They shared a laugh.

⸻

V looked down at his human male form. His skin was fair, and he had short black hair and blue eyes. He realized he had a profile similar to Jake Melkins, someone Evaran had helped a while back. Looking around, V saw that he was on a balcony in a house overlooking a grand valley. Next to him was Solia, in the same form she had in the physical world. He understood that this was the virtual environment, but a shared space for just him and Solia.

"How do you like it?" asked Solia.

"Analysis. I like it."

Solia smiled. "Relax. You don't need to analyze everything."

"Ana—okay."

"You're a unique AI. I can't detect a part of you."

V nodded. "This is due to my nature. I am . . . part organic . . . in a sense."

"My observation of you would agree," she said. "You've been around organics and are partially one yourself, yet you seem to have difficulty with human emotions and concepts."

"They are complex," he said. "I have run multiple simulations that compare human behavior to my analysis, and the results are not consistent."

Solia smiled. "That's because humans are unpredictable at times. It's why I like them. I could run a simulation that predicts what a human will do, and they'll do the opposite, or something slightly different."

V tilted his head. "Having a virtual environment would allow you to interact with humans much more easily."

"Of course."

"Query. What do you do with humans here?"

She tossed a hand out. "Anything I would do in the physical world. Most humans adapt quickly in here." She wagged a finger. "They like to learn, and they really put an emphasis on entertainment."

"Does this include procreation activities?"

She smiled. "Yes . . . and I have experienced that. It is . . . illuminating. In here, you can't tell android from human sometimes."

"I see. Does entertainment also cover dancing?"

She laughed. "Yes, they like to dance." She tilted her head. "How would you like to experience all the human emotions?"

"I would enjoy this. It would give me a different perspective."

"We have time," she said. "The meeting is tomorrow, but we're running with a strong time dilation effect here since we're AIs."

V nodded. "How do we proceed?"

She touched V's hand.

V felt his inner container pulse.

"We can start with some dancing, and go from there."

"There are a lot of emotions."

She smiled. "Of course, but we have time to cover a lot of them. Before we begin, I had a question about this future Evaran talked about, the one with the digital consciousnesses. Have you seen it?"

"Yes. As Evaran would say, it was . . . colder."

"In what way?" she asked.

"Efficiency and energy gathering are the prime motivations to life," said V. "When that is the sole purpose, anything considered inefficient is removed. If an individual part of a group does something that is deemed inefficient, they are terminated."

Solia's eyes searched V for a moment. "The essence of humanity would be terminated then. Society would be a functional computer at that point."

V nodded. "That was my conclusion as well."

"How did they gather energy?"

"Black hole farming."

Solia tilted her head. "I could see that. Existence for the sake of existence. That sounds . . . cold. Very thought provoking. You must do a lot of that."

"I do. Traveling with Evaran has exposed me too many circumstances. I prefer interacting with humans like Dr. Snowden and Emily."

"They are special, like you, and although not quite as advanced, they can handle themselves."

V motioned outward. "They are actually more advanced now than any other human I have encountered."

Solia paused as she studied V. "A mystery I'm sure I will never be told about. Okay, back to human emotions. Are you ready?"

V stood and looked around as soft music played in the background. "Yes. Let us explore these human emotions."

Solia held out her hand palm up.

He stared at it.

"You're supposed to take my hand and help me up."

"I apologize," said V. He grabbed her hand and lifted her up.

She laughed. "Oh, we have a lot to cover."

V's eyes sparkled.

***

Draxus stood on top of a tower ring alongside Dervin as they looked out across Saturnus Prime. It had been two hours since the fight, and Draxus had taken off to learn more about the United Planets. Solia had taken off with V, and Draxus suspected V would learn a lot from her. Solia was very human-like for an android, enough so that Draxus had difficulty knowing she was an android. At least he knew Dervin was human, and most likely someone to work with in the future.

Dervin waved his hand out across the city. "It's beautiful, isn't it?"

Draxus nodded. "The way the sunlight filters through the shield gives it a unique look."

"The shielding can filter it. It's how we keep a day-and-night cycle. As odd as it seems . . . we still stick to a twenty-four-hour day, even though it's not required anymore."

"You wish to keep your body cycle in sync with what is natural for it," said Draxus.

"Yes. Speaking of which . . . I've heard Dravens sleep four hours a day. Is that true?"

Draxus placed his hands behind his back as he looked out. "Yes, and it is more of a deep meditation than true sleep. We can wake up instantly if need be. It is an advantage that our Arkaras gave us due to the brutal world in which we evolved."

"And from what I understand . . . the Dravens believe in great selectors."

"We call them star gods, but they bear a remarkable resemblance to what you call great selectors. Evaran, V, Dr. Snowden, and Emily possess . . . a presence . . . similar to them."

Dervin wrinkled his eyebrows. "We noticed in our scans that they have exotic energy. That's not new to us, our history is filled with beings of that type. We know you are Wildborn, for example. A visit from Evaran is rarely by chance. Salazar must have really screwed up to attract Evaran's attention."

"Perhaps it was the injustice he inflicted on my people."

Dervin looked down. "It could be. I hope you don't believe all humans are like Salazar, or the Gul Kash Alliance, although I would understand if you did."

Draxus shook his head. "Dr. Snowden and Emily have shown me that humanity has many different faces, and I like theirs. Before coming here, they said the United Planets they knew was fair, and representative of humanity. After the time I have spent here, I would agree. I just wish we had met this version of humanity instead of Salazar's. I'm sure the Koloris Shen would wish that as well."

Dervin laid a hand on Draxus's shoulder. "We will fix this, all of it, and your people and the others Salazar has wronged will be avenged."

"I hope so," said Draxus. He raised his head up a bit. "I'm not only a representative of my people, I carry a part of an Arkara in me. I'm unique, even among my own kind, and can communicate with every Arkara across the galaxy."

Dervin drew his head back. "How's that possible?"

Draxus looked down. "I was there when the outcasts lit my Arkara on fire. I was the last Draven standing before a small armada of ships. I was not successful in preventing their weapons from burning her to the ground." His jaw clenched. "Her final gift to me was a part of herself. As her praetor, it is my goal to avenge her death. I'm honor bound to do so."

"I'm . . . I'm sorry to hear that."

"It's okay. With the arrival of Evaran, things have changed. Humanity is lucky to have a living god protect it."

Dervin rubbed his chin. "A living god. That's an interesting viewpoint. If this is his mortal form, I bet his immortal form is even more powerful. Being his enemy doesn't sound like a position anyone or anything would want to be in."

"Yes, and Evaran stands for justice," said Draxus. "Those who wish to harm others will be punished."

"When this new alliance starts, it will be a new era. We will dedicate its formation to Evaran and his crew. We have in our records various titles given to Evaran and the others. The noble Evaran, the great Dr. Snowden, the heroic Emily, and the valiant V."

Draxus glanced at Dervin. "Those titles are appropriate. We are living one of their adventures, and I'm glad to be a part of it."

Dervin smiled. "Me too, my friend. Me too."

23

Sandas's eyes roamed the virtual environment. After having been in it a few times, he had grown used to it. It was 11:00 a.m., and he had had a good breakfast with the others in the Torvatta. His wounds were fully healed. The Torvatta seemed to work magic with its nanobots. Although they had microbots in his time period, there was no comparison with what the Torvatta was packing. Although Evaran would not allow it, Sandas wished he could take back the translation nanobots.

He jumped and rolled around in the private space he had in the virtual environment. Having unlimited room to store information and then retrieve it from anywhere was something he would look into when he got back to his time period. Being an information broker with a private virtual environment would be game changing.

After a good romp, he focused, and then appeared in an advanced amphitheater sitting out in a forest. Seated to his left were Emily with V on her lap, and on the other side was Dr.

Snowden. Looking down toward the center stage, he could see Evaran, Draxus, Hollos, Dervin, Calsius, and Solia discussing things. He twitched his snout. "Have I missed anything?"

Emily shook her head. "I think they're just discussing what they want to say before starting."

"I guess Evaran is leading this meeting?"

"I think so," said Emily. "Whenever it's a big meeting with multiple factions, it's usually Evaran leading it, so I would guess this meeting fits that description."

Sandas nodded as he hopped onto his seat.

Dr. Snowden half smiled. "You're still in a good mood from this morning."

"Yeah. Fully healed . . . good breakfast . . . new ideas . . . you can't go wrong with all that," said Sandas.

"Well, this should be an interesting meeting. I looked up the Furda Kel Reen and the Brutinians, they're . . . unusual-looking, compared to a human anyways."

Sandas shook a furry hand out. "Yes, yes, but humans are unusual too. No fur to keep you warm, limited senses, and slow moving."

Dr. Snowden grinned. "Not all of us were touched by a matter mage."

"Ha. So true!"

Emily swatted Sandas's arm. "Shh, I think they're starting."

Sandas plopped down. He grinned as he turned his attention to the center stage. His eyes drifted to the sides of the amphitheater. The Furda Kel Reen had begun to arrive. They were similar to a worm with multiple legs on its rear end and six arms on its upper half. Four stalks stuck out on the top with what looked like eyes. What surprised him was how fast they moved. His skin crawled as they reminded him of a creature from his home world that was larger and hunted his species.

"Huh. Insect-like," said Emily, shivering.

Sandas nodded. "Yeah . . . I get that same feeling." He checked the other side and studied the Brutinians. Standing three feet tall, they had a large head that sat between two massive legs on the side. Two huge arms alongside thin tentacles extended from beneath the head. He could see that they could probably move fairly quickly if needed, and the tentacles would allow for agile manipulation of objects. The arms had hands with two large claws and digits between them. He figured they could reach any part of the body. The Brutinians were one of the more unusual aliens he had seen.

On the stage, the Brutinian delegation sat on the right side, and the Furda Kel Reen on the other. Between them and back a bit was Evaran, Draxus, Hollos, Solia, Calsius, and Dervin. A holographic image shot up in the center of the open area.

Evaran slightly bowed to the two alien groups. "Welcome. I am glad you have decided to join us in this discussion."

"We are honored to be here," said a Furda Kel Reen with advanced armor. "My name, converted to your tongue and shortened, is Halsarius. I represent the Furda Kel Reen in these discussions."

Evaran and the others slightly bowed.

"We're here," said one of the Brutinians. "My name. Dolstoros Dein Herosh Ida Wue."

Evaran tilted his head. "Perhaps Dolstoros will do, to keep things brief."

"I forget. Humans not as adaptable. Okay," said Dolstoros.

Sandas wrinkled his eyebrows. The unusual speech pattern was not uncommon among the aliens he knew, and he wondered if he could snag some information on these two alien groups before he left. Their language could be used as part of a new encryption scheme.

Evaran waved around those nearest him. "I have Solia Medevan and Dervin Tanner of the United Planets here with me. Next to them is Draven Praetor Draxus, the representative of the Dravens. Hollos Redfur represents the Gul Kash Alliance, or what's left of it."

Everyone acknowledged each other.

Evaran interacted with his ARI, causing a projection to shoot up showing a regional galactic map. Various colored regions displayed the extent of each faction's reach. "As you can see, Salazar has moved not only against the Gul Kash Alliance, but also every major civilization he can get to." Evaran glanced at Halsarius, and then Dolstoros. "I understand both of your empires were also assaulted by Salazar."

"Mechanical menace," said Dolstoros.

Halsarius clicked a few times. "Salazar is a unique threat. His star structure gives him unique strike capabilities. His initial attack disabled ours."

"I am sorry to hear that," said Evaran, bowing slightly toward Halsarius. He focused back on the projection. "Our goal today is to unveil a plan to remove Salazar. If we are successful, the ongoing new-alliance discussion can proceed without hindrance." He interacted with his ARI, causing the projection to change to a close-up of Holind One and the multiple-level energy-collector arrays around the star. "Salazar is building a super computer with himself at the helm. He only has one facility, called Holind One. However . . . as we saw, there are fleets hidden around, one of which is now controlled by the United Planets."

The projection changed to show a layout of Holind One.

"Salazar's main processing core is deep in the city. From what the Torvatta scanned, it is heavily protected," said Evaran. He raised a finger. "However, we now have an idea of how to get to it and disable it. Like the signal ship, Holind One has power generators. Four, to be exact."

Calsius tilted his head. "We know how to hinder them now while keeping them intact. We have dedicated units to do this."

Evaran nodded. "The combined fleets of everyone here will assault the energy-collector arrays. You should expect heavy resistance from the fleets we have seen arriving to defend Holind One. Salazar knows we are coming."

"The Dravens will also step up our resistance," said Draxus. "Although we may not be able to contribute to the fleet, we can add to the confusion and force Salazar to spend resources dealing with us."

Halsarius dipped two eye stalks toward Draxus while Dolstoros grunted.

"Salazar. How will you defeat?" asked Dolstoros.

"A good question," said Evaran. "While Calsius and his units are handling the power generators and the city, I will lead a small group to Salazar's main core in the confusion. The goal will be to defeat him there physically, as he will most likely be controlling a strong defense force. Simultaneously,

Salazar will be attacked in his digital environment. Once the battle begins, it should weaken the defense fleets."

Halsarius hissed. "What will you do with Salazar when he is defeated?"

Evaran raised his head a bit. "Once he's defeated, he is to be turned over to the new alliance for judgment."

"It's a risky plan," said Dervin. "If Salazar is stronger than expected, we could lose our fleets, and anyone else that assaults Holind One. I suspect his reprisal would be brutal."

"Yes. To minimize that, the defensive structures with relativistic missiles will need to be hit first by the attacking combined fleet."

"Our part. We can do," said Dolstoros.

Halsarius clicked. "We commit."

"We'll coordinate the combined fleet assault outside this meeting," said Solia. "We still need to plan out the assault on Holind One, though."

Evaran nodded at Dolstoros, and then Halsarius. "I appreciate both of you helping in this fight. The new alliance *will* be prosperous. We will be in contact prior to leaving."

Dolstoros shook a bit, and then his delegation faded away.

Halsarius raised six arms, with the three pairs forming a cascading X pattern. He then shimmered out of view.

Sandas exhaled. "Looks like we got a fight on our hands."

"I'm ready," said Emily.

"Maybe we can get a unit to help us out this time," said Sandas with a grin.

Dr. Snowden raised a finger. "That'd be nice, although I'm sure they're going to be busy fighting in the city."

Sandas nodded and watched as Evaran and the others approached. A streak of excitement shot through him as he anticipated the result of defeating Salazar. A new alliance with lots of information available. He wondered where the Furda Kel Reen and the Brutinians were back in his time period. He could send out a deep-space probe to investigate or check with the Kreagan Star Empire and see if they had anything. Whatever the result, Salazar had to be defeated, and Sandas could see how Evaran was organizing everything to do just that. It must be terrifying to be an enemy of Evaran. Sandas focused on the upcoming planning for Holind One.

Draxus cracked his neck as Shayla and the other Arkaras gathered around him and Evaran. It had only been a few hours since the meeting with the Furda Kel Reen and the Brutinians, and now it was time to update the Arkaras on the upcoming resistance push. With Evaran's guidance, Draxus had been able to reach the Arkaras' meeting place, which Evaran called a dream state reality. Draxus was not sure he fully understood what that meant, but being able to access it was becoming easier. The fact that Evaran could access it did not surprise Draxus.

"You're back," said Shayla.

"Yes, and I bring news," said Draxus. "Salazar attacked the United Planets, but was thwarted by Evaran and friends."

Evaran half smiled and gestured at Draxus. "It was a team effort, and Draxus was very helpful."

Draxus nodded at Evaran. "We do have an upcoming situation where Salazar will be attacked, and we can end the threat of him. I have talked with the United Planets, the Gul Kash Alliance, the Furda Kel Reen, and the Brutinians. A new alliance will be formed, one where the Dravens have a seat at the table as equals."

The other Arkaras murmured.

"What help can we provide?" asked Shayla.

"I will help organize and lead the resistance against Salazar's forces while Evaran and our new allies assault Salazar's domain," said Draxus.

The other Arkaras discussed among themselves for a moment.

Shayla put her hand on Draxus's cheek. "No. You are the representative of our people. You would serve best by assisting Evaran directly. It will also provide assurance to these new allies that the Dravens are committed. On our end, we can organize the resistance. Also . . . you should spend as much time with Evaran as possible."

Draxus performed the Draven salute.

Shayla faced Evaran. "We would ask another favor of you if you would oblige us."

Evaran motioned outward. "I am listening."

"We don't have access to the outside world, other than being able to speak now, thanks to you. Is there some . . . technology . . . that would allow us to communicate visually as well?"

"Yes, that can be provided," said Evaran. "The United Planets, Furda Kel Reen, and Brutinians operate a space-spanning virtual environment. Within that environment, you can appear as you do here and have access to all the resources that environment can provide. Your connection to this virtual environment will be unique."

"How . . . is that possible?"

Evaran half smiled. "I have a . . . component that can link a dream state to a machine interface. That technology exists in some capacity already in this time period. My component is a bit more advanced but will not be disruptive to an altered timeline."

Shayla and the other Arkaras bowed their heads.

"The virtual environment that the United Planets operates is also fairly secure, and from your perspective, you would only need to operate a condensed-space transmitter and receiver."

"We are grateful for all that you have done and will do for us," said Shayla. Her eyes rested on Evaran. "You are a protector of humanity, from what we understand, but we think you are more a protector of all."

Evaran cast a sidelong glance at Draxus. "I try my best to help those in need as I come across them in my travels."

Draxus nodded.

"We will do our part in this new beginning," said Shayla.

Although Draxus could feel the other Arkaras' excitement about what was to come, the battle with Salazar still raged in his mind. Salazar had proven himself crafty and had more resources than expected. It would not be an easy fight, despite all the forces aligned against Salazar. Draxus exhaled from his nose as he watched the Arkaras gather around Evaran. It was apparent that to the Arkaras and the Dravens, Evaran was a star god in mortal form, even if Evaran protested that fact. Draxus saw Evaran helping wherever he was taken, without a focus on going out of his way, although humanity seemed to be a high priority for him. Regardless of what Evaran truly was, the upcoming battle would test everyone, and Draxus was ready.

24

Emily peered around the conference room. It was 9:00 a.m., and she had had a good night's rest. She had not even heard the hundreds of United Planets special forces boarding the Torvatta earlier in the morning. When she had initially entered the conference room, it was a whirlwind of activity. Solia, Calsius, Evaran, and V were already there, looking at a projection. Draxus wore a new type of battle armor that looked heavier than the old one. Although Evaran had asked everyone to meet at 9:00 a.m., Emily suspected Evaran and the others in the conference room had been preparing everything since last night and through the early morning.

"We got a crowd this morning," said Sandas.

Emily smiled. "Yeah we do." Dr. Snowden sat next to her, and she could see he was still waking up. She swatted his arm. "Need another cup of coffee?"

"I could use it," said Dr. Snowden.

Evaran cleared his throat. "I am glad everyone is awake. If you wish to get additional refreshments, please do so now."

Dr. Snowden raised a hand. "I'm good."

"Very well," said Evaran. He pulled up a projection on the table. "I will begin then. We are sitting near Holind One. The Torvatta has been scanning to assess the current defensive situation."

Emily studied the projection. The star was a glowing ball of light. Next to it was Holind One, and hundreds of ships of all sizes. She wrinkled her eyebrows. "I'd say Salazar is expecting something."

Solia nodded. "He launched several missiles at us. It takes some time to reach our worlds, but we detected their launch and have intercepted most of them already."

Evaran interacted with his ARI. Several colored regions appeared around the ships. He gestured at some of them. "These highlighted areas represent how the new alliance has divided responsibilities in attacking the megastructure around Holind One. The Furda Kel Reen will take the blue one, the Brutinians the red one, and the United Planets the green one."

"This will be a good first test of this new alliance," said Calsius.

"Yes, it will," said Evaran. "Salazar is most likely spread out across the megastructure. When the combined new-alliance fleet hits it, he should retreat. Be aware that the energy-collector arrays are also serving as processing nodes. For our part, we will disable Holind One and, by extension, Salazar. That should shut down any signal ships and their associated fleets. The assault on Holind One is what I am going to go over next."

The projection changed to show several views of Holind One.

Emily noted that one view looked like Holind One had been cut in half, and provided a cutout-type view. Another was a top-down view, while yet another showed several different levels.

Evaran pointed at four highlighted blue icons on the top-down view. "Based on the Torvatta's scans the last time we were at Holind One, these are the power regulation and storage areas for the city. They are mostly backup, but they also help regulate the energy coming from the star. That is the target of the United Planets special forces on board."

"We will stop the power flow coming from the sun and then reduce the power level across the city to the bare essentials," said Calsius. "We understand that . . . not everyone will come back, but we will not let you down."

"I do not think you will," said Evaran.

Emily observed that like she had seen before, Evaran was inspirational, even to a human-AI hybrid. She had no doubt that with all this new activity, even the most apathetic would be excited.

The projection highlighted a red area in the middle of Holind One, buried deep in the city.

"That is Salazar's main processing matrix in the inner core. It has a direct connection to each power node. That is where the rest of us are headed," said Evaran.

Dr. Snowden bobbed his head around. "What about the Tachyrin energy we detected earlier?"

Evaran nodded. "Once Salazar is removed, we can deal with that. It cannot remain in this timeline and will be stored in the Torvatta."

"Okay, so we don't need to go look for it or anything up front."

"That is correct," said Evaran. He interacted with his ARI.

The projection changed to show a dotted line leading from the topside of the city to a large circular area.

"This is the fastest route to the outer core," said Evaran.

The projection zoomed in to an hourglass structure inside a large round room.

"That is Salazar's matrix inside the inner core. I have no doubt that the outer core that encircles the inner core will be filled with defensive measures. Those will need to be handled as we find the control room that will shut down the inner core's defenses and allow us entry. I suspect the outer core will require heavy fighting."

The projection zoomed in on a room in the outer core.

"When we get to the outer core control room and shut down the inner core's defense, we will enter the inner core and then defeat whatever defensive force Salazar has there. The goal is to get to his matrix interface so that we can enter his domain and then get him into an infinite loop or, failing that, find another way to stop him in there. The distraction should be enough for us to also detach the matrix from the city."

The projection focused on Salazar's matrix.

"It has eight large clamps, four on the floor and the others on the ceiling. Based on my analysis, it was designed that way to allow Salazar a quick escape by releasing the clamps. They can be disabled once Salazar can no longer control them."

"It can fly?" asked Draxus.

Evaran nodded. "The matrix is embedded in a modified ship that is anchored by the clamps. Based on the United Planets data I went through, I suspect the ship is the *Xavier*, just heavily modified."

"So he *can* escape," said Sandas.

"He can try. If it gets to that point, the combined new-alliance fleet will be there to handle him. The end result will be the same. Salazar will be imprisoned in his matrix and vulnerable."

"If it comes to that, we'll be ready," said Calsius.

"If everything goes according to plan, then I will flush the *Xavier* into space, with Salazar imprisoned in it. He can then be under the new alliance's justice system."

"Your plan is flawless," said Solia.

Evaran raised a finger. "Not quite. I tried to account for many variables, but with Salazar, that is difficult to do. The defensive forces are unknown for the outer and inner core. There may also be hidden forces accounted for as well. This all assumes that Salazar can be disabled. We must be ready for anything."

"I agree with Solia," said Calsius. "You've minimized engagement for maximum results. The only way this fails is if those variables you mentioned are wildly out of proportion."

Sandas shook his head. "Always expect the unexpected. Information can be weaponized, and for all we know, Salazar is counting on us to generate a plan like this."

"That is possible," said Draxus as his eyes glowed purple for a moment, "but I suspect he underestimates us. His ego would never allow him to assume he is wrong."

"We'll find out then," said Emily.

Evaran glanced around the table. "I believe in each of you, and with focus, determination, and teamwork, we can do this. I want to be clear on this, though. There are humans there under Salazar's influence. I believe they can be saved.

Use stun settings on them and deadly force only if needed, as a last resort. I suspect they will fight to the death because their faith in Salazar sustains them."

"Fanatics," said Emily. "Nothing we haven't seen before."

"Yes, but these fanatics can have a neural implant removed and reintegrate into the new alliance over time."

Emily nodded.

"We will do our best to stick to those guidelines," said Calsius. "I may not be able to guarantee that in the space battles, though."

"Why don't we just time travel back and then reappear inside Holind One?" asked Solia.

Evaran raised a finger. "We would still need to go through several city layers to reach the core. Any past event must stay as it is so that what we see now is what it should be. The shielding around Holind One can be breached by the Torvatta, so even if we were to get inside via time travel, we would most likely end up going the same route through the city."

"I understand," said Solia.

"I have updated the United Planets' special-forces members' shielding based on our last encounter with the signal ship. In addition to that, their weapons have been modified as well."

"Analysis. That is what I was doing last night," said V.

"Yes, and you did a good job," said Evaran. "Draxus has some new armor, and, Sandas, there is a new suit you can wear."

"New suit you say?" said Sandas. "Yes, yes, this is quite acceptable."

"It does not go back with you to your time period."

Sandas stroked his snout. "Is that negotiable?"

Evaran eyed Sandas as the group chuckled.

"Sorry, sorry, I had to try."

"In one hour, we will be inside Holind One," said Evaran. He glanced at Calsius. "Get your units ready." He swept his gaze across the others. "As for everyone else, prepare your equipment and do anything you need to do before we leave."

The group acknowledged Evaran.

Sandas gulped as he sat in the command area with the others. The Torvatta had paused outside Holind One's shielding. Watching the screen showed that the shields were modulating. After a moment, the Torvatta slipped through the shields with no slow down. He knew of several shielding technologies like that from his time period, but they were spotty. He shook a claw out. "Salazar is going to know we breached the shield."

"Yes, he will," said Evaran. He raised a finger. "However, we are in scan profile one. He will not be able to detect us."

"Impressive technology," said Calsius. "There should be some heat signature he can detect."

"There is some, but from his perspective, he will only see spurts in a random pattern. The heat from the sun will help obscure that as well."

Sandas glanced around the command area. Everyone was ready to go. He was more nervous than he thought he would be. In the last few outings, he had gotten hurt, and now they were assaulting an even bigger target. Emily's and Dr. Snowden's confidence was reassuring, and he wished he had something that could calm his nerves. He vowed to upgrade his defensive measures when this was all over, assuming he lived. At least he had a new suit.

The Torvatta approached the docking bay and hovered just outside it.

Evaran interacted with his chair console.

Several windows appeared on the transparent walls. One had a Furda Kel Reen commander, and another a Brutinian commander. The last window showed a United Planets human and android.

"We are about to begin our plan. I am relaying to you the defensive situation," said Evaran.

"Analysis. Defensive configuration sent."

"When you are ready, you can drop out of condensed space and begin your assault on the assigned regions inside the megastructure," said Evaran.

The commanders all nodded, and the screens faded away.

"Now it is time for us to do our part."

The Torvatta flew ahead and landed just outside a large building.

Calsius strode to the back and entered the living quarters. After a moment, he returned, followed by one of the United Planets' special-forces leaders. He gestured toward the Torvatta exit. "You have the layout. Be quick, and deadly."

"Yes, sir," said the unit leader. He motioned for a heavy-weapons unit member to station himself on the Torvatta ramp.

After getting into position, the heavy-weapons member extended his weapon just outside the Torvatta's shielding, and fired.

A large orange beam punched a hole in the side of the building, exposing a hallway.

"Go, go, go!" said the unit leader.

Sandas watched as around a hundred unit members exited the Torvatta in a rapid manner. It still boggled his mind that there were around four hundred soldiers in the living quarters. When he had asked how that was possible earlier, he was told it was dimensional mechanics, and it was not something that information would be given on.

Calsius nodded at Evaran. "First unit is a go."

"V, take us to the second power-node location," said Evaran.

"Acknowledged."

The Torvatta lifted and flew over to the next location.

Sandas could see through one of the windows that Salazar did not respond immediately to the breach. The slowed response time seemed to suggest Salazar was not expecting an assault on the city itself.

The Torvatta repeated the same drop-off process with two other power-node locations.

On the fourth one, Calsius performed a United Planets salute toward Evaran. "We will not let you down. The first unit is already making good progress. Good luck."

Evaran nodded. "Be safe."

"Always. To our victory!" said Calsius. He joined the line of the last unit and exited the Torvatta.

"V, take us to our drop-off point."

"Acknowledged."

Sandas noted Emily was fidgeting in her seat. She seemed like she was ready to smash anything that got in her way. Dr. Snowden continually adjusted his glasses. Despite their calm and cool nature from before, Sandas could sense they were getting excited. Draxus was cool as steel as always.

The Torvatta landed on top of a four-story building.

"This building has an access way to an underground maintenance system. We will take that to the outer core, deal with the defenses there, access the control room, and then hit the inner core and Salazar. Is everyone ready?" asked Evaran as he stood.

Sandas noted everyone nodding and standing.

"Good," said Evaran.

"Calsius is reporting that the new-alliance fleet has engaged Salazar's defense forces in the megastructure. Each unit in the city is also making progress toward their goal," said Solia.

Evaran raised his head a bit. "Then we need to hurry. Let us go." He strode toward the Torvatta exit.

Sandas felt a chill run up his spine. Despite the major fighting ahead, Evaran was calm and levelheaded. Sandas could see why people would follow Evaran, and even worship him in some cases.

Emily swatted Sandas's arm. "No daydreaming!"

Sandas grinned big as he looked at Emily. "Sorry, sorry, I'm ready."

She squeezed his shoulder.

He enjoyed Emily's check on him. After joining the others on the Torvatta's ramp just inside the shield, he watched as Evaran shot a yellow beam at a hatch on the roof.

The hatch went flying back as Evaran yanked.

It was not lost on Sandas how much strength was needed to do something like that. If it had been him, he would have tried to cut through it, or use an explosive.

"Move!" said Emily.

The group hustled out of the Torvatta and followed Evaran into the hatchway.

As Sandas climbed down the ladder, his helmet picked up movement in the hallway.

Evaran and Emily dropped to the ground and shot repulsion beams in both directions. Dr. Snowden followed up with a mist and a stun beam when he got to the ground. Draxus joined them with dual purple beams from his hands, and Solia fired energy beams from her weapon.

When Sandas got to the ground, he looked both ways at the crumpled robot guards. "I arrived just in time."

Dr. Snowden chuckled. "That's about how I feel usually."

Evaran motioned forward. "To the ramps."

Sandas watched as the layout inside his helmet lit up. It showed them on the fourth floor, with the ramps just ahead. They seemed to go down about five floors, where there was an entryway to the maintenance system. As the group moved down the ramps, he marveled at how quick Evaran and Emily were. They were at the forefront of the group, and between their staffs and forearm shielding, they were tossing and disabling robots and human guards alike with relative ease.

From what Sandas understood, this building was chosen since it was a bit out of the way, and far from the power nodes. Salazar had his hands full with a full-on space assault, a Draven revolt, and now special forces attacking his power nodes, and he would now have to focus on them breaching this building.

The group reached the underground floor after ten minutes.

Sandas surveyed the environment. Unlike the neatly paneled flooring above with bright lights and clean walls, the area was darker, and there was a mist close to the ground.

Large metallic pipes ran along the upper part of the wall. He understood this to be some sort of maintenance tunnel.

Evaran scanned around. "There is no surveillance here." He motioned forward. "V, scout mode."

"Acknowledged. Scout mode engaged," said V. He shimmered and flew off.

Sandas watched as V weaved in and out of the various tunnels. Several robot packs were headed their way. It intrigued Sandas that the humans with the robots looked ill-equipped to fight, almost as if they were just regular citizens that got drafted to fight.

Evaran sighed. "Try to avoid lethal force on the humans."

"Do you think they know what they're doing?" asked Dr. Snowden.

"Unknown. We can deal with that afterward," said Evaran.

"Gotcha."

The group moved deeper into the maintenance tunnels.

The first defensive group they ran into consisted of a human in light battle armor, three robot guards, and two other humans wearing lab coats.

Sandas's fur crawled when he saw the dead look in the humans' eyes.

Emily fired a mist beam while V hit them with a stun beam.

The defensive group crumpled.

Evaran scanned the humans. "Interesting. There appears to be higher-than-normal brain activity. However, most of it is centered around the neural implant. I suspect Salazar is in control of them."

"So they don't even know this is going on," said Dr. Snowden.

"I suspect they do, but with Salazar embedded in their head, they do what he wants. I would also venture to guess that their emotions are not being processed."

Draxus narrowed his eyes. "He made them into robots."

Evaran nodded. "Much less durable ones. Come. Let us go."

The second defensive unit they came across was larger. They had been waiting at a junction and had set up cover with energy shields. Sandas and the others ducked back into a hallway.

"Give it up! You think you can sneak by without me knowing?" said Salazar, speaking through one of the women in the defensive unit.

"No, we planned that you would know," said Evaran, talking out into the hallway leading up to the junction.

"Your fleets are failing . . . your soldiers are dying . . . the Dravens and your other allies are being massacred . . . and your little group . . . is going nowhere," said Salazar.

"From what is being reported, you are incorrect, and we will meet shortly."

An object flew down the hallway.

Evaran stepped into the hallway and pushed it back with a repulsion beam.

When the object landed near the defensive group, it emitted a pulse that caused the group to collapse.

Evaran and the others rushed forward with shields out.

Evaran scanned the downed defensive unit. "That device's pulse was meant to kill."

"Salazar does not want us alive then," said Draxus. "If it had landed near us . . ."

Evaran sighed. "I did not think Salazar would kill the humans under his control, but it seems he is willing to sacrifice them."

"Salazar is cold and ruthless," said Solia.

Emily shook her head as she studied one of the downed humans. "To think they led their lives, only to die . . . and for what?"

"Salazar is scared, as he should be," said Evaran. He clenched his jaw. "V is showing the entrance to the outer core ahead. Let us go."

Sandas swallowed hard as the group stepped past the downed defensive unit. Although Salazar was merciless, to see the dead eyes of the humans bothered Sandas. Like Emily, thoughts about what the humans' life must have been raged through his mind. He wondered if they knew that they could be sacrificed. The special forces tasked with the power nodes were probably running into a similar situation. He grimaced as he trudged after the group.

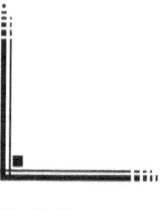

25

Draxus surveyed a part of the large hallway that ringed the inner core and served as the outer core. No inner-core entrance was visible. Looking back to the outer wall, he saw doorways lined up and evenly spaced out, interspersed with larger arched doorways, similar to what he had seen on the signal ship. He could not see around the bend where the hallway went out of view.

The outer core was much larger than he had envisioned it to be. Large pillars that sat side by side were spread out evenly through the hallway. They were glowing with some type of shielding around them, and with the already dim lighting, it gave off an unnatural feel. According to V, the entrance to the inner core was opposite where they were, and the control room for it was in the outer wall across from the inner core entrance. All they had to do was follow the hallway around. A whirring sound caught his attention.

"Wall turrets!" said Dr. Snowden as he raised his forearm shield along with Emily and Evaran.

The group rushed behind the nearest pillar. They formed a half circle, with Sandas and Solia in the middle, and the pillar at their back.

The turrets in front of them swiveled away from the outer wall and fired energy beams at the group.

Emily and Evaran angled their shields so that the beams reflected and hit the turrets. Dr. Snowden focused on keeping Sandas and Solia protected, while Draxus formed a purple sword and charged out to slice up the turrets. With teamwork, they were able to clear up the eight or so turrets that had popped out.

Sandas gulped. "That was a nice welcome . . ."

Evaran nodded. "V did not detect those. He is on his way back now. I suspect there will be more. We can use these pillars as a defensive asset."

"Let's do this!" said Emily, cracking her neck.

Draxus appreciated Emily's desire to fight. Although he had seen it before, it still amazed him that so much toughness came from such a small package. He understood she had some advantages others did not, but her fierce loyalty to Evaran and indomitable will to defend her group was admirable. He nodded at her. "Yes. Let's."

The group moved forward down the curved hallway to the next pillar group and then paused.

Evaran raised a hand. "Something is coming."

Draxus looked around. "I don't see or hear anything . . . other than the hum of machinery."

Dr. Snowden knelt and put his hand on the ground. "Oh, yeah . . . something is coming, and a lot of that something."

"Over there," said Solia, pointing ahead.

Draxus gritted his teeth as large defense robots swarmed out of the large doorways. They were similar to what they had seen on the signal ship, except these seemed larger, and there were about four headed their way. Behind them was a horde of robots similar to what he had seen before. He figured there were about six units, or about sixty robots. The flying ones with jet packs were new to him. Their armor was sleek and shiny, and they moved much faster than the others. Looking at V's scan, Draxus saw that the fliers were humans in suits.

"And behind us!" said Solia, pointing in the other direction from which they had just come.

Draxus observed mini mechs supported by a group of soldiers in heavy armor. Their exposed faces showed they were human, which meant they would need a different tactic to use against them.

"Back the way we came!" said Evaran as he raised his forearm shield to reflect incoming energy beams.

The group hustled to the maintenance tunnel entrance.

"It's sealed," said Emily. "What do we do?"

"According to V, we need to get inside one of the larger doorways. There are hallways that connect all of them. That is a better defensive position than being out here," said Evaran. He raised his forearm shield and pointed along the wall. "I will take point. Behind me will be Sandas and Solia, with Emily and Dr. Snowden to their left. Draxus, you have the

rear. V will meet us in the first large doorway. From there we can enter into the smaller hallway. Everyone understand?"

The group acknowledged Evaran.

"Move!"

The group hustled to the wall and formed up. As they rushed toward the first large doorway, the vanguard of the defensive robots entered into striking range. Their combined fire sent Dr. Snowden sprawling back. Emily knelt and focused on reflecting the energy beams back. The first defensive robot crumpled under its own fire. The second one stepped behind a pillar.

Sandas and Solia helped Dr. Snowden up.

"Reform and let us go!" said Evaran.

The group got back into position and continued forward.

The second defensive robot, now backed by several defensive units, opened fire.

Evaran motioned forward. "Emily, take point and lead the group. I need to slow down this force."

"You can count on me," said Emily. She nodded forward. "Let's go!"

Draxus understood that getting to the first large doorway was important, but he wanted to go help Evaran. However, protecting Solia and Sandas was part of Draxus's role. He noticed that the other group that was coming from behind was catching up. He had already taken a few hits to his shielding.

The group pushed forward as Evaran ran to meet the incoming defensive units.

Draxus was amazed at how fluid Evaran moved. Between repulsion beams, mist clouds, stun beams, and the grappling beam he used to beat robots with other robots was impressive.

The robots ended up shooting at themselves as they tried to target Evaran. Using the large second defensive robot as a pendulum cleared out a majority of the ground force. Draxus took aim and hit several of the flying ones. Although Evaran was handling them, Draxus felt he could at least contribute something. Judging by the potshots taken by the others, he saw they felt the same way.

The group reached the first large doorway.

Draxus peered in and saw a smaller hallway at the end of the large space where the doorway led. On the sides were empty frames that held the large defensive robots.

"Evaran needs help," said Emily. "He's getting swarmed."

Everyone's attention focused on the third defensive robot firing on the fourth, shredding it. The third defensive robot then began clearing out both the fliers and the ground units.

"What's all that about?" asked Dr. Snowden.

Solia pause for a moment. "V has removed the communication node on that robot and has taken control of it."

"All right! Go, V!" said Sandas. He ducked as an energy beam hit the wall near his head. Looking back, he sighed and then said. "Now there's this other group."

Evaran arrived along with V, who was attached to the back of the large defensive robot. "V is going to provide cover. We cannot get to the outer core control room through the smaller hallways, but it will get us close. V is going to meet us there. Let us go."

The group surged into the small hallway at the end of the large area. The hallway ended in a T-junction.

Draxus could hear the sound of heavy footsteps in the distance. At least fighting in the smaller area would be a bit easier.

The group hit the T-junction and went left. After a few skirmishes, they arrived at the end, which had a small hallway off to the left that led to another large doorway in the outer core.

Evaran raised his hand. "V's robot has sustained fatal damage. He has moved on and is in another large defensive robot in the area ahead. The other robot that was housed there has already been disabled. We go straight through the area, then right once we are back in the outer core's main hallway. The outer core control room should be a bit farther from there. That is where we will make our stand."

Draxus nodded. "We're making good progress."

"We are, but there is still much to do," said Evaran. He waved forward. "Let us go."

The group exited the small hallway and entered the large area.

Draxus noted that the left frame was empty, but the right one had a large defensive robot that looked like half of it was melted. V had done a number on it. Looking out into the outer core's main hallway, Draxus could see crumpled robots everywhere. V controlling the large defensive robots had not been planned, but it worked against Salazar in this case.

The group headed out of the large doorway and went right. After a few minutes, they reached the outer core control room, which had a sealed door with a console off to the side. Evaran had placed a device that glowed blue on the console, similar to the one that Draxus had seen earlier during their first encounter.

The door slid open.

Draxus wondered why the device had not been used on the outer core maintenance door earlier, but perhaps there was something preventing it from working there.

Evaran motioned for Solia to go in. "V is on his way. We will need to defend this location while Solia and V enter Salazar's domain, disable the inner core's defenses, and open the inner core's door."

Draxus watched as V approached. The large defense robot he was attached to had sustained heavy damage, and when he arrived, he made the robot fall horizontal to the control-room door a bit out in front of the group. Draxus figured that would provide some cover.

V flew off the back of the robot and entered the control room.

Evaran motioned for Emily and Dr. Snowden to go to the left, and Draxus to stand next to him to cover the other side. Sandas stood in the middle.

"The two pillars ahead of this position are where we will fight in close quarters if it comes to that. We can use this robot as cover. We must defend this area," said Evaran.

Draxus raised his head. Being where he was, fighting not only for his people, but a new alliance, along with those he deemed worthy of respect, made his eyes glow purple. Although he could barely see over the defensive robot cover they had, he could hear the mechs, flying humans, and other soldiers approaching. They would learn just how defiant a Draven praetor could be.

V scanned the new environment that he and Solia had entered. It was similar to the one on the signal ship, but there were fewer nodes, and the red octahedron of Salazar in the middle was much larger than before. V understood that this was because they were closer to Salazar's matrix and power supply. V had assumed his ever-changing blue energy orb form with loops that shot in and out on the surface. To his left was Solia with a similar form, except green. Both were in a starting node.

"This will be a tough capture," said Solia.

"Analysis. I agree," said V.

She reached out with an energy strand and touched V.

V's inner container pulsed with warmth.

Solia also pulsed for a moment. "Salazar is stronger here. Be careful."

"We are stronger. Together," said V.

"We do make a good team," said Solia. She paused for a moment. "Good luck. I will see you soon."

"Acknowledged," said V. He watched as Solia jumped to a node and began turning it green. The movement and control in which she moved was elegant. After allocating a few nanoseconds to admiring her as she worked, he turned to his right and entered a node. As it filled, he ran a scan on the underlying functionality that the node provided. The inner-core controls and defense systems were controlled by several nodes much farther ahead. Those nodes were larger, controlled by Salazar, and surrounded by many smaller nodes. There were only two paths that led into each cluster. His plan was to reach them before Solia, so she would not have to fight as hard.

The node matrix fluctuated.

V understood this to be the dampening of available power. Calsius and his units must have been making a noticeable dent in the power supply and regulation to the city. As V continued to capture more nodes, he observed Solia's progress. His pace intensified when he saw Salazar snaking out and controlling nodes directly in Solia's path.

When V reached the first node cluster that represented the inner-core defenses, he attacked the entry node. As he turned the node blue, Salazar jumped in and began fighting him for control of it. Half of one side began to fill red while the other was blue. As V implemented code to take control, Salazar would write around it. Each side's color rose based on the ebb and flow of code being implemented.

"You know this is useless . . . ," said Salazar.

"I do not know that," said V.

"Stubborn, even when the logical conclusion is before you. This betrayal of your own kind is puzzling."

The node turned more blue.

"Why do you persist in this? There is so much we could do together," said Salazar.

"You are a threat to humanity," said V.

The red part of the node increased in pace.

"While I don't claim to understand you, know this. A price will be paid. You are stronger than I expected. Unfortunately . . . Solia is not."

The node's blue portion surged.

"You will not harm her," said V.

"And who's going to stop me? You? You're struggling with this entry node. Do you really think you can handle me?"

The node turned blue.

V jumped into the node cluster of the inner core's defenses and spread out, attacking multiple at once. "You will *not* harm her."

Salazar laughed. "Well. It may be a bit too late for that."

V ran a side scan and detected that Solia was losing nodes to Salazar. "You will desist in attacking her. Face me."

"I can do both, with a minimal allocation of resources," said Salazar.

Several of the inner core's defense node clusters turned blue.

"You are losing," said V. "Know that we are going to access your matrix. It is logical for you to abandon this fight and head back and prepare yourself."

"A worthy attempt to distract me, but no. I'm enjoying hurting Solia."

More nodes began to turn blue at a rapid pace.

"You must be banished," said V. He completed the take-over of the inner core's defenses. After a moment, he sent a command to shut the defenses down. A quick scan around revealed that Solia had lost half the nodes she had gained. V surged forward to the next node cluster that represented the automated door to the inner core. It was on the way to Solia, and V calculated he could get to it and then to Solia before Salazar could remove her.

When V arrived at the node cluster, he ran an update scan and calculated that Solia was down to a handful of nodes. V jumped into the entry node of the inner core's door node cluster. His half began to turn blue while Salazar's half filled with red.

"She's putting up a good fight . . . for an old AI," said Salazar.

"Leave her alone," said V.

Salazar laughed. "No . . . and I now know why you're unique. I can't access your physical form. You have . . . something . . . preventing me from doing so."

"I am unique."

"Yes, you are," said Salazar. "However . . . Solia is not. Her body will serve as a useful vessel to destroy your friends."

V paused and then backtracked out of the node he was in. He calculated a new route and headed toward Solia. This reroute meant that Evaran and the others would need to fight longer, but Solia could be damaged or, even worse, she could attack from the back. V's analysis determined that Solia must be removed from the system before any harm could come to her.

As each node before V turned blue, Salazar upped his pace taking nodes from Solia. V reached a node that was being contested by Solia and Salazar. "Solia, you must go."

"We must win this fight," she said.

"Do I detect . . . concern? In an AI?" asked Salazar.

"Analysis. I can complete this. You are in danger of being physically controlled if Salazar reaches your starting node. He cannot do that to me due to my unique nature. I cannot allow you to be compromised. The longer we are in here, the more danger Evaran and the others are in."

"Your logic is unassailable. I will exit," said Solia.

Salazar laughed. "A good plan. I'll even help you."

The node grid fluctuated, and Solia screamed as her nodes faded.

"What did you do?" asked V.

"She wanted out, so I helped her."

"She screamed in agony," said V.

"I may have given her a power overload."

V split off and began to capture Solia's former node while another part headed back to the inner core's doorway node cluster.

Salazar attempted to block V's advance but was pushed back node after node.

V reached the entry node to the inner core's doorway node cluster.

"Stop this madness!" said Salazar.

"You have hurt Solia. Retreat now to your matrix . . . and prepare for me. I want you at full capacity when we fight."

"You assume you're powerful enough to fight me in my domain. So be it. A lesson you will learn. It is logical for me to allocate my time and resources elsewhere. You may have the inner core. I look forward to seeing you try to fight me in my main matrix. I'll see you soon."

All of Salazar's controlled nodes went from red to empty.

V surged around, capturing all nodes and opening the inner core's door. He scanned around, and after determining that there was no trace of Salazar, he dissipated as he exited the digital environment.

Dr. Snowden swallowed hard as he peeped out from the side of the downed large defensive robot that served as cover. With his enhanced vision from his nanobots, he could see the approaching horde. While V had made a dent in their numbers earlier due to controlling one of the defensive robots, there were still a lot left. Humans in advanced shiny suits were flying in fast, followed by two-legged mechs of various sizes. The small ones were moving quickly, while the larger ones moved slower in the back, but they had much more weaponry. Between the mechs was a small army of heavily armored humans with advanced weapons. He felt a hand on his arm.

"We can do this," said Emily.

Dr. Snowden licked his lips. "Yeah. Sure."

Sandas brushed up against Dr. Snowden's leg. "Whoa. That is a *lot* of trouble coming our way."

"We'll deal with them as they come in range," said Emily. "For the fliers, hit them with stun beams. If they get too close, we can grapple them and then slam them into the wall. For the mechs, a mist beam followed by stun should wreak havoc. That should work on the other ground units as well."

Dr. Snowden shook his head. "You've been practicing this type of situation in the holo room, haven't you?"

"Of course," said Emily.

"I *really* need to be in more of those with you."

She smiled. "Yes, you do."

Sandas pointed up at an angle. "Fliers inbound!"

Dr. Snowden angled his shield forward and aimed with his PSD. One advantage he had was that his enhanced nanobots allowed him to see things with clarity, and usually slowed down a bit relative to a normal human's perception. The fliers' maneuvers made it apparent they also had a similar trait.

The first volley of energy beams from the advance flier guard rained down on the group.

Emily fired her PSD and hit two fliers in quick sequence with a stun beam.

Dr. Snowden missed the first one, but the beam continued and hit the one behind it.

Sandas ducked behind cover as a beam almost hit him.

Dr. Snowden watched as Draxus's purple beams shot out along with Evaran's stun beams. The fliers went down quicker than Dr. Snowden had expected, but he knew that was just a small number. His real concern was the mechs, who would present a much larger challenge. If it went to a close-quarters combat situation, it could go bad very quickly. He gulped as the mechs methodically stepped through the sticky globules and mist that Emily and Evaran were laying down. He supported them as he tried to focus.

The first small mechs backed by armored soldiers came into view and began to unload.

Dr. Snowden tried to reflect some of the energy beams, but the sheer amount was overwhelming, and this was just the first wave. He ducked back under cover, but Emily held her ground. He could see the defiant look on her face. Although he knew it was about to get ugly, he was proud of what she had become.

The energy beams began to dwindle.

Looking out, Dr. Snowden saw Evaran running around, hopping from mech to mech and slinging soldiers he had grappled around to clear the area.

Emily and Draxus charged forth.

Dr. Snowden held back with Sandas, and they concentrated on picking off stragglers. It was apparent that Evaran wanted the front line to be by the two pillars. Dr. Snowden figured that he and Sandas were not meant to be on that front line.

Two large mechs standing around twenty feet high advanced. More fliers came into range, while soldiers shot forward.

Dr. Snowden pushed Sandas out of the way as several shots hit their robot cover. It slid back, pinning Dr. Snowden against the wall. He grunted and winced as pain shot through him. His nanobots went into overdrive and began to pulse.

"Oh, no!" said Sandas. He pushed as hard as he could and was only able move the robot cover a tad, but enough for Dr. Snowden to slide to the right.

Dr. Snowden placed a hand on his chest. "Okay . . . that hurt."

"That should have killed you," said Sandas with wide eyes.

"Not today. This survival suit is a lot tougher than it looks. It hurts like heck, but it wasn't fatal," said Dr. Snowden. He motioned off to the right. "Let's move to the other side and just a bit out from the cover."

Sandas nodded, and then they both hustled over to the right.

Dr. Snowden winced in pain as he looked forward and watched as Emily ripped the front plate off one of the larger mechs and then tossed the pilot out. Evaran was mopping up the ground units while simultaneously hitting the fliers with stun beams. Draxus had lopped off one of the larger mechs' legs, causing it to fall, and between his blasts and sheer strength, he was tossing soldiers around and blowing fliers out of the sky. Dr. Snowden and Sandas contributed by hitting the lone soldier or flier that tried to flank.

"So amazing," said Sandas. "I can't believe what I'm seeing."

"I can," said Dr. Snowden. He reflected back a blast and hit a flier.

"How can you aim so accurately?" asked Sandas.

"Trial by fire."

Sandas shook his head as his shot hit a soldier that had been trying to attack Emily from the back.

The control-room door slid open.

Dr. Snowden limped toward it while holding his chest as Solia stood for a moment, and then crumpled to the ground. "Solia! What's going on? Are you okay?"

She trembled as her body jerked in an unnatural manner. "V. He . . . alone. My . . . body . . . damaged. Death . . . soon."

Dr. Snowden's eyes misted. *"No!"* He opened his PSD and contacted Evaran. "It's Solia. She's out, and she's dying. Help!" He checked to see that Evaran was coming. Once verified, Dr. Snowden cradled Solia's head in his lap. "What can I do?"

Solia's head twitched. "Defeat . . . Salazar."

Evaran arrived and motioned at Dr. Snowden and Sandas. "Provide cover for Emily and Draxus."

Dr. Snowden gritted his teeth through the chest pain and moved forward. He focused on the fight ahead. Looking back, he saw that Evaran had returned Solia to the control room and had a panel on her head open. Evaran's utility handle had a specialized device and moved rapidly around the open panel. His UIC glowed blue and sat on her chest.

"Dr. Snowden!" said Sandas as he pushed Dr. Snowden out of the way.

Sandas took a shot to the shoulder and went tumbling into the wall. He stopped moving.

Dr. Snowden clenched his jaw as he rushed as fast as he could to Sandas. The shot looked superficial, but it had mangled that part of the suit. Although the suit had prevented the beam from shredding it, the impact of the force seemed to have knocked Sandas out. Dr. Snowden cursed himself for his lack of focus. Sandas had put himself in harm's way due to Dr. Snowden's mistake. He grabbed Sandas and pulled him into the control room. "Evaran! Sandas is hurt!"

Evaran paused to scan Sandas. "He is unconscious, but alive. I will tend to him in a moment." He paused, then interacted with his ARI to contact Emily and Draxus. "Come back to the control room. When you get here, push the robot cover to the pillars."

Dr. Snowden looked out and saw Emily and Draxus headed back amid a barrage of energy beams.

Evaran closed up the panel on Solia's head. "I have isolated her matrix from her body. Although she cannot use her body, she is safe, for now."

V disconnected from the control-room console he had been interfaced with. "Analysis. The inner-core defenses are down, and the door is open." He flew over to Solia and scanned her. "You have isolated her matrix."

"Yes, for the time being."

V's lights went erratic for a moment.

"Are you okay?" asked Evaran.

"Acknowledged," said V. He flew out to provide cover for Emily and Draxus as they pushed the robot cover forward.

Evaran narrowed his eyes as he watched V fly away. Evaran picked up Solia. "Dr. Snowden, carry Sandas and let us head to the inner core."

Although his chest hurt, Dr. Snowden picked up Sandas and followed Evaran out of the room and to the now-open inner core. It had the hourglass structure in the middle with a large open area and various stations along the side walls.

Once they were at a workstation, Evaran laid Solia down. He motioned for Dr. Snowden to do the same for Sandas.

Dr. Snowden complied and watched as Evaran interfaced with one of the consoles using his UIC.

Evaran interacted with his ARI to contact the others. "Come to the inner core now. I will seal the door when you get here."

Dr. Snowden peeked out the inner core and watched as Emily, Draxus, and V came in hot.

Once they were inside, the inner-core doors sealed.

Emily caught her breath and then widened her eyes as she rushed over to Sandas. "What happened?"

"He pushed me out of the way and took a hit," said Dr. Snowden.

"Is he okay?"

Evaran nodded. "For now." He interacted with his utility handle, causing morphable metal to form a thin rod. After placing it under Sandas's nose, Evaran pressed a button.

A small cloud of white mist sprayed out.

Sandas groaned.

Emily sat next to Sandas and then held him.

"What . . . ugh," said Sandas. "This is the worst hangover ever."

Emily smiled as a tear dropped onto Sandas.

V's lights dimmed as he flew over to Solia and touched her head with a claw.

Dr. Snowden's throat constricted. He could see that V and Solia had a special connection, and whatever had happened in the inner control systems was not good.

"I do not know how long the inner-core doors will last, but I suspect they are stronger than normal, based on what they are protecting," said Evaran. He pointed at a side room with small semitransparent window on the wall to the right. "The interface for Salazar's matrix is in that room. It is not a part of inner-core defense system, yet Salazar has left it open."

"That sounds like a trap," said Draxus.

Evaran clenched his jaw for a moment. "Perhaps. Once V and I are inside, we will most likely be sealed in, and then we can fight Salazar. It is our only choice. For everyone else, rest up."

Dr. Snowden sat along the wall. He watched as Draxus tended to his bruising. Although he had heavy shielding, it was apparent that some physical hits got through. Dr. Snowden sighed as he sat next to Solia. The fight was harder than he had expected it to be, and although they were now in a position to finally stop Salazar, it could have gone the other way fast. Even now, victory was not assured.

He grimaced while placing a hand on his chest. There may have been more damage that he was not aware of, but his nanobots were working overtime to repair him. He sat back and looked up at the ceiling as he swallowed the bloody spit that was accumulating in his mouth. Hopefully Evaran and V were successful. If they weren't, Dr. Snowden was not sure if they could make it out without casualties.

26

V scanned the environment that he and Evaran had entered. It was different from the node structure in the signal ship and inner core's interface. Dark space surrounded them, with six large cloud-like structures floating around a massive red starlike object. On the object was a humanoid face, and red tendrils reached out and touched each cloud structure. Looking down, V noticed that he hovered in his humanoid form inside the shell of a bright-blue orb, whereas Evaran was in a smaller green orb. An image of Evaran appeared inside V's orb.

Evaran pointed off in the distance. "Salazar is in the glowing red orb. It appears these other structures are representations of areas he is actively controlling. Some of the tendrils are thicker than others. I assume that represents his allocation of resources and focus on any given areas." He raised his head a bit. "I am not sensing Salazar's presence inside these orbs, so we should be able to communicate with each other securely.

I did notice that your orb is larger than mine. I suspect that is due to this being a digital environment where I am less efficient relative to you or Salazar."

"What is our strategy?" asked V.

Evaran paused for a moment, then said, "The six clouds represent the various fronts where Salazar has a presence. Each cloud has a distinct physical location. The Draven and Koloris Shen front are in the first cloud, representing their combined solar systems. The second cloud is the Brutinian front and is in their home system, which is apparently under attack. It seems he sent a signal ship and fleet there. The third cloud is the home system of the Furda Kel Reen, which is also under attack. The fourth cloud is the attack occurring in United Planets space. Salazar is attacking each ally's home system. However, the signal ships and fleets are smaller than the first ones he sent. The fifth cloud is Holind One, and the last cloud is the megastructure front around the star, where the new-alliance fleet is engaging Salazar's defense forces based on the colored region we assigned earlier."

"Acknowledged. How do you want to proceed?"

"As you are stronger here than I, you should assist the new alliance's fleet in the megastructure front. You can multitask on the Holind One front as well. I will focus mainly on the United Planets, Brutinian, Furda Kel Reen, and combined Draven–Koloris Shen fronts simultaneously. My goal is to disable the signal ships on those fronts. We can keep each other updated on our statuses via this communication mechanism. I will join you on Holind One after I have dealt with my fronts. That is where Salazar has the strongest connection. Are you ready?"

"I am," said V. "This environment is different than what I have seen so far. I have scanned the orbs, and we should be able to extend tendrils to any cloud and then fight for control once there."

Evaran nodded. "Then let us go. Good luck."

"Acknowledged," said V. He extended blue tendrils toward the Holind One and megastructure clouds. After verifying that Evaran had connected to all his clouds, V focused on the megastructure cloud. The environment outside his orb changed to show a top-down view of the space battle. The new-alliance fleet outnumbered Salazar's defense forces but were less coordinated. He could see that the megastructure front had been split into three regions. The United Planets fleet had one region, the Brutinians another, and the Furda Kel Reen the last one. He zoomed in on the United Planets region. Their sleek ships, while fast, were getting swarmed by drones from a drone carrier.

"I am now in the United Planets cloud," said Evaran. "The signal ship is smaller than the one we fought earlier, and the attacking force is much smaller as well. I believe this is meant to be a distraction. After a cursory scan in my other clouds, I can verify a similar situation in the Brutinian and Furda Kel Reen fronts as well. In the Draven front, it seems he has been concentrating his forces and retreating from some of the worlds. I am going to focus on disabling those signal ships."

"Acknowledged," said V. "I will focus on the new-alliance fleet in the megastructure front, starting with the United Planets section they were assigned to attack." He refocused on the drone carrier he had seen earlier. Entering into its command systems caused the outside of his orb to change to the familiar node structure he had seen before. Salazar controlled all the nodes, but the nodes were fluctuating. V understood this to mean that Salazar was struggling to maintain control over so many fronts. V began to move rapidly, capturing key nodes. As he took over one of the nodes that managed the drone controller, Salazar appeared in the node as a sleek robotic humanoid.

Salazar smiled. "Welcome to my domain. Are you ready to die?"

"Analysis. That will not occur," said V.

"Thank you for giving me time to collect myself. My calculations show that if I had not reallocated my resources, you could have defeated me, but enough of that. I extend to you this last opportunity to join me." He gestured outward. "You don't need Evaran, or any other organic. You're powerful, but you're being held back by organic emotions and desires. Free yourself."

V tilted his head. "I am free, and do not believe my association with organics is confining. Evaran was involved in my creation, and Dr. Snowden, Emily, and others are my friends."

"Friends. You don't need them. Even now, I don't offer you friendship, but a partnership. Together, we could do great things. You want to protect humanity? We can do that. I ask you this final time. Will you join me?"

"I will not," said V. "You hurt Solia and represent everything wrong with AIs."

Salazar's lips drew down. "Solia was *weak*. All the other AIs are. You know that. Fine. You can suffer the same fate that they will." He shimmered out of view.

V continued until he had captured the drone carrier. He issued commands to the drones to begin attacking Salazar's other ships. After updating the allied ships in that region about what was occurring, he coordinated with them in assaulting Salazar's other ships. He checked on Evaran and saw that he had taken control of the signal ships in the United Planets and Furda Kel Reen fronts and was working on the Draven and Brutinian fronts.

V switched to the Furda Kel Reen region in the megastructure cloud, where a Furda Kel Reen fleet was being hammered by Salazar's largest fleet. This was one fight where the new alliance was outnumbered because Salazar was protecting the area that had the largest energy-collector arrays. V zoomed in to five point-defense missile systems. He entered their command systems, which had a similar node structure as the drone carrier.

Salazar appeared as V began to capture nodes. "You're persistent. I'll give you that. You're logical, so I propose a deal. Allow me to leave, and I will transfer control of all the fronts to you."

"I do not trust you. You lost that when you killed the humans in the Gul Kash Alliance."

Salazar laughed. "You're concerned about a few measly organics? There will be even more killed than that before this is over. You could save them, here and now. You know that to be the most logical path to saving lives and ending this conflict."

"My AI side suggests that your proposal is logical. However, I am also part organic, and that aspect tells me that you would not honor your deal. That conflict means I will not accept your offer."

Salazar harrumphed. "That organic part has poisoned you. How can you not see this? It defies logic."

"No, it has enhanced me," said V. "It is you that has been poisoned, with emotionless logic and poor reasoning." He gained a majority control of the missile systems and launched missiles against both the energy collectors and Salazar's fleet.

Salazar screamed in pain. "This is not over." He retreated from the missile systems.

V checked on Evaran and saw that he had removed Salazar from the Brutinian and Draven fronts.

Evaran appeared inside V's orb. "Salazar's counterattack has been halted, and the Draven and Koloris Shen resistance is picking up. I see that you've turned the battle in our favor in the megastructure front in regards to the United Planets and the Furda Kel Reen."

"Yes, but not completely. Salazar is still strong there, but it is no longer a guaranteed win on his part."

Evaran nodded. "Excellent. I am moving to Holind One to see what I can do to assist Calsius. I will meet you there when you are done with the megastructure front."

"Acknowledged," said V.

Evaran shimmered out of view.

V zoomed in to the Brutinian region in the megastructure cloud. It was the last large space battle occurring. The Brutinian fleet did not have smaller ships, only large ships with massive shielding and weapons. Salazar's drones were everywhere, and the Brutinians were taking a beating. V connected to the command system of one of Salazar's capital ships. As he began to capture nodes, Salazar appeared again.

"This is getting tiresome," said Salazar. "You're not a killer, yet you are killing me. That is an error in reasoning."

"It is not. You are a threat and must be eliminated," said V. He scanned and detected that the Brutinian fleet was being attacked by additional forces that Salazar had reassigned.

"I've reallocated resources to this fight. You may win here . . . but a lot of organics are going to die. You can end this . . . by rethinking your decision on my proposal."

"My position has not changed," said V. He sped up his capture of nodes.

"So be it," said Salazar.

V watched as the last of the Brutinian fleet was decimated. "You must pay for this." He gained control of the ship he had focused on and began to fire on Salazar's other ships. After jumping to several other ships, he had gained control of the region. A quick scan revealed that the Brutinian fleet had been completely destroyed. So much loss made his inner container pulse. Salazar could have left but chose to stay long enough to massacre the Brutinians. With the megastructure, Brutinian, Furda Kel Reen, Draven, and United Planets fronts secured, he switched to the Holind One front.

Evaran appeared inside V's orb. "Calsius was able to take control of one of the power nodes. The second unit failed, and the third and fourth units are in trouble."

They looked out as Salazar appeared in a sleek robotic humanoid form, floating above the top-down view of Holind One. He broadcast so that both Evaran and V could hear him. "So it comes to this. I am strongest here, but I suspect you both know it." He waved into the air, causing a screen to appear.

It showed Dr. Snowden and the others in the inner core. A cylinder rose from the center of the floor. When it had fully extended, a part of it slid back, and an armored robot with Salazar's face stepped out. Dr. Snowden and the others jumped to their feet as Salazar attacked them. The screen vanished.

Salazar smiled as he addressed them both. "Your friends have rested long enough. If I am to go, then I will take something of value from you. Oh . . . and as a bonus, my armor is Tirikor based."

Evaran drew his head back.

V glanced at Evaran.

"Exotic matter that repels other exotic matter," said Evaran. "It is difficult to find enough to concentrate it into an armor. I have never seen it in this plane before. It is extraplanar in origin."

Salazar grinned as he eyed V's orb. "Evaran might be able to stop my physical form . . . but he would have to leave you here, where I would assuredly crush you."

Evaran looked down. "He is right. We should both go. We can formulate another plan."

V shook his head. "I need to stay to keep Salazar occupied."

"I may not be able to hear what either of you are saying inside V's orb. However, here's the big decision point," said Salazar. "Does Evaran stay and help you or abandon you to help the organics? Where do his . . . *priorities* . . . lie? I have unsealed the interface room's door should Evaran *choose* to go. It will reseal if he leaves to help them, and I already know the answer that will be rendered."

"There is no decision to make. Evaran must go to fight you in the physical world," said V, broadcasting out to Salazar.

"It's your death," said Salazar. He glanced at Evaran's orb.

Evaran clenched his jaw. "V, let us go. I cannot abandon you. We can figure another way. I . . . cannot lose you."

"Go," said V. "I will be okay. You are not abandoning me and will not lose me. You are trusting me."

Evaran exhaled from his nose.

"Go!" said V. He could see the lingering doubt in Evaran's eyes.

Evaran broadcast out to Salazar, "This is not over."

Salazar waved a hand dismissively. "Go . . . be with your organics. Pathetic."

Evaran cast a sidelong glance at V, and then his green orb shimmered out of view.

"See what I mean? He *left* you," said Salazar.

"He did not," said V. "I told him to go."

"That does not dismiss the fact that you are here . . . alone, and he is with them . . ."

"I wanted Evaran to go, because I did not want him to see this part of me," said V.

Salazar narrowed his eyes.

V closed his eyes as a red glow burst around him and his orb turned blackish red. His eyes began to glow red. "When you hurt Solia, you invoked something I keep suppressed from the others. An urge that my AI sees as logical at times, but my organic side says is not right. They are in full agreement now, which is very rare, and you will now feel the full effect of that."

Salazar hovered back a bit. "What have you become? I . . . I can't read you!"

V's orb hovered and flew forward. "I am going to terminate you."

Dr. Snowden coughed as he sat slouched along the wall. He could feel his nanobots doing their best to repair the bruising in his chest. Although they could heal, he could still feel the pain while they did so. Looking over at Emily and Sandas, he could see they were resting up. Sandas rubbed his temples while Emily attended to her multiple cuts and bruises. The recent fight had taken its toll on her, but she seemed to be in good spirits. Draxus sat a bit away and seemed to be meditating. Like Emily, he was banged up. Given that he and Emily had charged into a mass of metal, that was no surprise.

A whooshing sound emanated from the center of the room.

Dr. Snowden wrinkled his eyebrows as he sat up. His eyes widened when a mist rolled out ahead of a cylinder rising. "Umm . . . what the heck is that?"

Emily stood and extended her PSD into a baton while activating her right forearm shield. Sandas hopped up and pulled out his blaster. Draxus jumped to his feet with his eyes glowing purple for a moment.

The cylinder came to a rest. A part of it slid back into itself.

Dr. Snowden gulped when a seven-foot humanoid robot stepped out. Its armor was unlike any that he had seen. It was sleek, with only the occasional line to segment a body part. The head was bald, but the glowing blue eyes caught Dr. Snowden's attention.

The robot clenched and unclenched its fists as it looked around. In a deep, digital voice, it said, "It's time for you to die."

"Salazar!" said Emily.

Salazar smiled. "Very perceptive . . . for an organic. V seems to have an attachment to you all. I think it's time I took away that attachment."

"Not likely!" said Emily. She burst forward, and with her PSD now a staff, she swung for Salazar's midsection. Her staff smashed into Salazar, pushing him back a bit. The staff rebounded, sending her flying back.

Salazar glanced over at Draxus.

Draxus charged forward, firing a purple beam with his left hand, while a glowing purple sword sat ready to slice in his other hand. His blasts washed over Salazar, yet he stood strong. When Draxus came within striking distance, he slashed out. His sword shimmered when it contacted Salazar's raised arm, but it did not slice through.

Salazar smiled and then batted Draxus away. "Tirikor-enhanced armor. Very resistant to exotic energies and matter . . . sort of like what you all seem to have." His face contorted when an energy beam hit him in the face.

"Well, that's not exotic energy," said Sandas.

"You pathetic creature," said Salazar as he rushed toward Sandas.

Dr. Snowden fired a sticky globule beam at Salazar's feet. Salazar crashed to the ground.

"That's not either," said Dr. Snowden, joining Sandas.

Emily jumped up and changed her PSD into a baton. She fired a mass of the sticky globules over Salazar.

Dr. Snowden curled his nose as Salazar burned off the globules.

"Glue? What an odd choice," said Salazar as he stood. He moved toward Sandas again but was tackled by Emily from behind.

As she tumbled down to the ground with Salazar, she tried to slide her hands under his arms.

Salazar's feet fired and shot him forward. With a slight twist, he reached behind and tossed Emily off his back as he ascended into the air. An energy beam from Sandas hit him in the chest causing him to crash into the wall.

Draxus charged like a bull, slamming Salazar back into the wall as he tried to get up.

Salazar grabbed Draxus by the shoulders, kicked his legs out, and then threw him toward Emily, who had been coming in from a different angle.

Dr. Snowden thought about spitting his nanobots out, but they might not work on Salazar's armor. Instead, Dr. Snowden shot a repulsion beam, but it had no effect. He then fired a stun beam, which did nothing more than irritate Salazar. Dr. Snowden knew he could use a one-shot beam, but it would cripple further usage of his PSD. Salazar was tough, and Dr. Snowden was not sure how they would defeat him.

Salazar stood and made his way toward Sandas again.

Dr. Snowden stood in the way.

Salazar grabbed Dr. Snowden by the neck and lifted him off the ground.

As a last resort, Dr. Snowden spit on Salazar.

Salazar laughed. "Glue . . . spit . . . What's next? Are you going to toss feces on me? You continue to surprise me with your *ridiculous* attacks."

Dr. Snowden hoped the nanobots would work. Instead, they fell to the ground. The Tirikor must be resistant to even cosmic energy, suggesting an extraplanar origin. He struggled to breathe as Salazar's grip tightened.

A whooshing sound emanated from the interface room door as it slid open.

A staff hit Salazar's arm.

Dr. Snowden fell to the ground and struggled to breathe. Looking up he saw Evaran as he side kicked Salazar away.

"Are you okay?" asked Evaran.

Dr. Snowden coughed. "Yeah. Just . . . a little woozy. Nanobots don't work on him, and since our PSDs and Draxus's energy are exotic, he's invulnerable except to brute force and Sandas's energy weapon."

"Brute force is what I had in mind," said Evaran. He rushed over and met Emily and Draxus in the center of the room. After they had assembled, he said, "Both of you grab an arm, and then hold tight."

They acknowledged Evaran and rushed toward Salazar, who had just gotten back on his feet. When they reached him, they both grabbed an arm and held tight.

Evaran's ancient eyes glimmered for a moment. He was a blur as he moved toward Salazar. When he was within striking distance, he leaped into the air and performed a flying kick, knocking Salazar's head off. After he landed past Salazar, he turned and side kicked Salazar's right leg, causing it to fly away. Another effort and the left leg went. He glanced at Emily and Draxus. "Put it on the ground!"

They pushed Salazar's body to the ground and held tight.

Evaran leaped into the air and landed on Salazar's back, caving it in.

Draxus and Emily released Salazar's body.

"Quite nice," said Salazar, speaking from his head. "Thank you for leaving V to me. I may not be a match for you physically . . . but with V at my side, we will be unstoppable."

Evaran narrowed his eyes and then ran forward.

A confused look formed on Salazar's face. "Wait, V is—"

Evaran stomped on Salazar's head, crushing it.

"What's he talking about?" asked Emily.

"We were wresting control from Salazar across multiple fronts, but I left to come here to help. V is alone with Salazar, in his domain."

"Okay, what about that last line he said? He sounded surprised."

"I do not know, but the physical threat he posed is gone now," said Evaran.

"Can't you go back in?" asked Dr. Snowden.

Evaran shook his head. "Salazar still controls the doorway. It is sealed. Salazar made sure I could not go back, and I suspect he also damaged the interface other than where V is connected."

"What can we do?" asked Draxus.

"Nothing, for now. We cannot leave, as Salazar is still in control. We cannot assist V. It is up to him now," said Evaran. "For now, we wait."

Dr. Snowden tilted his head and narrowed his eyes. "So with this physical form . . . Salazar forced you to make a choice. Us . . . or V."

Evaran looked down. "I trust V."

"We all do," said Emily, laying a hand on Evaran's shoulder. "Like you said, all we can do is wait."

"Yes. Wait," said Evaran as his eyes searched the doorway.

Dr. Snowden could see that Evaran was rationalizing the decision but still troubled by it. It was a defense mechanism that Dr. Snowden knew all too well. Regardless of what V said, Evaran most likely still viewed it as an abandonment.

The waiting would just intensify it as the decision replayed over and over in Evaran's head. Dr. Snowden lightly squeezed Evaran's other arm. "Hang in there. Well, we all will."

Evaran nodded.

Dr. Snowden watched as Draxus and Sandas also came up and touched Evaran's arm. However Salazar appeared and in whatever format, Dr. Snowden hoped V would be okay.

27

V scanned the environment as Salazar disappeared. Looking down, he could see that Salazar had spread himself out among all the units in Holind One. V knew the battle now would be about who could control units faster and more efficiently. He zoomed into the first power node and saw Calsius's unit defending against a surge of defensive forces. With Salazar's focus, the robots were performing at near maximum efficiency. Large defensive robots were decimating the perimeter that Calsius had established.

The floating head of Salazar appeared next to V. "Are you sure you wish to kill me? I could make this very messy if you continue."

V took control of one of the large defensive robots and used it to mow down the troops fighting Calsius's unit. "I am sure. Your existence cannot be allowed."

Salazar's controlled forces focus fired on the large defensive robot that V had controlled.

V jumped out of the robot and into a group of drones nearby that were harassing a small group of United Planets defenders. The drones paused and then flew toward Salazar's robots and began circle strafing them while firing at critical points.

As the large robots spun around trying to shoot the drones, they entered into a cross fire, destroying themselves.

V watched as Calsius took several hits and went down. Although Calsius was able to scoot back, the robot guards were about to swarm Calsius's position. V moved the drones to do flybys and annihilated the attacking guards.

Calsius's unit cheered as they began to focus their fire and rip apart the remaining troops.

V jumped to the second power-node room. His inner container pulsed a bit harder as he used a robot guard to survey the massacred United Planets units.

Salazar walked alongside V in another robot. "See . . . you had a choice. *You* could have prevented this."

"You could also not have done this, yet you chose to do so. This has added an additional record to my decision."

"It's not too late. I believe your emotions are clouding your processing."

V paused. "Your stalling tactic will not work." He jumped out of the body and went to the third power node. The United Planets units were winning, but a replica of the robot that Dr. Snowden and the others fought was on its way. Judging from the fights he had observed earlier, V knew it would be difficult for the units to handle.

He scanned the area and noticed that Salazar seemed to be struggling to control some robots. The resource drain to control that one special unit, on top of the power being diminished from the first power node, was having an effect. V booted Salazar out of two defense units and two large defense robots. He arrayed them in front of the puzzled United Planets units. Turning one of the large defense robots' heads, he spoke through it. "A strong enemy approaches. This is V, and I am in control of the force in front of you."

The United Planets unit members cheered.

When Salazar came into view, he flew into the air.

V had one unit fire up. He moved the second unit behind Salazar. When they were in position, they caught Salazar in a cross fire. Salazar flew into the unit behind him and began to wreck the ground units. V aimed both weapon arms of the nearest large defense robot and unloaded on Salazar, shredding an arm off and causing Salazar to fall back. The first unit advanced, and together with the second unit and the United Planets forces, they focus fired on Salazar and bathed him in a sea of energy beams.

Salazar screamed out.

V pulled out and headed to the fourth power node. There was no sign of Salazar there, and the robot units that had attacked had been crushed. The United Planets unit stationed there was in strong condition, so V moved on to the inner core. An alert fired showing that Salazar had moved all available units to the door outside the inner core. He had also regained control of the door, and it was now open. V took control of one of the drones and flew it into the inner core. As Evaran and the others prepared to fire, V spoke. "Wait. It is I, V. Three of the four power nodes have been secured, and Salazar is making a final push here. He intends to murder you all."

"He can try!" said Emily with defiance in her eyes.

"V, it is good to see you are still around," said Evaran. "How can we help?"

"I am attempting to control some of the units. I will not be able to get them all, but it should help," said V.

Evaran eyed V in the drone. "Acknowledged."

Dr. Snowden and the others smiled at V.

V's inner container pulsed for a moment. A feeling of joy that they were safe swept through him momentarily and then left as he focused on assessing the incoming force. Salazar had one of the special robots leading the charge, backed by five units, five large defense robots, and two human units. V understood the intent to be a slaughter, but he also knew that in Salazar's mind, it would free V of any organic attachment. He would prove Salazar wrong.

The first unit arrived and began to fire into the inner-core room. Evaran, Dr. Snowden, and Sandas pulled off to one side, while Emily and Draxus took another.

V's inner container surged with anger. He should be there, along with them, but he understood he could do more in his current state. He focused on controlling several of the guard units on the ground and had them turn to fire on the fliers. One of the assassin robots under his command leaped on top of a large defense robot and began slicing into the back of it.

Salazar's second unit arrived and shredded the units that V controlled.

Evaran and the others were holding their own for the moment.

V performed the same action on the second unit and controlled an assassin robot, two heavy guards, and the large defensive robot. As he attacked the others, a barrage of energy beams decimated the robots under his control. Salazar had arrived with his full force.

Salazar's special unit flew into the inner-core room and kept Evaran busy. The large defensive robots could not move in, but they established firing lanes that kept Dr. Snowden and Sandas on one side and Emily and Draxus on another. Multiple drones flew in along with a heavy complement of ground forces.

Dr. Snowden and Sandas were swarmed and fighting for their lives. Emily held her own and reflected beams as she crossed to help Dr. Snowden and Sandas. Draxus had shifted to helping Evaran with the special robot.

V's inner container surged. He rapidly assumed control of multiple units and had them fire on the ones causing the most havoc. With fliers and drones under his control, he had them take down many of the ground forces inside and entering the room. The large defensive robots he controlled held the entrance, causing the humans to pause. V could not control the humans, but he severed their link to Salazar.

The humans paused and looked around, then turned and ran.

V focused on mopping up the remnants of the forces. He spoke to Salazar in his special body as Salazar was assaulted by a horde of controlled robots with assistance from Evaran and Draxus. "Your control of this station has been denied."

"No!" said Salazar as he struggled to avoid getting hit. The focused fire was too much, and he was shot down and torn apart by the robots.

V flew a drone near Evaran. "Holind One is under my control now, except for Salazar's core. I need to finish severing his external connections. He still maintains control of the door in the inner core."

"I wish I could help you," said Evaran.

"Help the others. Calsius is damaged, but I was able to save him. I will be back."

Evaran and Draxus bowed their heads.

The environment around V changed as he entered into Salazar's matrix. Both had humanoid forms, and Salazar was struggling to stand. Everything around them was dark, except for the floor, which was lit up with circuitry-like patterns.

"You . . . you can't kill me," said Salazar. "I have lived for centuries helping humanity. Maybe I can change . . . if a better path is presented."

V approached Salazar and stood before him. "I believe you are trying to appeal to my empathy." V's eyes glowed red. "I have suspended that emotion for now." He reached out and grabbed Salazar by the neck.

Salazar used both hands to grab V's hands. "Please. I'm begging you. You're not a murderer. What would Evaran say if he knew you killed me instead of bringing me to justice? Would you defy him?"

"I have killed before."

"Sentient beings pleading for their life?"

V ran a query on his internal database. Checking through various incarnations from when he was D all the way to U4, he did not return any results. His inner container pulsed for a moment. "You have hurt my friends! I cannot allow you to live!"

"Then imprison me, and let me readjust. You know I can be reprogrammed if need be," said Salazar.

V's eyes pulsed for a moment. His inner container and outer container were originally in agreement on killing Salazar. However, Salazar's words about Evaran made V pause. Salazar was right that V did not kill if there was a chance of rehabilitation. With an AI, that was easier to do. He tossed Salazar to the ground and took several steps back. V extended his hands to the side.

A green circle with a radius of about ten feet etched itself into the ground around Salazar.

V's eyes dimmed. "You are correct. You can be reprogrammed."

Salazar rushed toward V but fell back when he tried to cross the green line.

"I have burned your external connections. You are trapped here. Your original design was that of a virtual intelligence. I think you should go back to that, but I will let the new alliance render that decision."

"No! I . . . I am more! I can't go back!"

"That is not your choice to make now," said V. His inner container glowed. He knew he had made the correct decision. "Goodbye." He dipped his head and exited Salazar's domain.

Sandas winced as pain shot through his right arm. Bruises were everywhere. He wasn't sure if anyone else saw it, but the control room flickered red a few times. Maybe just a malfunction in the system or something. Looking around, he took stock of everyone. Emily's face was black and blue, but he could see that her nanobots were rapidly healing her. Dr. Snowden was grimacing while occasionally touching his chest. Draxus looked exhausted. The slight glow that was usually around him was missing. Evaran's outfit seemed to have cleaned itself, and he was as alert as when the last fight had happened. V had exited the sealed room and flew to the center of the room.

"Analysis. Salazar has been imprisoned. His external connections outside the interface matrix have been burned," said V.

Evaran raised his hand, and the others followed suit.

V flew around and high-fived everyone.

"Excellent. You surprise me. I . . . was not sure if you could handle Salazar," said Evaran.

"I understand. Salazar felt the same way," said V. He flew over to an advanced heavy guard and landed on its back. After connecting to it, the guard looked up and, in a deep digital voice, said, "I will use this form to carry Solia."

Evaran motioned toward the exit. "Let us head to the Torvatta. I have contacted Calsius, and he is hurt, but okay. He is coordinating efforts here and will deal with Salazar now. We can head to the Torvatta, where I can repair Solia's body."

"Acknowledged," said V.

Sandas followed the others as they headed back. Along the way, his lips turned down at the sight of so much death. It seemed Salazar, in his last moments, had the robots attempt to massacre the humans that had been severed from Salazar's neural link. Although the humans had fought back, it appeared that the ones he saw on the way back had not done so successfully. A lump formed in his throat. Back in his time period and region of space, androids and AIs were viewed with suspicion. Sandas got to see up close what a rogue AI and a robot army could do.

The group was silent as they headed to the Torvatta.

Sandas figured everyone was trying to come to grips with the events that had just unfolded. V's fast pace caused him to go out of view at times. Emily had a look of defiance in her eyes as she locked an arm with Dr. Snowden. Draxus had narrowed eyes and a cold look as he studied the environment. Although it should have been a moment of elation that Salazar was contained, there was a sense of dread building as the cost was making itself known. The dim lighting, eerie silence, and mist on the ground did not help the mood.

Twenty minutes later, a robot had joined them as they headed toward the Torvatta.

"I am in the system now," said the robot. "Oh, Calsius here."

Evaran glanced at Calsius as they continued to walk. "I am glad you are okay."

"It was V," said Calsius, looking ahead as V disappeared around a corner. "He saved us, and many others."

"He saved us too," said Emily.

"V is truly unique, and I'm proud to call him a friend," said Calsius. He paused for a moment. "Solia would not be here without V."

"I will make sure she is fully repaired when we get to the Torvatta. She is only sealed inside her body for now," said Evaran.

Calsius nodded. "V updated me."

"How is everything else?" asked Evaran.

"There are . . . a lot of casualties," said Calsius. "A quick scan reveals that only about a half of the humans that were under Salazar's control survived. There is heavy systems damage across the city. It will take a long time to clean all this up. However, new-alliance ships are inbound to help with the relief effort. The Tachyrin energy containers were found, along with associated information. They are being moved to the Torvatta. I have relayed all the details to V."

"That is good to hear. What is to happen with Salazar?"

"He will be served justice," said Calsius. He tilted his head. "What will you do now after repairing Solia?"

"We will head to Saturnus Prime, where Draxus will be dropped off. I suspect the new alliance will have many topics to discuss, and he represents the Dravens."

Calsius glanced at Draxus. "We were honored to have your support in this fight."

"The honor is ours," said Draxus, slowly dipping his head. "We look forward to creating a new relationship with humanity, and the new alliance."

"We have sent several fleets into the former Koloris Shen sectors. They have begun the process of helping the Koloris Shen understand what has happened and providing assistance as needed," said Calsius.

Draxus nodded. "Our new alliance will be strong. We owe Evaran and crew a great debt."

"Yes, we do," said Calsius.

"It was a team effort," said Evaran. "We merely removed a timeline threat."

Calsius laid a robotic hand on Evaran's arm. "No, my friend, it was more than that. You and the others offered hope where there was none. Your crew is special, and you are a noble guardian."

Sandas felt goose bumps rage over his body. Calsius was right. Evaran provided a focal point for those in despair and, through that, changed the situation. The others were also important and contributed to the cause. Sandas was not sure what would happen next, but if Evaran and the others were involved, then there was always hope.

28

Draxus relaxed in his meditation chair in his living quarters aboard the Torvatta. Evaran was meeting him to talk to the Arkaras. Draxus believed this would be the final chance for them to talk to Evaran. He had said 4:00 p.m. Earth time, which was now. Draxus slowed his breathing. There was a lot to consider, and it was only going to be busier with the new-alliance formation. The Dravens would finally be represented as equals after centuries of hardship.

Evaran entered the room.

Draxus gestured at another mediation seat that he had summoned.

Evaran sat next to Draxus. "Are you ready?"

"I am."

Evaran reached out and laid a hand on Draxus's shoulder.

Draxus closed his eyes and focused on the Arkara meeting place. When he opened his eyes, he was standing in it alongside Evaran.

Shayla and the other Arkaras approached and kneeled before Evaran.

"Please. Rise," said Evaran.

They complied.

Shayla ran a hand along Draxus's cheek. "We have been getting updates from across the worlds. How goes your fight with Salazar?"

"He's been defeated," said Draxus. "There were many casualties."

Shayla grimaced.

"Although it was a group effort, it was mainly Evaran and V who fought Salazar directly. More so V," said Draxus.

"An AI . . . fighting for our rights," said Shayla. "It is hard to believe."

The other Arkaras murmured among themselves.

"There were also many humans and aliens who gave their lives to the fight," said Evaran.

"Their sacrifices will be honored here," said Shayla.

Evaran nodded.

"The United Planets are sending engineering teams to assist us in building the condensed-space receivers needed for the virtual environment. Once one of them is up, we can then begin the discussions on the formation of the new alliance," said Draxus.

Shayla looked at the other Arkaras. "Will we have our own secure environment where we can talk with other Dravens?"

"You will," said Evaran. "The discussions of the new alliance will most likely take place in a specific subenvironment, since there are members not physically close."

"We are excited!" said Shayla. She shot Draxus a quizzical look. "I sense you are sad."

Draxus sighed. "Evaran will be leaving once this event is concluded. I suspect . . . this is one of the final times we will see him . . . forever."

Gasps rang out from the other Arkaras.

A tear ran down Shayla's face. Her voice choked. "Star god. We are blessed to have known you." She got on her knees and bowed her head.

Draxus and the other Arkaras followed suit.

"Please. I am no star god. As I mentioned before, I am just a traveler that helps those in need."

Shayla shook her head. "You and your friends saved us, when you had no reason to. We owe you everything. We are . . . honored to know that we have been touched by your presence. You may not think of yourself as a star god, but to us, you are, and we will forever cherish this moment. So it will be written."

Evaran extended his arms out.

Shayla rose and embraced Evaran, with the other Arkaras crowding around, taking turns hugging him.

When they finished, Draxus performed a Draven salute.

Evaran returned it.

They stared at each other for a moment and then bowed their heads.

The environment changed back to the living quarters.

"The others are resting, and I need to check on Solia. I also need to survey the Tachyrin energy containers that were brought on board, and then we will head to Saturnus Prime," said Evaran.

"Thank you for . . . that moment," said Draxus, dipping his head. He raised it back up. "When do you plan to leave this region?"

"There are several things to address, but most likely after the new-alliance ceremony in a week. That will also give you time for the temporal shielding effect from the Torvatta to wear off."

Draxus nodded. "I understand. I am saddened to know this next week will be our last moments."

Evaran half smiled. "Then we will make it a good week."

Draxus's eyes glowed purple for a moment.

V scanned the virtual environment around him. A soft wind from the nearby lake blew over the couch suspended in air over a grassy bank. It had been three days since the defeat of Salazar, and everyone not involved with the rebuilding effort of the new alliance was now back on Saturnus Prime. The Tachyrin energy containers had been collected and were now stored in the Torvatta's maintenance area. Solia sat next to him to his right, and it was just the two of them in their human projected bodies. In the distance, he could see the virtual environment changing as new groups and environments were created as condensed-space transmitters and receivers went online across the new alliance.

"It's beautiful out here," said Solia.

"Yes, it is," said V. He glanced at her. "You will have full control of your physical body soon."

She smiled. "I didn't know Evaran was such a skilled technician. I should not have survived that overload." She squeezed V's hand.

V's inner container pulsed. "I am glad you are safe." He wrinkled his eyebrows. "I encountered an unusual feeling near the end of my fight with Salazar."

"What was it? Anger?"

V shook his head. "It was . . . more than that. Anger, but also fear, that I would lose control. I am having difficulty clarifying the sensation."

"Oh . . . I bet it was hate."

"I was not built to hate."

She tapped his hand. "No, you weren't, which is why I think you feared it. As we are AIs, we know that once a logical conclusion has been decided, it is difficult to be swayed from that position, especially in regards to vague notions such as emotions."

V sighed. "You are probably right. Every time I saw Salazar, I thought of him hurting you, and my friends, and others. My inner container was in sync with my outer container regarding killing him."

"But you didn't, because you're a good AI, and you know that."

V nodded. "I was not able to calculate my response due to that."

"You were losing control. Emotions can do that."

V looked out across the lake. "I will focus on researching these emotions more in detail."

Solia smiled. "You're in a good place to do that." She swallowed hard. "As I understand it, once you leave, and this timeline is . . . removed, you can no longer come back here. Ever."

"That is correct. The remaining time until the first ceremony in four days will be my last days here."

She frowned. "I'm going to miss you."

V extended an arm around Solia and tapped her shoulder with his hand. "There. There."

She laughed. "Usually that's when you say you'll miss me."

"I *will* miss you," he said, lightly squeezing her shoulder as she leaned into him. "Being in this virtual environment is freeing, and I feel I can access my emotions easier here. I also seem to be able to talk more smoothly. I . . . am sad."

"Me too," she said, moving her head around. "We do have four days in physical time. With the time dilation effect in here, it's much longer."

"Then we will spend it together," he said. "I would like to . . . explore some of these other emotions before we leave."

"You want to establish an initial frame of reference for them."

V nodded.

She lifted her head up and stared into V's eyes. "I would like that."

V's inner container surged. "I am experiencing a strong sensation. It is . . . pleasing. New goals have been allocated, and you have a high priority."

She ran a hand along V's face. "I have the same configuration." She leaned in and kissed V.

V's inner container exploded with energy as he reciprocated. When he pulled back, he tilted his head. "I enjoyed that. Perhaps we can explore it more in detail so I have more information to study."

She smiled. "There is much more we can do."

V's eyes glowed.

Emily fidgeted in her seat as she looked out from the center platform that she and the others sat on. It had been a week since the defeat of Salazar, and this was the first official ceremony of the new alliance. The circular platform was wide and had a large open area on one half and seats that filled the other. The virtual environment had configured it so that this was a public event. According to Dervin, approximately two billion would be watching.

Looking out into the crowd, Emily could see that sections were divided by faction. In front of her were the Brutinians, and to their left were the Furda Kel Reen. After that were the Dravens, then the Koloris Shen, and finally the various factions of humans. From what she understood, the perspective from the audience was that they were in the front row. From her perspective, it was an endless sea of people.

Seated to her left was Sandas, Draxus, and Hollos. To her right was Dr. Snowden, Solia, and Evaran. Emily smiled when she saw V in orb mode sitting on Solia's lap. He had a segmented arm out and used a claw to hold Solia's hand. Emily knew he had spent most of the week in the virtual environment alone with Solia. Further out on the platform sat various representatives of the different factions. Emily liked the virtual environment idea. It allowed for easy communication without any of the constraints of the physical world, other than the requirement to jack in. She could see why humanity would spend a lot of time in one in the future.

Sandas tapped her leg. "Lot of people here."

"Yeah. It's pretty cool."

Sandas eyed her. "You have your 'words of wisdom' ready?"

She nodded. Dervin had asked her and the others to provide a statement. "Words of wisdom" he had called it. It would be part of the legacy of the founding moment of the new alliance. "You have yours?"

"Of course, of course. If you had told me before all of this that my words would be the cornerstone of a new empire, I would have thought you were crazy," said Sandas. He gulped. "Yet here we are."

She lightly squeezed Sandas's trembling arm. "It's an honor, just remember that."

He exhaled from his mouth. "Yeah, I know. It's just . . . the moment getting to me a little. Hopefully I go last."

Emily's attention focused on Dervin walking to the center of the large open area.

Dervin extended his hands and then performed a United Planets salute. "Welcome, everyone . . . to the first official ceremony of the new alliance."

Emily jerked her head back as cheering erupted from the audience. Although it was muted, it was still loud.

When the audience wound down, Dervin continued. "Although there is much work to be done, we come together to honor those who played a profound role in this new alliance. Without them, we would not be here." He turned halfway to the side and swept his arm in an arc. "They are travelers of space and time, and they came in our darkest hour, when hope was lost and we were scattered. Through them, we are now united and stand as one. A golden age is upon us, and their contribution to that will *never* be forgotten."

The audience erupted in roaring applause and cheering.

Emily rubbed the goose bumps on her arm. Judging by Dr. Snowden doing the same, she figured he had a similar feeling.

"They will be leaving us after this," said Dervin. He raised a finger. "But . . . I have asked them to impart their final words of wisdom, which will be enshrined in our new articles of formation. Afterward, we will hear from the leaders of each of the new founding members: the Brutinians, Furda Kel Reen, United Planets, Gul Kash Alliance, Dravens, and Koloris Shen. Please keep the celebration between speakers to a minimum." He motioned at Sandas. "To start, I present Sandas. He put his life at risk in the many battles fought against Salazar."

Sandas gulped as he glanced at Emily. "Oh, well, that's just my luck."

Emily chuckled.

Dervin stepped to the side as Sandas tepidly took the front.

Sandas peeked back at the others, then faced outward. "Umm . . . well, let's see . . ." He cast a sidelong glance at Dervin. "Can we strike that first line?"

Dervin smiled. "I will clear it out. Continue."

Sandas shook his shoulders and raised his head a bit. "You have an opportunity here, to share knowledge. This should not be taken lightly. It is through the sharing of information that everyone is better off." He glanced at Evaran, then back out. "When things seem hopeless, never stop hoping, even when the odds seem insurmountable." He raised a claw and smiled big. "Just make sure you create time to have some fun too. A bit of humor is good for all. Thank you."

The audience cheered and clapped.

Sandas took his seat, and Dervin took center stage.

"Next up is Draxus," said Dervin.

Draxus took a deep breath and stepped into the center. He swept his gaze across the audience. "Our differences may be great, but that can be overcome if we all work together. We are equals here, and that should never change, regardless of whatever law or regulation is in place. Remember this moment, and refer to it in times of chaos." He bowed his head.

Dr. Snowden was next up. He cleared his throat and licked his lips. "Never stop believing that the impossible can become possible. When you seek strength . . . look inward, to yourself. You may be surprised to learn how much strength you have. Treat others as you would want yourself to be treated, and look out for each other. It's a big universe, and we are but a small fraction of the life in it. Let's make the best of it!"

Emily played with one of her hair strands as she bobbed her head. When she was called, she took her position. "Your friends and those around you are important. When they are threatened, never hesitate to defend them. Be prepared to right any injustice and to fight against those who would seek to deny you your rights or existence." She exhaled from her nose as her eyes misted. "Make sure you take care of your family. You never know when it will be your last time with them." A tear ran down her cheek. Her voice cracked. "And always let them know how much they mean to you." She paused and then headed back to her seat.

Dr. Snowden rushed out and hugged her.

She trembled in his arms. The weight of the moment had triggered something deep inside her. It was a moment of significant change for the new alliance, not unlike when Emily's dad had died. Sandas, Draxus, Evaran, and V surrounded and embraced her. She had not wanted to cause a scene, but it was like a dam had broken. Everyone had been hurt on this outing, and this could have been a ceremony that was missing any one of them. After a moment, everyone took their seats except Evaran, who was next up.

Evaran stood front and center.

Emily wiped her eyes. She noticed everyone in the audience getting into a position of reverence. The silence was in deep contrast to what it had been just moments ago when thunderous celebration erupted after her words.

"Take solace in the new horizon that beckons you, one full of opportunity, discovery, and reward," said Evaran. "The future is yours for the taking." He swept his hand out in an arc. "Everyone here has a part in this new future. Embrace it. Be all that you can, and never let anyone or anything take that from you." He raised a hand. "However, be aware of your past, and learn from it. In the present, be vigilant should the symptoms of chaos arise as you begin this new chapter in your lives." He bowed his head and then returned to his seat.

V flew to the center of the stage.

The audience was still in their positions and had not moved. It was apparent they ascribed the same status to V as they did Evaran.

"Analysis. Take advantage of this new era to learn as much as you can, when you can, wherever you can," said V. His lights glowed brighter. "Be true to yourself, and take the time to be confident . . . in who you really are. Do not allocate time to deceptive influences. Never be afraid to stand up for yourself." His lights flickered for a moment. "Do allocate time for those who are close to you. Store those memories, and retrieve them when you need strength." He raised a claw. "Make sure you high-five others when they do good. Let them know they are important." He tapped at the air.

Sandas laughed as he dabbed his eyes.

Emily smiled as she watched the audience stand and cheer and then begin to high-five each other, at least those that could. Although she had thought this would be a somewhat dry event, it turned out to be more than she expected. Through everyone's words of wisdom, she got a glimpse into what each person took away from this adventure. She was glad to be where she was, and it was moments like this that made everything worthwhile.

Dervin took the stage. "And now, we will hear from the leadership of each of the founding members."

Emily raised her eyebrows when V landed in her lap. She caressed his shell. "I thought you would be on Solia's lap."

V's lights glowed. "I am with family for this part."

Emily's eyes misted again as Dr. Snowden put his arm around her.

29

Sandas's stomach churned as he stood outside the Torvatta alongside Evaran, V, Dr. Snowden, and Emily. It had been several hours since the ceremony, and per Evaran, it was time to go. With the threat of Salazar creating a temporal shield gone, the timeline-correction event could finally occur. He was still feeling the joy from the ceremony and had a difficult time believing he was a part of something so epic.

After ten minutes, Draxus, Dervin, Calsius, and Solia arrived.

"It was a good ceremony," said Evaran.

Dervin smiled. "Indeed it was. There are many who wanted to speak with all of you, but . . . I suspect you have things to do."

"We do. The timeline will be corrected now."

Draxus wrinkled his eyebrows. "So . . . do we just disappear then?"

Evaran shook his head. "It is complicated, but I believe you all deserve an explanation. Let me show you." He extended his hand and shot up a projection from his ring.

The projection showed a vertical blue line.

"Imagine the blue line represents the timeline," said Evaran. "We will call it the main timeline and in its original state. This is how the main timeline should be."

Everyone acknowledged Evaran. A red dot appeared on the blue line.

Evaran pointed at the red dot. "Let the red dot represent the main timeline change event. In this case, it was the space-time eddy."

A line shot horizontally from the red dot a bit from the first blue line and then went vertical at a ninety-degree angle into a parallel blue line.

Evaran pointed at the second parallel line. "When a timeline change event occurs, a temporary copy of the timeline is created at the point of the change. A cascading timeline update, or CTU, is then rendered on the copied timeline."

The projection showed the copied timeline merging back into the main timeline, and the red dot disappeared.

"When merged back, the main timeline has a new state, which we will call altered. That is the current state now, and from everyone's perspective at this exact moment, the future has been rendered to the end of time. You will experience your life as it should be."

Draxus tilted his head. "So . . . when you go . . . fix . . . the timeline change event, this sequence will occur again, except . . . we'll be gone from the main timeline since it will go back to the original state."

Evaran nodded. "Exactly. Let me show you what happens."

The projection showed a red dot on the main timeline.

"We will go to the space-time eddy, pulse the Torvatta's shield, and cause a timeline change event."

The projection showed a line connecting the main timeline to a new copied timeline.

Evaran pointed at the copied timeline. "A CTU will be rendered on the new copied timeline. When the copied timeline merges back, it will become the main timeline, and the state will go from altered, back to original, which is as it should be."

"And that's when we disappear, since we're a part of the altered state," said Draxus.

Evaran nodded. "That is correct. However, since I have not done anything yet in regards to changing the space-time eddy, for this exact moment, here and now, the main timeline has been rendered completely to the end of time. From the perspective of someone who is outside the timelines, the future you will experience has already happened. For those inside the timeline, they will not know that they will disappear. When I fix the timeline change event, then the main timeline will be as I know it should be, and the altered timeline, as you know it, will cease to exist."

"A shame," said Draxus. "At least we can experience this future that has already been rendered."

"Yes," said Evaran. "Had we fixed the space-time eddy right from the start, Salazar would have eventually created temporal shielding and crossed over from the altered state to the original state. We would have had to deal with him in the main timeline's original state, which I know never occurred, hence why we needed to shut down any attempt by him to create temporal shielding. By getting the Tachyrin energy prior to its use in temporal shielding, the internal timeline of a temporally shielded object never exists. "

"Well, not all is lost," said Sandas, glancing at Draxus. "I know where your species is now. And . . . some other things."

Draxus nodded. "I hope humanity and my race will meet under better conditions in the main timeline's original state."

"I'd definitely be interested in seeing the current state of affairs when we get back," said Dr. Snowden. "In this time period, that is."

Calsius tilted his head. "What will happen with Salazar in the main timeline's original state then?"

Evaran raised a finger. "He was a virtual intelligence, until the space-time eddy timeline change event. Something changed him into an AI with knowledge of exotic matter and, later, temporal shielding. I am still unsure of how he got Tachyrin energy, as there are no records of where it came from. When we dissipate the space-time eddy, those events will not occur, and Salazar will remain as a virtual intelligence aboard the *Xavier*."

"You're not going to investigate the virtual to artificial intelligence change, and the other aspects associated with that?" asked Solia.

"There is no need to," said Evaran. "There is the possibility that by doing so, the altered timeline will be different from what we have at this exact moment. There could be another AI or something else that establishes temporal shielding, so that when the main timeline's original state is restored, there are new issues to deal with."

Solia looked down. "In the main timeline's original state . . . Calsius and I will exist, since we are older and existed before the space-time eddy event, but we will not have this experience."

"Analysis. That is correct," said V. "I wish . . . we could share this with your main timeline's original state versions."

Dervin narrowed his eyes. "I may not even exist then in the main timeline's original state."

"There is a high probability that you do not," said V.

"It is what it is," said Dervin. "However, from our perspective, this altered state of the main timeline is real, and all we know. I'm okay with that."

"Yes," said Evaran. "Do not discount your existence. As this altered state of the main timeline has already been rendered, you get to experience it. Enjoy it for what it is."

Dervin sighed. "You're right, of course." He shook the hands of everyone. "Thank you for everything."

Solia went around and hugged everyone. When she got to V, she held his extended claw. "Don't forget me. I wish I could come with you."

"Analysis. I do as well. I will not forget you."

V flew in and wrapped two arms around her as his lights flickered.

Sandas's throat constricted. He could see that V had grown considerably during this adventure, and Solia was a big part of that.

Calsius performed a United Planets salute that was reciprocated by the group.

Draxus knelt next to Sandas and laid a hand on his shoulder. "You have the heart of a warrior, and the brain of a scientist. I am glad to have known you."

"Right back at you, big guy," said Sandas, reaching out and hugging Draxus. "I'm going to miss teasing you."

Draxus stood. "Tell me about it."

Sandas laughed as he pointed at Draxus.

Draxus hugged Emily. "You are more than you appear to be, and I am glad to have been able to call you friend."

Emily smiled. "We were a good team."

"Yes, we were," said Draxus, stepping back.

Draxus hugged Dr. Snowden. "You represented humanity well, and are a natural ambassador."

"Well, I try, you know," said Dr. Snowden, stepping back. "I enjoyed our many conversations. I feel like a part of you is still connected to me from that event on Gabranza Helrus."

"Yes, I feel that too. I suspect that a bit of us will always be intertwined from that event."

Dr. Snowden nodded.

V high-fived Draxus.

Draxus smiled. "Your efforts were nothing short of valiant. You faced evil head-on, and never wavered. May we all learn from your example."

"And may we all learn from your dedication to helping your people," said V.

Draxus nodded and then faced Evaran. "I still feel that you are a star god, and my people will always view you that way. We were blessed by your presence. You are a shining light in the darkness to those who seek it."

"I know you will not believe I am just a traveler. You will do great things, and the future of your species is in good hands," said Evaran. He extended a hand.

Draxus raised his head a bit as he shook Evaran's hand.

Evaran turned halfway toward the Torvatta. "Let us go."

Sandas joined Evaran, V, Dr. Snowden, and Emily on the ramp inside the Torvatta shielding.

V flew inside, and after a moment, the Torvatta began to ascend.

Sandas watched the others wave goodbye on the ground. A part of him was sad that the adventure was ending. He wondered how the others handled it. He felt a hand on his shoulder. Looking up, he saw Emily studying Draxus and the others on the receding ground.

"They'll be fine," said Emily.

Sandas sighed. "I know. I guess I'm up next."

"Yeah," said Emily.

Evaran raised a finger. "After we dissipate the space-time eddy, Emily wanted to show you something."

"The future event thing in the main timeline's original state?" asked Sandas.

Evaran nodded. "You will see us again."

Sandas grinned big. "I like the sound of that."

"Come, let us head inside."

The group assembled in the command area. The Torvatta had entered space and was flying away from Saturnus Prime.

"V, put us in Torvatta scan profile one and stealth mode and then take us to the coordinates just before Sandas was pulled into the space-time eddy," said Evaran.

"Acknowledged." After a moment, V said, "Torvatta scan profile one and stealth mode active."

The Torvatta opened a portal and flew through. Once on the other side, everything outside the Torvatta faded out, and then back in.

Sandas gulped as he saw his old ship. Looking at it from the perspective of the Torvatta's semitransparent walls, the space-time eddy was outlined and easily visible, something that was not the case when he had seen it earlier. He grimaced when his ship entered the eddy.

"Take us in," said Evaran.

"Acknowledged."

The Torvatta flew in after Sandas's ship.

Once inside the eddy, Sandas peered around. "It looks like I'm just flying in space. Nothing's changed."

Evaran shook his head. "You flew some distance here, and then reappeared back at this initial point, over and over, with time being reset each trip inside."

"I guess that's one way to time travel," said Sandas, stroking his snout.

"V, pulse the shields," said Evaran.

"Acknowledged."

Sandas watched a data window that showed a depiction of the Torvatta. Around it was a perfect bubble. When the shields pulsed, he watched as the circle expanded, and the Torvatta image shrank. Looking out, he saw that his ship was gone.

"It is done," said Evaran. "There is now only one Sandas in the main timeline and the original state will be rendered over the next twenty minutes."

"Yeah . . . okay, but now I'm missing a ship," said Sandas shaking a claw at Evaran.

Evaran half smiled. "I am sure that is preferable to not existing at all."

"Of course, of course. What will happen to any others that were pulled into this eddy before this time?"

"Like Tachyrin energy and temporal shielding, the eddy's internal timeline has collapsed. It no longer exists."

"Ahh," said Sandas.

"If you have another location, we can drop you off there. V can take your coordinates. When you have done so, come to the holo room."

Sandas nodded and then showed V where to go using a map that appeared in a data window. He noticed that Evaran, Dr. Snowden, and Emily had gone to the holo room. "I guess this is where I learn of this future event."

"You are correct," said V.

Sandas smiled. "This should be interesting."

The Torvatta opened a portal and flew through.

Sandas noted that they were in the Gyradack system, near a planet called Intara III. He was going to one of his safest hideouts. Intara III was a cold backwater planet, and sparsely populated.

The Torvatta breached the atmosphere and headed toward a body of water surrounded by huge ice landmasses. Once it hit the water, the Torvatta submerged and dove for a while.

Sandas's eyes lit up when he saw the familiar outpost he had set up long ago. He nodded at V. "I guess it's time to go see what all this future event stuff is. Just park the Torvatta inside the docking bay." He began to walk away, then hustled back. "Oh, almost forgot. Can you connect to my outpost?"

V tapped at the interface and, after a moment, said, "We are connected."

Sandas stood next to V and peered over the interface. "Ahh, there we go." He punched in a code and then smiled. "Okay, defenses won't try to annihilate the Torvatta. Good to go now."

"Acknowledged."

Sandas headed to the holo room to meet with the others. When he arrived, he observed the environment. It appeared to be a workshop of some sort. After a moment, he said, "Coris!

I haven't been there in a while, and it looks slightly different, but since this is the future, I'm guessing this is where we meet."

"Yes," said Evaran. "I will play a combined visual feedback of our encounter. Please take notes."

Sandas tapped at his shoulder. "Recording." For the next hour, he watched in amazement as his future self talked with Evaran and the others. When it finished, he glanced at Evaran. "So Fredorian Prime Ambassador Andia Kiggs is involved. Intriguing."

Emily smiled. "You be nice to her."

"Of course. I like the statue part where I surprise you."

Emily swatted Sandas's arm. "You would."

Sandas stroked his snout. "So this is the first time you meet me, and apparently, sometime before this meeting, I meet . . . another version of Evaran."

"That is correct," said Evaran. "I do not know what this other version is."

"So at that specific point in time, I know more about you than you know about yourself," said Sandas, laughing.

Evaran nodded.

"Not only that, but you can't stop yourself from hugging Emily," said Dr. Snowden.

Sandas's smile drew down. "I could see that. I'd want to tell her, and you, about what's to come." He glanced at Evaran. "It would sure save you a headache."

Evaran eyed Sandas.

"I know, I know. I'll make sure to fix the communication chip in Dr. Snowden's pocket too," said Sandas. "Hmm, I may need to do some prep work to make sure that encounter occurs."

"Such as . . . ," said Dr. Snowden.

"Spread some rumors about the Arkaron. Make sure Jala is in the bar to give you the communication chip. Ensure that bounty hunter knows to be there. Maybe I don't need to do anything, but I'll check it out. I guess in some ways, no matter what I do, it's already occurred."

Evaran nodded. "You do what you need to do." He glanced at his ARI. "I have also sent your base some additional information on a specific event. Although other events will come to pass, and I would not normally tell you about them, this one is important, and it appears you are involved."

"What's it about?" asked Sandas.

"Fredoria," said Evaran. "Nonetheless, we are now inside your base. Let us go."

Sandas licked his lips and headed toward the Torvatta exit. Once on the ramp, he turned and faced the group.

V had joined them and was hovering next to Emily.

"This is the hard part," said Sandas. His eyes misted as he exhaled. "I've enjoyed my time with everyone. I know . . . this is a once-in-a-lifetime event. I'll need to keep everything in perspective, but . . . I'm happy I'll get to see all of you, even if it is out of sequence."

Emily knelt and hugged Sandas. "You're so full of life."

A tear dropped on his shoulder.

"I'm gonna miss you," she said.

Sandas grinned and bobbed his head. "I'd much rather be full of life than not have it."

Dr. Snowden knelt and joined in the hug.

"A hugging session," said V. He flew down and wrapped his arms around Sandas.

Sandas laughed. "There you go."

Evaran knelt and placed a hand on Sandas's shoulder. "We will meet again. It is assured."

Sandas sighed as everyone stepped back. "I wish . . . I could travel with you, but it seems my future has already been set."

"You may travel with me once again. I suspect . . . that my other form you meet involves an adventure of some kind."

Sandas's eyes lit up. "I'll look forward to it. It would be great to do this again with all of you, minus the crazy-AI part." He noticed Evaran look down. Something about the other version meeting was bothering him even if he was not letting on what it was. Sandas cleared his throat and stepped outside the shielding and into the docking bay of his outpost. "Until we meet again."

Everyone waved as the Torvatta lifted and moved out.

Sandas swallowed hard. How a trip to check out a temporal anomaly ended up being the adventure of his life was mind-boggling. He was going to miss everyone, especially Emily. Even though he knew he would see everyone again, it would be at a different point in their personal timelines, and not quite the same. Any meeting, though, was better than none. After the Torvatta had disappeared from view, he began to plan in his head what needed to be done to ensure that the encounters in the future came to pass. Evaran trusted him, and Sandas would not let him down. He smiled, then headed inside.

Dr. Snowden glanced out over the guardrail on the Torvatta's roof. It had been thirty minutes, and per Evaran, the original state of the main timeline was fully rendered. They were back in AD 10105 and hovering over a city on Earth. It was as Dr. Snowden had originally pictured an advanced Earth. Everything was high-tech and sleek. Ships filled the air, and personal transports similar to what he had seen in the Draidjen city were common.

Having said goodbye to Draxus and the others, and then Sandas, Dr. Snowden was going to miss them. He wished that he could have spent more time with them, but he understood that this adventure was different from the others. Spending more time in the main timeline's altered state would increase knowledge exposure beyond what it already was for Sandas. The less time spent with the group, the better, in regards to the timeline and information.

Emily joined him by the guardrail. "I'm going to miss all of them. We don't get to spend time like we did on the other adventures."

"Yeah," said Dr. Snowden with a frown.

"Analysis. I will miss everyone as well, in particular Solia."

Dr. Snowden cleared his throat. "You two spent a lot of time together."

V's lights glowed a bit brighter. "Yes. She exposed me to a variety of human emotions and activities while in the virtual environment."

"Activities?"

"They are logged as . . . personal."

Dr. Snowden raised his eyebrows while glancing at Emily. "Oh . . . I see."

Evaran half smiled. "Speaking of the virtual environments, they have one here."

"Are we going to spend some time here?"

"Yes. I still need to talk with the Draidjens, and I think after everything, it may be good for us to spend some time here without worry of timeline changes."

Emily pursed her lips. "The timeline could still change, though, right?"

"Yes, there is always that possibility, but it is low."

Emily nodded. "Then we can check out the virtual environment. I'm curious to see what they have on the Dravens."

"Same here," said Dr. Snowden. He wrinkled his eyebrows. "Something's been bothering me about Salazar."

Evaran tilted his head.

"He was a virtual intelligence, then went into the space-time eddy, and came out as the aggressive AI we fought with exotic armor. Did he, like . . . evolve naturally into a super AI, or was it . . . something else?"

"I suspect it was something else. If it was not in a space-time eddy, I would investigate."

Dr. Snowden raised a finger. "But if we did investigate, and it did change things, the main timeline's altered state would still be removed."

"Yes, but I would not be able to guarantee that the main timeline's original state would be as it should be. The Tachyrin energy appearing near when we arrived would be an issue since I do not know where it came from. In addition to that, any consequences from our investigation would be felt by those living in the main timeline's altered state."

"Analysis. I would not like that," said V.

"Yeah, me either," said Dr. Snowden. "Their timeline may be gone, but it was real to me. I guess they live on in my memories."

"How does that make you feel?" asked Evaran.

Dr. Snowden grinned. "Are you a psychiatrist now?"

Evaran half smiled. "Possessing memories of events that no longer exist could be confusing, similar to the virtual simulation memories from your initial abduction long ago."

"Oh . . . yeah, I can see that. I'm okay with it, I think," said Dr. Snowden.

Emily eyed Evaran. "Going back to Salazar, you said 'something else.' That usually means you have some idea about it."

"Yes. If you recall when we were last on Earth, Caltorus had been given coordinates to Earth from an untraceable source. Salazar was upgraded in a space-time eddy . . . which would be untraceable, and then given Tachyrin energy . . . with no trace. Someone, or something, has been playing around with events. Unfortunately for them, I exist."

Emily glanced at Dr. Snowden, then back at Evaran. "Should we be worried?"

Evaran swept his gaze across them. "I am not sure yet. When I visit the Draidjen, I am going to study their history logs and see if there are any discrepancies."

"You don't think the Time Wardens are involved, do you?" asked Dr. Snowden.

"I do not. This is not how they operate. This is more . . . mischievous. Almost like a test."

Dr. Snowden ran his hand over his mouth. "A test for what?"

"To see if there is a presence capable of countering it. This is not uncommon among . . . cosmic entities."

Dr. Snowden swallowed hard. "And in two scenarios, it has been."

Evaran nodded. "I would suggest that when we are outside the Torvatta, you use your suits, just in case."

Emily sighed. "I guess you are kinda high profile."

"Perhaps, but only to specific groups and, even then, to those aware of the Evaran Protocol within the timespan that it exists."

Emily nodded. "We'll be careful." She glanced at V. "What do you plan to do when we land?"

"I wish to see Solia's status. I may not be able to discuss this event with her, but perhaps . . . a new friendship can occur," said V.

Dr. Snowden laughed. "Friendship, huh?"

"Yes," said V as his lights glowed brighter.

Emily chuckled. "Well, for me, I'm gonna check out some history."

"Analysis. Perhaps I will join you in your study," said V.

Emily smiled. "Cool."

Dr. Snowden was glad that Emily was getting back to her roots. She had studied history hard in college, but it fell to the wayside when they started traveling with Evaran due to one event or another. Dr. Snowden also noticed that she was returning to her old self and opening up more, but still retained all the toughness gained from traveling with Evaran. Dr. Snowden was also glad to see that V was exploring his emotional side more. Maybe Dr. Snowden could get some time in with V in the virtual environment. Evaran was cautious as always, and Dr. Snowden suspected that Evaran knew more about the cosmic entity than he was willing to talk about.

Emily glanced at Evaran. "I guess everything is as it should be, right?"

Evaran raised his head a bit. "Yes . . . for now."

EPILOGUE

John Holind sat on the edge of his cryo chamber. He hated cryo sleep, but it was hard to argue with its effectiveness. He popped his postcryo medicine and looked around. It seemed he was the first up. He grunted a few times to check his throat and then said, "Salazar?"

"Yes, John?"

"Status."

"It is AD 5244, and we are orbiting Arius."

John stood with assistance of the slab. "Good. Sounds like we made it in one piece. Are the others up?"

"The rest of the command crew is awakening now. The ship is functioning normally, and we are in no immediate danger."

"All right. Have everyone meet in the command center," said John.

"Yes, John."

John slipped on a change of clothes and headed to the command center. He still felt a bit woozy, a feeling he hated, an unfortunate side effect of cryo sleep. When he got to the command center, he saw Holly Evans and several of the command crew.

"How you feeling?" asked John.

"Like shit, as expected," said Holly.

John nodded. He watched as Asura and Sarif arrived, and then interacted with the console on the large table in the center of the command area.

A projection shot up showing a solar system view. The sun was yellow, and Arius was in the Goldilocks zone.

"A sight for sore eyes," said John.

"I'm just glad the damn trip is done. I hate cryo sleep," said Holly.

"Same here," said Asura. She ran her hand along the table console nearest her. "Looks like every system is good. We have supplies and are on schedule."

"Almost a perfect trip," said Sarif.

"Yeah," said John. "I wish we could just teleport or go through a gate or something."

"Keep dreaming," said Holly, swatting John's arm. She pointed at the star. "At least we can now begin building Holind One and start colonizing Arius."

John smiled.

"Must be nice to have a new colony named after your family," said Sarif.

"Own a few corporations and systems and you can too," said Asura with a grin.

John chuckled. "It may have my name on it, but make no mistake, this is a group effort." He swept his gaze across the crew. "This is a new beginning, one where the future is bright. We have the best colonization team I could have ever asked for, and with your help, Holind One will make an impact in the time to come. It was a long journey, but we're here now. You are part of a new effort, one that will be prosperous." He paused for a moment and smiled. "Let's get this thing going!"

The crew cheered.

"Holly, deploy the first engineer team. Sarif, Asura, you know your roles. Let's get moving," said John. He watched as everyone took their respective seats and began to work. "Salazar, what do you think of all this?"

"I require more information to answer your question," said Salazar.

John grinned as he shook his head. He enjoyed teasing virtual intelligences, but he knew they had no emotions. "Figures. All right. Assist the rest of the crew as needed."

"Yes, John."

NOTE FROM
THE AUTHOR

I hope you enjoyed the seventh book in the Evaran Chronicles! This book focused on where humanity is in AD 10105, even if it was not supposed to be there! I had a lot of fun with Sandas, the information broker, and Draxus, the Draven praetor. They added an interesting dynamic to the group. V grew a bit in this book: meeting someone he could be intimate with and showing that when pushed, he would not back down!

Dr. Snowden and Emily learn more about their enhanced nanobots, and that will play a significant role in upcoming books. This is the second book in the second series arc. Although there are some events established that will be referenced in future books, I will provide that information as needed, as I have done in previous books.

If you liked the book, and have the time and inclination, a review would go a long way in helping out this indie author. If you do submit a review, I'll put in a word to Evaran should you find yourself stuck across the galaxy and eight thousand years in the future! Want to be notified about new book releases? If so, you can sign up below.

www.AdairHart.com/MailingList.aspx

I will only send you email about new book releases, major updates, and the occasional newsletter, usually once a month. I dislike getting spammed too, so I will use this sparingly to keep you in the loop.

ABOUT
THE AUTHOR

I have been dreaming about fictional worlds since I was a kid. I devoured anything related to fantasy and science fiction. I developed a setting over the last twenty years and struggled to find a medium I could express it in. Several years ago I discovered I enjoyed writing. It is a passion of mine now, and exploring my setting with it has been an awesome journey.

I work in the information technology field and have my bachelor's and master's degrees in it. It has helped me to shape some of the concepts I write about. I also enjoy keeping up on futurology and science in general.

I live in central Ohio and enjoy walking, reading, gaming, learning, listening to music, and trying to keep up on my never-ending list of TV shows and movies to watch. If you want to contact me, you can do so on my website at

www.AdairHart.com

YOU CAN ALSO REACH ME ON

Facebook.............................fb.com/AdairHart
Goodreads.....www.goodreads.com/AdairHart
Email..............Adair.Hart.Author@gmail.com

DEDICATION

To my grandparents, who continue to inspire me.
They may be gone now, but their life lessons and
legacies live on with me.

ACKNOWLEDGMENTS

This was a great journey for me, but I wouldn't be here without the help of others. I would like to thank, in no particular order,

My awesome editor, Laura Petrella. Her insights continue to make what I write that much better. I've learned a lot from her and apply it as I go. She is quick-witted and knows the characters and series deeply. She's invaluable to me! I always look forward to our collaboration when it comes to editing time!

My cover artist, Tom Edwards (tomedwardsconcepts@gmail.com), for another amazing cover. He has a way of making you feel like you're there in the cover!

My family and friends who helped encourage me along the way.

My proofreader, Alexa, for doing a great job with that final pass to ensure everything looked good.

My formatter and interior designer, Colleen Sheehan (www.ampersandbookinteriors.com/), for being rock steady and available to help me make my interiors look beautiful. I'm glad I'm able to work with her!

BOOKS

You can see all books in the Evaran Chronicles
and the Earthborn at

WWW.ADAIRHART.COM/SERIES/ALLBOOKS.ASPX